Keep Me Close

Also by Jane Holland

Keep me close

jane HOLLAND

LUME BOOKS

LUME BOOKS

Published in 2021 by Lume Books
30 Great Guildford Street,
Borough, SE1 0HS

ISBN 978-1-83901-214-3

Typeset using Atomik ePublisher from Easypress Technologies

www.lumebooks.co.uk

In memory of my wonderful aunt, Marjorie Chapman, whose lifelong zeal for books, reading and storytelling has been a huge inspiration, both to me personally and to all our family.

About the Author

Jane Holland lives in Cornwall with her family and two inquisitive cats, where she enjoys gardening and coastal walks. A full-time novelist, she also writes historical, romantic and other fiction under a variety of pseudonyms, including Betty Walker, Beth Good, Victoria Lamb, Elizabeth Moss, Hannah Coates, and JJ Holland.

CHAPTER ONE

Sometimes, it feels as though life itself is conspiring against me. Back home after a long day in London, I'm hurrying to the chemist's before they close, hoping to grab some medicine for my mother, when someone catches my eye across the street and my carefully constructed world crumbles around me...

One glance, and the walls I've erected come crashing down, possibly to the sound of angelic trumpets. Only I can't hear a thing because of all the rumbling traffic on the high street as the early evening commute continues. All I can hear is the sick thump of my heart.

My first thought is: run. My second thought is: too late. My third thought is: please, whatever you do, Kate, don't cry.

But maybe he won't see me. Or won't recognise me. And maybe it's not too late. Perhaps if I were to dive into the next shop or look the other way...

He's standing outside the newsagent's opposite, head slightly bent, about to light a cigarette in the chill autumn breeze, when his eyes flash up and meet mine...

As though he sensed my presence. As though this is destiny at work. The universe forcing me to confront my past.

Why, though? Why can't the bloody universe just let it go for once? The unfairness of it all makes me want to scream in frustration. I've tried so hard to move on. God knows, I've tried. Yet here I am, confronted yet again with the full weight of guilt and misery, of my failure as a human being. Why can't life work with me, not against me, just this once?

It's definitely too late. He's seen me.

His eyes widen, and he lifts a hand. The one holding his elegant silver lighter, its front panel inscribed with: *To Logan, on your 35th birthday, love David and Kate.*

I can't pretend not to have recognised him.

I wave back, forcing a brittle smile to my face. Then I stop and stand there like a shop mannequin, clutching at my shoulder bag like it's a lifeline, as he waits for a break in the traffic, then dashes across towards me.

He's pushed the unlit cigarette back into its packet. To my relief, the lighter is slipped into his jacket pocket along with his fags.

I wish I could disappear that easily.

'Kate.' He hesitates, then hugs me briefly. 'How are you? I haven't seen you since...' He stops, and we both suck in a breath at the same horrible moment. Then his mouth quirks into a crooked smile. 'Well, not for ages.'

'Hello, Logan.' My smile feels like it's stuck in place with glue. I feel rigid too. Do I look as stricken as I feel? 'I'm fine, thank you. Work is quite stressful, but that's nothing new.' I pause. 'How are you?'

He tells me how he is while I nod politely and study him, devouring every inch while my brain shrieks at me in anguish.

Up close, there's a shock to the powerful sense of familiarity.

His dark hair is maybe cropped a little tighter; his face and neck are lightly tanned, perhaps from a summer spent mostly outdoors;

and there's a dark shadow under his eyes, not unlike the shadow u... my own. Otherwise, he's essentially unchanged. I always thought hi... attractive, though never as attractive as David. Tall, broad-shouldered and lean, with a face that turned women's heads, Logan could almost be a Mills and Boon hero, I used to say.

Two years. And it might as well be the day after the funeral for all the difference I can see in him.

Those two years have been a little less kind to me, and I know it. Those dark shadows under my eyes, for instance…

Why does life have to be so cruel?

'I see you still haven't kicked the habit,' I tell him, struggling feebly against the subject we're both avoiding.

His frown is confused.

'Smoking,' I elaborate, feeling awkward now for having mentioned it. 'I saw you across the street, about to light up.'

'Oh, that.' He looks embarrassed. 'Yeah… I'm actually trying to quit.'

'You were always trying to quit.'

'I suppose I was.' His smile, too, is fixed, like my own. A mimicry of polite friendship. 'Maybe one day I'll manage it.'

'You should take up running instead. That will help. Or swimming. Once your lungs get a taste for exercise, you'll quit more easily.'

He's silent for a moment.

'I'd forgotten that about you,' he says at last, his eyes narrowed on my face.

'My obsession with fitness?'

'Your need to fix people. Whether they want to be fixed or not.'

Now it's my turn to be embarrassed.

'I'm sorry.' I take a step backwards. 'You're right, of course; it's none of my business.'

'No, that was unfair of me,' Logan says quickly, half-putting out a hand to stop me from leaving. 'You just... care, I suppose. About other people, I mean. I didn't mean to be rude. It's not something I'm used to, that's all.' This time, his smile reaches his eyes, and his whole face lights up. 'Swimming, you say? I haven't been to the pool for years, but... Yes, maybe it's time I finally did something about my nicotine addiction. Do you swim?'

I'm taken aback by the question.

Of course I swim. I swim, and I jog too. I take aerobics classes twice a week at the local sports centre. I try to get in at least an hour's yoga every week. And sometimes I cycle, though not as often as I'd like these days. I used to belong to a club. But that was before...

I nod, wary. 'Whenever I can find the time.'

He looks at me very directly. 'We could try and find the time together some day. Maybe one evening next week?'

'Oh, erm, that's...' I flounder and stop.

Swimming together. Half-naked in a warm pool. The intimacy of it all...

'Or dinner, if you prefer,' he suggests.

I'm standing there like a statue, I realise. Clutching the strap of my shoulder bag so tightly it feels unnatural. Rude, even. As though I'm expecting the poor man to pounce on me at any moment. Which is insane. Not to mention insulting.

He's just being friendly.

But before I can say anything, Logan gives a groan and shakes his head. 'I shouldn't have asked you. I'm sorry.' He runs a frustrated hand through his hair, looking away down the street. There's a brooding quality to the man, which I'd forgotten about. 'I think about him all the time. Do you?'

I open my mouth, and then close it again.

4

There are no words.

'It's like my brain can't quite get used to the idea that he's not around anymore,' he continues, frowning. 'I'd known him since primary school, of course. Thirty-five years or so. You can't just switch off a friendship that old, can you? He's still there, at the back of my head, even now. Something funny happens at work, and I find myself thinking, *I must tell David about that.* And then I remember.'

'Don't,' I mutter.

We say nothing for a moment, both wrapped up in our own intense thoughts and memories. People flow past us.

I wonder how I can escape politely.

'Well, Kate,' he says, as though reading my mind, and sticks out a hand, oddly stiff and formal, like we're business colleagues meeting on the street, 'it was wonderful to see you again.' He hesitates, temporarily lost for words.

'Friday,' I say.

He stares at me. 'Sorry?'

'You suggested dinner.'

'I did,' he agrees swiftly, catching on. 'You're free Friday evening?' His smile widens, suddenly confident. 'Are you still in the same place? I can swing by and pick you up at seven.'

'That would be lovely, thank you.'

'Any preference for food?'

I feel flushed and uncertain now. 'Surprise me.'

His eyes widen slightly, but he nods. 'I will.'

Briefly, we embrace again, the handshake forgotten, and then he's gone, moving back into the stream of people going about their business.

I stand there a moment longer, breathless and flustered. What have I done? Why on earth did I agree to meet him for dinner?

I'm a mess. I mean, I can function at work, just about. But inside, when I look in the mirror, I'm in pieces. I'm certainly not ready for... whatever this is.

Dinner. A date.

Oh god, a date?

Panic sweeps through me.

I start walking compulsively, head down, so fast and blindly, I march straight past the chemist's and have to turn back a block later, bumping into people in my haste.

This is wrong. I should cancel.

But another voice inside me says more firmly, no. Don't be silly. Work has been mad recently. Permanent white-water. I've barely come up for air in months. And it's been so long since I thought of myself in that way. As date material. This dinner with Logan may be what I've been waiting for. An excuse to do something about my hair, my tired makeup, my dreary wardrobe.

It's only dinner. And it's only Logan.

After collecting the prescription from the chemist, I hurry on to the mini supermarket to grab a few essentials, and then stop dead on the way back to my car, staring at myself in the window of a small boutique.

In the excitement and near hysteria of a dinner date for the first time in forever, I've forgotten something rather important.

My mother.

CHAPTER TWO

My mother, Celeste Kinley, is only sixty-eight years old. Once, I would have called that being still in her prime. Except that, three years ago, my darling mum, my lively, dramatic, funny, brilliantly clever mother, was diagnosed with early onset dementia.

I'd known something was wrong for several years before that, of course. Mum had started to forget words occasionally, or to muddle them up in a quasi-comical way, like saying 'bread' when she meant 'bed'. We all do that now and then, of course, and have a good laugh about it. But for Mum, it began to happen with increasing frequency, her linguistic lapses accompanied by other, even more disturbing symptoms.

She would forget where her keys were or what her postcode was, or even which year we were in, and a few things I told her would sometimes slip away too, so I kept having to repeat information I'd already told her. Things I'd seen on the news, or local gossip overheard in the post office, or everyday domestic stuff.

It was like being caught in a time warp, where the same things get repeated ad nauseam. Only there was no magic reset button to get us out of the deadly loop…

After nearly a year of this 'muddled thinking' as Mum referred to it, I took her to our local GP, Dr Forster, a rather severe young female doctor, and was reassured this was all within the parameters of normal behaviour for a woman of Mum's age. Until she developed a urinary infection and took to her bed with a high temperature.

Her speech became slurred and incoherent, and for a while, she didn't seem to entirely recognise me. At the time, I thought this was because of her infection. But later, when the antibiotics had done their work and she was able to get up and walk about, I realised Mum was still confused about where she was, and even who she was at times. That was particularly unsettling.

So back we went to the GP.

This time, I put my foot down with Dr Forster and demanded a referral. And I was proved right. Once Mum had seen a consultant and taken a few tests, we finally received a diagnosis.

She had early onset dementia, possibly exacerbated by a stroke or 'cerebral event' during her illness.

Not knowing what was wrong had felt pretty bad.

But knowing is almost worse.

We live a few miles outside Guildford in leafy Surrey, as people love to refer to it, in a relatively green part of the county, not too built up.

I drive home from the chemist's in my flashy red Mazda and pull up on the gravelled drive, observing with a flash of irritation that the man who does our garden hasn't been to mow the lawns yet. It's nearly a fortnight since his last visit.

We have two large lawns at the front and back of the house, bordered with long-established flower beds, shrubs and a few trees. The last of the summer blooms are languishing now under foliage turning yellow and brown for autumn.

The house is detached, late Victorian with twelve rooms and

pretensions of grandeur. Wisteria covers much of the south-facing wall at the front, softening its sharp lines with trailing greens and yellows, while an open portico with two white pillars lends an air of distinction that pleased Dad enough to buy it twenty years ago, when I was thirteen and still easily impressed by displays of wealth. Nowadays, I'm more likely to fret over how much it costs to maintain such a large house.

Mum is watching television with Nurse Giorgios in the living room when I walk in.

That is, Giorgios is watching his latest Netflix crush, some new American cop show everyone's raving about, and Mum is staring into space with an abstracted expression on her face.

Guiltily, Giorgios snaps off the sound and stands up when he hears me come in. 'Miss Kinley,' he says, and his gaze shoots to the clock on the mantelpiece. 'I didn't expect you back until seven.'

'I took an earlier train back,' I tell him coolly. 'I wanted to collect my mother's prescription.'

I also wanted an excuse to avoid my boss's birthday party, hosted in a nearby restaurant with the rest of the office staff. Last year, Mark had made me sit next to him and then groped me most of the evening until I 'accidentally' knocked my water glass into his lap.

I throw my keys and the meds down onto the coffee table and bend to kiss Mum on the cheek. 'That's a pretty dress. How's your day been?'

'Fine,' she says, nodding.

'Fine' is one of her favourite words. She seems to have worked out that it stops most people from enquiring further.

It doesn't stop me.

I don't forbid Giorgios from watching telly with Mum. That would be absurd, considering how many hours he spends with her on those few days that I commute into London. But he's supposed to be keeping her mind active, not putting it to sleep with trashy TV drama she can't possibly hope to follow.

'Did you do the crossword puzzle with Giorgios like I suggested?' I ask, surreptitiously pressing her hand to check if she's warm enough.

Her skin is chilly, and I make a mental note to put the heating on.

Mum stares up at me blankly from her high-backed armchair, then looks across at Giorgios in mild surprise, as though she's only just realised he's in the room with us. Or perhaps she wasn't immediately sure who I was talking about. Some days her mind is sharper than others.

'I don't know,' she admits, and looks pleadingly at Giorgios. 'Did I?'

'We tried a few lines,' Giorgios tells me quickly, using the royal plural as always when talking about my mother, his large eyes expressive, 'but we weren't in the mood.' He shrugs. 'So we try harder next time. Not a problem.'

'I see.'

Right from the very start, Mum stubbornly refused to accept that she had dementia.

She still refuses to accept it.

One of the main issues is that she can't actually remember being tested and diagnosed. And because she's now struggling with the written word, her ability to understand the doctor's reports, even when shown to her as evidence that she's genuinely unwell, is limited. Which doesn't help when I'm trying to persuade her to take her meds or explain why she can't fly out to Spain or Greece for a solo holiday, something she's become obsessed by in recent years.

But that's not the worst.

The worst thing about Mum's dementia is how she's forgotten about Dad. Not that he existed. She remembers *that*.

But she's forgotten that he died five years ago.

And that my brother died with him.

That particular lapse in memory makes for some uncomfortable conversations – when I can be bothered to contradict her cheery assurance that Dad is about to walk in the door any minute, that is…

'Giorgios, how is she?' I ask quietly when we walk into the hall together to collect his jacket. He walks with a limp since some undisclosed accident a year ago, his build hefty, on the verge of corpulent, but his round face always cheerful. 'Did she eat anything at lunch?'

'A little soup.'

'Did you offer her the shepherd's pie like I asked?'

'She wouldn't even look at it. Or the vegetables you left.' He pulls a face, his Greek accent very pronounced. 'I'm sorry, I did try. But your mother has no appetite today. She is well though, I think.'

'Okay, thank you.'

'I'll see you on Monday as usual.' He opens the front door.

Giorgios only comes to sit with Mum one or two days a week. And very rarely looks after her in the evenings, unless I have a special class or event. Which almost never happens.

I stop him. 'Actually, Giorgios, hang on a tick.'

He looks back, surprised. 'Miss Kinley?'

'I have a… meeting to go to on Friday night. I agreed to it without thinking. Is there any chance…?'

'You want me to come over?'

'Would you?' I grimace, feeling awkward. 'I don't like to leave Mum on her own for too long, and the meeting… It could run late.'

'Sure, sure.' Giorgios gives me a charming smile. 'Only, late evenings… It will be double pay.'

'Of course.' I smile too, opening the front door for him. 'Should I pay you through the agency as usual?'

'Not for evenings.' He gives me a cheeky wink. 'Cash in hand, yes?'

11

'Got it.'

I watch him climb into his battered Ford Focus and raise a hand as he revs towards the gate, his tyres spitting gravel. Dad would have had a fit; he obsessed about his redesign of this driveway, needing everything to be perfect, and used to curse whenever delivery vans went too fast, chucking tiny stones onto our lawn.

My father was a property developer, and my brother Ciaran worked alongside him in the office, despite his yearnings to be an artist instead. The two of them were always so excited when a big investment finally paid off, celebrating with riotous champagne parties.

Both men were larger than life, ambitious go-getters in the office as well as on the golf course and on the piste. Highly experienced skiers and climbers, father and son had spent at least two weeks of every year skiing or climbing in small groups with other intrepid, like-minded souls.

That thirst for adventure had been an extension of their need to make the 'big bucks' as Dad had enjoyed boasting, and I'd loved that about them. Admired it tremendously too.

Until the avalanche that claimed their lives, that is, along with seven others, and left me and Mum grieving and alone.

I'd been living in my own flat in central Guildford at the time they died, enjoying some independence at last. Clubbing at weekends, commuting into London for work, a rowdy circle of friends for sport or drinking or art and museum trips.

That's how I met David for the first time, in fact. On the club scene, which I used to love so much.

But soon after my father and brother died, I made the difficult decision to move back in with Mum, to support her in her bereavement, and have lived here ever since.

While David was still alive, I used to go out all the time, even though my other friends had more or less dropped away. We went out as a couple for dinner and clubbing, or to the cinema, and even into central London a few times a month to catch a show.

But since David's death, my life has become much narrower, mainly just shuttling between work and my mother's care. There's not been much room for anything else, to be fair.

Only Mum.

I click on the central heating, change out of my work clothes and into loose jeans and a blouse, and go back to my mother.

To my horror, I find her tottering about the living room with a vase of flowers she can barely lift.

'What on earth?' I take the heavy glass vase away from her before she drops it. 'Mum, for goodness' sake... Sit down, I can put this wherever you want it.' I wait while she drops back into her armchair. 'On the sideboard?'

'What?' She looks at me, confused.

'You were moving these flowers,' I say patiently. 'Where do you want them?'

'I don't know.'

I take a breath, then return the vase to the table. Then I sit on the sofa and briefly check my phone before turning it off for the evening.

There's a message from Mark.

You're missing a great party here. Maybe we could grab lunch together next week. I've got a little proposal for you.

Oh Christ.

I have nothing to say to that. Not tonight, anyway. He can bloody well badger me on company time, not my own.

Wearily, I glance at the other message on my phone.

It's from Stella, a woman I know from Monday yoga. Some of us go for coffee and cake occasionally after morning class, much to the disgust of Beth, our yogi, and Stella and I are usually the last to leave the café.

Stella's older than me, nearly forty, but her dad suffers from dementia too, so I guess we have something in common.

Did you leave a blue cardigan at the studio? Beth found one after class. It's in the back of my car.

I reply, *Not mine, sorry,* and then add a smiley face icon as an afterthought.

Recently, I moved to working a four-day week, Monday to Thursday. One or two of those days I commute into London. The rest I work from home for a publishing firm, mainly on their non-fiction lines: travel, business, true crime, self-help.

I'm a commissioning editor, for what that's worth. It sounds good, but the publisher has cut back on staff in recent years, so these days I tend to do a little bit of everything. Commissioning, editing, marketing, promoting... I even read what comes in on the slush pile – and bring Mark his hourly black coffee when nobody else is in earshot.

The work can be chaotic at times. Unpredictable too. But that's why I enjoy it. No one week is the same.

I hate my boss though. Mark, the company director, is a total misogynist who makes my skin creep. I can't recall the number of times I've turned down the offer of a drink after work with him because I know it's just a random come-on. So of course he hates me.

In fact, I'm increasingly sure he'd love nothing better than to see me booted out of the industry altogether.

His latest office favourite, Debs, recently promoted to managing editor, has always made it clear how much she dislikes me. When she came to us two years ago, she had almost zero experience in publishing, straight out of an internship with a second-rate literary agency, and I was tasked with the job of making sure she learned the ropes.

Perhaps I was too short with Debs, irked by her slowness in grasping basic software or her apparent inability to remember the names of our more important authors and the titles of their books. But she soon developed a dislike for me that has since grown into what can only be described as hatred. And when we both went for the same senior position, Debs got it, despite my longer tenure with the company and what I personally felt was a strong interview.

I still suspect she had help beating me. Mark has never been one to let a little thing like professional integrity get in the way of his plans. But I've never dared voice that suspicion out loud. He's still my boss, after all…

I wonder what he wants to offer me.

'Someone was in the garden today,' Mum says vaguely.

I throw my phone back into my bag and stretch out on the sofa, my feet aching after a long day in heels. I really ought to start wearing flats. But I'm so short, I still feel I need that extra height in the office.

'Sorry?' I force a smile. 'You saw someone in the garden, did you? When was this?'

'Lunchtime.' She sounds very certain.

'Okay.'

I rub my bare feet and consider the situation. I wonder if this random visitor could have been Ron, the man who comes to mow our lawns and occasionally lop our trees and shrubs to keep things neat.

There was no sign of any gardening work having been done, as I'd noted on arriving home. But maybe Ron just popped by to check what needed doing.

'Was it the man who mows the lawn?'

'No,' she says, and tuts, as though annoyed by my stupidity.

15

'Then who was it?'

Mum shrugs. 'I don't know.'

I frown, bemused by this. Someone was in our garden? I wonder why Giorgios didn't mention it. But maybe it slipped his mind.

'Man? Woman?'

'I told you, I don't know,' Mum repeats, a little impatient now. 'You can't tell these days, can you? They all look the same to me.'

'Well, never mind,' I say briskly, and give her my broadest smile, pushing all other considerations out of my mind. If it had been important, I'm sure Giorgios would have mentioned it to me. 'What would you like for your supper? I believe there's a shepherd's pie in the fridge.'

'Oh!' She claps her hands. 'I love shepherd's pie.'

I smile. 'I know you do, Mum.'

CHAPTER THREE

'What do you think?' I ask, and perform a quick twirl for my mother.

I had intended to wear something colourful tonight – and perhaps a little more low-cut. My wardrobe is full of bold little numbers that I almost never have the nerve to wear. But, in the end, flicking through dresses and skirts that suited me when I was seeing David but now seem to belong to an earlier me, a previous edition of Kate Kinley, my hand stopped on a trusty little black dress.

The dress is a good ten years old now. But something about it hooks me. It's safe, maybe. The easy choice. And, to my surprise, it still fits quite well. Perhaps a little snug over the hips, but I'm thirty-three now. What did I expect?

'Hmm?'

Mum looks up from her lap tray with a distracted air. She's sitting in her armchair as usual, a crossword puzzle book open in front of her. She has a pen but hasn't lifted it. The puzzle is unstarted, though she's been poring over it for nearly an hour.

'My dress.' I smile, suspecting she's already forgotten what I told her five minutes before going off to change after my bath. 'I'm going out tonight, remember?'

'Going out?' She blinks; there's a note of outrage in her voice. 'Where? Am I going out too?'

'No, Mum.' I pat her hand. 'I told you, I'm going to have dinner with a friend tonight.'

'But what about me?'

I give her a reassuring smile. 'Giorgios is coming to sit with you.'

'Giorgios,' she repeats, staring into space.

I refuse to believe she can't remember who I'm talking about.

'That's right. You like Giorgios.'

'Do I?'

I frown, feeling guilty. 'You know you do, Mum.' I worry about how poorly she's getting and how fast the disease seems to be progressing. 'Honestly, Giorgios is one of your favourite people. That's why I arranged for him to be your usual carer.'

'I don't need a carer,' she insists gruffly.

'Well, someone to talk to when I can't be here,' I say, as gently as I can. 'You know how much you like to talk to people.'

Mum smiles then, self-indulgently. 'I'm a chatterbox.'

'And we love that about you.' I surreptitiously check the time on the mantel clock. Giorgios must be running late; he agreed to be here for six thirty, but it's nearly quarter to seven, and there's no sign of him yet. 'But it does mean you get super lonely when I have to pop out. And Giorgios likes to chat too. So, it's a good fit.'

I hurry into the hall and take a peek out of the door. It was an uncertain day, weather-wise, and the afternoon is already drawing in, long shadows falling across the lawn. I'll need a light jacket with my dress, though it's not cold enough yet for one of my winter coats. My black one is hanging in the hall, so I can easily grab that on my way out.

The drive is still empty.

When I return to my mother, she has put on her reading glasses. She peers down at her crossword puzzle book, lifts the pen to write something, then puts it down again, her air perplexed.

'Do you need help with that?' I ask.

She looks up at me, then seems to notice the little black dress and my hair, which I've pinned up in a chignon. 'You look nice.'

I beam. 'Thank you.'

'Why are you all dressed up? Are you going out?'

I take a deep breath and explain again about my dinner date. This time I forget to be cautious and mention that it's a man I'm meeting.

She stiffens at once. 'What's this man's name?'

'Logan. He was a friend of David's.' I pause, uncertain. 'You remember David.'

'Of course I do. Lovely boy. Bit dreamy, maybe.' She frowns at me, her look almost accusing. 'Why does he never come round anymore? I suppose you scared him off. You'll never manage to attract the really nice ones if you won't make more of an effort to be friendly. Men don't like women who ride roughshod over them.' She halts, staring at me. 'Whatever's the matter now?'

Tears have sprung to my eyes, and I try in vain to blink them away. She's forgotten about David's death. Of course she has. Of all the things you'd probably want to forget, your daughter's boyfriend committing suicide would be high on the list...

'Nothing, Mum.' My voice wavers as I fight off the tears. 'Yes, I suppose I did scare him off. In a manner of speaking.'

'Well, no point getting upset about it now. You'll ruin your mascara if you cry. Better tidy yourself up.'

I reach for a tissue from the box on the coffee table and dab under my eyes, checking my reflection in the oval mirror above the mantelpiece.

Behind me, through the windows that overlook the lawn, I see a dark shape at the far end of the lawn, just slipping out of view behind the trees.

A man, I'm sure of it.

I spin round, shocked to my core. 'Who the hell is that?'

'Language,' Mum says, tutting.

But to my surprise, the lawn is empty. There's nobody there.

Uneasy now, I stare out, leaning as far as I can over the windowsill to look round the corner at the drive.

Still no sign of Giorgios's car.

Mum said she'd seen someone lurking about in the garden earlier in the week. I'd dismissed it as another of her misunderstandings. She often misinterpreted things these days. It could have been anyone. Even a neighbour, come to retrieve a football. We do have a neighbour with young children who occasionally send a ball sailing over at that end of the garden. But neighbours tend to ring the bell first and ask for permission to collect lost objects, not just wander in unannounced.

'I thought I saw someone out there on the lawn,' I say.

'Hmm?' Mum takes off her glasses and slams the puzzle book shut. 'I can't do this. I can't see the damn thing. Take it away from me, would you?'

She hasn't been paying any attention, I realise.

I take the puzzle book away and give her the ball of knitting she sometimes plays with. She doesn't properly knit anymore; she can't follow the patterns. But she can still set stitches, and knit and purl for a while on a good day. Today, Mum just squeezes the ball of soft red wool rhythmically in one fist, like pumping a heart to keep it going, and stares across the room absentmindedly.

I pick up my phone and ring Giorgios.

Nobody answers.

I leave a brief message on the carer's voicemail, trying not to sound irritated that he's late.

He might be stuck in traffic, after all. Or he might have had an accident. And it's very good of him to come over to sit with Mum. Double pay, yes. But it's a Friday night and I know he's got a boyfriend tucked away somewhere, and would probably much rather be with him. Not minding an old lady, even if he does usually persuade her to watch something gory and unsuitable on the telly with him.

A few minutes later, the doorbell goes, and I heave a sigh of relief. Thank God he's finally arrived.

But when I fling open the front door, it's not Giorgios.

It's Logan.

I ought to have realised when the bell went, of course. Giorgios knows the code to the key holder. The nurse doesn't ring; he just knocks and strolls in with a cheery hello.

Logan is wearing smart trousers and a crisp white shirt under a black jacket. His hair looks damp as though he recently showered.

'Hi,' he says, and his eyes widen as he looks me up and down. 'You look fantastic. Ready to go?'

I smile, suppressing a flutter of excitement at his compliment. Stupid, really. But it's been so long since I've had a date, and I really wasn't sure if my little black dress would hit the vibe. It seems it has.

'Not quite,' I admit.

'Okay, there's no hurry.' He hesitates. 'Should I wait in the car?'

'God, no, you'd better come in. It's my mum, you see. She suffers from dementia and I can't leave her alone for too long. But the nurse who was due to sit with her hasn't turned up yet.' I grimace, catching a flicker of something unfathomable in his expression. 'I'm really sorry.'

'There's no need to apologise. We'll have to wait, that's all.' About to come inside, Logan spots me eyeing the garden behind him and stops, raising his eyebrows. 'Problem?'

I feel embarrassed. 'Oh, it's nothing.'

'Kate…'

'I thought I saw someone in the garden a few minutes ago. But I probably imagined it. Or maybe it was a neighbour.'

He doesn't smile, looking sombre instead. 'Would you like me to take a look?'

'Would you?' It's not very feminist of me to enlist his help, perhaps. But it'll be getting dark soon, and the thought of some unknown bloke possibly creeping about the grounds while I'm out gives me the creeps.

'Of course.' Logan turns to survey the garden. 'Whereabouts did you see this lurker?'

I point out the area, and he strides across the lawn without the slightest hesitation, disappearing into the undergrowth a moment later.

I nip back in and briefly check on Mum. She's got her eyes closed and seems to be having a nap, so I return to the doorstep.

Still no sign of Giorgios. Where on earth can he be?

Logan still hasn't returned.

Uncertain, I take a few steps down the gravel path and onto the lawn, though my heels sink into the damp, uncut grass.

Everything is still.

I listen hard for sounds of him searching the undergrowth; all I can hear is the steady hum of traffic on the main road and a plane somewhere in the distance. But there are birds chukking in alarm in the dark cluster of trees, and suddenly I catch a faint rustle from the shrubs where the lawn meets the undergrowth. Is that Logan coming back?

I take a step closer. 'Hello?'

Nothing stirs beyond the lawn. In vain, I scan the beech trees, elder and hawthorn, their roots shrouded in low-creeping plants and

22

shrubs. And there's the wide-girthed sycamore, with an old wooden swing still attached to one of the lower branches, that I used to play on as a teenager, swinging back and forth on my own or being pushed by my brother...

The rustling sound comes again. Louder now.

I step back, holding my breath.

Seconds later, Logan bursts out of the undergrowth, and a bird in a nearby tree clatters away in surprise.

'Nobody there,' he calls to me, heading my way. 'I went all the way to the back fence. Looks secure enough.'

He has mud on his boots. Mortified, I pull a face. 'What a wild goose chase. I'm so sorry, I must be seeing things...'

'It's not a problem.' His smile reassures me. 'Better safe than sorry.'

At the door, he wipes his boots on the outside mat and then follows me into the house. Mum is awake again, sitting up and craning round to see who it is.

'This is my mother,' I say awkwardly. 'Mum, this is Logan. He was one of David's friends.'

She stares at him, saying nothing.

'Hello,' Logan says, and gives her a friendly smile. Then, when she greets this with a continuing silence, he looks back at me. 'Did you ring the sitter? Just in case she forgot.'

'It's a he,' I say, and check my phone again. Still nothing from Giorgios. I'm so stressed out now, I don't know what to do. 'Maybe we should stay in. I could cook us a meal.' I haven't even checked what's in the fridge. 'Or defrost something.'

He looks amused. 'You don't sound too keen.' He gets out his own phone. 'Look, maybe I can ring one of my friends, who's in a similar situation. He might be able to recommend a carer at short notice.'

'Mum's used to Giorgios.'

'Of course, stupid of me.' He puts his phone away again. 'Dinner here would be fine. Maybe we could all eat together. Or watch a film.'

Together?

The horror of sitting down to eat dinner with him and my mother, who frequently needs help with eating and would certainly need her food cut up into little bits, and who tends not to eat much by way of an evening meal anyway, is too much for me. That's not how I envisaged tonight's date.

As for us all watching a film, I can already imagine Mum constantly interrupting to ask for an explanation that swiftly becomes circuitous as she asks for it to be repeated again and again.

I love my mother dearly. But there are limits…

'Give me a few minutes,' I say with a smile, trying not to sound too despairing, and slip into the hall.

The agency number is on the hall table. I try them, but it's only the voicemail service. There's a flier too, from a new carer. They might be worth trying. But I don't like having people in the house who aren't properly vetted, or at the very least recommended to me by a friend.

I hesitate, then call Stella from my yoga class instead. She's always waxing lyrical about her dad's marvellous nurse, who knows everything about dementia patients and is so thoughtful. It makes me quite envious to hear her talk about him.

To my relief, she answers at the second ring. 'Hello, Kate,' Stella almost shouts down the phone, a cacophony of noise in the background. 'Sorry about the racket; we've got the telly turned right up so Dad can hear it. He's deaf in one ear, did I ever tell you? Anyway, better speak up…'

Raising my voice, I explain that Giorgios hasn't shown up to sit with my mother, and Stella instantly sympathises.

'Do you want my carer's number? Francis is wonderful; he'll come right over.' Then, halfway through reading out his telephone number, she groans and says, 'I'm sorry, I just remembered, he asked me last week not to recommend him to anyone else because he's got no slots free at the moment. I've been giving his name out to everyone who asks. Very naughty of me.'

'Damn,' I mutter, panicking.

'Is it really that urgent?'

'It's my first date in years,' I say, lowering my voice and hoping that Logan can't hear me. 'I'm all dressed up, and now...'

'That's awful, you poor thing. I don't know what to suggest... Oh, hang on a tick. I forgot about Ruby.'

'Ruby? Who's that?'

'She was recommended to me by someone before I got the Fabulous Francis. Apparently, she's really sweet and utterly brilliant with dementia patients. So good you'll never go back to Giorgios.'

I grin. 'I don't know about that. I sometimes think Mum loves Giorgios more than she loves me. But if this Ruby can look after Mum tonight, I'll probably thank her on my knees.'

'She's not cheap, as I recall.'

'That's okay.'

'She put a flier through the door. But I don't know what I did with mine.'

'A flier?' I blink. 'Oh, I got that one too. It's right in front of me! Ruby Chambers? Thanks, Stella.'

I dial the number and it rings about seven times, while my heart thumps ridiculously. Please answer, I think grimly. I want this date with Logan to go well, and right now it seems doomed to fail.

At last, somebody answers.

'Hello?' It's a woman's voice, deep and rich and melodic. 'Ruby Chambers here, can I help you?'

I explain the situation, and to my relief, she agrees to come straight over. She insists on texting me her usual references so I can feel secure leaving her with my mother. I give her the postcode for the Sat Nav, we discuss a fee, and then I ring off.

When I turn around, Logan is in the doorway to the living room, watching me intently.

'Did you manage to find someone?' he asks quickly.

'Yes, no problem. A woman called Ruby is coming over right away to sit with her.'

Hurriedly, I check the two referees' names that she sent through and feel reassured. One of them is a woman I know from a charity I volunteered with a few years back, and another is one of our local councillors. Dad was quite active in the small community around here during my teens, so I know most people involved in local politics.

'Unusual name,' Logan comments.

'I suppose so. Once she's here, and I've introduced her to my mother, we can go out.' I catch sight of my flushed face in the hall mirror and feel a little self-conscious. All this nonsense must seem very chaotic and disorganised to him. 'I'm so sorry about this. It shouldn't be much longer. Ruby said she'd be about twenty minutes.'

My nerves are frayed, and no wonder. This isn't just any first date; this is one of David's closest friends. Part of me is pleased that we'll be able to go out for a meal tonight after all. But part of me is afraid of what he may ask me about David. About his death, in particular.

But Logan doesn't seem to notice my uneasiness.

'That's wonderful. Though I can still cancel the restaurant if necessary. I'll happily stay in with you and your mother if you feel at all uncomfortable.'

'No, I want to go out.'

'Okay.' He glances over his shoulder at the drinks tray on the sideboard. 'Well, I don't know about you, but I'm parched. Shall I pour us both an aperitif while we wait? Mine will be non-alcoholic, of course, since I'm the designated driver tonight.'

I force a confident smile to my lips. 'That would be perfect, thank you.'

CHAPTER FOUR

Ruby surprises me by being completely lovely, just as Stella had described her to me. She's quite tall compared to me, and a little on the well-built side, with comfortably padded hips and a prominent chest disguised by a long suede skirt and flowery overshirt, topped with a soft purple pashmina shawl that covers all sins. She also has a frank smile and intelligent eyes, though keeps referring to me as 'love', which I find a little overfamiliar.

But I'm ecstatic that she's here, so I accept her 'love' with a nod and a grateful handshake.

Briefly, I recap what I already told her on the phone so she's up to speed with Mum's medical condition, and then point her towards the soup I've been heating for Mum's supper.

'She doesn't tend to eat anything heavier than soup or a salad in the evenings,' I add, in case she thinks soup a bit of a miserly meal.

'Don't fret, love. I'll make sure she gets the soup.' Ruby also shakes hands with Logan, who's still lurking in the hallway when she arrives, having long since finished his non-alcoholic drink. 'Pleased to meet you.'

He nods, then flicks me a glance. 'I'll wait in the car, shall I?' he says diplomatically.

When he's gone, I take Ruby through to the living room to meet my mother. 'Mum,' I say gently, hoping she won't kick up a fuss, 'this is the lady who'll be sitting with you tonight.'

My mother looks up from under frowning brows. She's looking a bit confused, which worries me. I have a feeling she nodded off while we were out of the room and isn't quite aware of her surroundings yet.

'Lady? What lady?' Her bleary gaze swings past Ruby as though she doesn't see her. She does, of course. But she's often unwilling to acknowledge anyone she doesn't recognise or would rather *not* see. Mum can be stubborn that way. 'Where's Giorgios?'

I explain again about Giorgios's non-arrival, adding cheerily, 'Ruby, this is my mother, Celeste.'

'How do you do, Celeste.' Ruby bends forward to shake her hand, but Mum doesn't lift hers in response. Thankfully, Ruby's smile is patient and understanding. 'Or would you prefer Mrs Kinley?'

'Celeste,' Mum mutters. 'Ruby… That's an old-fashioned name.'

'Isn't it just?' Ruby perches on the sofa opposite my mother. She seems amused rather than offended. 'Though Celeste isn't a very common name either. Perhaps we should go on the stage together. Ruby and Celeste. Has quite a ring to it, don't you think?'

Mum looks astonished.

For a moment, I'm afraid Mum will launch into one of her tantrums and refuse to have Ruby sit with her tonight.

But Mum studies Ruby suspiciously, and then asks, 'Do you like crossword puzzles?'

'Not much,' Ruby admits.

'Good.' Mum looks satisfied. 'Neither do I.'

I check the time.

'It's only for tonight,' I remind her, darting a quick kiss to Mum's cheek, and edge out of the room. 'Ruby?'

Ruby follows me out to the front door.

'You've got my mobile number,' I say hurriedly, grabbing my jacket and handbag. 'I've pinned an information sheet to the kitchen board – dietary needs, meds, and her doctor's number. Though just call me if there are any problems.'

'You leave everything to me, love,' Ruby says calmly, and nods me off. 'You'll see, your mum and I will be the best of friends by the time you get back home.'

Dinner out with Logan is a marvellous experience. I've never been to the side street French bistro he's chosen, but it seems popular and is bustling with diners. There's low French music playing out of hidden wall speakers, and each table is set into a discrete high-sided booth with an engraved glass panel that prevents others from hearing our conversation, which is rather cosy. We order hors d'oeuvres and a main meal each, and sit opposite each other on softly padded benches, talking throughout the meal about... well, about everything under the sun.

Logan is an excellent conversationalist, I soon discover; steady in his opinions but perfectly calm when I disagree with him, and we move rapidly through politics, both local and global, to environmental issues, traffic concerns around Guildford and into London, and finally health, which leads us into less certain territory.

After our light hors d'oeuvres, our main meals arrive. Logan is an unashamed carnivore, happily devouring a fillet steak with fried mushrooms and a jacket potato. I also enjoy eating meat but like fish too, so tuck into trout with almonds, served with sautéed potatoes. It's absolutely delicious and a real treat, for my mother has never been keen on fish, so we rarely eat it these days.

Eventually, he asks about my family.

I talk about my father and brother, and how they died in an avalanche, and he nods with sympathy yet shows little surprise.

No doubt he heard all about it when the accident first occurred. My father was so well respected, the local papers covered the tragedy in horrific detail, meaning I had to walk past newsstands with my face averted for some weeks, just in case I saw something to set me off crying again…

When the topic of my mother's dementia comes up at last, I decide not to shy away from it as I ordinarily would. It's probably an illusion, given how little I know the man, but I feel as though I can trust Logan with anything. He just has one of those faces…

'But you've chosen to look after her at home,' he comments after listening to me explain her diagnosis and how rapidly the dementia is advancing now. 'That's brave.'

'What do you mean?'

His dark eyes survey me thoughtfully. 'Forgive me, I had an opportunity to speak to your mother while you were busy. She seemed confused. Not always aware of her surroundings, and probably unable to look after herself in any meaningful way.'

'That sounds about right,' I mutter.

'I imagine her care must be quite complex and demanding, to say the least.' Logan hesitates, then adds gently, 'Many people in your situation would have arranged for her to move into a residential home by now. To lighten the burden of care.'

'You think I should put my mother in a home?' I shake my head, giving a brittle laugh. 'Not likely!'

'As I said, that's very brave of you. It can't be easy.'

'No, it isn't,' I admit, feeling awkward at the way this conversation has swung so quickly towards a topic I hate even thinking about. 'But Mum wouldn't be happy living anywhere else. We discussed it

31

in the past. Before she got quite so… confused, as you put it. And she made it perfectly plain that she intended to stay at home for as long as possible.'

'Sounds like your mother's a forthright lady.'

'Oh God, you don't know the half of it.' I check the time on my phone and note there are no messages. 'I hope Ruby's getting on okay with her. Mum can be difficult. Especially with new people.'

I'm aware of a feeling of unease at leaving Mum with a stranger. But she seemed to click with Ruby straightaway, so I'm probably being foolish. Besides, Ruby looked to be a confident sort who wouldn't be bothered by any of the games Mum likes to play when she's in one of her tricky moods.

'I'm sure Ruby will be fine. I only met her for a couple of minutes, but she struck me as an extremely competent sort of woman.'

Logan nods to a waiter, who comes swiftly over in response. Logan has such an air of authority about him, I think, secretly reminded of my father. Dad too only ever had to raise an eyebrow to have people scurrying to do his bidding.

'Would you like a dessert?' Logan asks me, leaning back to allow the waiter to remove his plate. 'Or maybe some coffee?'

I shake my head reluctantly. I would like to linger over coffee, talking more, getting to know this man. But I'm also painfully aware of how long we've been out.

'I should get back. Check on Mum.'

'Of course.' To my relief, he doesn't look annoyed or attempt to persuade me to stay. Instead, he asks the waiter for the bill, then smiles at me reassuringly. 'I've really enjoyed myself this evening. Perhaps we could do this again sometime? There's a new Chinese place I haven't tried yet.'

'I love Chinese food.'

But when I get out my purse, he frowns and says, 'No, I invited you to dinner. I should be the one to pay.'

'There's really no need. Let's split it.'

Logan hesitates, then shrugs. 'If you insist. But let me take care of the tip, at least.'

I agree to this since there's no point putting his back up. And it is rather lovely to have dinner with someone so very courteous, even to the point of being a little old-fashioned. It's been a long time since anybody treated me in such a caring way…

Back home, I find the house in semi-darkness. Logan escorts me to the front door but insists on waiting outside while I pop in to check on Mum.

'Just in case you need me,' he says enigmatically.

Everything inside is still and quiet.

As I'm taking off my jacket, Ruby tiptoes out of the living room, smiling but with a finger on her lips.

'Your mum's tucked up in bed,' she whispers, pointing to the downstairs room that Mum now uses as a bedroom to save her having to negotiate the stairs every day. 'I've checked on her twice and she's asleep now.'

This is so unusual, I stare.

'Really? But Mum always takes ages to settle.'

Ruby nods with understanding. 'I expect she does, yes. But I put a little music on in her room, just very softly. She said she likes jazz.'

'She used to, yes,' I stammer, surprised by how quickly she's managed to gain my mother's confidence.

'I find music can be helpful for getting dementia patients to sleep. Music or white noise, it doesn't matter which. But they seem to prefer that to complete silence. It's playing on a loop, but you might want to turn the music centre off before you go to bed.'

'Thank you.'

I pay her what we agreed, and she heads out the door with a cheery wave.

Logan, a shadow in the porch, steps forward into the light as soon as she's gone.

I'm oddly nervous now we're alone together, without the noise of the bistro around us. The night seems very dark behind his head, a rack of sombre clouds masking the merest sliver of a moon. He dominates the space, very large and masculine. But not intimidating, I remind myself.

I suppose I've got used to not having any men in my life, that's all.

'Well,' he says deeply, 'that sounded promising.'

'It certainly seems to have gone better than I feared.' I smile up at him, suddenly awkward and uncertain. Is he expecting me to invite him in? However pleased I might have been to get a dinner date at last, I'm definitely not ready for that. 'Look, I'm a bit tired, so—'

'Yes, me too,' he interrupts me. 'I was only waiting in case you…' He stops, and laughs. 'It was a great evening. Thank you.' He stoops and kisses me on the cheek, close to my mouth, and then straightens. 'Good night.'

I close the front door and lock it, kick off my high heels with a sigh of relief, and tread softly, barefoot toward my mother's bedroom.

The door is partly ajar.

From inside, I can hear the gentle strains of jazz music…

Peeking inside, I find my mother fast asleep under the covers, exactly as Ruby had said, her breathing even and seemingly undisturbed by the saxophone playing in the background.

I stand over her for a moment, so pleased I can barely stop myself from grinning, and then tiptoe over to click off the music centre.

The silence feels suddenly oppressive.

There's a slight gap between the curtains, I realise, and pull them closer together across the window, feeling an odd sense of apprehension. I glance about the bedroom, wishing I had not asked Logan to leave quite so soon, though it's ridiculous to be afraid of the dark at my age.

A memory returns of that shadowy figure I'd seen earlier in the evening, creeping about in the shrubbery…

Unless I imagined it.

My mother doesn't stir, continuing to sleep soundly, unaware of the world around her. Her silvery hair streams over the white pillows, her skin smoothed out in sleep.

'Night, Mum,' I whisper, though I know she can't possibly hear me.

CHAPTER FIVE

Monday comes with no reply from Giorgios to my repeated texts and calls. I usually go into work on a Monday, and this week I have a big presentation that I spent all weekend prepping for.

I call the agency. 'Giorgios Baros hasn't shown up.'

I explain that I've been trying to contact him for several days, though I don't mention the Friday evening arrangement, because he doesn't declare extra sessions earned without agency input and I don't want to get him into trouble.

Suella, who runs the agency, is horrified. 'I'm so sorry. He hasn't been in touch to let us know he's ill or had to go away.' She asks me to hold the line for a moment, then comes back, sounding embarrassed. 'We don't have anyone available to cover for Giorgios today, I'm afraid. Everyone's already placed somewhere else. In fact, we have three people down with illness and won't have any cover available for you until Thursday at the earliest.'

'Thursday?' I'm speechless.

She hesitates. 'I could try one of our ladies who's meant to be on honeymoon, but I can't guarantee—'

'No, I don't want to interrupt somebody's honeymoon, for

36

goodness's sake,' I tell her, and run a hand through my hair, despairingly. 'Look, it's okay, I'll sort it out myself. I'll ring work and tell them I can't make it in today.'

'I can't apologise enough, Miss Kinley,' Suella says, sounding genuinely contrite, though it's not her fault at all, adding, 'I'd better try Giorgios myself, find out what's happened.'

'Good luck with that. His mobile number goes straight to voicemail every time.'

'How odd. But maybe he lost his phone.'

'Maybe.'

After I hang up, I wander into the living room where my presentation notes are still spread out across the table, and stare down at them, unsure what to do.

I keep hoping to hear the front door open and see Giorgios's cheery face. But it's almost nine thirty by the time I've packed my papers into my briefcase and helped Mum to dress for the day, and there's zero chance by then that I can still reach central London in time for my presentation, which was scheduled for late morning.

Grimacing, I call my boss to apologise.

Mark is, unsurprisingly, furious. 'What do you mean you can't make it into the office today?'

'The nurse didn't show today. I can't leave my mother on her own.'

'I thought she had dementia, not a physical illness. I have a neighbour with dementia. He lives alone and seems to manage okay. Why does your mother need someone there *all day*?'

'As I've explained before,' I tell him through gritted teeth, trying not to snarl, 'it's not that simple. Maybe your neighbour's dementia is still at an early stage. But my mother's case is different. This is early onset dementia, and she's also deteriorating quite rapidly. So she shouldn't be left alone for long periods of time. It simply wouldn't be safe.'

'But why not?' he asks, clearly impatient.

'Well,' I say, gasping a little as my anxiety levels begin to rise, 'she might leave the house and wander off in her slippers, or go for a walk and forget where she lives. Or she might put something on the hob to cook for her lunch, forget it's there and burn the house down. With her in it.' My heart is thudding now, and my palms are clammy; I hate this kind of confrontational discussion. I resist the urge to ring off; he is my boss after all. 'Do you see where I'm going with this?'

'Don't get smart with me, Kate,' he says irascibly, but to my relief doesn't pursue the point. 'Okay, so when *can* you get in?'

'I'll have to speak to the agency again. They said they might be able to arrange someone for Thursday.'

'Thursday?'

The note in his voice is pretty much how I sounded too when it was suggested to me. But it is what it is.

'I know, I'm sorry.'

'I need to hear your presentation today, Kate. It's that important.' He pauses significantly. 'Or I may have to give the project to some-body else.'

I suck in a long breath and control my temper with an effort. Bloody man!

Mark's a nasty piece of work; he smiles in public, utterly charming to top authors or those above him in the food chain, but behind closed doors, he has a history of making people suffer even for minor acts of rebellion. It's taken me a long time to get to commissioning editor. I mustn't blow it now by telling him what a bastard he is, even if it's true.

'I could try to get in for this afternoon,' I say with difficulty.

Mark says nothing.

I'm promising the impossible, but what else am I supposed to do? I can't let my career slide; it would be unthinkable. And I'm sure

Mum wouldn't want that either. If she could understand what was happening, that is, which I doubt.

I add into the silence, trying to keep the irritation out of my voice, 'Perhaps we could reschedule the presentation for, say, two o'clock?'

'That's more like it,' he drawls, and even down the phone line, I can hear him smiling. 'I'll see you later, then.'

I put the phone back on its charging cradle and step outside to check on Mum, who's pottering about in the garden now with a trowel, attempting to garden.

It hurts to see her bent over, stabbing ineffectually at the earth. Mum was such a keen gardener once, knowing the names of all the flowers and plants she tended. Now she struggles to remember any of them, or how they should be looked after, but does love to make herself busy in the garden.

'Mum?' I glance at my car, and then back at her, not quite sure yet what I'm thinking but aware of an idea vaguely forming. 'How do you fancy a little drive out in the car? Just for half an hour to see the scenery.' She straightens up, trowel in hand, staring at me in surprise. 'We haven't done that in a while, have we?'

'I'd like a drive in the car,' she says decidedly.

'Good.' I head back inside for our coats and the car keys. 'I'll need to stop somewhere for five minutes. But you can wait in the car.'

I've only been to Giorgios's flat once before, back when he first started caring for Mum and accidentally left his phone at our place one evening.

'You sit tight,' I tell Mum, parking on the narrow side street where he lives, as close to his place as I can manage. 'I won't be long.'

'Where are we? Where are you going?'

'This is where Giorgios lives. I'm just going to check if he's okay.'

I hesitate, worried she may wander off while I'm gone, and remind her not to leave the vehicle.

'Can I turn the radio on?'

'It won't work without the keys in.'

'So leave the keys.'

'I can't, it wouldn't be safe.'

'Oh, don't be silly. I'll look after the car.'

'Honestly, I won't be more than a few minutes. You won't need the radio.'

'I think I should come with you.' She starts fiddling with her seat belt, trying to unbuckle it and escape.

I stop her. 'No, you need to wait here. Please don't do anything, Mum… Just stay in the car and think happy thoughts. All right?'

She pouts, looking about herself a little wildly, as though about to rebel. Luckily, a delivery van drives past slowly, as though looking for an address, and her gaze follows it along the street, suddenly caught. 'Happy thoughts,' she repeats, with a huffing sound on the 'H'. 'Happy, happy, happy.'

'Well done, that's the spirit.'

I'm not particularly happy myself, but I leave her and hurry down the road to Giorgios's place.

The curtains are closed.

I go back and knock on his front window, though I can't see a damn thing through his tightly closed curtains.

Still no movement from inside.

Finally, I hear a door opening, and turn around, hugely relieved. 'Giorgios?'

Only it's not Giorgios standing there; it's a middle-aged woman in a flowery housecoat and slippers. I've never seen her before in my life.

'Hello,' the woman says, peering round the corner at me suspiciously. 'Can I help you?'

'I'm a friend of Giorgios Baros. Is he at home?'

'He's gone on holiday,' she says, still looking me up and down. 'Who are you?'

At these words, I feel all the air go out of me.

Gone on holiday? Now what the hell am I supposed to do? But I keep smiling politely, gritting my teeth against a gnawing sense of disappointment and frustration; it's not her fault he's gone away, after all.

I introduce myself and briefly explain why I'm there, even pointing down the street towards the car where Mum is still waiting.

'It was a bit of a shock when he didn't turn up this morning. If he's on holiday though, that would explain it.' I pause, still baffled and annoyed. 'Sorry, do you know why he didn't contact me before leaving? Was this holiday unexpected? Because if he'd told me in advance, I could have arranged for someone else to look after my mother today.'

'No idea. He didn't say.'

'I see.' My smile feels fixed in place now. She's not being very helpful. 'Did Giorgios say how long he'd be gone?'

'No,' she snaps. 'He put a note under my door to say he was going away and to keep an eye on the flat for him, that's all.'

She turns away, and I follow her back to the door, confused. That's when I realise she came out of the flat opposite, not Giorgios's flat.

'You're his neighbour,' I say slowly.

'That's right.' The woman goes back into her flat and gives me a hard look over her shoulder. 'Now, if you'll excuse me…'

'Of course,' I say automatically, and add, 'Sorry to have disturbed you.'

But she's already slammed the door.

I turn and study Giorgios's front door for the moment, wondering what on earth he was thinking, just disappearing like that. Then I take a deep breath and hurry back to the Mazda.

I don't know what to do, and that unnerves me. I'm someone who likes to plan everything ahead of time, down to the last detail, so when plans get derailed, I tend to panic. Which is not a very comfortable feeling.

I promised Mark I would be in the office this afternoon.

Time is ticking.

'Where's Giorgios?' Mum asks when I get back in.

I explain, and she looks crestfallen.

'On holiday?'

'Apparently. So it looks like I won't be able to make it into work today after all,' I say, unable to disguise the wobbly note in my voice as I imagine what Mark will say when I cry off from the presentation for the second time today.

'Are you feeling upset, darling?' Mum asks, looking at me astutely from under thin, frowning brows. She has these sudden flashes of lucidity every now and then, which I love; it's so comforting to feel she's still my mum at those moments, still her old self.

'A little,' I admit.

'But I'll be perfectly fine on my own. I can do some gardening… And some knitting.' Mum sighs, looking down at her hands clasped in her lap. 'I can't remember what I was knitting. But it'll come to me in the end, I daresay.'

I have a vision of Mum heading out into the garden in her wellies and then absentmindedly wandering off down the road, trowel in hand, never to be seen again…

'Perhaps I could ask a neighbour to check on you,' I wonder out loud, chewing nervously on my lip. 'Once every hour, for instance. Just to be on the safe side.'

I've barely spoken to our neighbours, but I know that at least one of them, a mother with three kids of primary school age, is likely to be home this afternoon. Her husband is a high-powered lawyer and she doesn't seem to work, except for volunteering at one of the local charity shops once or twice a week. She's been round a few times, in fact, collecting for them. Her name's Beatrice. But I don't know her particularly well. I can't even recall her husband's name.

Oh God. This is disastrous.

The last thing I want is to go knocking on some stranger's door and ask if she'll check on my mother every so often while I pop into London.

Grimly, I pull down the sun visor and check my reflection. I look washed out without any makeup on, and there are dark shadows under my eyes that are crying out for some concealer.

I used to thrive on stress. But these days, what with work pressure and having to deal with Mum's condition, things seem to be piling up, getting on top of me in ways that I don't recognise or know how to deal with.

I remember Friday night, and can't help smiling.

My dinner date with Logan was a break from all that intense pressure. He was such an interesting conversationalist, and a real gentleman too.

I'd like to see him again sometime.

'There's always Ruby, I suppose,' I add thoughtfully.

'Ruby?'

I sigh. 'You remember her, Mum. Ruby sat with you on Friday night while I was out with Logan.'

'Really?' She looks blank. 'Do I like her?'

'I thought you did, yes.'

Mum stares out of the car window. 'Ruby's a nice old-fashioned name.'

'That's right. In fact, you said the very same thing when you met her.' I study her face. 'So you do remember?'

She makes no comment.

'You seemed to get along with her quite well.' I hesitate, then find Ruby's number on my mobile phone. 'It's really short notice. She's probably not free, but…'

I don't see what else I can do, except not go into work, which feels like such a dangerous choice, I'm simply not prepared to make it if there's any possible alternative.

Ruby answers after only three rings, sounding a little out of breath. 'Of course I'm free,' she says cheerily in response to my hurried explanation. 'I don't usually work Mondays. But I can make an exception. If it's important.'

I look at myself in the visor mirror. 'It is pretty important, yes.' I pause, aware of Mum listening to this conversation, and not wanting to upset her with something she might not understand. Then I add self-consciously, 'I'm worried I might get the sack if I don't do this presentation.'

'Say no more. Give me twenty minutes.'

'Thank you.' I'm so grateful, there's a lump in my throat and I actually feel like crying. 'You're a life saver, Ruby.'

After I finish the call, I take a deep breath, starting the car engine, and allow myself to hope. Suddenly, the impossible is looking possible. I shouldn't have let Mark get to me earlier, or become so madly stressed about this.

Things are going to work out; I feel it in my bones. 'All sorted,' I tell Mum with a smile.

44

'I knew you could do it, darling.' Mum pats my hand on the steering wheel, her face indulgent. 'So there was no need to get upset, was there? Cinderella *shall* go to the ball.'

I laugh, feeling better already. 'Yes, you were right.'

Now all I need to do is grab my briefcase and give the best bloody presentation of my life...

'I wonder where Giorgios is,' Mum says as we head back to the house, echoing my thought. She sounds troubled.

'I know... It's all very strange. And inconvenient.' I try to sound cheerful though. 'But no doubt when Giorgios gets back from holiday, he'll explain the whole thing, and we'll have a good laugh about it.'

CHAPTER SIX

Mark strolls out of his glass-walled office as I stride through reception a few minutes before two o'clock en route to my desk in the open-plan area overlooking the city.

Habitually dressed like some fey nineteenth-century artist, today Mark is wearing a cream and plum waistcoat with a burgundy shirt and hideously clashing green corduroy trousers. The shirt is open-necked, but a silk scarf knotted about his neck hides his hairy chest – and for this relief, much thanks! Dark-haired and rather heavy-set, he has a goatee beard that he often strokes in an annoying way while speaking, and he has a tendency towards barbed comments and sarcasm that make office life a little uncomfortable. For me, at least. He seems much friendlier to some of the other editors, especially the females, who make up the majority here.

No beard-stroking today though. With both hands sunk into his pockets, jiggling his loose change thoughtfully, Mark positions himself in the gap beside two low bookcases that act as a space divider between editors and lowly editorial assistants, and through which I'll have to pass on my way to the meeting. It's an aggressive move that I deliberately ignore, pretending not to have even noticed his arrival.

Clearly irritated, he watches in silence as I sling my jacket over the back of my chair, open my briefcase and drag out various colour-coded folders I'll need for the presentation.

'Glad you could join us, Kate,' he drawls.

'Yeah, sorry for cutting it so fine…' Still breathless from my mad dash up the escalator, I log into my work computer and transfer my presentation files onto the office network so I'll be able to access them in the meeting. 'Like I said earlier, I had real difficulty finding someone to sit with my mother.'

I don't know why I think this excuse may soften his mood; Mark is never interested in our domestic arrangements, only in results. Which basically means book sales.

That's why he hasn't managed to get me sacked yet; I'm still handling a few of our long-term top sellers in non-fiction, and the company directors are worried one of them at least might jump ship with me if I were given the boot. Things are always on a knife-edge financially, so that's probably a risk they would only take as a last resort.

But I can't guarantee they won't sack me if I start failing to turn up on time. There are limits, after all. And Mark hates anyone who doesn't kiss his bottom on a daily basis. Which means me, basically.

Sure enough, when I glance at my boss, his gaze has risen to the wall clock. 'I wouldn't call this cutting it fine. You're late.'

'Only by about thirty seconds.'

'Even thirty seconds is too late as far as I'm concerned. I'm not psychic, Kate; I couldn't be sure you were even going to turn up. In fact, I was just about to cancel the meeting.' He jerks a thumb over his shoulder at the meeting room, where I can see the other senior editors and our marketing team already gathered. 'For the second time in one day.'

His ironic tone is not lost on me.

'This morning was a one-off problem, I promise.' I have an urge to cross my fingers in a superstitious gesture, as this isn't strictly true. But he's watching me, sharp-eyed and unpleasant, and I don't quite dare. 'I've got it sorted now.'

'I've forgotten, what exactly did you say the issue was?' Mark asks me impatiently, though he's famous for not caring about such things. I explain again about Giorgios's odd disappearance, and he shrugs dismissively. 'Sounds like a problem with a simple solution. Put your mother in a home. She's been ill a while now, hasn't she? It must be about time.'

I see two of the editorial assistants, Joan and Harry, glance up from their work, clearly shocked by this careless attitude, and know how they feel. I'm struggling not to snap back at the bastard myself.

But Mark only says things like that to bait me.

He wants to get a rise out of me; that's the simple truth. To make me lose my temper and lash out at him. Anything to give the man an excuse to get rid of me…

'She's fine with me for now,' I say as calmly as possible. 'Your message said there was something you wanted to say to me. Some kind of proposal?'

'Let's wait for a better time to discuss it. Over lunch, I believe I suggested. Maybe Thursday?' He crooks an ironic eyebrow. 'Assuming you can manage to be here on time, that is.'

'I'll be here, don't worry.' Gathering my folders, I tuck them under one arm, my chin raised. 'Shall we go through?'

My presentation on the true crime market goes surprisingly smoothly, given all the angst and drama that led up to it. But maybe the stress of getting to the office on time had driven all the fidgets out of my system, so I was free to give my presentation without looking too nervous. I know so much about true crime now, I really ought to try my hand at writing a thriller.

Afterwards, I grab a coffee and head back to my desk, sagging with relief. There's some mail waiting for me, which I hadn't had time to check before, so I sit down and work through the small stack of envelopes and parcels. Most people send work via email these days, which makes the snail-mail post easier to navigate. But a few die-hard wannabes still bombard us with paper submissions. These tend to get tossed straight into the slush pile. Today, one short sample catches my eye and goes into my bag to be read on the train home. The rest get shoved aside while I settle down to check my emails and internal memos.

'Here, you dropped one,' Harry says helpfully, stooping as he passes to pick up a small white envelope and hand it to me. 'Sorry about your mum, by the way. That sounds like a difficult situation.'

I give him a grateful smile and discuss my mother's care for a few minutes. I like Harry; he's an intern and a cheerful soul, always smiling, and the way he flicks back his shoulder-length curly brown hair while chatting is so endearing.

When he's gone, I break open the envelope he handed me.

It's marked with my name – handwritten in capitals, so presumably internal mail – and seems to contain only a single sheet.

With my gaze on my computer monitor, which is displaying a graph of last month's sales figures for one of my newest authors, I unfold the sheet and glance down at it absentmindedly.

I draw in my breath sharply and blink, shocked by the simple message printed in all capitals in a bold sans serif font.

YOU'RE SUCH A STONE-COLD BITCH. NO WONDER I KILLED MYSELF.

Beneath these words, the signature – also printed in capitals – reads DAVID.

Though, of course, it can't be from my boyfriend, David.

David's dead, as the message itself implies.

So this is some sick person in the office trying to upset me.

And it's working.

'What the hell...?'

There's a prickling sensation on the back of my neck as though someone's staring at me. Or is it just my guilty conscience? I've always feared that I could have done more to prevent David's death, despite everyone's reassurances that I wasn't to blame. Now it seems somebody else agrees with me. But who?

I glance swiftly around the office; nobody is looking my way.

Harry and Mark are deep in conversation by the coffee machine, and one of the design team, Abigail, is leaning over Joan's computer screen as the two women discuss a cover mock-up for our latest self-help book. Everyone else seems absorbed in their work.

Who could have sent me this? And why?

My hands are shaky as I fold the sheet over double and stuff it hurriedly back into its envelope, then drop it into my handbag. I'll examine it later, when I'm back home and feeling calmer. Or maybe I'll just rip it up and throw it into a bin, which is where it belongs.

I click on the screen graphics to see more detail on the sales stats. But I'm just reading the same figures again and again, not really taking them in, my mind still blank after the horror of receiving such a vile anonymous message. It's all I can think about.

Should I tell someone? Mark, perhaps?

I glance across and find his gaze on me. Harry has strolled away, coffee mug in hand, but Mark is still there in the tea and coffee-making area. He's stroking his goatee, dark eyes narrowed thoughtfully on my face, but looks away as soon as he realises I've spotted him.

No, not Mark.

I ponder for a moment whether he could be behind the note. But then dismiss it as improbable. My boss may be unpleasant, but he's upfront about it. He wouldn't bother hiding behind a poison pen letter.

Would he?

I stare back at the screen, clicking the mouse automatically, but in truth, I can't see a thing. My vision has blurred with sudden, unexpected tears. I blink them away, horribly embarrassed and afraid someone will spot me crying at my desk and think I'm losing it.

NO WONDER I KILLED MYSELF.

My stomach clenches in fresh agony at an old memory. Getting that late night call, the disbelief and guilt churning inside me, my terrified and erratic drive through a rainstorm to find blue lights flashing outside his place…

Thankfully, before my mind can go too far down that horrifying route, the mobile on my desk vibrates, and I snatch it up.

It's Logan.

I'm so relieved at the distraction that I don't register who it is at first. Logan hasn't been in touch since our dinner date on Friday night, and I'd started to worry that my issues with Mum's care had put him off seeing me again. He'd been polite and sympathetic at the time, of course. But how else could he have reacted?

'Hello? Kate?'

'Hi, yes…' Trying not to sound breathless, I get up and wander across to the external glass wall overlooking the city; it's such a fabulous view, and somehow super-calming right now. We're fifteen storeys up here and the glass walls make the office feel light and airy. 'How are you?'

'Great, thanks, and hoping you and I can meet up again this week,' Logan says crisply, wasting little time on small talk. No doubt he's at work too. 'There's a film on at the arthouse place – French with

51

subtitles. No idea what it's about. But I thought…' He hesitates. 'Well, since you work in the arts, maybe that's something that would interest you.'

'I'd hardly call publishing "the arts", but you're right, I am interested.' More in seeing him again than in watching a French film, but I keep that part to myself. 'I haven't been to the cinema in ages. I'm at work, but maybe you could text me the details when you get a minute?'

He agrees to this at once. 'And how's your mother? Did you ever hear back from that Greek guy?'

'Giorgios? No, I'm afraid not.' I guess he's asking in case I back out at the last minute, having failed to find a sitter for Mum. 'But it looks like I may have found someone to take his place, so it shouldn't be an issue. Ruby, in fact. The woman you met.'

'That's excellent news. I'm so pleased.' Logan pauses. 'You were clearly upset about it on Friday. A difficult situation for you.'

I swallow, a wave of emotion rising inside me, and hurriedly change the subject before my eyes can get misty again.

He rings off a few minutes later, and I turn to find Mark standing behind me, his eyes slitty and dangerous, like a cat watching a bird.

'Was that a personal call, by any chance?' he demands.

I feel a tide of panic rising inside me, and wish again that I am not such a mess where his bullying and intimidating tactics are concerned.

'Yes, I'm sorry,' I say swiftly, 'but I was only on for a few minutes.'

'It doesn't matter how long the call was. You're not being paid to chat, Kate. You only come into the office a few days every month now. I feel that I've been very understanding of your situation. Is it so much to ask in return that you give the job one hundred per cent of your attention while you're actually at work?'

People are staring. My cheeks are hot. Couldn't he have called me into the relative privacy of his office to give me this reprimand?

I begin to stammer something, but he's already turned away…

Putting away my mobile, I sit down at the desk and stare in a futile manner at my computer screen. I have no idea what I'm looking at. My heart is thumping; my palms are sweating. I hate confrontation so much. But I can't let him intimidate me. Or I'm finished. Not just in my career at this company but as a person.

I have always suffered with my mental health. As a teenager, I was particularly fragile, especially around relationships. Yet I somehow held it together until my father and brother died. That tragedy hit me hard. But, by focusing on my mother and her needs, I'd pushed aside my own pain and made it through our long bereavement. But then David killed himself. For a while after that, I tumbled into a bottomless emotional hell, and could barely get out of bed in the mornings. Thankfully, the publisher where I'd been working at the time had been very understanding and allowed me time off to recover from that second terrible blow. But this publishing company, and that awful man… I'm not in a safe space anymore, and that's the truth of the matter.

'Hey, are you okay?' Harry stops beside my desk, his face concerned. 'I couldn't help overhearing all that. Tell me to mind my own business, but I don't think you should let Mark talk to you like that. He may be our boss but there are limits… You should make a complaint to someone.'

'Who?'

'I don't know. Human resources? Or escalate it upstairs.'

I'm embarrassed but grateful at the same time. Harry means well.

'Thank you, but I'm fine, honestly.'

I click the mouse without even looking at the screen, pretending to be working, and force my voice to sound less shaky. Harry must think I'm such a flake.

'Well, if you ever need any advice, or just a shoulder to cry on, you know where I am.'

'That's very kind of you, Harry.' With some difficulty, because I'm feeling a little tearful, I manage a misty smile in a probably futile attempt to reassure him. 'But I'd better get on with my work, before he catches me chatting again. He's on my case at the moment. Though I don't know why.'

'I can guess,' Harry replies in a low voice. 'Your presentation was brilliant, and he couldn't stand it. I can't believe you didn't get that last promotion you went for. You certainly deserved it.' He glances around warily and then bends over my shoulder, whispering in my ear, 'If you ask me, it was Mark who made sure you got shafted.'

'Sorry?'

'It's just gossip but… Look, the word is he started sleeping with Debs over the summer, and that's why Debs got that promotion. So it would have been in his best interests to make you look bad during the selection process. Of course, I'm not saying that's what happened.' He makes a face. 'Only that's what people have been saying. Just thought you might like to know.'

I say nothing, feeling we're on dodgy territory with Mark only a few feet away in his office and Debs on the phone to someone at her own desk.

But once he's gone, I struggle to focus on my work, his words echoing painfully in my head.

Not getting that promotion to managing editor had been a real blow to me. At the time, I put it down to my problems at home and not being able to guarantee being in the office more than a couple of times a week. Working from home is more acceptable these days. But there are some tasks management still expect us to do face-to-face, so I was always going to be at a disadvantage there.

However, it had been a genuine shock when Debs, despite her lack of experience, bagged the job instead of me. I'd assumed my application must have been weak in some way. But if she really is Mark's latest squeeze, that would make better sense.

I grit my teeth and go back to the sales stats.

But underneath the embarrassment and turmoil raging in my head is the nagging question that I know will dominate my journey home and destroy my peace of mind for several days to come.

Who in this office could have sent me that poison pen letter? Basically, who hates me enough to do something like that?

CHAPTER SEVEN

It's getting dark by the time I reach home, a pale half-moon rising above the trees. The house looks lit up and welcoming, and I can hear the faint roar of the heating boiler. My feet are aching and I'm longing to kick off my shoes and collapse onto the sofa with a large glass of gin and tonic.

But of course it's not Giorgios, who is practically a member of the family these days, with Mum this evening, it's Ruby. I would feel awkward behaving like that in front of her.

As I put the key into the lock and open the front door, I catch a burst of laughter from inside. Not one woman laughing, but two.

No, not laughing.

Giggling.

I haven't heard my mother enjoy herself like that in a long time.

Astonished, I walk through to the living room, still shrugging out of my jacket. 'Hello?'

Mum is in her armchair, a chaotic pile of knitting and balls of wool in her lap. Beside her on the floor, kneeling with both hands held up, is Ruby. Her hands are tied together with long fluffy strands of wool, red, blue and a garish yellow-orange, all wound round in a hopeless tangle.

'What on earth…?'

'We've been playing a game while we waited for you to come home,' Ruby tells me, smiling broadly.

'I'm sorry it's a little later than I said,' I say stiffly, checking the clock on the mantel. 'I'll cover the extra time, don't worry.'

'Oh, I don't mind,' Ruby insists.

'So, what's this game you're playing?' I ask my mother. 'You certainly seem to have been enjoying yourselves.'

Mum winds another strand of wool around Ruby's raised hands. 'Cat's Cradle, of course,' she informs me proudly. 'Didn't I ever show you how to do it?'

'Maybe when I was young.'

'I used to love playing Cat's Cradle when I was a child. My grandmother showed me how to do it. Round and round until you run out of wool…' Mum frowns at the messy tangle, and then gives another merry laugh, seemingly unconcerned. 'Though this isn't quite right.'

'No, it does seem to have gone wrong.'

'I'm her prisoner. See?'

My mother giggles again. 'Kate, help her, would you?'

I just want to pour myself a large gin after today's trials and maybe put the news on, something to drown out the fears circulating in my head. But Ruby holds up her hands, looking at me expectantly, so I smile and help her remove the mass of wool strands binding her hands hopelessly together.

Ruby explains apologetically, 'After the first few times, I suggested we mix colours. But it got a bit confusing. So we gave up trying to keep the wool untangled, and just kept going. This is more fun though.' She winks at my mother. 'Isn't it, Celeste?'

'Definitely.' Mum grins, sitting back in her armchair with a contented sigh. 'I'm so tired now, I could go to sleep.'

I'm surprised. 'Did you not take a nap this afternoon?'

'Was there supposed to be nap time?' Ruby looks contrite. 'My fault. I must have missed that in your notes.'

'No, it's fine. She doesn't always take a nap. And maybe I forgot to mention it, anyway. Everything was so rushed today.'

'Don't fuss, Kate,' Mum says, without opening her eyes.

'I'm not fussing. Besides, if you were enjoying yourself, then why stop for a nap?' I finish unwinding the last strands of wool from Ruby's hands and collect up the knitting from Mum's lap. 'Have you eaten supper yet?'

Mum says nothing. Her eyes are still closed.

She looks exhausted.

'Not yet. We were having too much fun, I suppose.' Ruby catches my frustrated look and gets up from the floor. 'Sorry, I'll heat up some chicken soup before I leave.'

'No, it's fine.' I put away the knitting and spare wool in Mum's embroidery bag. 'I'll do it. You should get off home. I've kept you late enough as it is.'

Out in the hallway, out of my mum's earshot, I pay her what I owe for today's session and ask how it went.

'Your mother's a dream to care for,' she tells me warmly. 'I had no problems at all.'

I'm surprised but say nothing. My mother can be pretty hard work at times. But maybe she's only that way with me. It's true that Giorgios always seemed to keep her in a good mood. But he's a good-looking young man, and Ruby can't be ticking any of Mum's boxes in the same way he does. Though I suppose she's very smiley.

'Do you think you could come back on Thursday?' I ask tentatively. 'I have a working lunch in London.'

'Thursday?' Ruby pulls on a thick black coat and matching bobble hat. 'You're in luck,' she says indistinctively, wrapping a thick cherry-red scarf about her neck. 'The old lady I've been caring for passed away last weekend, very sadly. Poor dear was ninety-three, and poorly, but I do miss her. So I will be free on Thursday.'

'That's brilliant, thank you.'

'The only thing is,' she adds, frowning slightly, 'I prefer to have some continuity in care. That is, I'm not keen on dropping in and out of old folks' lives on an occasional basis. It's much kinder if they have the same person caring for them full-time.'

'I agree,' I begin, but am interrupted.

'I just think it would be best if we could make this a more permanent arrangement.'

'Oh.' I hesitate, uncertain. 'But Giorgios is only on holiday. I expect he'll be back in a week or two.'

I'm worried she wants to press me into a contract of some kind, and I'm not ready to go that far. She's only cared for Mum twice so far, and while she's clearly a very nice woman, we barely know her.

'I see.' Ruby nods, smiling again. 'Well, I'll have to check my schedule. I should be able to make Thursday. But if something else comes up—'

'No, please, wait.' I touch her shoulder briefly as she turns to the door. 'Of course you're right. It's not fair on you to keep it on an ad hoc basis; I can see that. So why don't we make it permanent for now, and maybe you could share care with Giorgios when he comes back?'

'That's a good idea.'

We shake hands, and then she pulls on her woollen gloves, the same cherry-red as her scarf.

'Goodnight,' she says, and then calls back to Mum, 'Goodnight, Celeste. Have a good evening!'

It's chilly outside.

I watch Ruby walk across to her small white Fiat, wait until she's safely inside and has started her engine, and then close the door with a final wave and a sigh of relief.

It's vitally important that I make that lunch date with Mark on Thursday. Much as I dislike the man, he's still my boss and I need to get him onside if I want my career to go more smoothly.

'Now, Mum,' I say cheerily, kicking off my shoes and heading back into the living room barefoot, 'how about some warm chicken soup?'

It's about three o'clock in the morning when I wake with a start, sure that I heard the sound of breaking glass.

Snapping on the light, I stumble out of bed and grab my dressing gown. All is silent and dark on the landing.

Did I imagine that noise?

A lamp is always left on downstairs in the hallway, for Mum's sake, as she often needs the toilet in the night or just gets up and wanders about in a daze, unsure of her surroundings. Without a light constantly on, she might trip and fall.

Tonight, the soft glow of the night light feels very comforting. I hurry down to check on Mum first. The door of her downstairs bedroom is closed, but when I take a quick peek inside, she seems to be fast asleep. So I shut the door again quietly and tiptoe into the dark living room instead.

Everything seems to be fine in there, and in the kitchen too. I check the other rooms, and then hesitate at the front door.

I'm sure now that breaking glass was what roused me from sleep.

Was someone trying to steal my car, perhaps?

But if they'd broken the window, wouldn't the car alarm have gone off? Or had they somehow managed to disable it?

My heart is thumping so loud, I feel almost sick.

But it's ridiculous not to check.

I can see the car from the front door, but not the windows. Uneasily, armed with a torch, I unlock the front door and peek outside.

The car looks fine.

Everything is still in the dark garden beyond it, the lawn empty under the moonlight, the trees thick with shadows.

But then, at the very edge of my hearing, I catch a tiny sound.

A kind of grating that lasts maybe a fraction of a second, and is followed by deep silence again.

Gasping with fright, I shut and lock the door, and then fumble to put the chain on too, something I haven't done in years.

I stand before the shut door, my mind flicking through the various possibilities at lightning speed. Perhaps it was an animal that had slipped hurriedly back into darkness when the door opened. Or my imagination, in fact. Like the sound of breaking glass when nothing seemed to be broken.

But I can't escape the idea that somebody is out there, watching the house. Watching *me*. Because that noise had sounded uncannily like a foot readjusting its weight on the gravel drive, or turning slightly in my direction.

In the morning, going out first thing to investigate before breakfast, I stand in my dressing gown and listen to birdsong from the trees.

Everything looks so normal and innocuous in the daylight, I'm embarrassed to remember how scared I was during the night. But then, things always feel so much more threatening in the dark.

But then, I wander a little way along the house wall, having spotted glass glinting on the gravel, and discover that someone has smashed the front security light. The one that illuminates the drive when people approach the house from the road. Not by accident – by a neighbouring child's stray ball, for instance – but deliberately and comprehensively. The outer glass has been smashed to pieces, and the bulb too. It will all need to be replaced.

The positioning of the light is quite high up. Higher than I can reach, even on tiptoe. But I'm only just over five foot.

I doubt it's much beyond the stretch of the average man, especially one armed with a long-handled implement. Like a hammer, for instance.

I stare down at the glass shards among the gravel, and then glance around at the quiet garden, more than a little panicked. Somebody stood here last night, presumably at around three in the morning, and smashed our security light, the unexpected sound waking me up.

I can't remember when I've felt this frightened before. Which is stupid, I tell myself, given the likeliest explanation that this is sheer vandalism. The work of some bored, destructive local kids who wandered in off the road during the night and had a bit of fun at our expense.

Because what else could it be?

CHAPTER EIGHT

Irina is our twice-weekly cleaner. She's often strangely deaf to my requests when I ask her to perform tasks she considers beneath her dignity or not in the job description, which I find infuriating. But she's punctual, reliable, and not too bad at what she grudgingly does about the place.

She's been with us for the past three years, another recommendation from one of my friends, whose large, lovely house she also cleans.

I've sometimes made the mistake of asking Irina if she'll keep an eye on Mum while I pop out to the shops. While she doesn't usually refuse, it's made clear by her eye-rolling and noisy tutting that such requests are resented and seen as a vast imposition, which makes me reluctant to repeat them. But no doubt that's the point.

On Thursday morning, Irina lets herself in at eight thirty on the dot, nods cheerlessly in my direction and drags the vacuum cleaner out of its cupboard under the stairs.

I tell her about Giorgios as she bustles about the hall, dragging off her faux-fur lined jacket and plugging in the Dyson.

'Giorgios's lucky,' she comments, with just a hint of underlying bitterness. 'I could do with a holiday.'

'But don't you think it's strange? I keep trying his mobile, but there's no reply. He could at least have given us some warning.'

She shrugs, tying a lurid headscarf over her dyed blonde hair, her nails coated with sparkly pink nail varnish that glitters as her nimble fingers move back and forth. 'So you get another carer. So what?' Her bracelets jingle noisily as she pushes both sleeves up to her elbows. 'Easy come, easy go.'

'Actually, it's not been that easy to get a replacement. Not at such short notice.'

I'm fishing, and we both know it. But it would be so convenient if someone Mum already knows well, like Irina, could look after her occasionally.

'I clean, Miss Kinley.' Irina flashes me a narrow-eyed look, her meaning unmistakeable. 'I don't *care*.'

I force a smile and try not to comment on that statement. Though it's obvious she doesn't care.

'Well, we did find someone. Her name's Ruby. She'll be here at eleven, in fact. So you should get to meet her.'

Irina makes a non-committal noise, checking her makeup in the hall mirror.

She loves to wear bright, colourful clothing, regardless of any clashes, and today she has surpassed herself, clad in skin-tight purple leggings teamed with a neon pink baggy shirt, unbuttoned to the navel over what looks like a garish yellow leotard. Some days, I half-expect her to put the radio on and launch into an exercise routine instead of cleaning the house.

Today, she's in a fierce mood, wheeling the Dyson into the living room and clicking it on. I scoop up Mum's knitting bag just in time and clear it safely out of the way as the vacuum cleaner roars past the armchair. Then I hurry down the hall to Mum's bedroom to check she's ready to get up.

Mum's still in bed, her gaze unfocussed.

'You haven't forgotten that I'm going out today, have you?' I ask cheerily. 'Which means an early start for both of us.'

Of course, Mum will have completely forgotten. But I try to keep up the pretence that her memory is still in working order, knowing how much she hates me to suggest otherwise.

'You're going out?' She sounds bewildered.

I tweak her curtains open, letting a little natural light into the room, though not too much as it hurts her eyes first thing.

'That's right,' I say firmly. 'I'm taking the train into London in a couple of hours, and Ruby's coming to sit with you again.' I turn to face her with a determined smile. 'I thought you two might like to play chess this time. I can set the board up before I leave.'

Mum used to love chess. But although Giorgios was very good at coaxing her to play, she has become increasingly reluctant even to try. The frustration of not remembering the rules or even understanding the game is too much for her these days. Still, Dr Forster has advised me to persevere with chess and crossword puzzles, anything that will keep her brain active and challenged, so I'm determined to keep trying.

'Come on.' I help her out of bed and to the downstairs toilet before encouraging her to dress.

I used to feel embarrassed at first, helping Mum disrobe and into fresh underwear and clothes. Now it's just routine.

She can occasionally dress herself unaided. But that's becoming rarer these days, and always takes ages. Plus, when Mum dresses herself, there are often odd choices that mean we have to return and start again.

Washing and dressing, followed by the usual lengthy discussion of what to have for breakfast, takes almost an hour. She wants bacon and egg; I've been advised to give her porridge oats with blueberries and a sprinkling of seeds. The daily tussle is draining and repetitive, but something we just have to get through to keep her healthy.

As I'm finally clearing away Mum's breakfast bowl, my phone goes. It's Ruby.

'I'm so sorry, but I'm running a little late,' she says breathlessly. 'Maybe another half an hour. Are you okay to hang on until I arrive?'

I check the time, and am shocked. My train leaves in a little over twenty minutes. It takes at least ten minutes to reach the station car park.

'Oh my God, that's a complete disaster.' My heart thuds almost painfully. I stand in silent consternation for a moment, trying to work out whether or not I can ring and delay my meeting with Mark. For the second time this week. But everything inside me is screaming a refusal. I need to look reliable right now, not flaky. 'I'm sure you're doing everything you can to get here, but I have to say, that's desperately inconvenient. I really can't miss my train.'

'Can't you take a later train?'

'It's a lunch appointment. I'd be late. As it is, I'm cutting it fine.'

'Perhaps you could call the person you're meeting and let them know you're running late?' Her voice is encouraging. 'Half an hour, and I'll be there. I promise.'

My teeth are gritted. But I need to stay polite. 'Are you sure you can't shave that down to fifteen minutes?'

'I'd love to, but it's just impossible.'

Out of the corner of my eye, I spot Irina strolling out of the downstairs toilet in a desultory fashion, stripping off a pair of yellow Marigolds and dropping them into her cleaning tray.

'Okay, look,' I say hurriedly, 'just get here when you can. I may have to leave Mum alone for a few minutes, that's all.'

After ringing off, I hurry out to grab my coat and speak to Irina, explaining briefly that Ruby will be late and asking if she could stay a little longer than usual.

Irina stares at me with hard eyes. 'I'm due to leave at eleven o'clock, Miss Kinley. I always leave at eleven.'

'Just this once?'

'I have something else to do.'

I bite back a complaint about her inflexibility; I still need someone to look after Mum on Friday evening for my next date with Logan, and I'm by no means sure Ruby will want to come round two Friday nights in a row. The poor woman probably wants some kind of social life, after all.

'*Please?*'

Irina rolls her eyes, but seems to soften at my pleading look. 'Okay, fine. I can stay maybe fifteen minutes. But after that…'

'Thank you so much!' I snatch up my shoulder bag and head back into the kitchen to kiss Mum goodbye. She's still sitting at the breakfast table with a cold cup of tea, just staring into space. 'I'll be back later this afternoon. Irina will wait with you until Ruby's here.'

When she nods, seeming to understand, I whisk out of the house, trying not to panic about the situation.

'See you later!'

I force myself to be optimistic about this. I can't believe Irina would leave Mum alone, and maybe Ruby will reach the house earlier than stated. There's no reason to prophesy doom and gloom, even though my inner critic is doing just that as I weave the car hurriedly through busy traffic towards the railway station.

Besides, I need to focus on my career right now, or risk losing serious ground to my peers. This is no time to be cowardly.

CHAPTER NINE

At lunch, Mark is in a surprisingly cheerful mood. We walk from the office to a nearby, family-run Italian restaurant, which we sometimes use to wine and dine our authors. We're given a secluded corner table and order a simple pasta course each with side salads. To a background of lively Italian music, Mark crunches on breadsticks while I select a few green olives from the bowl the waiter set between us.

'How's your mother?' Mark asks, surprising me with unexpected small talk. 'Any better?'

I nearly choke on my olive. My unpleasant boss is asking after my mother's health? Can this be for real?

'Erm, not really. Dementia is a progressive disease, so she's much the same as ever.'

'Right, I see.' He pulls a face. 'That's a shame.'

There isn't much to say to that, so I merely nod, scooping up another tasty green olive as I try to conceal my dislike for him.

Mark smiles.

Now I'm really suspicious. Just getting asked out to lunch by Mark was alarming enough. But discussing my mother's health, and then *smiling* at me? This is a thousand miles from Mark's usual curt manner.

I wonder fleetingly where Debs is today, and if his new girlfriend knows about this intimate tete-a-tete over lunch.

I bet she doesn't.

Perhaps a little too abruptly, I ask, 'Mark, you wanted to talk to me about something?'

'Yes.' He seems more relieved than offended by the change in tone. 'So, here's the thing. You like Calum Morgan's work, don't you?'

I stare, taken aback.

Calum Morgan is one of our top self-help authors. His bestselling title on mental health, *Twenty-Seven Ways to be Happy as F**k*, kept the company afloat two years ago when sales went through a difficult patch.

'Of course.'

That much is true; I like his books. They make sense to someone like me who's always struggled with mental health issues like depression and low self-worth. But what I'm not admitting to my boss is how much I dislike the man himself. Although a major social media phenomenon, always supportive and generous in public, Calum is a nasty piece of work in private. He's notorious for being vile to his editors and marketing team, and is reputed to be an undiagnosed narcissist.

To his readers, Calum comes across as sweet and vulnerable, a real 'touchy feely' guy who gets hurt by mean comments on Twitter.

But I've heard horror stories from female editors who've found themselves alone with Mr Sweet and Vulnerable after conference spots or festival appearances and had trouble escaping unscathed. Not that anyone would dare make a complaint against him. He takes offence at the slightest criticism either of him or his books, and he has an entire army of faithful followers on social media who pile onto his detractors and drive them off the platform if Calum so much as subtweets.

A woman editor tried to raise a complaint against him once, back at his last publisher, and was never heard from again, his legal team having pounced on them swiftly and without mercy. I have no idea what the accusation would have been, but this apocryphal anecdote is scary enough to make me enjoy the books but keep the author himself at arms' length.

'Good,' Mark says with obvious satisfaction, and suddenly his smile has turned gloating, 'because you're taking over as his editor.'

My eyes widen in horror. 'I beg your pardon?'

'Cheryl's on maternity leave from the end of next month, and Donald can't possibly take him on. He's snowed under with the entrepreneur section. It's so popular right now; everyone seems to be launching their own pop-ups.' Mark passes me the basket of bread-sticks, and I take one automatically. 'But you're free, aren't you?'

I can't think of an excuse. 'Erm…'

'It's a big leap for you, I know.' He nods, seeming to dismiss my hesitation as fear of being out of my depth. 'Calum's a major name in self-help, and you'll have your work cut out with him. Apparently, his next book needs a little TLC before we can release early review copies.'

'TLC?' I echo faintly.

'Cheryl thinks he's been a bit off his game lately.' He lowers his voice conspiratorially. 'Between you and me, his wife left him recently.'

'I didn't know.'

'Yes, he's kept it off social media.' He shrugs. 'It was always on the cards. He likes to play the field, and I guess she got sick of being messed around. But his new book has suffered because of it. I'll get Cheryl to send you the manuscript, and then schedule a meeting between you and Calum before she leaves.' His smile terrifies me. 'You should be honoured. Calum asked for you by name.'

'Me?' I swallow the breadstick and gulp down some water. My mouth is dry. 'I can't imagine why; I barely know the man.'

'Really?' Mark crooks a disbelieving eyebrow at me. 'He spoke to you at last year's Christmas party. Or so he says.'

I remember the incident, vaguely. I think 'groped' would be a better word than 'spoke', but it's probably best not to mention that to Mark. He hates any suggestion that our authors are less than perfect human beings. And we'd both had a few drinks by that stage.

'Yes, he did,' I agree, 'but I'm travel and true crime. I haven't got much experience with self-help.'

Mark leans back as the waiter arrives with our pasta dishes. 'Then this is your chance to learn. And don't worry about getting overloaded. Harry can take over some of your travel authors for now. He's eager to learn the ropes, and he's just come back from backpacking round the world. A perfect fit for travel.'

'But if Calum's book needs a lot of editorial work—'

'I'm sure it's not as bad as that.'

A dish of cannelloni is placed in front of me with a watercress and spinach side salad. It smells delicious. I thank the waiter, who bows and disappears like my appetite.

'Can I think about it?' I ask tentatively.

Mark is frowning and tapping the table with his fingernails. A dangerous sign. 'Are you refusing to take him on? I'm doing you a favour here, Kate.'

'I know, I know,' I say quickly, and drag a smile to my lips. 'And I'm grateful to you, I really am. It's an amazing opportunity. I'm just a little taken aback, that's all.'

'You'll be terrific,' Mark says smoothly, but I know he's secretly sneering at me, mocking my lack of enthusiasm. He raises his wine glass to my water, and I accept his toast with a sinking feeling. 'To you and your new career in self-help. With Calum Morgan as your new prize author.'

'And to Calum's new book,' I add.

'Absolutely.' Mark knocks back his wine and then pours himself another large glass. I wonder how he manages to drink so much at lunch and still function in the office. 'Let's hope it sells as well as his last one. Or better.' His eyes glint with grim amusement at my expression. 'Bon appetit, Kate.'

'I'll do my best with it,' I stammer.

He laughs and begins to eat, our conversation over.

I pick up my knife and fork too, determined to enjoy the expensive Italian meal I'm being treated to, despite the fear churning in my belly. But there's no hiding the fact that I'm deeply uneasy.

Mark's hiding something from me. I just don't know what it is yet.

What I do know is that Calum Morgan is a vile, obnoxious character, and I've often wondered how on earth Cheryl could stand working with him. If it wasn't too ridiculous, I'd even suggest she got pregnant simply in order to escape him and his books, at least for a few months. But Cheryl's quite hard-nosed herself, and an experienced editor after ten years in the industry, so maybe she was able to rebuff Calum's advances without too much trouble.

I, on the other hand, am unused to authors who torment and gaslight anyone who doesn't agree with them. Especially women.

Mark's right, though. Whatever his motives, he's doing me a favour by giving me such a well-known author.

Now I have to justify his belief in me by making sure Calum Morgan's new book is a bestseller.

* * *

By the time I turn down our road, it's already getting dark. I see flashing lights ahead of me in the dusk, and stare transfixed as a fire engine pulls out of our drive and chugs slowly along the road towards me.

'What the hell…?'

CHAPTER TEN

There's a car in the drive, parked alongside Ruby's. I'm not one hundred per cent sure but it might be the doctor's, a possibility that floods me with dread.

The front door is slightly ajar.

I go inside, calling out, 'Mum? Ruby?'

There's acrid smoke in the air; it makes me catch my breath and cough.

I'm suffused with guilt, so gut-deep it actually hurts.

Whatever this is, it must be my fault. I was so intent on getting to that lunch with Mark on time, I didn't wait to make sure Mum's carer got to the house before Irina had to leave. And this is the result…

I find Mum in the living room, seated in her armchair with a worried look on her face. She's nursing a bandage wrapped professionally around her right hand.

Our private care doctor is with her, packing various items away in her kit bag.

Dr Forster is dark-haired and only a little taller than me, but the kind of person who gives off a deeply centred air, radiating energy like she has a nuclear core. I find her difficult to deal with, perhaps because her direct gaze is a little intimidating. But she's been very good with Mum's care and always comes out in person when requested, so I try my hardest to get along with her.

'Mum? Are you all right?' I dump my work briefcase on the table, staring at her. 'I saw the fire brigade were here. What on earth—?'

Dr Forster has turned at my voice. 'Ah Kate, I was hoping you'd be home before I left.' Her smile is calm and professional as she takes in my shocked expression. 'Now, don't worry. It looks worse than it is. Your mother will be fine, trust me.'

'But how did she hurt herself?' I touch Mum's shoulder, and she looks up at me, startled, as though only just aware that I've entered the room. 'Mum, what have you done?' I frown at her bandaged hand, confused. 'Did... Did you have a fall?'

'It's a minor burn, that's all.' Dr Forster closes her medical kit. 'But I've covered it, all the same, to make sure there's no chance of infection. She'll need the dressing removed in a day or two, so the skin can air.'

'A burn?' I put a hand to my mouth. 'Is that why the fire brigade was here? Oh my God.'

'I believe there was a small fire in the kitchen. A tea cloth caught light from the gas flame and set fire to a few things. Nothing to fret about, just a bit of a mess in there. But the fire service was called as a precaution.'

I resist the urge to see how bad the damage is. If it was only a small fire, then it can wait.

'But how did she get hurt?'

'Apparently, your mother tried to put out the fire herself, and burnt her hand in the process.'

'Oh, dear God.'

Mum meets my anguished look with a stare of blank bafflement. 'I don't remember any of that. Well, I remember my hand hurting.'

76

'I don't understand. You shouldn't have been using the oven at all.' I take her bandaged hand and very gently turn it over, wishing I knew how this calamity could have happened. 'Was Irina still here? And what about Ruby? I saw her car in the drive. Surely you weren't here on your own?'

At that moment, Ruby comes bustling into the room with a glass of water and stops dead at the sight of me.

'Oh,' Ruby says, looking distraught. 'Miss Kinley, thank goodness you're back. I thought I heard a car pull up.'

'Ruby?' Carefully, I release Mum's hand and straighten up. My heart is hammering with guilt and incredulity, but I don't want to accuse her of anything without knowing the truth. 'Why did you let my mother anywhere near the cooker? I'm sure I noted in my instruction sheet that she shouldn't be allowed to operate it, or even to go in the kitchen unsupervised. There have been dangerous incidents before. That's why she can't be left alone.'

'I'm all right,' Mum mutters, shaking her head. 'It was an accident. Everyone, just stop fussing over me like I'm a child.'

'It was an accident, yes,' I agree with her, my tone softening, 'but it shouldn't have happened. Not if you had someone else in the house.'

'Well, that's just it.' Guiltily, Ruby puts the glass of water on the side table next to my mother's chair. 'I wasn't here. Nobody was.'

I'm stunned. 'But... But I left Irina to look after her until you arrived. I made it clear Mum mustn't be left alone.'

'Your cleaner left before I got here; I must have just missed her, I suppose.' Ruby seems a little flushed and off-balance, her voice rushed. 'I'm so sorry. This is all my fault.'

'I can't believe Irina would do that. Exactly how late were you?'

'I got here at about a quarter to twelve.'

'What?' I stare at her in disbelief. 'You said you'd be here as soon as possible.'

'I know, and I'm really sorry. I can't say it often enough. Everything went wrong for me this morning.' Tears spring into her eyes as she adds thickly, 'I know it's not an excuse, but… my grandfather died this morning.'

This silences me.

Mum looks round at her, wide-eyed. 'Oh no!'

'I… I'm sorry,' I say, feeling awkward. 'That's awful news.'

'He didn't live with me. In fact, I've barely spoken to him in years. But it was still a shock. And I couldn't leave home until I'd made a few phone calls. To my brother and sister. They needed to know.'

'Of course, I totally get that.' I feel the anger slowly draining out of me, and recall only too well how it felt to get that awful phone call on the day my own father and brother were lost. 'It's not your fault, Ruby. Obviously that changes things.' I take a deep breath. 'I'll have to speak to Irina though; I asked her specifically not to leave before you arrived. It was too bad of her not to stay.'

But even as I say that, I know Irina won't care. Besides, I don't really have the right to criticise her. She's not employed to look after my mother, so it would be unjust to reprimand her for not staying beyond her agreed time.

I'm not happy, though.

'My hand hurts,' Mum announces, eyeing her bandage miserably.

'Your poor thing,' I say, and bend to kiss Mum on the cheek.

'You can have more painkillers at five o'clock,' the doctor tells her, and Mum pulls a disgruntled face.

After saying goodbye to my mother, Dr Forster asks me to walk to the door with her. While Ruby sits with Mum, I follow the doctor into the hall and shut the living room door behind us for a little privacy.

'It's not a bad burn, as I said,' Dr Forster tells me, unsmiling now. 'But it shouldn't have happened.'

'I know.'

'Given the rate at which your mother is deteriorating, she really can't be left on her own anymore.' She pauses, seeing my embarrassment, and her tone softens. 'I realise today was unusual. But I also have a duty of care towards your mother. I have to report any patients who may be at risk of neglect.'

'It won't happen again,' I insist.

The doctor looks at me without saying anything, but I get the feeling she doesn't believe me.

On her way out the front door, Dr Forster asks, 'Look, have you given any more thought to the idea of a residential home for her? I know you decided against it when we discussed it last time, but things change rapidly in this disease and never for the better.' She gives me a sympathetic smile. 'Even a taster week would afford you a few days' respite if you're struggling.'

'I'm not struggling,' I state firmly. 'And put her into a home? No, I won't hear of it. Besides, Mum wouldn't go willingly. You know that.'

'Yes, getting her consent is paramount. I'm afraid your hands may be tied if your mother refuses to go. At least while she's still able to discuss her choices in a reasonable manner. That's one of the dilemmas with dementia. There's no clear-cut moment when a person ceases to have the capacity to make those decisions for themselves. Often, it's just a matter of wait-and-see.' Dr Forster sighs. 'It's a real pity, though. I happen to know that Fairview has a few beds available at the moment. It's one of the best residentials in the area, if you ask me, and though it's pricey, their levels of care are second to none.'

I shake my head. 'I'm sorry. We're not at that stage yet.'

'Well, that's a decision you may need to make together. Let me know if you have any further concerns about her hand, won't you?'

'Of course.' I watch her walk across the gravel drive to her car. 'Thank you for everything you've done, Doctor.'

She nods, but waves me back inside. 'Better keep an eye on her.'

The doctor definitely doesn't think much of me as a carer, I realise, and feel heat in my cheeks. But can anyone really blame her after what happened today?

Closing the door, I hurry back into the living room, guiltily aware that Ruby must also want to leave and that I'm holding her up.

I find Ruby talking soothingly to Mum, down on her knees next to the armchair.

Poor Ruby.

She must have had such a traumatic day, I think, first learning of her grandfather's death, then rushing over here, only to discover that Mum had nearly set fire to the house, burnt herself in the process and needed the doctor to visit.

'I can take over now,' I tell her. 'It's okay if you need to leave. You must have things to do.'

Ruby gets up slowly. 'I do,' she admits, still with tears in her eyes. 'But I need to say something first, if I could have a word in private?'

I feel so bad about the way I practically accused her of neglecting my mother that I follow her to her car, hoping she too isn't going to give me a hard time like the doctor did. She's my mother, after all, and I did leave her with only the cleaner in the house. I'm the one ultimately to blame for today's accident.

It's chilly outside, the dusk slowly thickening around us. Our next-door neighbour's small dog is outside and barking for some reason, something I always find stressful. But I wait to hear what Ruby has to say, trying not to let its incessant yapping get on my nerves.

80

'I'm so sorry about the fire and your mother's accident,' Ruby begins to say again, but I hold up a hand.

'It's okay,' I tell her quickly. 'It was my fault, not yours. I ought to have hung on until you arrived, even if it meant I was late for my lunch meeting. It was wrong of me to expect Irina to wait.'

'Well,' Ruby says tentatively, 'it occurs to me that this kind of thing could be averted if...' She stops, and shakes her head as though dismissing some idea.

I'm surprised by her hesitancy. 'Go on.'

'No, I don't want to make you feel uncomfortable.'

'Ruby, for goodness' sake!' I smile at her encouragingly. At least she's no longer looking so miserable. 'Tell me what you're thinking.'

'I was just wondering if it wouldn't be better for me to move in and care for Celeste full-time. I noticed you have several spare rooms, and...' She comes to a halt, seeing my expression. 'I'm sorry, I wasn't poking around. I ran upstairs to turn off the smoke alarm after the fire and opened some of the bedroom windows so the house wouldn't reek of smoke all night.'

'That was very thoughtful of you.' I frown, considering what Ruby has said. 'Moving in though... What about your own place?'

'My tenancy is coming to an end, anyway. The owner wants to sell up. I've been looking about for a small place but they're all so expensive.' Ruby bites her lip. 'That sounds awful. Like I'm trying to grab a free ride or something.'

'No, it's... Actually, it's very sensible.' I glance over my shoulder; the front door is still open and the house will be getting cold. 'Look, let me think about it. Will you be able to sit with Mum tomorrow night?' I smile, a little embarrassed. 'I have another date with Logan.'

'Have you? But that's marvellous. He looks like such a nice man; I hope you have a great evening. Of course I can come over.' Ruby seems relieved by my attitude and doesn't press me for an instant answer, which I appreciate. 'What kind of time?' She gives a quick chuckle. 'I promise faithfully I won't be late.'

That night, while locking up the house at around midnight, I again hear someone moving outside in the garden. Just the faintest sound, a kind of rustling, which could be a wild animal, but followed by a few grating steps across gravel.

I freeze in the hall, listening, and the sound stops, as though whoever it is knows I'm there.

There's no garden security light now, of course. In all the frantic chaos of the past few days, I forgot to get it fixed. And indeed, I'm not even sure how. The whole thing would need to be replaced, not just the bulb.

I wish I was daring enough to go outside with a torch, but I'm not. Instead, I simply stand there, listening, my heart thumping, and wonder who on earth can be out there – and why.

After several minutes have passed, I check the rest of the downstairs, including Mum's room, but everything seems quiet again.

When I go up to bed, I leave several lights on downstairs, blazing away in the night without anybody around. Ridiculous, perhaps, but it makes me feel safer.

CHAPTER ELEVEN

'I think it's an excellent idea,' Logan says as we walk out of the arthouse cinema, having spent rather too much time whispering to each other instead of watching the French film with subtitles we'd come to see.

At any other time, I might have been content to sit back and watch it and lose myself in the story and characters. But the guilt over my mother nearly setting fire to the house in my absence, not to mention her burnt hand, coupled with fears over my seeming 'promotion' at work, had left me too on edge to enjoy anything, except perhaps a drink.

'What, hitting the pub before last orders?' I smile, not bothering to hide my enjoyment, and am surprised – perhaps even shocked – when he takes my hand, interlacing his fingers with mine. Yet why shouldn't we hold hands as we walk along the street together? 'I agree, I'm terribly thirsty.'

Our elbows rub against each other, our hips brushing too, and I feel ludicrously self-conscious.

Perhaps this was too soon after David, I think, wondering if I will offend him by pulling my hand free. Though it's been two years. If I'm not ready for a new relationship now, then when?

'No, I meant about Ruby moving in.' Logan peers down at me when I say nothing. 'I take it you're still undecided?'

I mentioned Ruby's suggestion to him earlier, just as we were leaving the house. He came to pick me up as arranged and spotted Ruby in the hall. When he asked after Giorgios, I explained that our previous carer still appeared to be on holiday, and since Mum had taken such a shine to Ruby, I was seriously considering allowing her to move in.

'Oh, that. The thing is, if I do decide to go down that route, it could only be for a few weeks. Just until Giorgios comes back.'

'And if he doesn't?'

That surprises me. 'Why wouldn't he?'

Logan shrugs, looking vague. 'People do funny things.'

'Maybe.' I frown. 'It's true that I'd feel more confident leaving Mum alone if Ruby was living-in with us. There'd be no more of this "running late" business, for starters.'

'Much safer too, given your mum's propensity for arson.' He nods, stopping outside the pub and glancing about at the tables that habitually clutter up the pavement. 'Sitting in or standing out?'

'Inside, please. It's far too cold to be outside.' I see his expression and grin. 'You want to smoke, don't you?'

'I'm happy not to, if you'd rather go inside.'

'You're supposed to be giving up anyway,' I remind him, and we crowd into the warm interior, the counter bristling with punters. 'There,' I say promptly, spotting a table that's just been vacated, and steer him over to it. 'Shall I buy this time?'

He raises his eyebrows. 'Not a chance. What would you like?'

I give in, and he brings our drinks over a few minutes later. It's a good feeling, being out with someone on a date, but I'm unsure how far I want this new relationship to go. Not least because he knew

David so well. That complicates things. It's not a completely new slate, that's the thing; I keep being reminded of times when we went out as a threesome, or in a group, while David and I were together and Logan was just a friend. Perhaps I'm being oversensitive. But the feeling of awkwardness is still real.

'So, what did you think of the film?' Logan asks as he squeezes next to me in the cramped space and leans forward, taking a quick sip of his pint.

Our thighs press together, and I'm very aware of him physically, which increases my unease. I find him sexually attractive; there's no doubt about it. But it's too soon for that. Way too soon.

'Well, it was very… French.'

He laughs.

We discuss the film for a few minutes, then I decide to check on Mum and pick up my phone. He watches me without comment, though he must think me overprotective. She's my mother, after all; not my child.

I text Ruby.

How's it going? Any problems?

Her response is surprisingly quick – and reassuring.

Just fine. Celeste is having a shower, then getting an early night. You enjoy yourself.

Logan smiles when I read out the text message to him. 'See? Nothing to worry about.'

'You think I'm a snowflake.'

'Not at all. I think you're charming.' It's noisy in the packed pub, but his voice is deep and warm in my ear as he bends towards me, adding, 'I wish I had someone to look after me the way you look after your mother.'

I turn my head to look at him and have a sudden impulse to kiss him. Luckily, common sense kicks in, and I give a wry smile instead, picking up my pink gin and tonic.

'It's a full-time job, to be sure.' I pause. 'Actually, I'm not sure how much energy I have left over for… for a relationship.'

He's silent for a moment. Then nods.

'Of course. Your mother's welfare has to come first at the moment. That's perfectly understandable. But I'd still like to give this a try, Kate. Whatever this is. And tell me to get lost, but I suspect you'd like to give it a try too.' He's watching my face closely. 'Otherwise, why agree to a second date?'

Why indeed?

'Maybe I needed a break. I've been having a difficult time lately,' I say carefully, looking away from him. 'Not just with Mum, but at work too.'

'Yes, you said. Though I'd hardly call being handed such an important author something to be worried about.'

I'd texted him soon after my lunch meeting with Mark, not just to check when we were meeting up tonight but to tell him about Calum Morgan, whose self-help books I was sure he would have heard of, at least. Which he had, sending back a suitably impressed message within minutes.

I worry Logan might think I was boasting, telling him about Calum Morgan like that. And maybe I am. Which is a sobering thought.

'It's not just that.'

Logan raises his eyebrows. 'What, then?'

Haltingly, I explain about the poison pen letter I received, and his face soon changes.

'Show me,' he says without hesitation, pushing aside his pint, and holds out a hand.

Embarrassed, but eager to get a second opinion, I take the envelope out of my bag and let him look at it.

'Good God.' Logan studies the printed sheet, his brows knitted together. 'This is appalling. And a disgrace to David's memory. Did you show this to anyone at work?' When I say no, he stares at me. 'Why ever not?'

'I don't know. I'm not sure. Maybe because I didn't want anyone else to know about it?'

'I don't understand.' He reads the note again. 'This sounds like a threat. You should have reported it at once.'

I shrug, feeling heat bloom in my cheeks, and not just because of the large gin I'm sipping.

'Making it public would have felt too intrusive. Especially with David's name attached. The way he died… I prefer people not to know my private business.'

'All the same, you should take this letter to the police,' he says decisively, and hands it back to me.

I put the horrible letter away. 'What good would that do?'

'It's clear that someone has it in for you at work. A secret enemy of some kind. You want my advice?'

'Please.'

'Let the police deal with it. You need to flush this person out. Straightaway. If you don't, you risk an escalation.'

'Meaning?'

'They may feel emboldened to send another letter like that. More poison intended to upset you.' Logan sounds sombre. 'Or worse.'

I meet his serious gaze, wishing I'd never shown him that stupid bloody letter. Now I feel under pressure to do something about it. And I'd rather just forget about the whole thing.

'Worse?'

'That's just a letter. Maybe they're testing the waters. Seeing how you'll react. If you stay quiet, they may take their campaign to the next level. So, something more shocking.' Logan shrugs. 'Become physical, perhaps.'

'You think I'm in real danger? Because of a nasty letter?'

'I don't know anything. And that's what worries me. It should worry you too.' He downs the last of his pint in one long swallow. 'Take it to the police. You'll feel better when you have.'

Would I, though?

I don't voice my uncertainty, merely nod and smile. But already I'm imagining a long, pointless wait at the police station, or filling out one of those onerous online forms, and for what? To be told what I already know, which is it's insignificant and there's nothing they can do about it. And to have some police officer look at me with pity or even suspicion. Perhaps I was to blame for David's death, after all. Because I didn't foresee it or do anything much to prevent it, did I?

Stone-cold bitch.

I wonder what Logan made of that, and whether he believed it or secretly agreed with it. A thought that's unworthy of me, perhaps. But I can't help worrying…

I could never tell what David was thinking. But his suicide note made it obvious he blamed me for his depression.

And maybe Logan does too.

Three days later, with no further update from the absent Giorgios, I ask Ruby to move in with us. The spare room – the one that used to belong to my brother – is cleaned out by a reluctant and clearly brooding Irina, and the bed made up, and Ciaran's dusty stuff put into cardboard boxes and stored in the attic.

My brother had dabbled in oil painting in his spare time, privately indulging an artistic streak Dad had advised him to suppress at school because it wouldn't pay the bills. There are numerous canvases stacked against the desk in his room, and his favourites are framed and already hanging on the walls. I dust these off and redistribute them about the house.

There's a wonderful family portrait he painted a few months before his death, capturing us together on the lawn under the large sycamore. Dad has his arm around Mum, standing proud and smiling in a characteristically wide-legged stance, while Ciaran and I, on either side of our parents, grin at each other rather than looking outwards. And at my side is David, his hand on my shoulder, his head turned away slightly as though looking at something beyond the picture frame…

I hang this oil painting in Mum's room, opposite her bed, and she seems both pleased and disturbed by our likenesses, her gaze frequently moving back to the scene in wonder.

'Who did that painting?' Mum asks more than once.

'Ciaran,' I tell her repeatedly.

'And is… is that your father?' She points to my dad at the centre of our group, frowning. 'I think it might be.'

'It's all of us together, Mum. See? This is me, and that's David…' Slowly, I name each of us in the painting, one by one, and see her confused stare move away, as though rejecting what I'm saying. But I persevere. 'He really captured Dad there, I agree. It's a brilliant self-portrait too, of course. Ciaran was an impressive artist. And with no real training either. I sometimes wonder if he shouldn't have gone to art school instead of taking that business degree. He had so much raw talent.' I shrug. 'But he always took Dad's advice. And I suppose it felt like the right thing at the time, steering him towards a private sector career instead of art.'

She says nothing, and I worry that she's forgotten who Ciaran is. It hurts to see her so blank-faced, and I long for one of her better days to roll around, when Mum remembers all our names and history and things feel almost back to normal.

Clearing out my brother's room ought to have been done long ago; it's been years since Dad and Ciaran died. I put it off for a good reason, though. It makes my heart ache horribly, sorting through his old sketchbooks and artwork, skim-reading his letters and private journals with a vague sense of guilt, and then bundling up the best of his shoes and clothes to go to various charity outlets.

But at least once it's done, I feel better. Lighter, almost. As though a terrible weight has been lifted…

Ruby brings her own boxes and stores them in the garage, which I rarely use. She exclaims in pleasure at her room, and thanks both me and Irina profusely for having prepared it for her so quickly.

'I won't get underfoot,' she insists, tweaking the curtain to gaze out across the leaf-strewn back lawn, 'so please don't worry.' A recent storm has denuded the trees and I haven't got around to going out with the leaf-blower yet, to disperse the scattered wet yellow and red detritus building up across the garden and drive. 'I'll keep to my room unless you need me to look after your mum.'

'Oh no,' I stammer, embarrassed by this suggestion, glancing about the sparse bedroom, 'you mustn't… You live here now. I can't expect you to stay in your room when you're not working. That wouldn't be fair.' I hesitate. 'You should consider the house as your own… Use the kitchen, watch telly, walk in the garden.'

'Thank you so much,' Ruby says, and I can see tears in her eyes. 'You're so sweet.'

'No, I'm very grateful to you. My mother is too, trust me. Having you here will make a world of difference to us both.'

I leave her to settle in, and head downstairs to check on my mother, whom I left napping on the sofa under a blanket.

Irina is quietly tidying the room but straightens at once when I come in, shooting me an irate look. 'Miss Kinley,' she begins, but I warn her with a shake of my head not to wake my mother and we talk out in the hall instead.

'What's the matter?' I ask softly.

'Ruby, that's the matter.'

I stare, perplexed by her venomous tone. 'But she's only just moved in. What's she done to upset you?'

'That thing with your mother… When she burnt herself.' Her voice has risen slightly, and she's flushed. 'That wasn't my fault.'

'Nobody said it was.'

'But Ruby told you I left before she arrived, and that's why it happened.'

I'm surprised. 'You mean you didn't?'

Her flush deepens. 'I did leave, okay. But only because Ruby rang to say she was five minutes away. Otherwise, I would never have left your mother alone.'

'And you think she took longer to arrive than five minutes?'

Irina bites her lip deeply. 'How do I know? I wasn't here. But your mother, she burnt herself. She nearly set fire to the kitchen. How could she do that in five minutes? Five minutes!' She shakes her head, looking scornful. 'I don't believe it. Do you?'

I don't know what to believe. Though I do recall her being very anxious to leave. Maybe this is her guilty conscience speaking, knowing she left my mother alone and wanting to shift the blame for what happened onto Ruby, the newcomer. But I soothe her with a few conciliatory words, and then head into the kitchen to start making Mum's lunch.

'Oh, Miss Kinley?' Irina calls me back; she draws an envelope out of her blue overalls and hands it over. 'This arrived for you a short while ago.'

'So late?' The post usually arrives around breakfast time, and it's nearer midday.

She shrugs, her lips pursed. 'It was on the mat. I think someone put it through the door. But it's got your name on it.'

I thank her and take the envelope into the kitchen. While the kettle is boiling, I tear it open and stare down in dismay at what is now a familiar sight: a plain sheet of paper with a few pithy words typed out in a sans serif font.

I DIED BECAUSE OF YOU, KATE. NOW IT'S YOUR TURN.

Again, it's signed DAVID.

Who could have sent this to me? I'd assumed the writer must be someone at the office. One of my colleagues, jealous of me perhaps, or trying to get rid of me. But why send such a letter to my actual home? This seems a thousand times more sinister…

I check the envelope.

I think someone put it through the door.

Irina's right.

There's no stamp, no postmark. The message was delivered by hand, put through our letterbox *in person.*

My accuser strolled down our drive, in full view of the house, in broad daylight, dropped this poison pen letter onto the mat like it was some random piece of junk mail, and then walked away.

The sheer audacity of this leaves me shocked and silent.

I DIED BECAUSE OF YOU, KATE.

So personal. So cruel.

So painfully true.

My chest constricts with horror and I find myself struggling to breathe, my vision misting over as I re-read the message.

I suddenly wish Logan were here to advise me, maybe to give me a hug or a kiss, somehow comfort me.

But I'm alone.

He suggested I should hand the matter over to the police. I wasn't convinced that was the best way to handle it. But now…

I feel my heart beating hard, and swallow, re-reading the words for a third time, trying to look at them calmly and rationally.

I should take both this and the other letter to our local police station. Someone is trying to upset me, that's all. For some unpleasant reason of their own. Yes, I should let the police deal with it. That's the sensible thing to do, isn't it?

But my insides are churning, and all I can think about is getting rid of this attack on my nerves, pushing it away from me, pretending it simply isn't happening. That way I won't have to face it, won't have to ask who is doing it or why.

But deep down, I know why this is happening, don't I?

It's awful, but the letter writer isn't wrong. I'm the one to blame for David's death. If I had made more of an effort to understand what he was going through… But I didn't bother. Over time, I just became impatient with his constant weakness and uncertainty. I was too bound up with the idea of a man being macho and suffering in silence, or not suffering at all. I mocked his mental anguish; I turned away from him.

And now he's dead…

Guilt infuses me. I crumple up the accusing sheet of paper and shove it into the bin, followed by its envelope, and stare blindly out of the kitchen window.

Behind me, Irina is getting her coat on and saying something

I can't focus on, though I'm aware she sounds unhappy. I respond automatically, and a moment later, she's gone.

NOW IT'S YOUR TURN.

After a few minutes, I retrieve the letter and envelope from the bin and take them up to my bedroom. There, I smooth them out, put the sheet of paper back into its envelope and then find a see-through plastic folder to keep it in.

Yet even after I've filed it away in a drawer, safely out of sight, I can't get those sinister words out of my head.

My turn to what?

The only possible explanation stabs through me like a knife in my back, shocking me out of frozen bewilderment.

My turn to die.

CHAPTER TWELVE

A few days later, Cheryl emails me the manuscript of Calum Morgan's newest book – the one we're hoping to release next spring – and I sit down with a large glass of wine to peruse it, hoping it will help me calm down. That's what he's good at, isn't it? Helping people with their problems?

But the real problem is with the manuscript.

I've only read about ten pages before I see precisely why Cheryl, one of our senior editors, was so eager to foist the project onto somebody else before swanning off on maternity leave, and why Donald, her long-term assistant, had also declined to handle Calum's new book.

It's riddled with nonsensical passages and dubious comments about mental health issues, especially where women are concerned. Calum Morgan has always trodden a fine line between pious sentiment and mocking self-parody, and this time he's tumbled right over the fence into dangerous territory. Of course, it's possible his early drafts are commonly like this, and Cheryl merely lacked the energy to tidy this one up. Because the only other explanation is that Calum's lost it. The ability to charm a reader, that is.

I can't say I'm sorry. The man's a beast. But my own neck is on the line now; somehow, I need to fix this book asap, and make it a bestseller.

I start off by making notes on the document itself, but the screen is soon awash with red underlining and yellow sticky note boxes. That's bad enough, but all I'm doing is correcting his grammar and crossing out infelicitous phrases. It's his fundamental ideas that are at fault, and no amount of meticulous line-editing will fix *that*. Basically, I'm straightening the book's tie, when what it really needs is a whole new wardrobe.

Hurriedly, I grab a notepad and pen, and start scribbling down thoughts on paper instead.

I'm so preoccupied that I don't notice Mum wandering out of the room on her own, nor do I pay much attention when I later hear the telephone ring and someone talking in the hall. Part of me thinks it must be Ruby, as Mum almost never answers the phone these days. It's not that she's forgotten how, more that it unnerves her to conduct a conversation without being able to see the other person's face. I know the feeling...

Then Ruby comes in, wearing red checked leisure pants and a loose red top, and at once starts busying herself by clearing away some dirtied tea mugs, though she isn't here to act as an unpaid cleaner. She looks a bit like a flushed, happy Mrs Santa. 'Who was that on the phone?' she asks. 'Your mum seemed very interested in them, whoever it was.'

'What?'

I had glanced back at my notepad, but now look up at her again, frowning. 'Sorry?'

'When I came downstairs just now, your mother was on the phone. I just wondered who it was.' She hesitates, misreading my shocked expression. 'None of my business, of course. I'm sorry.'

'No, it's not that…' I throw aside my notepad and jump up. 'Mum? Where are you?'

There's no reply.

I head out into the hall, and Ruby follows me, mugs clasped to her chest. My mother's not there anymore and the handset is lying on the telephone table. I pick it up, but it's dead, so I return it to its charging cradle.

'She's not supposed to answer the phone. She gets too confused. I heard a voice… I thought it was you.'

'No, I was up in my room.' Ruby has put down the tea mugs. She knocks on my mother's bedroom door at the other end of the hallway. 'Celeste? Are you in there?'

She must have heard something inside because she opens the door and goes in. I follow her in, and find my mother bent over, scrabbling through the drawers in her bedside cabinet, pulling out old packets of headache pills and creams, her expression abstracted. There are books and papers on the carpet that she's jettisoned in her determination to find whatever she's lost, along with ancient sweet wrappers from the back of the drawer.

'Mum? What on earth are you doing?' I touch her arm, and she peers up at me through a floppy fringe of hair, her eyes wide. 'What's the matter?'

'I need, um, that thing that you use when, um, you need to…' She pauses, dissolving into vagueness, and gestures wildly with her hand. 'Pay for things.'

Ruby starts picking up the debris on the floor. 'I think she means a cheque book.'

'Cheque book, yes!' Mum nods excitedly and returns to her digging through the drawer, flicking things aside without really looking at them, as though she's already forgotten what she's looking for but needs to keep searching.

I'm bemused. 'I don't understand, Mum. What do you need to pay for?'

'The man on the phone… He said I had to give him my bank details. Or he'll turn off my account. Like a tap, he said.' She mimes turning a tap, a worried frown knitting her brows together. 'I can't have that.'

The man on the phone…

Some kind of scamster, I realise, and am horrified at myself. I was so intent on my work, I did nothing to stop her receiving that bogus call.

'Oh my God.' I catch her swiftly moving hands and still them between my own. 'Mum, look at me. You didn't tell him anything about your account, did you?'

'What do you mean?'

'It wasn't a real call.'

'Of course it was,' she insists. 'He was from the bank. He told me. And he knew my name and where I lived.'

I go cold.

'No, he wasn't from the bank. He must have found those details from somewhere else. The electoral roll, perhaps. It's not real; it's a scam.' I shake my head, glancing at Ruby. 'How to explain it to her?'

'I'm sure Celeste can understand,' Ruby says. 'Can't you, love?'

'I'm not stupid,' Mum says indignantly.

'Nobody's saying you are,' Ruby reassures her.

'He was a criminal,' I say.

Mum's eyes widen. 'What?'

I take a deep breath. 'He rings up, pretends to be from a bank, and asks for your details. Then, when you give them to him, he steals all your money.'

'Oh no,' Mum says confidently, and wriggles her hands free to start searching again. 'That can't be true. He was a very nice man. Not a criminal.'

'Trust me, he was after your money.'

'Really?' Mum hesitates, and looks from me to Ruby, who nods sadly. 'Oh goodness. You must think I'm such a silly woman. But darling, are you sure?'

'Yes, Mum.'

'Really, truly sure?' Mum steps back and chews on her lower lip, fear in her eyes. 'He said he'd ring back in a few minutes, while I found my cheque book. That's got all my numbers on it, you see,' she adds to Ruby, who helps her sit down on the bed. 'You know, all my account details.'

'It's all right,' Ruby says comfortingly, patting her hand. 'Don't fret.'

'Stop it. Don't treat me like a child,' Mum snaps at her.

Ruby moves away, shrugging with a half-smile on her face. I imagine she's used to that kind of reaction from the people she cares for, and is unbothered.

I'm nettled by it though, and have to control myself with an effort. 'Don't worry, Mum, I'll answer the phone if this "man from the bank" rings back. I have a few choice things to say to him.'

It was meant as a reassurance. But this promise only agitates my mother further.

'But what if he really was from the bank and my account gets closed? Have you thought about that?' Mum struggles up off the bed, staring at the emptied-out drawers, the mess on the carpet. 'And that's another thing. I'm sure my cheque book was in there. I've always kept my bank things in that drawer. So where's it gone?' Her voice rises. 'I think someone must have stolen it.'

'I've got your bank statements and your cheque book,' I tell her soothingly.

99

She turns to eye me suspiciously. 'Why?'

'You asked me to look after them for you.'

She looks outraged. 'No, I didn't.'

'Actually, Mum, you did.' I bend to help Ruby clear up the mess on the floor, my head pounding. A sudden stress headache, no doubt. I've become prone to them lately. 'About a year ago. You've forgotten, that's all.'

'I have not forgotten. It didn't happen.'

'Mum, you gave me your bank cards. So I could pay your share of the household bills and get you anything you needed.'

'Why?'

'Because you couldn't use them in shops anymore. You kept forgetting the number for the PIN machine.'

Mum blinks. 'Did I? That doesn't sound like me. You're making things up now. Why do you tell me such lies?'

'I'm not lying, Mum.'

But she's clearly unconvinced, her expression disapproving.

I leave her with Ruby, worried that I'm going to lose my patience with her, and wait in the hall instead for this man – whoever the hell he is – to ring back. But the telephone remains silent.

Eventually, I try discovering which number rang us. But it was withheld. Irritated and wound up, I slam the handset back on its cradle just as Ruby appears from my mother's room.

'Did you give him what for?' she asks.

'Nobody rang.' I run a hand through my hair, feeling off balance. 'I was checking if there was a number that I could report to the phone company, but it was withheld.'

'You should report it, all the same. In case this scamster calls back. Now he knows she believed him, she'll be down on their list as an easy target.'

Now she's beginning to sound like Logan, which irritates me. But I suppose she has a point.

'Yes, you're right. I probably should.' I manage a smile for her, though by this point I'm feeling tired and more like bursting into tears. 'Thank you for your help in there, by the way. I'm sorry she was so cross.'

'Water off a duck's back. I've heard it all before.'

'You're very understanding. God though, what a nuisance! And to think, if you hadn't mentioned that phone call to me, I probably wouldn't have known what she was up to.' I roll my eyes. 'She could have been cheerily handing out her bank account number and PIN to all callers, and me none the wiser.'

'Just as well you're keeping that cheque book safe for her.' On her way to the kitchen, Ruby stops and hangs on her heel, looking back. 'You know, one lady I was caring for, her son had a Power of Attorney drawn up to stop scams like that from happening. But you have to get them in place early on. Before the dementia really takes hold.'

'We did. That was all sorted out ages ago.'

'Oh.' She seems surprised. 'But your mother still has her own bank account? That seems awkward.'

I blink, hesitant. 'Well, when we first set it up, Mum was still perfectly capable of handling her own affairs. It was something for the future. And then, once her condition started to worsen, I kept meaning to transfer everything into a joint account, to make life easier. But you know how it is. There's always so much going on, I simply never got around to it.'

'Perfectly understandable.'

'Besides, I don't like the idea of using the Power of Attorney. I mean, running my mother's bank account for her… It's a last resort, isn't it?'

'Of course.' Ruby smiles, nodding; I get the feeling she thinks I'm a poor, weak-willed sap, but is too polite to say so. 'Well, I'd better get on.'

She disappears, and I hurry into what used to be my father's study, unlock the filing cabinet where I keep Mum's bank statements, to check on the folder.

Everything's still in there, safe and untouched.

But Ruby's comment has got me thinking.

Have I been neglecting Mum's financial affairs? It's an embarrassing possibility. And she's right. I really ought to use my Power of Attorney for once to sort out her bank account. It's clear Mum's never going to be well enough again to deal with anything monetary, and though it goes against the grain to make decisions for her, it's in her best interests for me to do so.

I just hope Mum will understand why and not complain that I'm trying to 'steal' her money or something awful like that. Because I saw the suspicion in her face just now, and it made me horribly uneasy…

A few days later, I stop trying to put off the inevitable, and make an appointment with our family solicitor, Mr Adeyemi.

Shortly after lunch, I leave Mum poring over a crossword puzzle with Ruby and drive over there alone.

The weather having turned atrocious, I park as close as possible to the solicitor's firm and run the rest of the way in pouring rain, sheltering under an umbrella that threatens to turn inside-out in the strong winds.

Abayomi Adeyemi is a big man with a smooth head and dark sideburns. Mum always calls him a snappy dresser, but today his blue pinstriped suit seems too large for him, his long sleeves brushing the backs of his hands.

When the receptionist buzzes through to let him know I've arrived, he comes out of his office to greet me, shaking my hand with a broad smile. 'How are you? And your mother?' While I assure him that Mum is well, he ushers me into his small office behind the reception desk and closes the door. There are no windows, which always feels odd to me, but the fluorescent overhead lighting is bright enough and the constant whisper of an air conditioning unit somehow gives the illusion of fresh air. 'That's good, excellent.'

Mr Adeyemi sits opposite me, behind the large, cluttered desk, and swivels back and forth on his leather chair, nodding at me encouragingly. 'So, to what do I owe the pleasure of this visit, Miss Kinley?'

'It's about the Power of Attorney that we set up in case of future need. Do you remember?'

'Of course. How could I forget?' There's a twinkle in his eye now. 'Your mother is a very charming lady.'

'Indeed, she is. But I'm afraid the time has come for me to put the Power of Attorney into action, and I need your advice on how to go about doing that.'

His smile fades. 'I see.' He picks up a gold pen from his desk and fiddles with it, not looking at me. 'What you're saying is that Mrs Kinley is no longer able to manage her own affairs?'

'Sadly, that's about right.'

Briefly, I explain what's been going on with my mother and mention the unfortunate changes I've noticed recently, such as her increasingly wandering attention. He's not a doctor, but I'm sure he must understand that she's now coming to the point where she can no longer handle her own financial affairs.

He listens intently, nodding occasionally, sometimes frowning. 'Hmm, I don't like the sound of that. Have you spoken to her doctor about this?'

'Dr Forster says it's all par for the course. She says dementia is a one-way process, so my mother's only likely to get worse, not better.'

'Just a moment…'

Mr Adeyemi gets up and opens his filing cabinet. After a moment's search, he withdraws a file and sits down again, opening it and producing my mother's Lasting Power of Attorney.

He reads through the document with what feels like unnecessarily close attention while I wait in silence, glancing about at the windowless walls, mostly adorned with framed certificates or information posters about making wills and legacies, and listening to the hiss of the air con unit.

Eventually, he finishes reading and turns back to the front page of the document. 'May I ask why Mrs Kinley has not accompanied you here today?'

I stare, a little bemused. 'Mum's not capable of… I left her at home because it was raining heavily today and she wouldn't understand what was going on, anyway.' The solicitor seems unimpressed by this explanation, and it does now sound a little thin even to my ears. But I don't know what else to say. 'She gets flustered when she has to leave the house. Especially in poor weather. I didn't want to upset her unnecessarily, I suppose.'

'Well, without speaking to Mrs Kinley in person, I'm not sure how I can advise you.' He taps his copy of the Power of Attorney in front of him. 'This document is drawn up in her name, not yours.'

'Sorry?'

'Your mother is not deceased. She may have medical issues which prohibit her full understanding of legal and financial matters. But she still has rights.'

'I'm not sure I understand what you're saying. She has dementia, yes. But isn't that why we drew up the Lasting Power of Attorney? To allow for this eventuality?'

'The Power of Attorney can only take effect when your mother's mental faculties have been incapacitated beyond a certain point.'

'And I believe she's reached that point.'

'Ah.' He inclines his head, smiling faintly. 'But unless I am able to speak with her myself, and verify that to my own satisfaction, I can't condone your use of the Power of Attorney to access her money. Regardless of how you feel about it, it's still your mother's decision, and that proviso is noted in the Power itself.'

I'm stunned. 'It... It is?'

'Certainly.'

'Should I ask her doctor to contact you?'

'That would only be useful in regard to a specific health issue, in which case the decision would be made between you and her medical advisors. For financial matters, the law tends to frown on any use of an LPA before mental capacity is deemed to have been lost irrevocably. That's my take on it, though you're entitled to seek a second opinion if you prefer.' He straightens one arm, the too-long sleeve of his suit shooting back as he swiftly checks his heavy silver wristwatch, then smiles at me again. 'I'm very sorry, but you were late and I have another appointment. Maybe you should come with your mother next time, Miss Kinley. Then I can talk to her myself and make a determination on those grounds. Until then, I suggest we keep things as they are.'

'Right.'

My voice sounds small and inadequate. I'm angry and frustrated, but a little intimidated too. The solicitor is so sure of himself, it feels almost like he's mocking me.

He stands up and goes to the door.

I am being dismissed.

'Now, unless there's something else you wish to discuss…' Smiling in a genial way, Mr Adeyemi holds the door open for me.

I bend to collect my handbag and get to my feet, feeling hollow inside. It had all seemed so easy, but now…

'No, thank you. I'll come back with my mother.'

'That's an excellent idea. I would love to see your mother again. You can make an appointment with Lucy.' He nods to the smart young woman on the reception desk, who beams at me. 'Whenever is convenient for you.'

We shake hands, but I don't smile; I'm too annoyed. I came here today, thinking our family solicitor would help me. Instead, I'm being given the brush-off. Like he thinks I'm up to something shady, not merely trying to protect my mother from scamsters like the guy who rang, pretending to be from the bank. He doesn't even seem to consider that a threat.

'Though perhaps I should call at the house instead,' Mr Adeyemi says slowly, studying my face. 'It's true, the weather is getting colder now. I wouldn't want your mother to become ill on my account. We were good friends at one stage, you know… Before your father's death. Such a sad business.'

'No, I didn't know,' I say, surprised.

'I meant to stay in touch with her. But then she became ill, and…' He nods, seeming to reconsider. 'Yes, I will come to see you both at the house. Lucy can suggest a few times when I'm free over the next week or so, and you may pick one. How about that?'

After he ushers in his next appointment, I settle on a date and time with Lucy behind the desk, and leave the solicitor's feeling a little happier. Even the rain has stopped falling, which is a plus.

Heading back to my car, I can't work out why I got so upset in there. It's actually quite simple and straightforward. If Mr Adeyemi needs to speak to my mother before agreeing that the Power of Attorney can be implemented, there's no problem with that. It should only take the solicitor a few minutes to see how much she's deteriorated, and then we can proceed from there with perfect legality.

As I'm starting my car, my phone buzzes in my coat pocket.

I turn off the engine and check the screen.

It's a text from Cheryl at work.

You free for lunch with Calum Morgan next Tuesday? He wants to discuss the new book, so I hope you've read it.

I feel a stab of guilt.

I haven't finished reading the manuscript she sent me. I'm barely a third of the way through, in fact. Things have been so hectic recently, and there are so many issues with the book, it's taking ages to annotate. But admitting that could be disastrous for my career, given Morgan's status.

I text her back with a little white lie instead, grimacing at my own duplicity.

Of course. You can tell Calum I love it! A few minor problems but nothing we can't fix.

By the time I reach home, Cheryl's reply is already on the screen.

Tell him yourself. I'll email the venue/time later. FYI, he always records his meetings, so stay sober and watch what you say. And never be alone with him.

CHAPTER THIRTEEN

Calum Morgan greets me like a long-lost friend. 'How are you, darling?' he gushes, while pulling out the chair opposite him in the crowded restaurant above London's Borough Market. Several people wave a hello to him from nearby tables, and he nods indulgently in their direction before sitting down again and smiling at me. 'I'm so glad you were free to be my editor. Of course, I shall miss Cheryl. I've been with her since the beginning. But it's only until she's popped out that baby of hers, and fresh blood is always a teensy bit exciting, isn't it?'

'Oh yes.' I'm prattling, too nervous to know what to say. 'I'm delighted too. It's going to be amazing.'

His hard, clever eyes watch me like a snake's. 'God, yes.' He summons a waiter by crooking an eyebrow and orders champagne. 'Let's celebrate.'

'I need to drive later, but...' My voice tails off as Calum turns that gaze on me. 'I suppose a glass or two won't hurt. I can always get a taxi home from the station.'

'That's the spirit.'

We study the menus, discussing what's most warming for a winter lunch. A bottle of water arrives, along with breadsticks. We order our meals, and then chat briefly about the weather – it's turning colder all the time, chill air striking into one's bones in the early mornings – and then, abruptly, the conversation pivots to his book.

'So,' he says, with an air of disarming casualness, 'have you read it?'

'Absolutely.'

'And what do you think?'

I'm utterly terrified – of saying the wrong thing, of upsetting this man and blowing my chance to rise in the company – yet somehow I manage to keep smiling.

'It's… very interesting.' I swallow, and reach for my water glass. 'I think there may need to be a few changes.'

Calum pounces on that, his brow suddenly furrowed. 'Changes?'

The wine waiter arrives with a bottle of champagne in a cooler. He pours a glass each, waits for Calum to approve the choice, and then moves away.

I stick with my water for now.

Calum seems calm enough, enjoying the champagne, so I plough on with my take on his book, ignoring the warning bells ringing in my head. 'I could be wrong, but I'm not always sure you're striking the right note of… Well, of sympathy with the reader.'

'Good God, who cares about the reader? You only need them to buy the book; you don't need them to read it.' His eyebrows have risen steeply, and his voice with it. Then Calum seems to notice heads turning curiously in our direction. He puts down his champagne flute and leans forward, saying in a low growl, 'Very well. You think I'm unsympathetic. Millions of readers would disagree with you, darling, to judge by all my five-star reviews and my vast following on social media. But you're my editor now. So I'm open to suggestions. Perhaps you'd care to elaborate on that startling analysis?'

He's upset. But I can hardly withdraw my comments now. And besides, if I have any hope of rescuing his book, I'll need to get him to see where it needs to be changed.

'It's a self-help book about unhappiness,' I begin tentatively. 'So it's likely most of its readers will be suffering from mental health issues of one kind or another; otherwise, they wouldn't have picked it up. Certainly they'll be more inclined towards unhappiness than the average reader. And occasionally – just occasionally, mind you – it can feel a little as though you're…'

I run out of tactful ways to make my point, and gulp down some chilled water instead, staring at him over the rim of my outsized water glass.

'As though I'm what?' he presses me, holding my gaze.

'Making fun of them,' I whisper.

'Making fun of them,' he repeats blankly.

'And some of your recommendations to avoid unhappiness come across as a little… self-entitled.' Hopelessly, I reach for an example from my memory. 'For instance, when you suggested taking a long holiday somewhere hot to get over the blues. That might put some of your readers' backs up. I mean, given how badly the economy is suffering, a foreign holiday may be beyond the reach of many readers.' I pause. 'Especially those who may be reading your book precisely because they're depressed after losing their jobs.'

'Is that so?'

Hurriedly, I try to soften the blow. 'It's just your tone. I'm sure with a few tweaks—'

'My tone?' He almost doubles at the waist to reach across the table, his face close to mine, his voice an angry hiss. 'My *tone* is part of my style, darling. My style is what makes people buy my books in droves. And my sales are what keep your sad fucking company from going under.' He pauses, his eyes locked on mine, a hint of spittle on his lips. 'Am I making myself clear, Kate?'

I push the water glass away, my hand trembling.

'Perfectly.'

The waiter arrives with our hors d'oeuvres, and Calum leans back, throwing a white cloth napkin over his lap, an urbane smile on his lips again.

'Soupe à l'oignon,' he declares loudly, watching as the dish is placed reverently before him on the damask tablecloth. 'It looks delicious, thank you so much.' He nods as my own plate of olives and assorted spicy salami is set before me. 'Marvellous.'

The waiter smiles and moves away.

'I'm sorry,' I say falteringly, aware that I've screwed things up. I ought to have waited until we were more comfortable together as author and editor before making critical comments about his book. Now he must hate me.

But he's already got himself under control again. 'Don't give it another thought,' Calum says smoothly, and reaches across to grasp my wrist. 'I like women who aren't afraid to give their opinion.' His cold fingers, curled about me, tighten inexorably on the narrow wrist bones until I'm in actual pain. Tears start in my eyes and I blink them back, my lips closing on a barely audible moan. 'I find it... exciting. But I expect you know that, don't you, Kate?'

He releases me, and I have to resist the urge to rub my throbbing wrist.

'Know what?' I manage to ask, wanting to yell at him in fury but not quite daring. If it had been anyone else...

I can't risk losing this author. Not now, not with everything else that's going on in my life. Mark would kill me. Not literally, perhaps. But it would be a black mark against me, and my career

111

might not survive a bust-up with Calum Morgan. Besides, I should be grateful he isn't playing footsie with me instead of roughhousing me, given his reputation.

'You know about men who like feisty women.'

There's a strange inflexion in his voice… The inference being that I'm supposed to find this comment significant. Only I don't.

'I don't understand,' I begin to say, but he cuts me off with a thin smile and a raised hand.

'David,' he says softly.

My stomach plummets and for an instant, I can't breathe, let alone speak. It feels like someone's punched me in the stomach.

How the hell does he know?

'D-David?'

He nods, leaning back comfortably in his chair. 'Your fiancé.' His hooded eyes watch me without expression. 'Or should I say, your *late* fiancé?' When I still don't speak, his lips curl into a cruel semblance of a smile. 'What's the matter, Kate? Don't tell me you've already forgotten his name? What's it been…? Two years? Poor David. I wonder if he realised how little impact his suicide would have on the love of his life?' He shrugs. 'Maybe he did. Maybe that's why David killed himself. Because you drove him to it with your heartless—'

'Shut up,' I hiss under my breath, my eyes burning, locked furiously on his face. 'How dare you?'

Calum's smile broadens, and he gives a little chuckle. 'Ah now, there's the real Kate at last. I was beginning to think I'd have to slap you to see her.'

'Excuse me?' I'm shocked.

'Apologies if I touched a nerve but I can't stand working with an editor who's too timid to speak her mind. Cheryl and I have stayed together for so long because she never baulks at giving me the bad news about my manuscripts. When I met you, Kate, I knew immediately that you'd be the same. Fearless and hard to intimidate.'

I can scarcely believe what I'm hearing. Is the man crazy?

'So you thought you'd put that theory to the test by nearly breaking my wrist, and then all but accusing me of murdering my boyfriend?'

'Murder?' His eyebrows shoot up again. 'I asked Cheryl for some juicy background on you, that's all. She mentioned your fiancé. But she told me he'd committed suicide. Did I say you killed him?'

I pull myself up short, and swallow the words I'd been about to say. Wild, angry words that would have made me sound mad as well as guilty. Even though I am neither.

I DIED BECAUSE OF YOU, KATE.

It's those bloody poison pen letters. They've polluted my mind. Now, every time I hear David's name mentioned, I leap instantly to defend myself against that accusation.

'No,' I admit reluctantly, 'but you implied neglect. It wasn't my fault David died. He'd been depressed for a long time. I stuck with him through his illness, but in the end, it wasn't enough.' I rub my sore wrist at last, looking away. 'You hurt me.'

'Did I?' Calum reaches for my hand again, and I can't help but flinch and draw back as he does so. He stops, noting the involuntary movement. 'For that, I'm truly sorry. It was unintentional. Sometimes I don't know my own strength.' He pats my hand gently, and then sits back, his gaze on my face. 'Look, Kate, I was baiting you to get a reaction, I can't deny it. But I didn't mean what I said. Especially about the book. If you genuinely think it needs work, send me your editorial notes and I'll see what I can do.'

My head is all over the place. He was only pretending to be angry? And the thing about David was him *testing* me? I can't believe that.

I take a deep swallow of champagne, needing the courage of alcohol in my veins. 'Okay, I will.'

'Good.' Calum picks up his spoon and begins drinking his onion soup. His face changes as the first taste hits, his expression suddenly warm and sensual. 'Um, spicy. Utterly gorgeous.' His gaze moves to my plate, which I haven't touched. 'How's yours?'

I nibble some salami, pop an olive in my mouth, and smile mechanically. 'Delicious,' I say indistinctly.

But inside it's hard not to hate him.

Calum Morgan may be a bestselling author. But he's also as changeable as a wind vane, his mood swings not just mercurial but violent and disturbing. Working with this man is going to destroy what little peace of mind I have left, given everything that's been going on at home.

But I don't have a choice, do I? Not if I want to hold onto my career...

CHAPTER FOURTEEN

Logan takes me out for a lunch date on Friday, my day off, which is lovely. The contrast between the lunch with Calum Morgan and this one with Logan is so marked, it's almost absurd.

We choose a pub at random, chatting as we wander along the street together, and find a cosy table on a raised level overlooking the street. He's taken a long lunch break from work, which I suppose he's allowed to do because he's one of their senior executives, and shows no inclination to leave after we finish eating.

Logan is warm and friendly and makes me laugh with anecdotes about the office where he works, which sounds very cut-and-thrust.

He works for an estate agency like David did, having got into the business after university through David's recommendation, landing a job at a rival company. It seemed to amuse David, staying best friends with the 'enemy' – as his boss angrily referred to Logan whenever he saw them together. There was always banter about it when we went out to the pub as a threesome or in a group, the two men tossing ridiculous insults back and forth.

But I knew David wasn't really bothered by any of that business rivalry. He liked and trusted Logan, as do I.

Over coffee, he asks about the poison pen letters. His tone is casual, but I'm not deceived. 'Did you take them to the police station?'

'Not yet.'

His brows draw together. 'Kate—'

'Look, if there are any more, I'll speak to the police about them. You're right, it has to be done. But there are only two letters so far. It seems like a bit of an overkill to get the police involved over *two* letters.'

'One came to your workplace though, and one to your house.' He shakes his head. 'It sounds to me like you have a stalker.'

'God, don't!'

'I'm not trying to scare you, and I'm sorry if I have. But you need to face facts. Someone has threatened you. And they know where you live.' He finished his coffee. 'I don't like the thought of it, that's all.'

'I'm sure it's nothing.' But even I am not convinced.

'Let me take the letters to the police, then. On your behalf.' His gaze is serious. 'Or we could go together, if you're uncomfortable doing it alone.'

'I'm not scared to talk to the police about this,' I say sharply, offended by what I consider a patronising male tone. My cheeks feel hot as I meet his gaze with my own stormy look. 'I don't want to overreact, that's all. Is that so hard to understand?'

'Not at all.'

For an instant, I'm reminded of Calum Morgan and his verbal duelling, and how he grabbed my wrist so painfully, later pretending it hadn't been his intention to hurt me. Which I still don't believe.

'Bloody men,' I mutter, looking away.

'I'm sorry.' His smile is crooked. 'I suppose that must have sounded a bit high-handed. Am I coming across as a complete misogynist?'

I feel bad, then. Logan's nothing like Calum; he's only trying to help, not baiting me.

116

'No, of course not,' I lie, and force myself to relax. 'But I'd prefer to wait and see what happens.' I push my coffee away, unfinished.

Logan shrugs. 'It's your decision, of course.'

I stand up, feeling off-balance. 'I need to get back home. Sorry to dash off like this, but…'

He gets up too, reaching for his jacket. 'Can I see you again, at least? I hope I haven't blown it.'

His smile is so engaging, I find myself softening. 'I'd love to see you again, Logan. I'm sorry if I sounded abrupt. It's been a long week. A long month, actually.'

He looks at me keenly. 'This new guy… the big author… You've barely mentioned him. Is the transfer not going as well as you hoped?'

God, he's astute.

I hadn't gone into much detail with him about Calum Morgan or that awful lunch the other day, fearing what I might reveal of my mindset if I did. I'm wildly uncertain about being his editor though still continuing to work on his manuscript without comment. Yet, despite my careful reticence, Logan somehow guessed that things had gone badly between us.

'I'll cope,' I say, my chin up. 'Look, how about you come over on Monday? I'll cook something. We could watch a film together after dinner.'

'That sounds perfect.'

I hesitate. 'Monday is Ruby's night off this week, and Mum goes to bed quite early, so we shouldn't be disturbed.' I don't know why I said that. My cheeks fill with heat again under his caressing look. 'How about Italian food?' I say to cover the awkward silence. 'I could make a lasagne with a green salad.'

'I'd love that, thank you. I'll bring the wine, shall I?'

Outside, he kisses me briefly on the mouth, and heads off into the cold wind with his coat collar turned up. Back to work, I assume.

I watch him cross the road, considering whether I should let him go a little further after our next dinner date. We'll be alone, after all. And I do find him attractive.

But my frazzled mind can't move that far ahead, or even gauge if I would like to become intimate with Logan. Everything seems to be moving so quickly these days, I feel somehow out of step…

When I get back to the house, I find Mr Adeyemi coming down the drive in a smart black Jag. I pull to one side and lower my window. He does the same.

'Hello,' I say, faintly confused. 'I thought you were coming on Monday afternoon? Did I get the day wrong?'

'Not all,' he says smoothly, smiling. 'I have to go away this weekend, on a personal matter, and it's possible I won't be back until Tuesday. So I've been trying to squeeze in my Monday appointments before I go.'

'I see.' I glance at the house, but the front door is shut. 'Have you spoken to my mother, then?'

'Yes, indeed. We had a good conversation over a nice pot of tea that your housekeeper was kind enough to offer me.'

I blink, not understanding who he means; Irina's not in today. Then I realise he must be talking about Ruby.

'So how did you find her? Do you see what I mean about her needing me to take over her financial affairs?'

To my dismay, he shakes his head. 'I'm afraid not. She seemed perfectly alert and had no problems understanding me. I discussed the issue of her bank account, but she's adamant she wants to keep control of it.'

'But she's not capable,' I burst out, and see his eyes narrow. 'That is, I don't think it's safe. Not with so many con artists around.'

'We covered that too. She's happy to continue the way she always has, and frankly, who are we to try and take her money away from her?' He sees my eyes widen and raises a hand. 'No, I'm sorry. I do appreciate your concern for her well-being, Miss Kinley. But your mother is my client, and has been for many years. I like to think we have a strong relationship. So I would be remiss in my duty if I ignored Celeste's insistence that she is well enough to handle her own finances and handed that control over to you instead. I accept it's a delicate matter, but consent is everything in the eyes of the law. I'm sure you must appreciate that too.'

I don't know what to say, but everything inside me hurts.

'Well, goodbye,' he says calmly, and raises his electric window with a brusque nod, making it clear my opinion as her daughter means nothing to him.

I watch helplessly in my rear-view mirror as the powerful black car purrs down the drive and pulls away into traffic.

'Damn it,' I mutter, dragging my coat around me as I get out of my car. The wind tears at my hair in great gusts and whips at my skirt, our trees bending and rustling above me in the thickening gloom, the last of their leaves whirling about the gravelled drive.

I hurry inside, incredulous that Mr Adeyemi could have sat talking to my mother even for as little as half an hour, and yet not spotted that her grasp on reality is slipping away. Though even Dr Forster said something similar about Mum needing to 'give consent' to going into a care home. It seems I've been premature in my attempt to keep my mother safe. I feel a great bitterness inside at this irony, but push it aside as best I can. They're both experts and must be used to dealing with people in this situation, so perhaps I should accept their judgement. I certainly won't help my mother by stirring up trouble for no good reason.

Ruby has an apron on and is whisking something sweet-smelling in a large metal mixing bowl. 'Chocolate cake,' she says when I stare at the gooey mess, and points with her dripping whisk down the hall. 'Your mum's lying down in her room. The solicitor was here just now. Did you see him leaving?' When I nod, she smiles, continuing in her bright, bubbly way. 'Celeste was so exhausted after his visit, poor pet, she was stumbling about. I didn't see any harm in letting her take a nap. I hope you don't mind?'

'Why would I?' I kick off my shoes and hang up my coat, then knock on Mum's door. 'It's Kate. Are you okay, Mum?'

There's no answer. Perhaps she's already asleep.

After a moment, I tiptoe away.

'You all right, love?' Ruby gives me a concerned look, unfastening her apron. 'Can I get you something to drink?'

Briefly, I tell Ruby what Mr Adeyemi said, and she tuts, shaking her head in disbelief.

'That's not right. Do you want me to talk to him instead? Let him know what's what?' She hesitates. 'Because it might come better from me.'

I stare at her. 'Why do you say that?'

'Well, I haven't got an axe to grind, have I?' Ruby bustles ahead of me into the living room, scooping up the tea tray that they must have used during his visit. The cups rattle noisily together, setting my teeth on edge. 'It makes no difference to me what happens with the Power of Attorney. But if the solicitor says yes to you, that puts all her money in your control. So it stands to reason he'd be less likely to listen to you than to me.'

I haven't thought of it like that before, and stop dead in front of the window, staring blindly out at the garden. As dusk falls, the wind snatches at bushes and bends trees violently, the evening wild now.

The realisation that Mr Adeyemi may think me underhand and a thief makes me quite sick with anxiety.

'You're saying he thinks I'm after her money?'

'I'm not saying anything, love.' Ruby gives me a reassuring smile. 'I'm just trying to see it from his point of view. I know you don't mean harm by it. But it might look a bit fishy to some people.'

'What would?'

'Why, you saying Celeste can't look after her own bank account, of course, and that you want to do it for her.' She nods and her smile widens, seemingly oblivious to my frozen horror. 'But if the solicitor came here to talk to your mum about it and still doesn't see the need… Well, that's the end of that, isn't it?'

'Yes, I suppose it is.'

I draw the curtains across to hide the stormy evening, and then drop down onto the sofa, reaching vaguely for the television remote.

'Would you like some company?' Ruby asks, lingering in the doorway, still holding the tea tray. 'You seem a bit down, if you don't mind me saying so. I could put on some coffee. We could watch some soaps together.'

I don't watch soaps, in general. But tonight the idea of easy watching appeals to me.

'Yes, why not?' I click on the television and smile up at her. 'And then maybe I can help you eat that cake.'

But after Ruby has hurried out to make us both coffee, my mind shifts back to what she said about Mr Adeyemi, and I become uneasy again.

Does the solicitor really think I would try to steal from my own mother? Is that the real reason why he's refusing to let me use the Power of Attorney?

Perhaps I should ring Dr Forster and get her to write him a letter explaining how much my mother's mental capacity has deteriorated lately. She may have said that Mum needs to consent to being put into a home, but handling her finances is surely different. I just want to make sure my mother can't give away all her savings to some scam merchant.

But the embarrassment of both our family doctor and the solicitor imagining me grasping after my mother's money is too horrible to bear, so I quickly dismiss the idea. Under the circumstances, it could only do harm to put the two of them together...

CHAPTER FIFTEEN

The next day being a Saturday, I treat myself to a lie-in, blissfully secure in the knowledge that my mother now has a live-in carer. It's a luxury I haven't been able to indulge in for months, maybe even years, and it's with a real sense of pleasure that I finally yawn and throw back the covers at nearly eleven o'clock. The sun is warming the bathroom tiles as I take a leisurely shower, the weather outside cold but bright, a perfect autumn day.

But when I finally wander downstairs in search of a late breakfast, I find Ruby on her own in the kitchen. She looks round at me with a worried expression on her face.

'Good morning,' she says uncertainly, and bites her lip.

'What is it?' I ask, immediately apprehensive. I'd put my head round Mum's door on my way past but seen no sign of her, and assumed she must be in the living room, perhaps hard at work on a jigsaw puzzle or her knitting. Now a range of alarming possibilities run through my head. 'Ruby? What's the matter?'

She doesn't answer for a moment, her brow furrowed as she works, intent on spreading butter lavishly on two slices of toast. 'I don't want to alarm you,' she begins slowly, which panics me.

'I'm already alarmed. Please tell me what's wrong,' I demand.

'It's probably nothing.' Now she's chewing on her lip, practically eating it. 'I mean, obviously it is *something*. But it could be nothing.'

'Ruby, for God's sake! Where's my mother?'

'In the living room.' When I turn, she drops the butter knife and jumps in my path. 'No, please don't disturb her. She doesn't know. That is, I don't think she's even noticed.'

I'm stunned, both by the way she's behaving and her continuing mysterious utterances. 'Noticed what, exactly? I swear, Ruby, if you don't tell me right now—'

'She has some bruising,' she mutters, her gaze lifting to my face. Her eyes are full of foreboding. 'Do you know anything about it?'

'Me?' I shake my head, horrified. 'What kind of bruising? How bad?'

'Just a few blotches on her upper right arm.' She touches her own arm to indicate the place. 'I only noticed them this morning when I was helping her get dressed. Celeste says she doesn't know how it happened. That she can't remember. But I'd swear they weren't there yesterday morning.'

I'm struggling to understand. 'You think she hurt herself in the night?'

'I don't know.' Ruby shrugs helplessly. 'I can't be sure, obviously. But it looks… Well, it looks as though someone's grabbed her by the arm. Not one of us, of course.' She hesitates, blinking in confusion. 'It wasn't me. And I'm sure you would never… Oh well, maybe she just banged herself.'

I stare, my mouth open. 'Grabbed her? But she hasn't been anywhere but here. Who on earth… ' I break off, suddenly realising what she's suggesting. 'You think it could have been Mr Adeyemi?' My eyes widen. 'He was alone with her, wasn't he?'

She nods, a look of chagrin on her face. 'Sitting at the table together,

124

they were. Looking at a big folder of documents he'd brought. Oh, I should never have left Celeste on her own with him. But he asked me to leave the room. So what else could I have done?'

'He asked you to *leave*? Why?'

'They needed privacy, he said. So I took the tea tray through, like he asked. Then I went out and shut the door behind me.' Ruby looks distraught. 'Perhaps I ought to have left it open, in case she needed to call me. But I didn't want him to think I was eavesdropping.'

I feel sick to my stomach. 'How long was Mr Adeyemi alone with her?'

Ruby considers. 'Maybe half an hour?'

'I can't believe he would have hurt her. They've been friends for years. He knew my father really well.'

She nods reassuringly. 'I can't believe it either.' She pauses. 'Though maybe he did it accidentally. He looks quite strong, don't you think?'

'Accidentally?'

'Maybe he just…' Gingerly, Ruby reaches out and squeezes my upper arm. 'Touched her. Like that, to make a point while he was talking. Only he didn't realise his own strength.' She releases me. 'Or maybe she was going to wander off… You know the way she does sometimes, halfway through a conversation, and he tried to steer her back to the table.'

I study her face, my heart beating hard. 'You think Mr Adeyemi was trying to coerce my mother in some way?'

'I don't know what that means, sorry.'

'Coerce?' I hesitate. 'It means… force her to do something against her will.'

Ruby looks shocked. 'Oh no! He was such a nice, polite man. Like I say, I expect it was just an accident. Or maybe she did genuinely bang her arm in the night.'

'How?'

'Sometimes she gets up in the dark and tries to reach the toilet on her own, and knocks things over.'

I'm less convinced. 'I'd better go and look at these bruises.'

Ruby nods approvingly. 'I thought you might. So I gave her a short-sleeved top to wear, and popped a thick cardigan over it for warmth.' She looks worried as she returns to buttering her toast. 'I only hope she won't be feeling the cold.'

My mother is napping when I go in, closing the door quietly behind me. She doesn't stir. 'Mum?'

Pulling up the footstool, I sit next to her armchair and touch her hand gently, not wanting to startle her. Slowly, her eyelids flutter, and then she opens her eyes, gazing at me in an unfocused way.

I say, 'I'm really sorry to disturb your forty winks, especially when you're looking so comfortable. But can I have a word?'

Mum makes a little moaning noise and straightens up, yawning. 'Did I get any tea?'

Her cup of tea sits untouched on the low table beside her.

'It looks like it's gone cold,' I say. 'Don't worry, I'll fetch you a fresh cup in a minute. First, I wanted to ask you something.'

She waits, looking at me with a faintly surprised air.

I wonder how to broach such a delicate topic. Mum has always waxed lyrical about Mr Adeyemi, telling me what a kind man he is and how well he looks after her affairs. I find it hard to believe he would have put such a good relationship at risk by behaving unpleasantly to her. But if there's any chance at all that she's at risk, the question has to be asked.

'Ruby tells me you've got some nasty bruising on your arm,' I say carefully. 'Do you mind if I take a look?'

Mum stares. 'Bruising?'

'She saw it when you were getting dressed this morning.' I nod to her upper right arm. 'I think I ought to see what she means, if that's okay.'

Blinking, Mum makes no comment as I ease her cardigan off and push up the short sleeve of her top to reveal her pale skin.

I suck in my breath, stunned by what I find there.

Sure enough, her skin shows marks of having been manhandled, and recently too, the blotches quite distinct. I fit my fingers to the bruising, and can imagine a man's hand closing about her narrow arm and squeezing, perhaps even shaking her.

'Oh God, Mum…'

She's angling her head to see what I'm looking at. 'What is it?' Her eyes widen. 'Oh, now where did that come from?'

'Can you remember?'

Slowly, Mum shakes her head, her face blank. 'I remember my arm hurting… Ouch, yes.' She pushes my hand away, dragging her sleeve back down and fumbling for her cardigan. 'I… I'm cold.'

'Of course, sorry.'

I help her cover up, and she seems happier once she's snug again, wrapped up in her thick cardigan. But I'm far from happy.

'Mum,' I say with difficulty, 'who did this to you? Who hurt your arm?'

But my mother's already looking away. She frowns down at the tangle of knitting on her lap. 'Where's my pattern? Have you seen my pattern?'

I sigh.

She's forgotten that she can't follow a pattern anymore and just prefers to knit freestyle, for something to keep her hands occupied…

'You don't need one, Mum,' I remind her, impatient to return to the subject of her bruised arm. 'Remember?' I tap the knitting needles. 'Patterns only confuse you. So you don't like using them these days.'

She shakes her head stubbornly. 'I need a pattern.'

'Don't worry. You've forgotten that you don't like them anymore, that's all. Why don't you just set a few stitches, see how that goes?'

She picks up her needles, stares at the ball of wool, and then drops them again. 'I don't want to do this today,' she bursts out, and suddenly pushes the knitting off her lap, almost angry. 'I don't like it.'

'Mum, you love knitting.'

'No,' she insists, and pulls a face. 'Nobody cares what I want.'

'That's not true.'

'I'm not stupid,' she says vehemently. 'I know what's going on.'

'I'm lost, Mum.' I crouch at her feet, gathering together her discarded knitting. 'What do you mean? What do you think is going on?'

But she refuses to answer, staring into the distance as though thinking about something in her past.

I put away her knitting and stand over her, unsure what to do for the best. 'Mum, we need to talk about your arm.' She says nothing, but I press on regardless. 'It looks to me like somebody hurt you. These bruises on your arm... How did you get them?'

'I don't know,' she mutters.

'Then maybe I should tell someone else about them. Dr Forster, for instance.' I hesitate. 'Or the police.'

Finally, this gets her attention.

'The police?' Mum echoes in astonishment, raising her head to stare up at me. 'What on earth are you talking about?'

'Your arm, Mum. The bruises.'

'Oh, that.' She waves a dismissive hand, and I'm still not sure she understands what I'm talking about. 'It's nothing. Nothing.' Her gaze falls on the cold cup of tea again, and she tuts loudly. 'Now, look at that. All this chit-chat, and my tea's gone cold.'

'That's not a problem. I'll make a fresh pot for you.'

Yet although I pick up the offending cup, I don't move towards the door.

I don't want to send her into one of her rages, but it's important to ask before she forgets this episode entirely. I'm not sure I want to escalate this to a police matter. After all, it is possible she simply banged herself and has forgotten. But I need to be sure.

'Mum, one last question. Did Mr Adeyemi hurt you yesterday?'

'What?' Her eyes are wide and startled.

'Did he grab your arm, maybe? Did he argue with you?' I give her an encouraging smile. 'Or was it an accident, perhaps?'

'Mr Adeyemi?' She blinks and looks troubled, clearly trying to think back to their meeting. 'He… came to see me. We had a cup of tea together. And biscuits.' She points to the table. 'We sat over there.'

'Yes, Mum, that's right. I was out at the time, but Ruby told me about his visit.'

'Ruby,' she repeats slowly, as though the name is unfamiliar to her. Which I suppose it is. It often takes her a while to put names to faces these days.

'Do you remember what you talked about?' I take a deep breath and decide to be frank, afraid that her attention may already be wandering again. 'Was Mr Adeyemi unkind to you, Mum?'

'Unkind to me? Mr Adeyemi? What on earth makes you say that? Don't be so silly,' she says emphatically, looking almost offended by the suggestion. 'You do say some stupid things.'

'Sorry, but I had to ask.'

'Mr Adeyemi is a lovely man. I like him ever so much.'

'I know you do, Mum. But your arm—'

'In fact,' she says, interrupting me a little aggressively, 'you might as well know, I'm leaving him something in my will. It's what your father would have wanted.'

Surprise leaves me momentarily speechless.

Putting the cup down, I manage to ask, 'Wait, you're going to leave something to Mr Adeyemi? Are you sure about that? We're talking about your solicitor, right?'

'I know who he is,' she says testily.

'Okay.' I'm bemused. 'Sorry if I'm being stupid again. But I don't understand. Are you saying you've *changed* your will?'

'Not changed it, precisely. Mr Adeyemi is one of my beneficiaries, and he always has been. Well, since your father's death. They were good friends, you know.' She smiles. 'They played golf together all the time. And we had dinner parties here, just the four of us, though I suppose you would have been too young at the time to remember. Me, your father, Mr Adeyemi… and his wife, of course. I forget her name. But such a lovely woman. Your father liked her tremendously.'

I can't believe what I'm hearing.

I had no idea Mr Adeyemi would benefit from Mum's will. I'm not even sure if that's legal, for a solicitor to benefit from their own client's will. It doesn't seem like it could be. But maybe she means a small specific gift. Maybe something that belonged to Dad, for instance, that might have some sentimental value to Mr Adeyemi. His golf clubs, perhaps, which are still stored in the attic.

'Just to clarify, do you mean you're giving him money? Or have you left him something personal?' I press her, though I can see my curiosity is upsetting her. 'Something to remind him of Dad.'

'Of course I mean money,' she snaps, and waves me away. 'What a stupid question. You're always wasting my time with nonsense.' She shakes her head. 'Go and get me some more tea; I'm thirsty.'

Dumbfounded by this sudden change of mood, I move automatically towards the door on her command, and then stop.

This is insane.

'Mum,' I say more gently, hoping to catch her out with an unexpected question, 'when Mr Adeyemi was here, did you try to change your mind about leaving that money to him? Is that why he hurt you?'

But my mother's not listening to me anymore. Instead, she's humming an old dance tune as she stares at the framed wedding photograph of her and Dad that sits on the mantelpiece. They're dancing together at their wedding, many decades ago, Mum twirling under Dad's arm, both smiling for the camera. And in the shadowy background, a familiar face swims out from among the crowd of wedding guests watching them.

Mr Adeyemi, smart in a pinstriped suit and tie, with his arm about his own smiling, beautiful wife...

CHAPTER SIXTEEN

My mood descends into gloom on Monday when I receive a brief note from Irina through the post, giving in her notice, effective immediately.

I'm not entirely surprised, of course. Our cleaner barely spoke to me last week, hurrying around the house with the Dyson and doing more of a rushed job than usual in the kitchen and bathroom. Now, I realise she must have been planning her departure for some time…

I ring Irina at once, frantic to get her to change her mind. It's so hard to find trustworthy cleaners in our area, and there's also Mum to consider. She was destabilised enough by losing Giorgios, so God knows how she would react to another unfamiliar face around the house.

'Look, whatever the problem is,' I promise Irina, 'we can sort it out. Just come back on Thursday and we'll talk about it. A proper sit-down chat.'

'I don't want to come back,' she says stiffly. 'Anyway, I've already agreed to clean for someone else in your slot. I'm very sorry, Miss Kinley.'

She cuts the call abruptly and I sit there with the phone in my hand, staring at nothing. Now we have no cleaner. What on earth am I going to do?

After checking with the office that it's okay to work from home today, wanting to get properly stuck into Calum's manuscript, I lose myself in work for the rest of the day. With Logan coming round for dinner this evening, at seven o'clock I push aside my laptop with a sigh of relief and head downstairs into the kitchen to start tidying up the place and preparing a romantic dinner for two. I ought to have started earlier but Calum's book is a mess of errors and tricky issues that need to be resolved, and picking through that minefield without offending the author is driving me crackers…

Ruby, having helped Mum shower and get ready for an early night, has decided to go out for her evening off. She's already in the hall, buttoning up her black winter coat and checking her phone, when I emerge from the kitchen, dish cloth in hand.

'Ruby, did Mum eat okay tonight?' I ask, my guilty conscience nagging at me. Mum and Ruby had eaten together at six o'clock in the dining room while I was working. 'She's started nibbling at her food lately. I'm worried she's not eating enough. Did you manage to get her to eat something substantial?'

'Chicken salad,' Ruby tells me cheerfully, and pulls on a chunky bobble hat before checking her reflection in the hall mirror. 'She didn't do too badly. More salad than chicken, it's true. But that's probably a good thing if you don't want her to get indigestion and spoil your big date.'

I feel embarrassed. 'It's hardly a big date. I'm making a lasagne, that's all. Then we're going to watch a film together.'

'Sounds lovely.'

'Listen,' I say as she turns away, 'I'm sorry about all the mess lately. I did mean to have a proper tidy-up yesterday but I've been snowed under with work.'

'That's all right. I like a lived-in house. Much more comfortable than one of these immaculate show homes.' Ruby looks back at me curiously. 'So Irina's not coming back, I take it?'

'I'm afraid not. I seem to have offended her, somehow.'

'Well, never mind. I didn't much like Irina anyway. Several times I caught her snooping about upstairs, looking in drawers and so on.'

I'm shocked. 'Seriously?'

'I wasn't going to tell tales while she was working for you, but now…' She shrugs. 'Good riddance to bad rubbish, eh?' She hesitates. 'Is it a romantic film, this one you're watching tonight?'

I laugh awkwardly. 'I haven't decided yet. Besides, maybe he's not into that kind of thing. Men tend to prefer car chases and exploding helicopters, don't they?' I'm genuinely uncertain what kind of film Logan would prefer to watch; I'd been planning to wait until he arrived before making that decision. 'My father always did, anyway.'

'Even action films usually have a few smoochy moments, though.' Ruby winks at me. 'Might as well make the most of it, eh? He looks like a good kisser, your Logan.'

On that note, leaving me hot-cheeked and speechless, she slips out of the front door with a wave, adding quickly, 'I'll let myself back in. No need to wait up.'

It's only after she's gone that I realise I didn't ask Ruby what she had planned for her evening off. I don't even know if she has a boyfriend. But it's none of my business, and she probably would have told me if she was in the mood for sharing such private information.

We're not friends, after all. She's my mother's live-in carer. Though it's becoming hard not to think of Ruby as one of the family, now that she's installed in the house and almost constantly around. And Mum seems to adore her.

In fact, the only person unhappy about the new arrangement

has been Irina. And she's gone now, so maybe I can look forward to some peace and quiet at last.

All the same, while cooking the lasagne, I find myself fretting over what Ruby said about Irina, that she'd seen her looking through our bedroom drawers. It worries me. Why on earth would Irina be rummaging through our private things? But in the end, I push the thought aside. It's more likely Irina was putting something away, not stealing or snooping, and that Ruby merely misinterpreted what she saw.

Logan arrives on time, almost uncannily so, ringing the doorbell just as I've checked on Mum – who's already asleep, bless her – and taken the lasagne out of the oven before it over-browns.

Logan gives me a kiss on the lips, and then hands me a bunch of magnificent, tall white lilies and a bottle of expensive Burgundy, already chilled.

'Thank you, these are lovely.' Pleasantly surprised, I find a vase for the flowers and hurriedly put them in water while he's opening the wine for me. 'Mum's asleep, so we'll be eating on our own in the dining room. I've laid the table if you want to take the wine glasses through.'

He does so, sniffing the air appreciatively. 'Dinner ready, is it? Smells delicious.'

'Yes, your timing is perfect.' I put the flowers on the dining table and then carry in the lasagne, and serve us both at the table. 'There's a bowl of green salad and some sliced baguette too. Just help yourself.'

'It all looks very impressive.' He smiles, watching me. 'And I love the pinny. I didn't realise you were such a domestic goddess.'

A little flushed, I swiftly undo my apron and shove it under the table before taking my seat. I lift my glass, enjoying the heady aroma of the wine, and say breathlessly, 'Cheers!'

'Cheers!'

I take an exploratory bite; to my intense relief, the lasagne is near perfect. I've never been a great cook, but I have a few signature dishes I can pull off tolerably well, and lasagne is one of them.

While we eat, Logan tells me about his day at work, and then politely asks about mine. It's clear he's still curious about Calum Morgan, as he listens without interrupting while I describe the famous author in detail – his appearance and mannerisms, which Logan seems to find fascinating – and then outline a few of the issues with his manuscript, being careful not to be too indiscreet. It would be disastrous if news got out that Calum's latest book wasn't as good as his previous bestsellers. Unless his books are always that bad, and Cheryl has been in the unenviable position of fixing them for years…

'Sounds like you've got a lot of work on your hands there,' Logan says, pushing away his plate. 'That was so good, by the way. You're a great cook.'

'Thank you.' I finish my own meal, ridiculously pleased by this small compliment. 'Well, the book is a challenge, it's true. But I'm sure I can get it ready in time for publication.' I feel like crossing my fingers as I say this, hoping my optimism is not misplaced.

'You said earlier that Calum Morgan has a bit of a reputation.' Logan refills my wine glass. 'What did you mean by that?'

'Only that he's always been difficult with editors. Especially women.'

Logan frowns. 'Difficult in what way?'

'Oh, he tries it on sometimes. And then likes to get his revenge when they slap him down.'

'Seriously? And they still publish him?'

I hesitate, worried that I shouldn't have said that. 'Well, you know… Some authors are like that. It's all part of the job.'

'Putting up with sexual harassment is part of your job?' He sounds incredulous, and I can't blame him.

'When you put it like that…' I laugh awkwardly. 'He's never laid a finger on me. Well, not in that sense.'

Logan leans forward, staring at me. 'So he has laid a finger on you?'

'He grabbed my wrist.' I rub my wrist unconsciously, even though it no longer hurts, and then realise he's now focused on that movement. 'Look, it's not what it seems. He didn't mean to hurt me. He was trying to emphasise a point, and…'

'And he manhandled you,' Logan says flatly. 'You need to tell someone. Your boss.'

'Mark?' I gulp down some wine, and then laugh, a high-pitched note in my voice that wasn't there before. 'You're kidding, right? Run to Mark with tales of Calum Morgan's hands-on abuse? That would be just the excuse Mark is looking for to sack me.'

'It would be unfair dismissal if he did.' Logan seems angry. 'Good God, you can't just shrug your shoulders and let him get away with that. The man's clearly a menace.'

'Frankly,' I admit with rather too much candour, and mentally blame the wine I've been knocking back for not being more guarded, 'I've got bigger issues to worry about than Calum Morgan's bullying ways.'

'Your mother?' Logan smiles wryly when I look surprised. 'No, I'm not a mind reader. You get a certain look on your face when you're upset about your mother.'

'I'm sorry.' I bend my head, wishing my hair was longer and I could hide from his clever stare from under it. 'I didn't mean to burden you with all my troubles. This is meant to be a date.'

He laughs, and I look up, surprised.

'That was a delicious dinner, and I'm really enjoying being with you,' he says, his gaze locked on my face. 'That sounds to me like a perfect date. And if you have "troubles", then I want to hear about

137

them and to help you solve them, if that's possible. I'm not a fair-weather boyfriend. That's not my style.'

I smile, a warm glow spreading through me as I realise he's serious.

'Thank you. It does help to know I'm not completely alone in all this.' I stand up, a little unsteadily, and scoop up my wine glass. 'Shall we take this conversation through to the living room? I've got more wine in the fridge if you need a top-up.'

'I should have brought two bottles, I'm sorry,' he says ruefully.

'It's not a problem.'

We settle on the sofa with the new bottle of wine, his knee brushing mine from time to time, and talk for a while about my mother and her health issues, and how Irina has given in her notice, which hasn't helped. Eventually, I touch on the difficult topic of Mr Adeyemi, his veto of my Power of Attorney, and his recent visit to the house.

'I know something happened between them,' I say uneasily, sipping on my wine, 'but I can't be sure what. And Mum insists she can't remember.' I explain about the bruising to her upper arm and see him frown. 'Plus, she keeps insisting that he's going to benefit from her will. Financially, I mean.'

'Good God.'

'Yes, I was surprised too. Shocked, actually. I don't know what to think. But it all seems very fishy to me.'

'To me too.' Logan hesitates. 'Talking of things that are fishy, did you ever go to the police about those letters like I suggested?'

I'm baffled, thrown off balance by this unexpected question. 'What's that got to do with it?' I search his face. 'You think Mr Adeyemi sent them to me?' When he shrugs, giving nothing away in his expression, I exclaim, 'But why on earth would he do something like that? I can't believe he even knows where I work. Don't forget one of those letters arrived for me at the office. Through internal mail, in fact.' I dismiss it as a possibility, though the idea he's put into my head is certainly intriguing. 'No, I don't see the connection.'

'Maybe it will become clearer in time. Meanwhile, it would be easy enough for a man like Adeyemi to discover where you work and just pop the letter through the front door of your office building, surely? A hand-delivered letter shows no postmark and could easily be mistaken for internal mail.'

'I suppose.' I chew on my lip. 'But why? What would Adeyemi stand to gain by sending nasty mail like that?'

'Put you on the back foot, in case you're tempted to block the terms of your mother's will.'

'I don't think that would be possible.'

His eyebrows rise. 'When she has dementia? And he's stopping you from utilising your Power of Attorney? No, it sounds to me as though this solicitor has something to hide.' He takes the glass from my hand and puts it on the coffee table while I stare at him, astonished. 'The only question is, what?'

'I don't know,' I begin to say, but am silenced when Logan leans forward to kiss me.

When he pulls back, there's a curious look on his face. 'Good? Bad?' His sudden smile is crooked. 'Indifferent?'

'Good,' I whisper huskily.

His smile straightens out. 'Oh well, in that case,' he whispers back, 'I'd better do it again.'

Although Logan has kissed me before after our dates, it's usually been in a semi-public setting, a fleeting moment of pleasure. We've never been alone together in such an intimate, comfortable setting with the opportunity to take things further. Seated close together, we nestle against each other, our bodies sinking into the deep, soft cushions of the couch while his hands move restlessly over me.

It's been so long since I've been kissed so passionately; my body is soon aching, my breath coming short and fast…

Then, as if on cue, the door to the living room creaks open, and my head turns.

Mum is standing there in her flannel nightie, blinking at the brightness of the light and swaying slightly on the threshold.

'Oh,' she says, staring at us with a bemused expression, 'I thought I heard noises. Who are you?'

Mortified, I jump up, awkwardly smoothing down my hair and rumpled dress. 'This is Logan,' I remind her. 'You've met him before.'

'Have I?' She peers at him suspiciously.

'Hello again, Mrs Kinley,' he says politely, and stands up too. 'Did we disturb you?' He looks at me, and runs a hand through his own hair, acting as unsettled by this embarrassing interruption as I feel. 'Maybe we were talking a little too loudly. I'm sorry if we woke you.'

'Mum, what are you doing out of bed?' I steer her out of the room, throwing an apologetic look over my shoulder at Logan. 'Choose something for us to watch on Netflix, would you? Sorry.' Closing the door on him, I turn to my mother. 'So, did you need something? The toilet, maybe? Or a glass of water?'

At first, my mother shakes her head, then abruptly changes her mind. 'Both,' she says decisively, and smiles, patting my arm. 'You're a good girl, Kate,' she continues, surprising me by saying my name, which she rarely does these days because names don't come easily to her anymore, not even mine. 'You're always there for me.'

I wish that were true, I think with a pang of guilt, remembering how she burnt herself in my absence.

She peers at me, frowning. 'You won't leave me, will you? You won't go off with that man and leave your mother all alone?'

'Of course not, Mum.'

'Because I know what it's like when you meet someone you like. When you fall in love… Sometimes you just can't help it.'

I'm not sure now if she's talking about me and Logan or her and Dad, or some misty past even I don't know about.

'Don't be daft, Mum. I'm not going anywhere. Now, come on. Let's get you sorted out, shall we? Glass of water first?'

By the time Mum's had a few sips of cold water and a trip to the loo, and I've gently manoeuvred her back into bed, it's almost half an hour later.

I return to the living room to find Logan on his knees in front of the television, playing with the remote control.

He turns to smile at me. 'In your absence, I made an executive decision. I opted for the latest Bond film. I hope that's not too mainstream.'

'No, it's perfect.' I sink down on the sofa again, my nerves a bit frazzled. He joins me there a moment later, adjusting the volume as the film begins. 'I'm so sorry about my mum. The way she walked in on us… I didn't know where to look; I was so embarrassed.'

'Don't be ridiculous.' He moves a lock of hair off my cheek and tucks it behind my ear, his face relaxed. 'She's your mother and this is her house. She has every right to come looking for you.'

'But you've had to wait all this time…'

'Because her needs come first.' He shakes his head at my chagrin. 'No, that's why I like you so much, Kate. You care deeply for your mother. You're a caring person, and that's a quality very few people possess these days.'

I feel myself blushing, and don't know what to say.

'Thank you,' I whisper.

'You're welcome. And you should never apologise for needing to look after your mother. It's a wonderful thing.'

I hesitate, thinking back to our earlier conversation. 'So you think

I should go to the police about that bruising on Mum's arm? And mention the nasty letters at the same time? I mean, assuming you still suspect he might be the one who sent them. There could be a connection there…'

He looks at me seriously. 'You said your mother really likes this Adeyemi guy. Did I get that right?' When I nod, he pulls a face. 'Then you know it's going to upset her if you openly accuse him of abusing her or sending those letters. If there's any chance she could have hurt herself, it might be better to wait and see if it happens again. Or just make sure she never sees him alone again.'

I consider that. 'Yes, I suppose you're right. Mum wouldn't understand if I made an official complaint against Mr Adeyemi.' I sigh, feeling crushed by the hopelessness of the situation. 'Besides, since she claims not to remember how that bruising happened, it's unlikely the police could do anything about it anyway.'

'Except blame you,' he says softly.

I'm shocked. 'Me?'

'You live with her, Kate. You're the one the police are most likely to assume has been mistreating her. Most assaults on older people are domestic, i.e., another family member turns out to be responsible.'

I hadn't thought of it like that before, and the horror must show in my face, because he leans forward and kisses me on the lips again.

'Hey, don't worry about it. Just let it go.' Logan settles back against the cushions, our bodies brushing up against each other with easy warmth. The opening sequence has started, and his gaze has strayed back to the television screen. 'Now, it's time to enjoy some spy action. With a few car chases thrown in, I hope. I haven't actually seen this one.'

'I have to admit, Ruby and I were pretty sure you'd choose an action film.'

He laughs. 'You and Ruby been discussing me, have you? Am I that predictable?'

'Well, the rest of the films on my Netflix wishlist are romcoms or historical dramas—'

'So I noticed. God spare me!'

I laugh too, and allow myself to snuggle against him as his arm slips about my waist. 'To be honest, I'm glad you're predictable,' I admit shyly. 'There's enough in my life that leaves me guessing right now without adding you to the list.'

Logan doesn't reply to that, and when I turn my head in surprise, I find him already watching the film with an intent, narrow-eyed expression. But I have the oddest feeling he heard precisely what I said and simply chose to pretend he hadn't.

CHAPTER SEVENTEEN

There's a text on my phone when I stretch out to check it early next morning, turning over sleepily in bed to find a man where there's usually a cool space.

Logan spent the night with me. I didn't plan for that, but by the time midnight came along, I was open to the possibility, and when his goodnight kiss turned hotter, I chose to go along with it. It felt like the right thing to do.

And I've been lonely in recent months, wondering what it would be like to try a new relationship. The horror of David's sudden death still haunts me today. But at least with Logan, I don't need to explain any of that.

It's not easy though. David's suicide hangs between us in a silent, uneasy way, the elephant in the room, but it's been a mutual decision not to discuss it in any depth. And while it does feel strange and a little unsettling to wake up in bed with a new man, I'm also liberated by the experience.

I've finally moved on.

The text on my phone is from Ruby. It seems to have arrived unnoticed sometime during the early hours.

Sorry for the last minute notice. Staying out all night. Back 8am.

'Shit.'

I struggle up out of bed, abruptly awake, and Logan stirs as the bedsprings depress, opening sleepy eyes and yawning.

'Morning,' he drawls, and then seems to catch on to my tension. 'Something wrong?'

I hadn't realised that Ruby wasn't in the house and so didn't bother to check on Mum during the night, which I used to do faithfully at about three or four o'clock. Mum tends to be a bit of a nocturnal wanderer, and can sometimes forget where she is and get in a tizzy over it.

'Hopefully not. Can I get you a tea or coffee?' I go to the door. 'I need to check on Mum.'

'Doesn't Ruby do that for you?'

'She didn't come back last night. I just spotted a text from her.'

'You need help?'

'No, it's fine. With any luck, she'll still be in bed.'

But my luck is out.

Downstairs, I find Mum's bed empty and no sign of her in either the kitchen or the living room.

'Mum?'

Standing in the hall in my dressing gown, I shiver, feeling a cold draught, and realise the front door is slightly ajar.

Horrified, I drag the door open and rush outside in bare feet.

'Mum?'

My mother is lying on the drive, a little way from the house. Ignoring the tiny stabbing pain of gravel digging into the soles of my bare feet, I stumble over there and help her up. She's groaning, almost incoherent, and her face is as pale as a wax figure.

'Come on,' I pant, struggling to support her weight back inside

145

the house, and am relieved to see Logan, fully dressed, charging out to help. 'Yes, we need to get her back to bed. And maybe call an ambulance. She's had a fall. I only pray she hasn't broken anything.'

'What was she doing outside?'

'God only knows.'

As we carry her between us back into her bedroom, I spot that she's wearing her slippers. That's a mercy, at least. I shudder to think what damage she might have done to her fragile skin if she had left the house barefoot, as I did. Though I can't understand what prompted her to leave the house in the first place. And I was so sure I had locked the front door before going upstairs with Logan a little after midnight.

But I must have been mistaken, because it's been a long time since Mum was able to let herself out through a locked door. Though not impossible, I suppose. The keys are hanging up next to the door, after all.

'She has a tendency to wander off. I usually check on her at some point during the night, but…'

'But last night I stayed over. That distracted you.' He looks grim.

In her room, we lay her down on the bed, and I gingerly remove her slippers. Her feet are freezing, nonetheless, and I try to chafe some warmth into them, rubbing gently.

'It's not your fault,' I tell him, so crushed with guilt that I can barely look up at him. 'It's my fault. I had too much to drink last night; that's what it was. On a weeknight too. If I'd been sober, I would have noticed that text from Ruby and known to check on Mum earlier.'

'Kate, you can't blame yourself for this.'

'Then who should I blame? You? Ruby? Mum, perhaps?' I'm speaking in a low, savage voice, and I can see the effect that it's having on him, but I don't care. 'That's ridiculous. Her care is my

146

responsibility, and when something like this happens, it's my fault, and mine alone.'

I straighten up, my gaze on the woman resting now on the bed, her eyes closed, no colour in her cheeks whatsoever.

'I should have kept a closer eye on her. I was too busy enjoying myself. Now look what I've done!'

'Probably best to discover exactly what's happened before beating yourself up over it.' Logan, his hands sunk in his trouser pockets, regards my mother sombrely. 'She looks very pale. Does she need an ambulance, do you think? Or should we call out her doctor? It's a private practice, isn't it?'

I'm surprised that he knows Mum sees a private doctor, but maybe I mentioned it to him on one of our dates.

I check Mum over assessingly; although she's stopped making the little moaning noises, her breathing is faster than I would like, and as Logan said, she looks very unwell. 'Mum, can you hear me?' I drape a warm tartan throw across her body. 'Are you hurt at all?'

Her eyes open, and she stares around the room in a strange, wondering way, her gaze resting briefly on Logan.

'It's my hip that hurts, that's all,' she says in a hoarse whisper, looking back at me. 'I... I must have banged it when I fell.'

I check her hip gingerly, but she gives another moan at my touch, so I leave it and turn to Logan. 'An ambulance would be best, don't you think? She needs to be checked over at a hospital. The phone's in the hall.'

He nods and disappears.

'What were you doing outside?' I ask her, struggling to understand. 'And so early too?'

'I don't know,' she says plaintively. 'I can't remember, darling. Did... Did you tell me to go outside? I thought you did.'

'No, I certainly didn't. Why would I do such a thing?' My voice rises slightly as the full horror of the situation floods over me. 'How long were you lying out there on the gravel? Minutes? Hours?'

'I don't know.'

'You could have died of exposure. Oh God, I can't bear it…'

I sink down next to her on the bed and burst into tears, unable to hold it back any longer.

My mother peers up at me, clearly astonished. 'Goodness. Whatever's the matter?' Her voice sounds almost normal, and if it weren't for her pallor, I would think nothing was wrong. 'I just had a little tumble, that's all. Why are you crying?'

'Because I did this to you. I'm so useless… I ruin everything I touch.'

Mum's silent for a moment, as though digesting this. Then she shakes her head and says slowly, 'This isn't like you, Kate. You're not a crier. You're not the sort who gives up just because something's difficult. Whatever would your father say?'

I give a gurgling sob at her coherence, and the use of my name, and make an effort to pull myself together. If she can be strong in the face of this overwhelming despair, so can I.

'I know, Mum, I know.' I try to drag the tartan throw higher up her chest, to keep her warm, but she bats it away impatiently. Even now, when she must be so chilled, she hates me fussing. I arrange it over her legs instead and she seems to accept that. 'It's just been so hellish lately. I'm finding it hard to keep smiling.'

'Well, dry your eyes, darling,' she whispers, 'and just go get him. He'll sort everything out, you'll see.'

I sniff, and pat my damp cheeks with the backs of my hands. I'm feeling calmer now, thank goodness. And Mum's not unconscious, at least. She's talking clearly and making sense. That has to be a good sign, surely?

148

Then her words slowly filter through to me, and my brows draw together in puzzlement.

Just go get him.

I hear Logan's deep voice in the hall, speaking to someone at the emergency services, explaining what has happened.

'Go get who? Do you mean Logan?' I reach for a tissue from the box on her nightstand and blow my nose. 'You want me to fetch Logan?'

But her face is blank. 'Who's Logan?'

'My… My friend.'

Has she forgotten him already? He only just left the room.

Mum seems as confused as I am. 'I meant your father, darling. You'd better go and tell him what's happened. Of course, he'll be furious that I was so careless… You know what a temper he has, the big brute. But he'll tell us what to do.' Her smile is satisfied as she closes her eyes again. 'Your father can cope with anything.'

I don't know how to respond to that, but gulp and sit staring at her in horrified silence instead.

Dad is dead.

He's been dead for five years.

Her dementia has been steadily worsening over time, it's true. My name escapes her frequently these days. It's rare that she can remember what date it is. But never before has she forgotten that her husband is dead.

I can only assume it's the trauma of falling outside in the cold and damp, and being unable to get back inside without help. This incident may have exacerbated her memory problems and made everything worse. I ball the tissue up in my fist and dry my eyes with it. My legs feel so shaky, I don't even dare stand up. My guilt is like an ocean inside me; I'm drowning in it, barely able to function. Though I must, for Mum's sake.

Soon, I hear noises down the hall.

Logan comes back into the room shortly afterwards, a contrite-looking Ruby following closely on his heels.

'Oh my God!' Ruby stops dead on seeing my mother lying on top of the bedcovers with her arms by her sides, for all the world like a carved stone figure on a church tomb. Her eyes fly to mine in a wild enquiry. 'Logan says your mum had a fall in the garden. Is that right?'

I nod silently.

'I don't understand.' Ruby is incredulous. 'Why was she outside at this time of day? How on earth did this happen?'

The note of accusation in her voice almost sets me off crying again. But I grit my teeth and stand up, trying to stay in control.

'We don't know,' I say doggedly. 'I've been trying to find out. She was already out there when I got up.'

'The ambulance is on its way,' Logan says to me, paying no attention to Ruby, who has bent over my mother now and is fussing with the tartan blanket. This time, my mother doesn't resist, and is soon wrapped up more warmly, her eyes peacefully closed.

'Thank you,' I tell him huskily.

'Perhaps we should go and make your mother a cup of hot, sweet tea,' he suggests. 'For the shock.' He studies my face thoughtfully. Presumably, I must look ashen, because he adds in a softer voice, 'We could all use a cup of tea while we wait for the ambulance, don't you think?'

I suddenly realise he's probably meant to be heading off to work and will be late because of this.

Leaving Ruby to sit with my mother, I follow him numbly to the kitchen. 'Will you get into trouble?' I ask him. 'It'll be past nine before you get to work.

150

'Later, I imagine,' he says carelessly, filling the kettle and then glancing about the kitchen for mugs. 'I plan to go home first to shower and change.'

'I'm sorry.'

'Nonsense, this is more important.' He holds up his mobile. 'I'll give the office a ring, let my boss know I'll be in late. She'll understand.'

I think about Mark and his utter lack of interest in my domestic issues. The contrast couldn't be greater. 'You're lucky,' I mutter, head bent. I'll have to ring the office myself, let them know what's happened.

'No, they're used to me coming in late.' Logan frowns and takes my hand. 'Hey, you okay? The ambulance is on its way, and for what it's worth, I don't think your mother can have hurt herself that badly. She seemed a little shaken, yes. But she was lucid and in control.'

I don't bother telling him about Mum thinking he was my father. What would be the point?

'I should go and wait outside,' I tell him raggedly, trying not to dissolve into tears again; I need to stay strong for Mum's sake. But his kindness will be my undoing. 'Watch for the ambulance so they know where to come.'

He's looking me up and down, clearly concerned. 'Okay. But there's a nasty chill in the air this morning. Maybe get dressed first? I can hold the fort while you're gone.'

I nod, and run upstairs to my bedroom, dragging off my dressing gown and throwing jeans and a jumper on without really caring.

When I come back down, Ruby is tiptoeing out of my mother's room. Leaving the door ajar, she says in a whisper, 'She's resting. Poor thing, it sounds like she took a real tumble. How did she get out?'

I shrug helplessly. 'I really don't know.'

'But you locked the front door before bed, I presume?'

'Of course,' I say automatically, and then hesitate. 'At least, I think so.'

'You *think*?'

'I'm pretty sure I did. But…'

Glancing away from her troubled look, I hurry down the hall. The keys to the front door are still hanging up in their usual place. I touch them, struggling to remember what happened last night after we kissed…

But the misty wine haze keeps getting in the way.

I can't actually recall for sure locking the front door before going up to bed with Logan. But that doesn't mean I didn't do it.

Is it possible I forgot? Yes, I have to concede that. But even so, what would have prompted Mum to go for a walk outside in her nightie and slippers so early in the morning? She's never done that before.

'So your date stayed the night, then?' Ruby says in a confidential tone, looking over her shoulder towards the kitchen door. It's partly closed, but we can both hear Logan whistling as he moves about, presumably still making the tea. 'I expect that's why you can't remember locking the front door. I'd have been a bit distracted too.'

'I wasn't distracted. I did lock the door,' I say, with more irritation than certainty. But it shuts her up.

I hear tyres on the gravelled drive and dart outside to find an ambulance backing slowly towards the front door. A paramedic jumps down with a pack slung over her shoulder and comes towards me, smiling. She's in her thirties with short blonde hair and a capable air.

'Good morning. I'm Sue. Where's the patient?'

Briefly, I explain the situation and then show her into the house. A moment later, the driver joins us in Mum's bedroom, cheerfully announcing her own name as Belinda.

Logan has just delivered a mug of tea, and Ruby has already

manoeuvred my mother into a semi-sitting position against the pillows in order to drink it.

'I don't take sugar in my tea,' Mum is explaining to Ruby impatiently. 'Take it away. I won't drink it.'

Ruby tries to coax her, holding the cup to her lips. 'It's good for you, Celeste. You've had a shock; you need the sugar.'

'No, I don't... And who's this?' Mum stares wide-eyed at the two women in their green uniforms, now standing about her bed. 'Where did they come from?'

'We're paramedics. You had a fall, my love,' Sue says bracingly, unzipping her pack. 'Now, if I could just ask everyone to leave except for Celeste and her daughter?'

Logan pats my shoulder on his way out. 'I can stay if you need me.'

'No,' I say, smiling. 'But thank you. You should get to work.'

'I'll call you later.'

Ruby follows him out of the room and closes the door.

The two paramedics check my mother over, asking questions all the time and showing the most wonderful gentleness with her.

'How did she fall?' Belinda asks while Sue is examining my mother's hip. The skin is bruised, and Mum shrinks away when it's touched, her brows contracting in pain. 'That doesn't look good.'

'I'm not sure.'

'How's that?'

Guiltily, I try to explain without mentioning Logan. 'I came downstairs to find she'd somehow managed to unlock the front door, and when we – that is, when I went outside, I found her just lying there on the drive.' My voice sounds high and breathless. The stress of it all, I suppose. 'I can't even tell you how long she'd been outside, I'm sorry.'

Belinda gives me an odd glance, but turns to my mother. 'Why did you go outside this morning, Celeste? Trying to escape?'

I can't believe she's put it like that. 'I'm not holding my mother prisoner, you know,' I say, a little tartly. 'She gets into mischief if she wanders off alone. As you can see. That's why we keep the front door locked.'

'Oh, don't mind me, I was only joking,' Belinda insists, but something tells me she wasn't. 'Come on, Celeste, let's have it. Why do a runner?'

To my relief, my mother laughs. If she'd agreed that she was trying to 'escape', things could have become awkward.

'I can't remember. Not properly. It all happened so quickly.' She frowns, seeming confused. 'I heard a voice, I think. Calling me. Telling me to go outside.'

'What?' This admission astonishes me. 'You didn't say any of that before, Mum.' I take her hand and rub it gently between my own; her skin still feels frighteningly chilled. 'Whose voice was it? Did you see anyone? Were they outside in the garden too?'

'I don't know. I… I don't feel well.'

Sue looks up, having finished her examination, and nods to her partner. 'She needs to go into hospital,' she says quietly, and then turns to me. 'I can't be sure this is just bruising. We need to check whether your mother's broken anything. She's still on the young side for a broken hip. But better safe than sorry.'

'A broken hip? Oh God.' I feel sick.

'It's just a precaution.'

Mum has cottoned on to what's happening. 'No, no. I don't need to go to hospital,' she says stoutly. 'I'll drink that tea now. That'll do the trick.'

'Sorry, Celeste, but we can't leave you here. You need an X-ray, my love,' Sue tells her, and asks Belinda to fetch a wheelchair. 'Your daughter can follow us in her car, if that makes you feel better about

154

it. How's that? Kate can keep you company at the hospital while we transfer you to Accident and Emergency. It could be a long wait.'

I nod, and get out of their way while they work, preparing my mother to be conveyed out to the ambulance in a wheelchair.

The phone rings in the hall.

Snatching up the handset, I peer at myself in the hall mirror; to my horror, I look a mess. But I didn't even get a chance to comb my hair this morning or put on so much as a lick of makeup.

'Hello?'

The voice on the other end of the phone fills me with dread.

It's Dr Forster.

'Hello, Kate. I got your call, asking me to get in touch. Apparently, your mother's had a fall. Is that right?'

'What?' I'm stunned. 'I… I didn't call you.'

'Oh, my mistake.' Dr Forster hesitates. 'The message was quite muffled. And whoever it was didn't leave a name. But it sounded urgent, so I thought I'd better ring. I take it your mother's fine, then?'

'Actually, no.' I explain what's happened, and she exclaims a few times during my account of Mum's accident, sounding horrified. 'It's just a precaution, but they're taking her to hospital.'

'I see.' The note of disapproval in the doctor's voice is beginning to grate at my nerves. 'Well, I was worried about her. It's still my opinion that Celeste ought to be in a residential setting, given how seriously her condition has deteriorated over the past few months. Look, it's no reflection on you, Kate.' Her voice softens. 'But maybe it's time to hand her care over to the professionals. Will you consider it, at least?'

I close my eyes and hang up on the doctor without another word.

Behind me, I can hear the paramedics wheeling Mum carefully down the hall, with Ruby chatting freely to the two women about

155

my mother's habit of 'escaping' the house and how we were lucky to find her when we did.

It seems everyone is determined to grind my face in my failures. And why shouldn't they? I've failed my mother, there's no denying it. She's my responsibility, nobody else's. Yet instead of caring for her this morning, I slept late with my new boyfriend while Mum let herself out in her nightie, wandering about in the cold until she stumbled and fell...

'Right,' I say brightly, grabbing up my purse and car keys before turning to face them, 'I'll follow the ambulance to the hospital. You're going to be fine, Mum. I promise.'

But my smile doesn't fool anyone, and I know it.

CHAPTER EIGHTEEN

'Well,' Mark says, breaking into my explanation of the past few days with an impatient gesture, 'at least your mother hasn't broken her hip. It sounds as though she's going to be fine. So all's well that ends well.' He perches on the desk next to me, looking at me from under his brows in an expectant manner. 'Let's hear it, then. How is Calum's book going?'

I cross my legs and fold my arms, still defensive about this difficult project he dumped in my lap.

'Fine,' I say, not entirely accurately but not really caring at this point. 'We had lunch together. We talked about the manuscript. Calum was open to my suggestions. Now, I just have to finish going through the text and then email my notes to him.'

I suppose it was too much to ask for Mark to be interested in my personal life. But I'm grateful that he allowed me to shift my work days this week so I could be with Mum while she got over her little 'escapade' in the garden, as she insists on referring to her accident. I find such casual remarks about her bruised hip troubling. Mum treats the episode as unimportant, when in fact it's highlighted how vulnerable she is at home and allowed Dr

Forster to put additional pressure on me over a residential home placement.

I can't put Mum in a home, though.

Besides, she would never consent to go, so it would be a pointless discussion.

'Calum doesn't like editorial suggestions,' Mark says sharply. 'What exactly did you tell him to do?'

I lay out for him more or less what I told Calum Morgan about the book, though slightly watered down and without too many details. I don't want him to hound poor Cheryl, demanding to know why she didn't deal with these problems before going on maternity leave.

'Will this impact the publication date?' he demands, interrupting me before I've even finished.

'I doubt it.'

'Good,' he says crisply, 'because the marketing budget is already allocated. We've had several bites from supermarkets, plus confirmed review space in magazines, and Harry is organising some high-profile signings for him. I wouldn't want to jeopardise any of that over a few editorial notes.'

Listening to him, I realise I've seriously understated the sheer scale of the changes Calum's book needs. But I don't correct him, merely smile wanly. I'm not feeling strong enough to engage in battle over this.

'Of course.'

To my relief, Mark accepts this with a grunt and a jerk of his head, and goes away to pester someone else instead.

I settle to work for an hour, dealing with minor queries for some other authors whose books I handle, and only look away from my computer when my phone pings.

It's a text from Ruby.

Mr Adeyemi is here, talking to your mum. I told him she was resting after her accident, but he didn't take any notice. What should I do?

I swear under my breath, and then text her back.

Find an excuse to stay in the room, or keep the door open so he's not alone with her. I won't be back until later, remember. Can you cope?

Twenty minutes go by while I attach some JPG cover images to an email, nervously awaiting her reply.

Finally, it arrives.

Big date with Logan tonight? Of course I can cope. You enjoy yourself. Adeyemi just left.

I'm so relieved, I send her a row of smiley face icons and a GIF of a dancing dog in a tutu.

What would I do without Ruby?

The afternoon gradually thickens into dusk, and then it's dark outside, all the city lights across London twinkling in the wintry sky. I send my last email and check my phone again. No new messages, which can only be good at this time of day.

I'm just about to head home, pleased over a good day's work and excited by the prospect of a dinner date with Logan, when I hear my name being called.

'Kate? Can you step in here for a minute?'

It's Mark, hovering in the doorway to his office. He's unsmiling and his voice is sharp, almost accusatory. It seems something has upset my boss, and he's clearly decided it's my fault.

Oh God, what now?

I pin a fake smile to my face, drag on my coat to make my imminent departure look like a done deal, and head over there.

'I was just on my way home, actually,' I begin, glancing into his office, and then stop dead. Because he's not alone.

Calum Morgan is sitting round the corner on the white leather sofa reserved for visiting bestselling authors, and he's not looking happy. I hadn't noticed him arrive in the office. But my attention has been on my computer screen most of the afternoon.

'Hello, Calum. This is a pleasant surprise.' My gaze shoots to Mark, standing with his arms folded and his lips tight. 'Problem?'

'I'd say so, yes. Come inside and shut the door. Calum tells me you've practically rewritten every word of his book.'

'Sorry?' I close the door behind me but stay where I am, clutching my shoulder bag and feeling cornered, like an animal in a trap. 'That's not true. I perhaps made a few suggestions… Calum, you know I'd never force you to make any changes you weren't happy with, right?'

Calum's smile is malicious. 'Do I?'

'I'm going to take over from you on this project,' Mark says abruptly, and holds up a hand when I protest. 'No, my mind's made up. You're too inexperienced to deal with an author of Calum's stature. I thought you could handle it. But it's clear I was wrong.'

I stare at him and feel sick inside. To talk to me like that would be bad enough at any time. But in front of Calum Morgan…

It's nothing short of mental cruelty.

'Please, give me another chance.' I look pleadingly at Calum, though secretly I'm relieved to be shot of him. The man's a monster. But my career in publishing is too important to me; I can't bear to see it damaged like this. Not when I've sacrificed so much to hang onto my job. 'Let's talk about this. I'm sure we can work out a compromise.'

Calum stands up, and I back away automatically. He seems to fill the office. His clever eyes note the instinctive movement, and I see a faint mockery in his face. But he shakes his head. 'Kate, I don't see how that would be possible. Not when you want so many changes.'

160

He gives me a sad spaniel look. 'To be honest, I don't think you like my book at all.'

Mark has been looking admiringly at his top author, but at this, his head swivels back to me. 'You don't like his book?'

His gaze unnerves me. It's like being sized up by a vulture.

'No, I love his book,' I lie valiantly. 'I mean, Calum, your new book is... Well, it's wonderful. It's life-changing. Life-affirming, in fact.' I spread my hands wide in a conciliatory gesture. 'All I want is to ensure it reaches the widest possible readership. Which means making a few minor tweaks. That's all.'

Calum, after listening to this in silence, transfers his attention to my boss. 'You see? I'm not happy, Mark. And can you blame me?'

'No, I can't.' Mark opens the door and jerks his head for me to leave. 'Kate, I'm moving Calum to another editor. Whatever you've done to his manuscript, you can forget it. Just forward the original book file to me, and I'll either edit it myself or find someone better suited to the task than you.'

Speechless, I leave the office.

Mark returns to Calum, leaving the door wide open, as though he doesn't care who hears what's going on.

'I thought it would be inspiring to work with Kate, I really did,' I hear Calum saying in his most sorrowful voice. 'There's something so vulnerable and feminine about her. The creative eye is instantly drawn to her. But you're right. As an editor, she's too much trouble.'

I can't believe what I'm hearing.

There's something so vulnerable and feminine about her.

Mark begins to say something soothing, but I stumble away, my hands over my ears, trembling with sudden, almost uncontrollable rage. My vision is tinged red, like I'm seeing the world through a blood mist.

161

I feel like ripping my computer out of the wall, charging back to the office with it and chucking the whole thing at the odious man's head. Both of their heads, actually.

Except I don't.

That would be childish and merely get me sacked. Not to mention arrested for assault with a deadly computer.

God though, it would feel so fantastic, just for that one moment. Just for the sheer pleasure of seeing their shocked expressions…

Logan takes one look at my face when I charge into the restaurant back home in Guildford, over twenty minutes late for our date, and almost flinches.

'Bad day?'

'I've had better.' I catch a passing waiter, order a large gin and tonic and sit down opposite Logan. 'I've just narrowly avoided getting the sack. And lost Calum Morgan.'

'I'm sorry to hear that,' he says carefully, watching me.

'I'm not,' I admit, grabbing an olive from the dish in the middle of the table, and a breadstick to go with it. 'God, I hate that man.' Briefly, I describe what happened and the things Calum said about me. 'If I thought it was worth the emotional trauma, I'd sue him for harassment and the company for constructive dismissal.'

'Do it,' Logan says, also munching on a breadstick. His smile is encouraging. 'If it makes you feel better.'

'But it won't,' I point out bitterly. 'It will make me feel worse. And how could I prove it? Those two bastards will back each other up and deny everything. Meanwhile, I'd be out of a job. And I need to keep the money coming in, especially if…'

I tail off, not sure what I'm thinking. Well, not sure if I should be thinking it.

Logan looks at me enquiringly.

I sigh. 'Dr Forster thinks my mother should be moved into a home. She all but accused me of neglect on the phone. And maybe she's right.'

'I thought you were dead set against that idea.'

'I am. And Mum will be too. But that accident… her fall.' I shake my head, staring away at nothing. 'I wasn't there for her. Too wrapped up in my own life. She could have broken her hip.'

'But she didn't.'

'No thanks to me.' My large gin and tonic arrives, and I thank the waiter with a grateful smile, then gulp some down. 'I haven't drunk this much in years. Now look at me. I was dreaming about gin all the way back on the train. I could demolish ten of these.' I take a more leisurely sip, smiling ruefully at him over the rim of the chilled glass. 'Sorry. But my throat feels like the Sahara.'

'Go ahead, it sounds like you deserve it.'

He's so understanding.

'What about you? How was your day?'

He hesitates, looking uncomfortable. 'Not too bad.'

'Logan?'

'Oh, it's nothing. It's been a tough few years for us. Apparently, the company may be downsizing. Losing a few people.'

'You?'

Logan shrugs. 'Too early to say for sure.'

'Oh God, I'm so sorry.'

'It may not happen.' He raises his own glass to me in a wry salute. 'To things that may not happen.'

'Or have happened, but we don't give a toss about.'

We clink glasses, and I down another few fingers of gin, wishing I didn't feel so crappy. But I'm pretty sure Mark will call me tomorrow and gloat horribly as he gives me the bad news down the phone…

That man's never liked me. He's been hunting for an excuse to get rid of me for ages, and Calum's furious tirade will have given him just the ammunition he needs.

And if he sacks me, what will I do? How will we pay the bills? There's Mum's money, but we can't live off that indefinitely, and if she does move into a residential home, it will wipe out all our reserves.

I may have to sell the house.

Always assuming Mum's solicitor will allow it, of course. Given that he's been blocking me at every turn.

I gasp. 'Do you think Mr Adeyemi is preventing me from using the Power of Attorney so he can make sure I don't sell the house? He's always been so insistent that Mum's brain is working just fine and that she doesn't need to go into a home. But what if that's because the money he stands to get in her will is tied up in the house?'

'So he doesn't want you to sell the house, because you might use the money to pay for your mother's care instead of him inheriting it?'

'Precisely.' The waiter arrives and we order our food. I just pick something off the menu almost at random, not really caring. Once the man has gone, I lean across to Logan, saying in a low voice, 'I hadn't thought of it like that before. It seems outlandish. Impossible, even. Yet everything tells me I'm right. My God, the man's a ghoul. I wish there was some way to prove it.'

He nods but shifts in his seat, his gaze wandering around the busy restaurant.

'Logan,' I say, recalling his gaze back to me, 'what's the matter? You've been acting uneasy ever since I walked in the door. What's happened?'

His eyes meet mine. 'I can't hide anything from you, can I?' With obvious reluctance, he turns to the jacket slung over his chair and produces a folded sheet of paper from an inside pocket. 'This was on my doormat when I got back from work tonight. No envelope, no indication of name or address. But since it was shoved through my letterbox at some point during the day, it's obviously meant for me.' He hesitates. 'Have you been to the police about those notes yet?'

'I haven't had a chance. Besides, I thought you advised me against accusing Mr Adeyemi of sending them.'

'Well, that was before this one arrived.' His jaw is tense. 'Kate, I think it's time you started taking these letters seriously.'

'Give it to me.'

'Are you sure you want to read it?'

I thrust out my hand, glaring at him. 'If it's something to do with me, then yes. Absolutely.'

He hands over the sheet, and I unfold it, already guessing what it must be, butterflies in my stomach.

'Shit.' I read the note through twice, and then crumple it up in my fist before downing the last of my gin. 'This came to you? At your flat?'

'Yes, which makes it less likely it's from your mother's pet solicitor. I've never even met the man. How would he know where I live or even that we're seeing each other? Yet somebody hand-delivered it while I was out at work.' He stares at me. 'Kate? Are you okay?'

'My mother saw him today,' I say slowly. 'Mr Adeyemi. She may have mentioned you. Or maybe Ruby did. The two of them are always cracking jokes about…'

My head is swimming. Too much gin, drunk too quickly on an empty stomach. And now this shock.

I blench. 'Sorry. Back in a minute.'

I stumble to the ladies' restroom, which is not empty, cram myself into a narrow cubicle and promptly throw up my olives and breadstick.

I kneel on the cold lino beside the loo for several minutes, gasping, tears in my eyes, and wish I never had to move again. Then someone knocks on the cubicle door to ask if I'm okay, and I give some kind of husky assurance, at which the woman moves discreetly away.

The letter is still scrunched up in my fist.

Gingerly, I open it up again and smooth it out, force myself to read it again through teary eyes, wincing at David's signature at the bottom.

THAT BITCH YOU'RE BANGING IS A MURDERER. GET OUT WHILE YOU STILL CAN.

CHAPTER NINETEEN

I finally give in to pressure and go to the police station. Logan accompanies me. We wait for about half an hour before one of the officers is free to see us, and then we're ushered into a small side room. Logan and I sit side by side, and I feel like this is a declaration of intent. It's like I'm telling the world we're together, that we're a couple. I'm not sure how comfortable I am with that idea. But I'm also glad I'm not here on my own.

The police officer is a woman in her late twenties with short-cropped hair, watery blue eyes and a thin-lipped mouth, who introduces herself as PC Plimley.

She's perfectly pleasant to us at first, but when I explain about the poison pen letters and describe how I've heard sounds outside the house at night, and once thought I saw someone lurking in the shrubbery, her manner gradually changes.

I can tell she not only thinks we're time-wasters, but that I'm bonkers.

'Did you bring any of these letters?' PC Plimley asks me, somewhat sceptically, as though expecting me to say I have thrown them away. Which I nearly did, in fact, but am now glad I thought better of it.

I produce the crumpled letters in their see-through plastic folder and pass this across the table to her. She unsnaps the folder and takes out the letters, shooting me a dubious look. She then spends several minutes reading through them in silence, her mouth moving from time to time as though shaping the words, though the notes are hardly long enough to merit so much time.

I can't tell from her expression what she thinks of them.

Having read them, she turns them over and studies the paper itself in minute detail, even holding the letters up to the light, as if expecting there to be some kind of clue as to the identity of the sender on the reverse of each sheet, or on the two envelopes that accompanied them.

Finally, the constable shakes her head. 'Miss Kinley, why did you wait so long before bringing these to us?'

I feel like I'm being accused of something. This makes me defensive.

'I didn't think they were important. Not at first. But then I found the outside security light smashed, and Logan said…' I stop myself. I dislike women who rely on men to guide their every move. 'That is, I decided it was time. That enough was enough. When Logan got his letter, you see, it was no longer just about me. I could handle it being about me and David. It somehow didn't seem as serious. But when he drags Logan into this—'

She interrupts me, raising thinly arched eyebrows. '*He?*'

I feel awkward, unwilling to come straight out with it and name Mr Adeyemi. It suddenly feels ridiculous to do so. Dangerous, even.

I lapse into silence instead.

'We have a possible theory.' Logan glances at me for confirmation, but when I say nothing, he continues more cautiously. 'There is someone who might be sending these letters. But obviously, we don't want to accuse that person without proof. They might be completely innocent, after all. So we hoped… I mean, Kate thought the best idea would be to bring the letters to you and allow the police to investigate.'

PC Plimley looks faintly amused. 'For that, I'm afraid we're going to need more than a few hand-delivered letters.'

Logan frowns. 'Does that mean you're not going to do anything?'

'We can investigate, of course. Especially if this escalates. Sending threatening letters is against the law. But frankly, there's not a great deal to go on here, and police officers are not mind readers. Besides which, the force is pretty stretched at the moment. Serious crime has to be our priority.'

'And in the meantime, if someone tries to kill Miss Kinley…?'

'Oh, come on. That's a little melodramatic, isn't it?'

'You've read those letters, PC Plimley. You may not find them very credible. But they still contain threats against Miss Kinley's life, pure and simple. And what about the broken security light?'

'Hmm.' She studies his face, scans the three letters again, and then puts them slowly back inside the folder. 'Your boyfriend committed suicide?'

Again, I feel like I'm the one being accused of something, not the victim. 'Yes, like I told you at the start.'

She nods. 'Just trying to get things straight. Is there any chance this suicide might have looked suspicious to other people?'

'Of course not.'

'Okay.' She snaps the folder shut, and then starts scribbling down some notes. 'I'm going to keep this as evidence. If you get any more letters, bring them straight in and drop them at the front desk for me. Try not to handle them too much. If you can wear gloves to open your mail for the next few weeks, that could be useful.' She looks up from her notepad. 'You said "he" before. Can I have a name?'

'I'd rather not,' I mutter.

'Miss Kinley,' she begins, and then pulls a face. 'Kate…' She taps the folder. 'These letters are pretty nasty. To be honest, I'd be inclined to dismiss them as empty threats. Some crank winding you up about your boyfriend's death. Except for one thing.'

'What's that?' I ask sharply.

'The fact that there's been evidence of an intruder at the property recently, along with damage. That's an escalation. A physical intrusion into your life. So if there's someone who you suspect may be behind these letters – perhaps someone with a grudge against you, or an axe to grind – then you really ought to give me this man's name upfront.' She pauses, looking from Logan to me, and then adds with a sigh, 'I can assure you, we'll be discreet in our inquiries.'

I bow my head for a moment, conflicted.

Then warm fingers close over mine, and I glance up, startled, to find Logan has taken my hand. He smiles at me encouragingly.

'The man's name is Mr Abayomi Adeyemi,' I say abruptly, and transfer my gaze to the constable. 'And he's my mother's solicitor.'

The cold wind cuts through my coat outside the police station. It's late afternoon and already heading to a pearlescent darkness, the streetlights on and the sky glowing with that faint eerie orange you get above urban conurbations.

Logan gives me a hug. 'Well done,' he says softly, and then kisses me on the lips. 'I know that wasn't easy for you. But it's done now, and you can put it behind you.'

'Until Mr Adeyemi discovers I've accused him of sending me threatening letters,' I point out.

'You heard her. They'll be discreet. If it wasn't him, he'll probably never know. And if it was, then the police will nab the bastard.' He squeezes my hand again, smiling. 'And then he won't be able to claim that inheritance from your mother, will he? Not if he's found guilty of intimidation.'

'I hadn't thought of that.'

'Well, you should. That's your money he'll be trying to claim.'

I frown, thinking that possibility through. 'But why would Mr Adeyemi send me letters like that about David? And to you too. I don't get the why of it. Maybe I'm missing something, but it doesn't make sense.'

'Who knows? Maybe Adeyemi's hoping to drive you away.'

'To make me leave home, you mean?'

'It's possible. You said your mum is sweet on him. And he disapproves of her going into a residential home, probably because you might have to sell up to finance it long term. She's still relatively young, after all.' He sees the confusion on my face and explains, 'If you weren't around, Adeyemi would be free to court her himself. Maybe even marry her.' He shrugs. 'Why hang out for some piddling gift of money when you can get the whole thing, including the house?'

I stare at him, aghast. 'You can't be serious? She's not a well woman. And he's a professional. Her solicitor, for God's sake.'

'But that's a big house with large grounds. And look at its location. It must be worth several million, at least.'

'Probably,' I admit, uncomfortable with the direction of this conversation.

'So there you go. That kind of money can be a huge temptation. And Adeyemi's been stepping up his visits lately, especially when you've not been there to interfere or send him away. You don't need to look much further than that for a motive, do you?'

'I suppose not.' The cold wind makes me shiver, and I can't help fretting over the idea of Mum falling into the grip of a fortune-hunter. Especially when he may be hurting her. 'Should I have told the police what I suspect about him? That he may have bruised her arm?'

'Not without proof.'

I nod, finally agreeing with him on something. 'Look, I should go home and check how she is. And poor Ruby too. She's been stuck alone with Mum almost every day this past week or so, and I'm suspicious she's been doing some housework too, to help out now that Irina's gone. She's certainly earning her pay.' I smile up at him. 'Thank you for coming with me today. That interview would have gone quite badly without you there.'

'I'm sure that's not true. You didn't want to accuse a possibly innocent man, that's all, and quite right too.' Logan puts an arm about my waist and half-lifts me, his kiss a little more searching this time. 'I love that about you. You're a fair person, Kate Kinley. But I'm glad I was able to speak up for you in that interview. I don't like to see you suffering because of this creep. I want him stopped.'

I touch his cheek. It's slightly bristly, in need of a closer shave. 'I know you do. And I appreciate your help. But I'd better get back. Maybe we could have dinner again later this week? Or tonight, in fact?'

'I've got a better idea.' Logan looks deep into my eyes, smiling. 'How about I move into the house with you?'

I stare, taken aback. 'Sorry?'

'I hate you being alone at night there, Kate. Especially when you're constantly hearing noises or finding the front door unlocked...'

'I'm hardly alone,' I protest.

'Your mum and Ruby are not my idea of protective companions.' He grins. 'Though I imagine Ruby could give any intruder a run for their money. Especially armed with a rolling pin. She'd probably frighten them more than they could frighten her.'

I laugh, but uneasily. 'Do you really mean it, Logan? You want to move in with me?'

'Only temporarily, while all this is sorted out.' He searches my face, and a troubled look enters his. 'Of course, if you don't like the idea, just tell me to get lost. Or to mind my own business. I won't be offended.'

'It's not that.'

'Am I coming over all Neanderthal again? Trying to protect the little woman when in fact she doesn't need protecting at all?' He grimaces at my hurriedly bitten-back smile. 'Oh God, I'm sorry. Forget I spoke.'

'No, I think it's a great idea. I just wasn't sure how serious you were. Or how serious all this is.' I pause. 'You and me, I mean.'

Logan seems to consider this point, then bends his head to kiss me on the lips again, this time more lingeringly.

'Just about as serious as it gets,' he whispers. 'How's that?'

CHAPTER TWENTY

I take what feels like a massive step and clear out my parents' old double bedroom. It makes sense that if Logan is to move in on at least a semi-permanent basis, we should stop squeezing up together in my modest single room and take over the more lavish space my parents used to occupy, which includes a luxurious en suite bathroom with white marbled tiles and gold taps shaped like dolphins. Not my taste, but I can see Logan is impressed when I show him round a few days later.

'We'll need a new mattress, of course,' I say, and feel ludicrously embarrassed when he tests the springiness of my parents' bed, which has a massive wrought-iron frame, painted a sombre black with gorgeous scrollwork at the foot and head. 'I'll order one online.'

'We need to talk about division of bills. I can't expect you to pay for everything. Let's sit down in a few days' time and work out a system.'

'Okay.'

Logan walks about the room, pausing to look out of the window through a gap in the heavy curtains.

Those curtains probably also need to be changed, I think, and start wondering about a colour scheme, automatically redecorating the room as I look about the place. A black and white theme would work well with the wrought-iron bedstead…

'This seems like a really nice room,' he says, turning back to me. 'Why doesn't your mother still sleep in here?'

'Mum couldn't manage the stairs anymore. Not on her own. It was easier to convert the second lounge into a bedroom and install a shower cubicle in the corner for her. The loo's not too far away either.'

'Very sensible.'

'It was her idea,' I say, maybe a little defensively.

'But you sorted it out for her.' He comes close and touches my cheek. 'You're a dutiful daughter. I'm sure Celeste's very proud of you.'

I'm not sure how dutiful a daughter I am, but I kiss him back when he leans forward.

When he pulls back, he's smiling. 'It's a big house, isn't it?' He goes to the open door and glances idly along the landing. 'Which room is Ruby's?'

'Two along, next to the bathroom. That's my room next door. I'll have to move some of my things in here once the new mattress arrives. My work clothes, for certain. I can't be walking back and forth for everything.'

Still feeling awkward, I pivot away and start throwing open their closets. Mum's clothes were cleared out ages ago, her old evening gowns and fake fur coats taken to a charity shop, while her everyday clothes were moved to the new built-in wardrobe downstairs.

It stung to let go of some of those lovely clothes, but I would never have occasion to wear them, and besides, we don't share the same taste. Back in the day, my mother loved to wear daring backless dresses or sequinned gold affairs with plunging necklines and mid-thigh hems.

I'm not entirely a jeans with everything girl, but leaning that way. At work, they expect us to dress sharply and with 'wit' as Mark calls it. I've never quite managed to capture the look, unfortunately, but I know nothing my mother ever owned would be fit for our office.

'I'll clear all these out and then you can hang your stuff up in here,' I say, flicking through rows of my dad's work shirts.

'Nice ties,' Logan remarks over my shoulder.

'Take any of this you want. Shirts, ties, sweatshirts…' I see his surprised look. 'I mean it. They'll only go to a charity shop. Who else would want them? Though they're probably a bit out of fashion now. I really ought to have done this years ago.'

'Why didn't you?'

'Too painful, I expect. I had to sort through Ciaran's stuff…' I hesitate. 'Do you remember Ciaran, my brother?'

'I think we met a couple of times, here and there.'

'He was such a lovely boy, though a bit of a handful at times, and was becoming a lovely man too. I do miss him awfully, and wish we'd had a chance to…'

I break off, feeling myself well up with tears.

'You okay?' he says softly, at my elbow.

'Yes, I'm fine.' I take a deep breath. 'Anyway, I tidied out Ciaran's room quite recently. When Ruby started living here, in fact. But chucking out my dad's stuff felt like a step too far, then.' Sadly, I run my hand along the white and pastel-coloured shirt lapels, remembering how handsome and well-turned-out my father always looked when he came downstairs in the mornings. 'Dad loved looking smart for the office.'

'What changed?'

'Sorry?'

'You said you couldn't face it before. So why now?'

'Oh, necessity, I suppose.' I manage a wry smile for him. 'Let's face it; we can't keep sleeping right on top of each other in my little bed, like a couple of sardines in a tin. This room is much better suited to a couple.'

He strokes my hair. 'Agreed.'

'Besides,' I say, twitching the curtains open, 'this room has a better view of the drive and the front gate. I'll feel more secure being able to keep an eye on who's coming and going.'

Logan stands beside me, looking down towards the front gate. His face is speculative. 'I wonder if the police have got anywhere with their investigation.'

'Oh, don't. I still feel unsure about that whole thing. I mean, what if it isn't Mr Adeyemi and he finds out I suggested him as a possible… well, criminal.' I put my hands to my hot cheeks. 'It doesn't bear thinking about.'

'Then don't think about it,' he says calmly.

'I wish I could. But it's driving me mad, Logan. The thought that someone out there hates me enough to write such awful things to me, and about me. To send them to you.' I make a small sound under my breath, shuddering. 'Another man might have believed what that letter said, and stopped seeing me.'

'Just as well I'm not another man then, isn't it?'

I look at him sideways and wonder how this happened so quickly for us. It seems such a short time ago that I spotted him in the street and we got chatting. Now he's moving in…

Having a man under the same roof will protect my mother better, both against possible intruders and her nocturnal wanderings. I'm a fairly independent woman, but under the circumstances, I'm not embarrassed to admit it'll help me feel more secure too.

Yes, letting Logan move in feels like the right thing to do.

Doesn't it?

* * *

At the weekend, the new mattress arrives, covered in thick plastic, and together, Logan and I heave it up the stairs to my parent's old bedroom. We have to keep stopping because of its weight and sheer unwieldiness, and I burst into fits of helpless giggles at one stage when it slips from between my hands, pinning Logan against the wall. Even Mum comes out of her room to see what's going on, and has to have it all explained to her again by Ruby, for about the tenth time.

'Mum, you're supposed to be resting that hip,' I point out, leaning over the bannister. 'Better go back to bed.'

'I'm sick of that bloody room.' Mum starts to wander off down the hall, and is gently guided back to her bedroom by Ruby, complaining all the way in a loud voice, 'No, I don't want to go back in there… It's too dark, and I can't see what's going on.'

'There's nothing to see, Mrs Nosy,' Ruby says firmly, and a moment later Mum's bedroom door closes behind them both.

'Okay, let's try this again, shall we?' Logan hefts up the mattress. 'You got your end?' He looks a trifle dishevelled, but is still smiling. 'This time, please try not to drop it again. Especially on me.'

'I'm sorry.'

'Yeah, I got that impression.'

'No, really…' I bite back a snort of laughter. 'Though you did look funny, flattened by a mattress.'

'Pick up your end.'

I obey, still grinning, but I'm a little worried about my mother's complaints. 'I hope my mother's hip will improve soon,' I say, starting to back up the stairs with the mattress. 'She's not supposed to be moving about too much, the doctor said. But Mum's right. We can't keep her in that room forever.'

'More's the pity,' Logan mutters.

'Excuse me?'

He grins. 'Nothing.'

I narrow my eyes at him, but decide he's joking. At least, he'd better be.

We carry the mattress up to the bedroom and heave it breathlessly into place on the bedstead. I bend to make sure it fits the space properly, and turn to see Logan hesitating in the doorway.

'What is it?'

'I'm sorry, I need… you know. The loo.'

'Oh.' I try not to laugh at his obvious discomfort. 'Well, don't let me stop you.'

He disappears, but doesn't use the bathroom on this floor, heading for the downstairs loo instead.

I adjust the mattress to exactly where I want it, and then make the bed up, even putting a black cover on the duvet and finding the matching pillowcases. Once it's done to my satisfaction, I run downstairs to check on my mother.

Logan is nowhere to be seen, but the front door is slightly ajar, so I imagine he's gone out to retrieve something from his car. He's been gradually moving things from his flat to our house over the past few days, and keeps producing yet another tool kit or bag of knick-knacks from the recesses of his car boot.

Ruby has gone back into the kitchen; I can hear her humming to herself as she starts preparations for dinner, which we're all sharing tonight.

My mother's bedroom is in semi-darkness, her bedside lamp off and the curtains drawn to shut out the glow of lights from the road on her side of the house.

'Mum?' I peer into the room, thinking she must be napping. But she's not. Instead, she's pottering about in her nightie, her back to me, a ghostly figure in the gloom. I shake my head in disbelief. 'You just can't keep still, can you?'

Mum starts at the sound of my voice, and immediately climbs back into bed. 'It wasn't my fault,' she says, not looking at me but clasping her hands together in front of her chest. 'Not my fault, no.'

Puzzled, I go further into the room, snapping on the overhead light. 'What are you talking about? What isn't your fault?'

She blinks and raises a hand, shielding her eyes from the light. 'Too bright,' she says, sounding suddenly frail.

'I'll turn it off in a minute, I promise. I just want to check…'

I stop dead.

There's a trail of dirt on the green carpet.

I bend to examine the debris more closely. 'What's this?' I pick some up, smelling it, surprised by the crumbling texture between my fingers. 'Is this… soil? Compost?'

'I'm sorry,' is all she says, repeating the words several times in the same worried way. 'I'm sorry.'

'It's all right, Mum,' I reply mechanically, 'there's no need to keep apologising. But I don't understand. Where on earth did all this mess come from?' I follow the trail of dirt around the bed and find one of her tall pot plants has tumbled over. 'Oh dear, did you knock the plant over?'

There's compost everywhere, and the bamboo stick that was keeping the plant steady is some three or four feet away. It must have fallen out when the pot was knocked over.

'Well, never mind.' Carefully, I right the pot, try to steady the tall, fleshy houseplant and then go to retrieve the bamboo stick, as it refuses to stay upright without it. 'I'd better get the Dyson, get this lot vacuumed up. Just as well I've had a bit of practice at hoovering lately, now Irina's not coming in to clean anymore.'

I feel I've been reassuring and jokey, and not a bit accusatory. Yet when I glance her way, my mother gives a kind of whimper, and buries her face in her hands, muttering, 'Sorry, sorry,' over and over.

'Goodness, Mum,' I say, abandoning my attempt to fit the bamboo back into the pot and leaning the plant against the wall instead. I'm confused by her overreaction to what is clearly just an accident. 'Are you crying? Did you hurt yourself?'

Mum shakes her head.

'There's no need to get so upset over a little spilt compost on the carpet.' I hurry round to give her a hug, but she resists. 'Honestly, I'll soon get it tidied up. Oh, come here.' I hold her tight, and rock her back and forth like she's a child again and I'm her mother. Her unhappiness communicates itself so strongly to me, I feel almost frightened. 'Please calm down, Mum. What's all this about?'

But she refuses to say anything more, shaking her head and rubbing her eyes, something akin to terror in her face.

CHAPTER TWENTY-ONE

My birthday comes and goes without any contact from the police. I leave a couple of messages for PC Plimley on the number she gave me, but she never gets back to me. Too busy, I assume, and perhaps she has no information to give me. Which isn't surprising. A few poison pen letters can hardly be top priority for the police. The more days that go by, in fact, the more embarrassed I am that we took them to the police at all. What a snowflake the constable must think me, getting wound up over some malicious person sending me hate mail.

Though it was disturbing to see David's signature on those letters, almost as though he were still alive...

Which he isn't, of course.

I was chief mourner at his funeral; I saw him cremated. There can be no doubt that he's gone, and anyone who says otherwise is a liar.

But whoever it was clearly knew David too, or was able to find his signature and copy it, because it's a near-perfect match. At least to my untrained eye.

We celebrate my birthday with a small cake and some champers at home with Mum and Ruby, and then Logan and I slip away into central London for the evening. Logan has bought tickets to Cats, which I have to admit to never having seen, and we spend an enjoyable evening at the theatre, followed by a late dinner and drinks in a posh and very crowded West End restaurant after the show.

It's the first time I've been out in ages. Despite Ruby's constant presence at the house, which ought to have liberated me, Mum has been in such a fragile state since her accident that I don't like to leave her too much. She's become rather withdrawn, almost sullen at times. Logan is perfectly pleasant to her, so I don't blame him for her change in mood. But I have noticed that Mum seems fidgety and nervous in his presence, and sometimes refuses to speak while he's in the room.

Thankfully, Logan has taken this shyness in good part, and will often take himself off to browse the internet or clean his car just so that Mum can feel more comfortable. It embarrasses me, though, and I frequently find myself apologising for her hostile attitude towards him.

Tonight, though, after today's birthday celebrations, she seemed happy with the idea of me going out to enjoy myself. So I fully intend to do that.

'Happy Birthday,' Logan says softly, toasting me with the bubbly we're drinking. There's a candle in a jar on the table between us, and his eyes glitter strangely in the candlelight, but he's smiling. 'Have you had a good birthday so far? What did you think of the show?'

'I loved it,' I tell him enthusiastically, and take his hand across the table. 'Thank you so much for the tickets. What a lovely birthday present. And so unexpected!'

'November,' he says musingly, playing with his champagne flute. 'What star sign does that make you? Are we supposed to be compatible? I'm a Virgo.' When I grin, he raises his eyebrows. 'No giggling, please. It's purely an astrological definition. As you can surely testify.'

He's so charming like this, I can't seem to stop smiling, my lips fixed in a permanent up-tick. 'Scorpio,' I say, and raise my own brows when he draws back his hand in mock horror. 'Hey, don't look at me like that. I know Scorpios have the worst reputation in the zodiac. But I can assure you, none of it is true.'

'None?'

'Well, maybe the sexy bit.'

He throws his head back and gives a hearty laugh. 'I'm happy to swear to that effect in court.' His eyes twinkle at me. 'But what about the temper? Aren't Scorpios notorious for losing their rag?'

'Mum always said I used to throw the odd tantrum when I was a toddler. But I like to think I've mellowed over time. And since school, I've become almost a model citizen.'

'Ah, *almost*.' He nods. 'That word leaves you a lot of leeway, I'm guessing. Should I be worried for my life?'

'That depends on what you do.'

His gaze drops to my cutlery. I've been playing idly with my knife throughout this conversation, and he pretends to look uncertain.

'Can I just put it on record that you, Kate Kinley, are the sexiest woman I've ever met? And I've never heard you so much as raise your voice, so that bad temper thing must be a total fabrication.' He mimes wiping imaginary sweat from his brow when I put down the knife. 'Thank God; I was afraid you were going to stab me with that.'

'Oh, I wouldn't have done that,' I say sweetly. 'Not before the bill arrives, anyway.'

He laughs, and takes my hand, squeezing it. 'Funny too. My ideal woman. Why did I wait so long before asking you out on a date?'

My smile stiffens. 'Well, let's see. It might have something to do with the fact that my boyfriend – your best friend – killed himself. That probably put you off dating me. It seems to have put everyone else off.'

My brittle words fall like icicles between us, and I feel his hand release mine. I'm not looking at him, my gaze on the white tablecloth. But I feel his intent gaze on my face.

'Kate,' he begins, but I interrupt him.

'No, let me apologise. That was uncalled for.' I swallow against my embarrassment, and am horrified to feel tears brimming against my lashes. 'I'm sorry. What were we saying about Scorpios and a bad temper? I'm my own worst enemy, I really am. Now *that* has been said about me with alarming frequency, if you're looking for a character reference.'

'What, that you are your own worst enemy?' he repeats, watching me.

'Basically, yes.' I lift a hand to wipe away my tears, and realise he's holding out a hanky. I take it, dabbing at my eyes, and hope that my mascara isn't running. Judging by the wet black smears on his hanky, I'd lose that bet. 'It's not your fault. I'm still touchy about David, I suppose. It's those letters… God, those letters! Whoever wrote them is reading my mind.'

His dark brows knit together. 'Because you blame yourself?'

'Who else is to blame? I knew he was depressed and I did nothing. Well, I took a step back. And look how that worked out.' I blow my nose, and give a hysterical laugh. 'I seem to do a lot of crying on dates with you. I'm sorry. It's not a nervous tic, believe me. I've just had a bad year. Or a bad few years. Here's to next year instead.'

I lift my champagne flute and clink it awkwardly against his, almost knocking it over. Luckily, Logan grabs the glass before it can fall, his eyes on my face.

'And to us,' I add, suddenly uneasy in the spotlight and keen to move his attention away from me.

'To next year, and to us,' he repeats, seeming to find this double toast fascinating. He holds his glass aloft for a few seconds longer, and then gulps down his wine with a fervour to match my own. 'Look,

185

Kate, there's something I've been meaning to ask you. And maybe this is the worst possible time—'

'Because I'm drunk and emotional?' I interrupt him.

He blinks. 'Because it's your birthday, and I don't want to spoil the moment for you.'

Spoil the moment?

'Oh God.' I thump my glass down on the table and bury my face in my hands. I'm half-laughing, half-crying now; the other diners around us must think I'm off my head. But the pain inside is all too horrible and real. 'You're going to break up with me, aren't you? That's what this "dinner and a show" thing is about. You're kissing me goodbye.'

'No,' he exclaims, and grabs my hand across the table. I glance up at him in surprise as he adds, 'It's the polar opposite. I thought you knew. I thought you could tell just by looking... Women are supposed to be the observant ones, aren't they?'

'You've lost me,' I stammer, staring at him.

'I'm in love with you.'

'Sorry?'

'Didn't you hear me? Or don't you believe me?' Logan groans, and closes his eyes briefly. 'This isn't a good start, is it? I tell you I'm in love with you, and you think I must be pulling your leg.'

I shake my head, speechless.

He takes a deep breath, then produces a small black box from his jacket pocket and pushes it across the table towards me.

'I'm... in love with you,' he says again, with the air of a man who had a carefully rehearsed speech but has now abandoned it or possibly forgotten what he intended to say, and who is now improvising wildly. 'I know this is super fast. I know we've only just found each other again after... well, after David. I know you're probably not over him, and I don't expect you to be. But I'm willing to make a go of it if you

186

are, and in short…' He nods at me to open the black box. 'Will you marry me, Kate Kinley?'

I can't seem to breathe. 'M-Marry you?'

I glance around us at the other diners, and people whose heads had been turned towards us in fascination swiftly look away.

'Are you serious?' I open the box, and stare down in utter bemusement at the silver and emerald engagement ring sparkling in a nest of black silk. 'Oh my God. You are serious. Logan, I don't know what to say.'

'Saying *yes*,' he says quietly, 'would be a fantastic start.' Then he seems to pull back, as though forcing himself to be patient. 'But I know you may need time to think about this.'

'I need lots of time. It's so sudden.'

'I accept that, absolutely.' Logan nods, leaning back in his seat. His face is a little flushed, maybe from the champagne. Maybe from the stress of proposing. 'But it's not sudden for me. I've always held a torch for you, even back when you were seeing David. We clashed over it a few times, in fact.'

My eyes widen. 'You argued with David over me?'

There's a look of chagrin on his face. 'I wouldn't put it as strongly as that. But I felt David wasn't treating you as well as you deserved, and occasionally gave him the benefit of my advice about it. Which of course he rejected out of hand. But that was David.' There's a brooding, distant look on his face now, as though he's looking back at the past. 'He hated anyone telling him what to do. Especially when it came to you.'

'I had no idea.'

'Why should you?' Logan lifts his chin and smiles at me, rather too brightly. 'All water under the bridge now. But no, it's not sudden for me. And as soon as we started seeing each other, and then when you were so happy to let me move in, I thought…' He stops, seeming to correct himself. 'I *knew* from early on that this was right. You and me. That I wanted to marry you.'

I touch the engagement ring wonderingly with a fingertip. 'Logan, it's beautiful.' Then I close the box. 'But I can't say yes.'

He looks devastated, but asks calmly enough, 'Why not?'

'I don't deserve it.'

'Rubbish.'

'No, I mean it.' I push the box back towards him. 'I've messed up my life in so many ways. David was the pinnacle of my mistakes, yes. But there've been others. And I don't want to add you to the list.' My smile is wan. 'I'd rather just keep things as they are, if that's okay. Girlfriend, boyfriend. And maybe take it from there?'

'Of course,' he says, nodding, and puts the box away again, but the expression on his face nearly breaks my heart. 'Girlfriend, boyfriend is something. No, more than something. It's marvellous.' He pours out the last of the champagne, sharing it equally between our glasses, and then dumps the bottle upside down in the ice bucket. 'Thank you for not breaking up with me, at least.'

'Good God, why would I do that?'

'For being so selfish and spoiling your birthday with an unwanted marriage proposal. And nobody would blame you in the slightest. I should never have asked. Stupid of me.' Logan manages a smile despite the bitterness in his voice, and lifts his glass. 'Happy birthday, Kate.'

I drink too, smiling back at him, and wonder if I've done the wrong thing in rejecting him. He's been no trouble since moving in, after all, and he's pretty good in bed. But I was simply shocked, the way he sprang that proposal on me so quickly and without warning. I couldn't think straight, and I still can't.

Marry Logan?

No, my brain refuses to grapple with the idea. It's simply too soon and I'm not ready to think about him in those terms yet.

There may be another reason for my refusal, though. A deeper and more disturbing reason. Because it was roughly when David and I started to discuss marriage that things began to fall apart for us.

Maybe it's ridiculously superstitious of me to push Logan away just at the time when we ought to be growing closer.

But I'm afraid.

I don't want lightning to strike twice.

CHAPTER TWENTY-TWO

I manage to keep Mr Adeyemi away from my mother for several weeks, but in late November, he sneaks in another surprise visit while I'm at work. Ruby calls to let me know, sounding flustered, and I ask her to put the solicitor on the phone.

While I wait, I stare out across the familiar vista of London's rooftops, skyscrapers and church spires, but I'm not really taking in the spectacular view. I'm still smarting from having Calum Morgan's book taken away from me. In some ways, of course, it's made my life less stressful. I no longer have to fear what my email inbox may bring each morning, and there are no more uncomfortable phone calls from Calum to squirm through, or endless demands from Mark to know where I'm at with the manuscript.

The ice wall between me and Mark has not thawed, however; I'm still getting sharp stares from across the office and facing thinly-veiled hostility in meetings. Not for the first time, I wish I knew why he dislikes me so much. My best guess is that he's finding Calum every bit as challenging to work with as I did, or that the task of 'tidying up' Calum's manuscript is proving more onerous than he expected.

Mr Adeyemi's deep voice comes on the line, startling me. 'Hello, Miss Kinley? Can I help you?'

I greet him curtly, still suspicious he may have manhandled my mother during his last visit. But suspecting something and being able to prove it are two different things, as Logan has impressed on me whenever I've considered going to the police about him.

'Mr Adeyemi,' I say, 'I'd rather you don't visit my mother without me being present. Unfortunately, I'm at work right now. Could I ask you to reschedule for a day when I can be there?'

He doesn't seem cowed by this speech. 'May I remind you that your mother is my client, and she has a legal right to see me privately?'

Yes, I think. But not to be mauled about by her solicitor.

Silently, I count to five, rather than let myself explode. There's no point getting sued over voicing my thoughts too unguardedly.

'That's as may be. But Mum was upset after your previous visit, Mr Adeyemi. She's not good with visitors these days. That's why I'm asking you to reschedule. Not because I'm trying to interfere with her right to speak to you privately, but because I have a duty of care towards her. My mother has dementia, and I need to ensure that she's kept safe.'

He doesn't answer at first, but clears his throat. The noise is jarring. 'Miss Kinley, are you suggesting that your mother isn't safe during my visits? Because I must tell you that I find that idea offensive and abhorrent.'

'Not at all,' I lie, gritting my teeth against the desire to yell at him. 'And I'm sorry you feel like that. I'm merely asking you to come back another day when I can be there to support my mother.'

'I appreciate your concern for her; it does you credit. But it's wholly unwarranted. The suggestion that she would need your support to manage a few minutes alone with her solicitor is ridiculous.' He pauses and clears his throat again, and it strikes me as a nervous sound.

191

'Besides, I only need to speak with her very briefly on this occasion. There are some papers of hers that she wanted to see again.'

I'm amazed. 'Wait. You're saying my mum *asked* to speak to you?' I don't believe him. 'How? Because I haven't seen her use the telephone in months. And even then, I had to dial the number for her.'

'There's no mystery, I assure you. Last time we spoke, Celeste indicated that she would like me to return for further discussion. Unfortunately, I wasn't free to do so until today.'

'Further discussion about what?'

'Obviously, I can't be specific, as there's client confidentiality to consider. While I understand your protective urge, I also need to fulfil my professional obligations to your mother.'

Bloody patronising man. My protective urge is about ready to kick him in the…

'Of course.' How convenient, I think bitterly, but try to stay calm. There's not much I can do at this distance. 'Very well. Will you mind if her carer, Ruby, stays in the room during your discussion?'

'I can't allow that, I'm afraid. But I'm willing to schedule any future visits to fit in with your timetable. Or better still, you could arrange to bring your mother to my office instead. How's that?'

I grind my teeth in frustration. 'Thank you,' I say tightly. 'Could you put Ruby back on?'

Ruby comes back on the line a few seconds later. She keeps her voice low, saying, 'Did you ask him to leave? Because he's gone straight back into the living room to talk to your mother. And now he's closing the door.' She sounds breathless and outraged. 'What should I do, Kate? Do you want me to call the police?'

'Good God, no.'

'No, you're probably right. I'm sure he won't try anything. Not now he knows we're onto him.'

I close my eyes. I like Ruby, but she does have a tendency to get a bit trigger-happy where my mother's concerned. The last thing we need is to go bothering the police over a simple solicitor's visit. Not without concrete proof that something untoward is going on.

'Look, it's fine. Just keep an eye on my mum, and if there are any problems, call me again.' I hesitate. 'Or you could always try Logan. He's only ten minutes away, after all.'

'Good idea,' she says enthusiastically, and rings off, agreeing to monitor the situation for me.

As the line goes dead, I turn to find Mark behind me, his look supercilious.

'More personal calls during office hours, Kate?' he drawls, but then waves a dismissive hand when I start to explain. 'No, I'm really not interested. I have something more important to discuss with you. Come on.'

Mystified, I follow him back into his office, the scene of my last ignominious meeting with Calum Morgan.

To my surprise, my boss nods me towards the white sofa reserved for VIPs. 'Take a pew.' He thrusts his hands into his trouser pockets, jiggling his loose change. 'Coffee? Tea?'

I shake my head.

Mark sits beside me, which is alarming in itself. His eyes bore into mine. 'I won't bother beating about the bush. Calum wants you back.'

'Excuse me?'

'You heard. I don't approve, of course. He's our top author, and I'd rather have a more experienced editor working with him. To avoid any further mishaps.' His lips tighten. 'But my hands are tied. It seems Calum has decided he likes a tough editor. Someone who'll call him out on his bullshit.' His eyes hold nothing but contempt for me. 'So you're back on the job.'

I stare at him, unsure what to say.

I'm also unsure I want to work with the lecherous, game-playing Calum Morgan on his awful bloody book. But to say no would only strain my relationship with the company further, and I can't afford to risk losing my job. Not even over a matter of principle.

I guess I'll just have to find my own way of dealing with Calum Morgan's wandering hands.

Luckily, Mark doesn't give me a chance to comment, continuing irritably, 'I've done some work on the manuscript myself. I'll let you have my notes asap. Timing is crucial on this now. I need you to meet up with Calum again and talk pre-publicity. Take one of the marketing team with you. He hates promoting, so a pincer movement is probably best. Get him to nail down some dates when he'll be available for signings, plus radio and TV interviews. Make sure he can't wriggle out of them.' He pauses, grimacing. 'And get that bloody book sorted out double quick. It's an unholy mess.'

I resist the urge to say 'I told you so' and nod instead. 'Don't worry, I will. Leave everything to me.' I hesitate. 'Though it's a good idea to take someone else with me to any meetings. A third party might be useful. Calum can be a bit… hands-on, if you see what I mean.'

His gaze, which has been roving bitterly about the office, flashes back to mine. 'Is that so?' His lip curls. 'Well, keep it to yourself.'

'I'm not an idiot, Mark,' I say sharply.

He gives a reluctant laugh. 'No, you're not. Or he would hardly have wanted you back. Calum Morgan despises stupid people.' Abruptly, he stands up, and I guess the meeting to be at an end. As I head for the door, he calls me back. 'Look, if Calum gives you any more hassle, and you know what I'm talking about, don't try to deal with it on your own. Come straight to me. Is that understood?'

Surprised by this unexpected solicitude, I nod. 'Thank you.' Though

I can't believe he's serious. He and Calum have much in common when it comes to manhandling women, and besides, Mark would never put my welfare over that of a bestselling author.

He shrugs. 'Calum tried it on with Cheryl once, and I made him regret it. Can't have the talent pawing my staff, if you'll pardon the expression, be they ever so mighty.' With a laconic smile, my boss nods me towards the door. 'Now, go do your job.'

I return to my desk, smiling, and almost miss the jingle of a new text message arriving on my phone.

It's from Ruby.

He's gone at last. But your mum seemed upset, so I called Logan anyway. He's with her now. All well here. Rx

CHAPTER TWENTY-THREE

I take Harry along with me to meet Calum for lunch the next day. We meet in a small, family-run bistro not far from our offices, a familiar place that feels like safe enough territory. I half-expect Calum to find it too downmarket for his tastes. But to my amazement, the famous author is at his most charming; he praises the décor and the menu, and even goes on to congratulate me on my meticulous editing of his book, as though we had never clashed over my changes in the first place. He graciously allows the company to pay for lunch, but gives me a gift of a pendant necklace with a gold heart strung on its delicate chain.

'Please, I want you to have to have it,' Calum says when I try to give the jewellery box back. 'I picked it out for you specially.'

I protest, feeling awkward about an author giving me such an expensive gift, but he insists that I accept it.

Under the circumstances, I don't see how I can refuse.

'No hard feelings, I trust, Kate?' Calum indicates that I should put the necklace on in front of him, which I reluctantly do, fiddling with the catch while Harry grins.

'About what?' I ask, confused.

'My little temper tantrum over your edits, of course.' Calum rolls his eyes as though mocking himself. 'It took me a while, but I finally sat down the other day and re-read your notes. When I saw how much sense they made, I realised what a fool I'd made of myself.' His smile is satisfied as I straighten the gold heart on my chest. 'There, I knew that pendant would suit you. The editor with the heart of gold.' He glances at Harry, clearly nettled by another man's presence at our lunch but determined to be friendly. 'Don't you agree?'

'Absolutely, Mr Morgan.'

I shoot Harry a fulminating look, and then smile at Calum uncertainly. 'It's lovely, thank you. I'm not sure I deserve it though. I was just doing my job.'

'I love your modesty too.' Calum laughs, leaning back in his seat as though to study the effect of the shining gold heart against my white jumper. 'You've shown such care and attention to detail in looking after my book, Kate. That little gift is the least I can do in return.'

'Well, I'm simply glad we're moving forward with the book again. It's going to be a big launch. One of our biggest ever. Harry will talk you through the proposals.'

Our food arrives, and with great relief, I focus on my plate for a few minutes. The gold pendant around my neck feels heavy and conspicuous, like he's marked me out as his possession. The thought alarms me.

While we eat, Harry begins to explain what we have planned for the publicity campaign, both before and after publication, but after a few minutes, Calum waves him to silence.

'Send me the rest of those details in an email, would you? I'll only forget if you start listing endless events over lunch.' When Harry tries to protest, he gives him an assessing stare. 'Don't be offended, but you look and sound about twelve. Are you?'

Harry's eyes narrow but he laughs with an effort. 'Hold on, I'll have to check my passport.'

'Nice one. I can see I'm going to have to watch you, young man.' Calum's eye is caught by a passing woman in a tight-fitting dress. 'But never mind the jokes. I'm here to speak to the organ grinder, not her monkey.'

Appalled by his rudeness, I pick up my wine glass and take a few sips to disguise my reaction.

To my horror, Calum's foot suddenly bumps me under the table. I'm wearing opaque tights and a knee-length skirt, which has ridden up slightly since I sat down. With a leering smile on his face that tells me he knows exactly what this is doing to my nerves, Calum rubs the side of his leather shoe up and down my calf.

I'm too shocked to react, frozen in my seat, staring back at the author while my brain scrambles for a plausible next course of action.

'I'm thinking of doing a book about relationships between the sexes next. Maybe for the workplace. What do you think, Kate? Is that a *hot* topic these days?' On the word 'hot', Calum's foot rises, shifting under my skirt to brush my thigh. 'Would you be *open* to that suggestion?'

I jump up, scraping my chair back noisily, and see people's heads turn around us. Even Harry looks surprised. 'I'm sorry,' I say breathlessly, dumping my napkin on the table and making a grab for my handbag. 'If you'll both excuse me, I'll be back in a few minutes.'

Calum's eyebrows rise in surprise, but he doesn't try to stop me. 'Take your time,' he murmurs, his gaze unashamedly studying my figure as I brush past him on my way to the ladies.

In the quiet of the restroom, I take a moment to steady myself, and then text Mark.

Calum's playing footsie with me at lunch. I'm not sure what to do. Should I confront him? Throw my wine in his face?

I'm not entirely serious about the wine-throwing, but my hand was itching to do precisely that when Calum met my shocked gaze across the table and actually *smiled*. The man's a total creep and probably ought to be locked up.

I wait there for five minutes to get myself under control again. As I'm drying my hands, my phone finally jingles.

I'm in a meeting. Just sit out of his reach. I'll talk to him later.

So much for supporting me, I think grimly.

When I get back to the table, Harry has gone. I stare at his empty chair and then look accusingly at Calum. 'What did you say to him?'

'Nothing,' he says vaguely. 'Harry had to be somewhere. He said to apologise, and he'd speak to you later.' His smile flickers. 'Nice lad, isn't he? Not quite old enough to shave but that's publishing these days. Are you sleeping with him?'

'No,' I exclaim hotly, unsure I even want to sit down and carry on with this appalling lunch. 'Not that my private life is any of your bloody business.' I look about for the waiter. 'I should go too. I'll arrange for the bill to be paid.'

'Oh, sit down and stop flapping, woman.' He pushes my chair out with his foot. 'I won't touch you again. For God's sake, anyone would think you were a blushing virgin. So I touched your leg under the table. So what? There was no need to rush off and blab everything to Mark, you little tattle-tale.'

I fight the impulse to walk out without paying, and sink into the chair opposite him instead, my heart thudding hard.

'What are you talking about?'

'Your knight in shining armour just texted me.' He holds up his phone, and I see a brief message highlighted on the screen. It's all in caps. Mark's trademark bollocking technique. 'Mark says I'm to behave, or he'll find me a male editor. I can't work with a man. Not if I want to stay sane. A few days listening to Mark bleat on about "textual errors" in my book was enough to teach me that.' With a wan smile, he sticks out a hand. 'Truce?'

I'm tempted to tell Calum where he can stick his truce and then leave him with what will undoubtedly be a large bill for our three meals.

But part of me still wants this assignment. And I know Mark will be furious if I disobey him again.

I hesitate, looking at his outstretched hand.

I don't shake it.

Instead, with careful deliberation, not bothering to hide what I'm doing, I shift my chair backwards out of reach of his foot.

'All right,' I say, and take a quick sip of wine to steady my nerves, 'I'll play the game, Calum. But this time, it's by my rules. No more squeezing or grabbing or playing footsie. And no more gifts.' I wrench off the gold heart pendant and drop it into my bag. 'Is that clear?'

Calum takes a deep breath, his gaze moving restlessly about the restaurant. 'Spoilsport,' he mutters, and then adds hurriedly, when I start to stand up again, 'Fine, just sit down. Have it your own way. Your rules.' He grimaces. 'So, let's talk edits.'

When I get back that evening, the house is in partial darkness. On first moving in with us, Logan swore he would fix that broken security light, but he hasn't got around to it yet. Not his fault. I know he's been busy with work, and it's hardly his area of expertise. But it does mean I feel a little unnerved, walking from the car to the front door in near darkness, a cold wind stirring the bushes and trees. A distant memory tugs at me, of seeing a shadowy figure at the other end of the lawn, and I glance that way instinctively. As I do so, the door is jerked open.

It's Ruby, wearing an apron, and with a mixing bowl cradled in her arms. I catch a brief, tantalising whiff of chocolate.

'Thank goodness you're back,' Ruby says eagerly, light streaming around her like a full-body halo, the noise of the television on full blast drifting out along with it. 'You'd better come in quick. Your mum's beside herself. I didn't know what to do, so I've just been waiting for you to get home.'

Wearily, I follow her inside and hang up my coat. 'What's happened now? And why in God's name is the telly on so loud?' I'm having to raise my voice to be heard. 'Can't you turn it down?'

'She won't let me,' Ruby says darkly, and nods when I look round at her in surprise. 'She's been in quite a pickle, I can tell you. Yelling and so on.'

'But why?'

'Don't ask me, love. She's been like this most of the day. Keeps going on and on about men.'

'*Men*?'

'You may well stare. I don't know what it's about. Maybe Adeyemi's visit yesterday upset her and she's been thinking about it. Or Logan.'

I pause in the doorway. 'Logan? Why would he have upset her?'

'Well, I don't know for sure if he did. But he was here at lunchtime.' Ruby bustles off to return the mixing bowl to the kitchen, and returns without her apron, drying her hands on a striped tea towel instead. 'He ate his sandwiches at the same time she had her soup. At the table there.' She nods towards the living room; a small pine table has been set up in there with a couple of pine chairs, allowing Mum to eat her meals without having to walk through to the dining room, which faces north and gets quite chilly in the winter months. 'They had some kind of argument. At least, I heard raised voices, and when I came back into the room, Logan had gone outside, probably for a cigarette, but his chair was knocked over, and your Mum…'

She pauses, looking at me uncertainly.

'Yes, go on. My Mum… what?'

'She was crying.'

'Oh my God, why?' I'm horrified.

'I've no idea, sorry.' Ruby pulls a face. 'Logan never came back. I think he went straight back to work. I asked your mum if she was hurt, but I couldn't get her to talk to me. Whenever I tried, she started yelling at me to mind my own business, and even swore at me.'

My eyes widen. 'My mother *swore* at you?'

'Oh, I don't think she realised she was doing it.' Ruby taps the side of her head. 'It happens sometimes with dementia. They get a bit rude, and a bit shouty. I wouldn't worry, love. I certainly didn't let it upset me. I just put the telly on for her and gave her the remote control, like she asked me. Only Celeste turned the sound right up, and it's been deafening in there ever since. So I decided to make a chocolate cake.' She grimaces. 'It's quieter in the kitchen.'

Shocked, I hurry through to see my mother.

The remote control is lying on the floor a short distance from her armchair. Mum is huddled on the sofa, which is unusual, as its deep, soft cushions mean she finds it hard to get up again. Her face is pushed into the upholstery, and she's clamped both hands over her ears, covering her head.

Not surprising, given the decibel level.

'Mum? Are you okay?'

I grab up the remote and turn off the blaring television. The abrupt silence feels almost as disturbing as the noise.

'It's Kate, Mum. You're safe now. The telly's off.' When she doesn't move, still hunched over and shaking, I sit beside her on the sofa. I touch her shoulder and she flinches away, giving an odd groan under her breath. 'Hey, what on earth's the matter?'

She looks up then, and I see she has indeed been crying. Her heavily bagged eyes are red-rimmed, damp with tears.

'It hurts,' she whispers, and pulls down the shoulder of her dress to reveal a round, red-raw patch on her shoulder, a few inches down.

For a moment, I can't breathe, I'm so stunned.

'What the hell…?' I call Ruby into the room, and we both stare at the rough red mark, sunk into her skin like a tiny brand. 'What is it, do you think? How did it happen?'

Ruby shakes her head, looking equally horrified. 'I've no idea,' she whispers, and then touches my mother's arm very gently. 'How did you get that, love? Do you remember?'

'No, no,' Mum says, pulling away and closing her eyes. She drags up her dress to hide the mark. 'I… I don't know. I don't remember. Can't remember!'

I look round at Ruby. 'You said Logan was here with her? At lunchtime.'

'That's right.'

'And they had a row.'

'Well, I couldn't say for sure. I wasn't listening.' Ruby chews on her lip. 'But that's what it sounded like to me, yes.' Her eyes widen. 'You think he did this to her?'

'Well, it didn't get there on its own, did it? You said she was ranting about men afterwards, didn't you?' I close my eyes, barely able to cope

203

with the dark thoughts rushing through my mind. That any man could have done this to a woman was bad enough, but to a woman of her age and in her condition? I can't believe it of Logan, but at the same time, maybe I can. There's a kind of intensity about him at times that frightens me. 'Oh God, this is awful. Get the phone, would you? I'd better call the police.'

'Not the police.' Mum cries, looking round at me with huge eyes brimming with tears.

I suck in a long breath, considering. 'The doctor, then. Dr Forster will need to see this. She'll know what to do for the best.'

'No, please, don't call anyone. You understand?' Mum seems terrified. 'I don't want them to take me away.'

'Nobody's going to take you away.'

'Please!' Her hands grip my arm with surprising strength. 'I won't go, you hear me? I won't be taken away. You mustn't let them come here. Promise me you won't call anyone.'

'Mum—'

'Promise me, Kate, promise me!' Tears flow down her cheeks. Her voice is ragged. 'Say it!'

I can see Mum's likely to make herself sick if I don't give in. And it's certainly true that after Dr Forster's last visit and her dire warnings about neglect, this is going to look very bad for us.

The last thing I want is to lose my mother to a hospital or residential home. I swore that I would look after her for as long as I possibly could, and we haven't reached the end of the line yet.

'Very well, I promise.' I shake my head, torn between the need to report this to the authorities and my wish to calm her down. 'I won't call anyone if it makes you unhappy. But Logan's not coming back here. Not after what he did to you.'

'Logan,' she repeats, and shivers. 'I don't like Logan.'

'Neither do I,' I say grimly.

I ask Ruby to fetch the first aid kit, and then set to work, tenderly cleaning and dressing the tiny circular wound on my mother's shoulder, a wound that looks for all the world like a cigarette burn.

CHAPTER TWENTY-FOUR

I'm waiting for Logan when he gets home an hour and a half later. I hear his car on the gravel and step outside, pulling the door shut behind me.

He climbs out of the car, a lit cigarette in hand, looking every bit as exhausted as I feel. But as soon as he sees me on the doorstep, his demeanour changes. 'Kate?' He locks his car, tosses his cigarette away into the shrubbery and comes towards me, smiling. 'I'm sorry I'm so late. There's been some trouble at work, and—'

Logan stops, noticing my stillness and silence. His tone changes. 'What is it? What's wrong?'

There's a faint light coming from the living room window to my right. By its glow, I study his face, wondering if the man I've been gradually falling in love with could be guilty of the most appalling cruelty, attacking a vulnerable woman in her own home…

'You came home at lunchtime today,' I say softly, not wanting Ruby to overhear us. She's still in the kitchen, putting the finishing touches to her cake, but I know she's curious about how my mother got that mark on her throat. 'You ate lunch with my mother.'

'That's right. I thought she might be lonely.'

'And then you argued with her.'

His brows draw together. 'I wouldn't exactly categorise it as an argument. She had an odd turn, that's all. Nothing to get excited about.'

'An odd turn,' I repeat, and clench my hands into fists, itching to slap his face.

He peers down into my face, still frowning. 'You look upset. Shall we go inside and talk about this?'

'Not yet.'

'You want to talk about this on the doorstep? In the dark? In this bitter weather?'

'Yes.'

'Okay, if you *insist*.' Logan puts down his briefcase, but there's a ripple of impatience in those last two syllables that tells me he's unhappy. 'What is this exactly? The Spanish Inquisition? I take it Ruby told you what happened at lunch.' He grimaces. 'I knew I could hear her eavesdropping on us, bloody nosy woman.'

'Excuse me? If it wasn't for Ruby, I wouldn't have known what happened.'

'Fair enough.' Logan shrugs, shockingly casual about his behaviour. 'So I raised my voice to your mother. I lost my temper. I'm sorry. But do we really need to make such a big deal out of it?'

'When I came home, I found my mother crying.'

'Oh, Christ.' He runs a hand over his face, and then nods. 'In that case, I'm genuinely very sorry. I'll go and apologise. It won't happen again.'

'What exactly did happen, Logan? Because before I let you put so much as a toe over this threshold, you're going to tell me the truth,' I say through my teeth. 'All of it, please.'

He sighs and folds his arms. 'Right, you want the gory details. Well, we were sitting at lunch together, and your mother just flipped, with no warning. She glanced up at me from her soup and said something bizarre like "Who are you?" As though she'd never seen me before. I was surprised, as you can imagine. But I know she has dementia, so I replied simply that I was Logan, and your boyfriend, and she started shouting at me, claiming I was an intruder, an imposter, and insisting that David was your boyfriend.' He swallows, looking away suddenly. 'I was unnerved, I admit it. So I told her…'

'Go on.'

He looks guilty. 'I shouted back at her. I'm sorry, I know it was incredibly wrong of me, but she caught me off-guard and I… I lost my temper.'

'What did you tell her, Logan?'

'That David was dead. That he was never coming back, and I was your boyfriend now, and she needed to come to terms with it.'

I realise that I'm trembling, possibly with cold, but also perhaps through shock. I fold my arms and stuff my hands under my arms to keep them warm. 'And then?'

'And then… nothing. I left.'

'Are you sure about that?' I stare at him, disbelieving. 'You did nothing else? You just left the house?'

He hesitates. 'She called me a murderer, Kate. She said if David was dead, then I was the one who killed him. And she was going to make me pay. It was awful.' His voice is uneven. 'I know I ought to have stayed calm. But it really hurt me, you know? David was my best friend.'

'So what did you do?'

'Just what I've said. I yelled back at her. And then I walked out.' He pauses, looking embarrassed. 'I may have knocked my chair over on the way. It was all a bit childish and melodramatic, and I'm very sorry that I upset her. Now, will you let me go inside and apologise properly?'

I wait, unmoving. 'I think you left something out of that story.'

'Sorry?'

'Your cigarette?' I nod towards the bushes where he flipped the lit one he'd been smoking when he arrived. 'You didn't, in fact, light a cigarette at the lunch table and then stub it out on my mother's shoulder?'

His face seems to be carved from stone. 'What? Are you serious?' When I say nothing, his eyes widen. 'Did you just accuse me of…' His voice is hoarse. 'I don't believe this. You must be crazy.'

'One of us may be crazy, but it's not me. Now tell me the truth, Logan. Did you give my mother a cigarette burn?'

'No, of course I didn't.' His expression is incredulous. 'Why would I? This is insane.' He seems to catch himself on that word. 'Wait, you're saying she has a burn on her shoulder? For real?'

'Yes, Logan, that's precisely what I'm saying. As if you didn't know how it got there.'

'Well, I bloody don't. Were her clothes burnt too?' He frowns. 'She was wearing that blue dress today. Was it damaged?'

I think for a minute, then shake my head slowly. 'No. But maybe that was deliberate on your part. To throw me off the scent.'

'So, what?' His eyes are incensed. 'You think I pulled her dress off her shoulder in order to burn her, and she didn't struggle or call out to Ruby while all this was happening?'

'I don't know; I wasn't there. Maybe she was too scared. Or maybe Ruby was banging her pots and pans in the kitchen at the time, and didn't hear her.' I want to cry; I feel so cold and hollow inside at his lies and betrayal. 'Look, I've had enough of this conversation. We're just going round in circles. It's obvious you're never going to admit it—'

'Because I didn't do it,' he exclaims.

'Fine, if that's your story. I'm going inside now to call the police. Mum doesn't want me to. She's terrified someone will take her away

209

if I do, maybe put her in a home. But this is abuse. I have to report it. I can't turn a blind eye to what you've done.'

He grabs my arm as I open the front door. 'Wait, Kate. Please don't.' His voice is urgent. 'You know I could never do something like that, right? Torture your old mum? For God's sake, I don't have it in me.' He fumbles for his packet of cigarettes in his jacket pocket and throws it away. 'See, I've given up. No more ciggies. Christ, I didn't do this, Kate. It wasn't me.'

I stare at him, wishing I could believe him, and then shake my head. 'Then who did? Because there's still a burn on her shoulder.'

'I don't know. Ruby? Mr... Mr Adeyemi?'

'Now you're being ridiculous. Ruby is her carer. And Mr Adeyemi wasn't even here today.'

'Wasn't he? I thought Ruby said she'd had a visitor earlier... or was that the day before?' He looks confused. 'I'm sorry, I'm not sure. Work has been so demanding these past few weeks, I'm barely holding it together.' He sees my expression and shakes his head. 'Not in that way, though. You have to believe me. I'm not cracking up. And I would never, ever hurt a woman.'

I don't know what to think, but stare at his face in the semi-darkness. I badly want to believe him. And I did smell a faint whiff of cigarette smoke on Mr Adeyemi when we met in his office. It's possible Mum did get another visit from the solicitor today and that Ruby forgot to mention it, or perhaps didn't know, if he only popped in and out while she was busy elsewhere.

There's also an outside chance that Mum got that cigarette burn the day before, when Mr Adeyemi was alone with her, and none of us noticed it when she was undressing at bedtime. Yesterday, she'd been wearing a short-sleeved top with a loose fit under her cardigan. If she'd taken off her cardigan at any point, which she sometimes does when the electric fire is on next to her chair, it would have been the work of a few seconds to lift her sleeve, touch a lit cigarette to her skin and put a hand over her mouth to stifle her scream.

The mental image sickens me. I sway, and put out a hand to steady myself.

Has Mr Adeyemi grown impatient with waiting for my mother to die and is trying to force the situation by terrorising her? Or maybe his plan goes deeper and involves discrediting me as her carer too. Well, he's certainly doing a good job so far…

'Kate? Are you okay?'

'I don't know what to do anymore.' I close my eyes and feel his arms close about me. I just want to lean back into his strength, to trust him implicitly, as I always trusted David. To rely on him as I relied on my father and brother. Gone now, all of them gone, my world stripped down almost to nothing. Life is so unfair… 'You swear to me you didn't do this?'

'I swear it on my life.'

I let him into the house, and listen while he apologises solemnly to my mother, and to Ruby too for having stormed out the way he did, and then I help my mother take a shower.

About half an hour later, Ruby comes into my mother's bedroom, her curious gaze on my face. 'Did you ask him? Did he do it?'

'He says not.'

'And you believe him?'

I shrug helplessly, and sit my mother on the edge of her bed while I dress the tiny red wound on her shoulder again. It seems to be getting better.

Ruby lays out a clean nightie for my mother and brings over her woolly pink bed socks. 'So you won't be telling the police, then?'

'I should do, by rights. She's been assaulted, for God's sake.' I see the panic in my mother's face, and shake my head quickly. 'But I won't. Not if you don't want me to, Mum.'

My mother's lip quivers but she says nothing. I suspect she's too exhausted, poor thing.

After I've finished with her shoulder dressing, and she's tucked up in bed with her eyes closed, I take Ruby aside. 'Listen, I've been thinking. I really must inform the police. I'm as guilty as whoever did this if I don't. But I'd like to tell them without getting Mum involved, if that's possible.'

Ruby looks dubious. 'Won't they want a police doctor to examine her?'

I realise she's right.

My shoulders sag in defeat. 'This is intolerable. I'm damned if I do and damned if I don't.'

'Here's an idea,' Ruby says softly, steering me out of the room and clicking off the light. 'Why not think about it overnight, and then report it tomorrow if you still feel you should? I'll cover for you if the police come round asking awkward questions.'

'What do you mean?'

'I'll say we only noticed the burn tomorrow morning. Then nobody can blame you for waiting a few hours before ringing the police.'

I can see the sense in that little white lie, though it makes me uneasy. 'Okay,' I agree, too bone-tired to make a report right now and be forced to sit through a long and difficult interview, not to mention deal with Mum's hysteria when she realises what I've done. 'We'll talk about it tomorrow.'

'Goodnight,' Ruby says, and collects a hot drink from the kitchen before heading up to her room.

The living room feels warm and cosy. My bare feet ache as I pad across the fluffy white rug and collapse on the three-seater sofa. I hear the clink of glasses behind me, and accept with silent gratitude the large gin and tonic with a slice that Logan has poured for me.

'Yes, it's been one hell of a day,' he says in a weary voice, sinking down beside me with his own glass. His arm comes about my shoulder, and I don't resist, though I know our budding relationship has been horribly mangled by today's events. 'Thank you, by the way.'

'For what?' I sip at the gin with my eyes closed.

'For believing me earlier. For not throwing me out into the night and calling the police.'

I open my eyes and peer at the clock on the mantelpiece. It's a little after ten o'clock.

'Oh, don't get too comfortable. There's time yet.' He laughs, but it's not funny and we both know it. 'I'm going to have to call the police about it tomorrow. I can't just pretend I didn't find a cigarette burn on my mother's shoulder.'

'I know,' Logan says, in a voice so flat and emotionless there's no telling what he's thinking.

I realise I haven't even told him about Calum.

But that's another conversation that can wait until tomorrow.

CHAPTER TWENTY-FIVE

When I come downstairs early the next morning, having spent a dreadful night unable to sleep, there's a white envelope lying on the mat.

I stand there a moment, just looking at it. Then I pick it up and tear it open, my hands shaking with anger.

It's not a poison pen letter. It's a bundle of bank statements, folded together. I stare at the top one blankly, then realise the name on the account is Logan's. I check the envelope again, thinking I've opened his mail accidentally. But it's addressed to me.

I blink, confused, and slowly my gaze focuses on the figures. Which are very bad. According to the top statement, dated only a few weeks ago, Logan is more than ten thousand pounds overdrawn.

One of the other statements seems to belong to his savings account, which shows a steady withdrawal of funds over the past three months, leading to a balance of zero. And a third sheet lays out lending terms for a massive loan taken out a few months ago, to be repaid over five years at very disadvantageous terms. That one's not from a bank but what looks like a dodgy loans company.

Ten thousand overdrawn at the bank, with a massive unsecured loan on top. It has to be unsecured, as I know he only rents his town flat; he doesn't own it.

Ten grand isn't a huge amount on its own. I myself have quite a sizeable overdraft, though not quite at that level. And if his salary is substantial, then a few months' payments would easily cover that overdraft. Except that I can't see funds going into his current account, only out. And with the loan on top, which still has almost five years to run, it's clear he's in a heap of financial trouble.

Logan is coming down the stairs, yawning, still in his dressing gown. He stares at the papers in my hand. 'What's that? More trouble?'

I hand them to him silently, and watch his face.

'Jesus Christ.' He looks blank at first, and then furious, a dark flush coming into his cheeks. 'Where the hell did you get these?' When I point to the torn envelope on the mat, Logan stoops and retrieves it. But it can't reveal much, being plain and having only my first name on the front. 'I don't believe this... These are my bank statements. I keep them at my flat. Someone must have broken in and stolen them.'

'That's a fairly hefty overdraft.'

'I have a few money troubles, it's true. But that's nobody's business but my own.'

I say nothing.

He rubs his forehead, staring at the envelope. 'My God, someone's trying to... What is this? I don't understand.'

'I think someone's trying to tell me you're in need of a large amount of money,' I say slowly, working it through on my own. 'The same person who's been sending me the poison pen letters, at a guess.' A thought hits me, and I take a step backwards, catching my breath. 'That's why you asked me to marry you. I thought it was incredibly sudden. But if Mum goes into a home, and I sell the house, that would free up so much capital... If we got married,

215

you could ask me for that cash, and wipe out your overdraft and loan in one payment.'

His mouth works silently, as though he's trying to come up with a counter-argument or an excuse, and then he bows his head. 'I did think about that possibility, yes. But only for a second, I swear it.' He looks up at me, his face haggard. 'That's not why I asked you to marry me, Kate.'

I go into the kitchen and start automatically putting on the kettle and laying out the breakfast things. I don't want to think about it. But it feels like I've been cut inside and am bleeding out silently.

'Besides,' he points out more firmly, leaning against the door frame and watching me, 'you said no, remember? I haven't tried to force you to change your mind. I accepted your rejection. So this...' He scrunches up one of the statements in a ferocious gesture. 'This means nothing. It's someone's idea of a sick joke. And whoever did it is a criminal. They've been in my flat.' He looks grey-faced. 'I'll have to go round there before work today. See what else they've taken. What they've touched.'

'Are you actually still working?'

'What do you mean?'

'Those statements... I didn't see any income for this month.'

He says nothing for a moment, then swears under his breath. 'Look, I was going to tell you. They let me go.'

'When?'

'A few weeks back. Just after we first started dating. It was a shock. A real shock. But things hadn't been good there in a while.'

'Why didn't you tell me?'

'I don't know. At first, I didn't know how to tell you. I thought you'd cut me loose if you knew. Who wants to date a bloke who's unemployed? And I figured if I kept going to job interviews, I'd soon

216

land another post. But it's proved a little harder than I thought.' He laughs without humour. 'Plus, the longer the charade went on, the harder it was for me to be honest with you. If you'd said yes to marrying me, I would have found a way. But you didn't, so I thought…'

'You thought you'd lie to me a bit longer.'

He flushes more darkly. 'I deserve that, I suppose. That was never my intention, for what it's worth. But it's how things ended up.' He closes his eyes, and exhales heavily. 'I'll go and pack.'

'Yes.' I turn away to fiddle with the kettle. A tear rolls down my cheek, yet somehow I control the shake in my voice. 'That's probably a good idea.' When he moves away, I call over my shoulder, 'Is that why you did it, Logan?'

'Did what?'

'Is that why you moved in here with me? Why you pretended to be in love with me? Why you gave my mother that cigarette burn? To force us into a situation where Mum might have to go into a home and this house would get sold?' My voice is shaking now, uncontrollably. 'Did you do it for the money, Logan?'

He comes back and grabs me, dropping the bank statements. His face is dark with emotion, a hard red along his cheekbones. 'How dare you? You think I'd do something like that? To you and your mother? For *money*?' He glares down at me, and then forces his mouth against mine in a cruel mimicry of a kiss before pushing me back against the sink. 'Fine, do your worst.'

Dazed, I rub a hand across my mouth. My lips feel bruised. 'Wh-What?'

'You're going to the police today, aren't you? And I suppose you'll try to pin everything that's happened onto me.'

I say nothing, staring at him.

'You can tell the police whatever you bloody well want,' he

continues. 'I didn't do any of it. And I certainly didn't move in here so I could… what, intimidate you? Control you? Or whatever it is you think I came here to do.' He strides out, knocking a tall gin tumbler off the surface with one flailing elbow; it smashes on the floor behind him and I jump, giving a tiny cry as glass shards spatter my bare legs. He turns briefly to see what's happened, and then keeps going. 'I never want to see you again, Kate. But something tells me I will. In court.'

A few minutes later, shakily sweeping up the glass with a dustpan and brush, I hear him thumping about the bedroom overhead, opening and slamming drawers. So he wasn't kidding about packing his stuff. I can't decide whether I'm glad or sorry that he's leaving. My head is so full of contradictions that I can't reconcile, it feels like I'm going to explode.

Ruby comes downstairs and stands in the kitchen doorway, looking at me. The sympathy in her eyes is almost too much to bear.

'I'm so sorry,' she whispers, 'I couldn't help overhearing most of that. You were both speaking quite loudly.' She crouches to pick up a large jagged piece of glass near the door that I missed. 'Did he hurt you, love? Do you want me to call someone?' I shake my head, holding out the dustpan, and Ruby drops the glass shard into it gingerly. 'I'll be a witness if you need me to.'

'It's fine. He's leaving anyway.'

She doesn't seem surprised, nodding. 'Easier, I suppose. Especially on your poor mum.' Her gaze moves to the bank statements strewn about the kitchen floor, and she bends to pick one up, clucking her tongue. 'So he was in financial trouble all along. That's awful.'

I take the bank statement away from her and collect the others. 'These belong to him. Not us.' I put them in a little stack on the hall table, where I hope he'll see them when he leaves.

Who sent them to me? Someone who wants me to know what Logan is really like underneath the charm and the lies about how busy he's been at work. But is it the same person who sent me the poison pen letters? Because although the delivery method is the same – a hand-delivered envelope with just my name on the front – I'm not sure if the handwriting is the same. It might be, but right now, I can't get my brain to engage. Besides which, I no longer possess those letters; the police kept hold of them for their investigation. Though 'investigation' is a bit of a joke, seeing as I've heard nothing from them since. Too busy dealing with *real* criminals, no doubt.

'You poor thing; you look done in. Shall I make us both a nice cuppa? And one for your mum too. I can't believe she'll have slept through that row.' Ruby touches the kettle with the back of her hand. 'Looks like it only needs a quick reboil.'

'Thank you.' I stop in my tracks, staring at my reflection in the hall mirror; she's right, I look awful. My cheeks are intensely pale compared to my red-rimmed eyes, the lids of which are swollen. I'm crying again and can't seem to stop, the taste of salt in the corners of my mouth.

'I… I'm sorry I woke you.'

'Don't be silly, love, I was getting up anyway.' Ruby looks at my face, and then gives me a quick hug. 'Hey, no more of these waterworks. Do you hear?' She tidies my dishevelled hair, tucking a few strands behind my ears. 'Who needs men, eh?'

'Me,' I stutter, though in fact I've managed fine without a boyfriend for the past two years.

If being lonely and depressed counts as 'fine'.

'Even so, there's no point worrying. With your looks, and this beautiful big house, you'll soon find another man. A better man.' Her smile is reassuring. 'Trust me.'

CHAPTER TWENTY-SIX

I'm supposed to be working on Calum's book as a matter of urgency, but instead I spend the whole of the day with my mother. It feels like the right thing to do after the horror of what she's been through recently. Also, part of me doesn't want to face the reality of my sudden, cataclysmic split with Logan or that I have to go to the police about Mum's cigarette burn. Could it really be Logan who hurt her? Or Mr Adeyemi, perhaps? Either way, it happened because I was too busy looking the other way to notice.

I feel so consumed with guilt and fear, my stomach turns over whenever I think about it, and I can't breathe.

But I need to tell somebody about this.

Today.

Much to her bemusement, I snap a few photos of Mum's bare shoulder with my phone's camera while changing the dressing on her burn.

'Don't worry,' I tell her when she tries craning her neck to see what I'm doing, 'it's just so I can ask the... the doctor about it later.' I've decided not to mention the police to her. She would only get frightened.

'Ask her about what?'

I push the phone into my jeans pocket. 'Never mind.'

To my relief, the circular red mark on her shoulder is healing. It's grown paler overnight and looks a lot less gruesome than when I first spotted it. Mum seems to have lost interest in it altogether. But that doesn't mean I can just forget about it. She's been *tortured*, basically, and it may turn out to be my fault to some extent.

I'll have to live with that guilt for the rest of my life.

Determined to see my mother happy again, I make a last-minute appointment with a mobile hairdresser who specialises in dementia patients. She turns up late morning with her scissors and an endless selection of amusing anecdotes about her job, which keeps Mum happy for a few hours.

'I swear, it's taken ten years off you,' the hairdresser insists, showing her the back view with a hand mirror. 'You look gorgeous, Celeste.'

Mum smiles and pats her hair. 'I do a bit, don't I?'

Afterwards, I look out some pretty clothes for her to wear, and we watch a black and white movie together on the sofa, one of her favourites with a drawling Humphrey Bogart in the lead role.

Ruby makes fruit shakes in the blender, and the three of us drink them together while listening to music and chatting about Dad and Ciaran, the glory days when we used to go skiing or climbing as a family and nobody could have predicted the dark days we inhabit now. Ruby sits with Mum to look at old photograph albums, exclaiming over Ciaran's good looks and admiring Mum and Dad's wedding photos, and Mum looks radiant, tracing her husband's face with wonder and trying his name for the first time in ages.

'Peter,' she says, tentatively at first, and then with pleasure and increased certainty. 'I was so in love with him, you know. Perfect Peter.'

Ruby nods. 'He does look perfect, your husband. And Peter's one of my favourite names.'

Mum gives a happy noise under her breath, and hugs her. 'I like you,' she tells her deliberately. 'Ruby. One of *my* favourite names.'

Later, I nip to the loo, and while there, feel a notification chime from the mobile in my pocket. Wishing I could just ignore it, I hook the phone out and stare down at the lit-up screen in dismay.

Need you at the festival tonight. Here's a link to the event. Meet me in the green room 6.00 pm.

I groan.

Bloody Calum Morgan.

I'd forgotten; he has a festival interview tonight at a London venue, one of those on-stage events where an expert or fellow writer grills the great author for an hour in front of a paying audience, the two of them probably in leather armchairs with a projected image of Calum and his various books on the wall behind them.

The 'green room' is the hospitality area at festivals like this for authors and their guests, such as editors or agents. Calum dumped his agent last year and hasn't signed with a new one yet, so I guess I'm his only possible plus-one.

Festival interviews or panel discussions are the kind of publishing-related event I particularly loathe and have always avoided attending in the past. It's always hot and crowded, and we're expected to smile and look upbeat no matter what. Calum is notorious for hating them too, yet has agreed to this one, and it's hard not to question that uncharacteristic decision. He'll be surrounded by hundreds of adoring fans tonight. So why does he need me there as well?

It's not hard to find the answer. Now I'm his editor, it seems I'm expected to form part of that rapt, sycophantic audience too.

If only his fans knew what a sleazy, self-serving git Calum Morgan is, I think, maybe they wouldn't be so quick to buy his books or swallow the worthless snake oil he peddles at these events.

But then again, it's the age of the self-serving git. So maybe they wouldn't care.

I can't go, however. He'll be furious but there's no help for it.

This evening has been earmarked for a very different kind of outing; I still need to go and show the police those photos I took of Mum's burn mark, and admit my suspicions about who did it. Delaying overnight while I weighed up my options was one thing. But if I wait until tomorrow to report what is essentially a physical assault, they'll quite rightly ask why on earth I didn't call them the same day I noticed it.

I can already imagine PC Plimley's face, the taut cheeks and narrowed lips, like she's sucking a lemon. 'You ought to have come to us straightaway, Miss Kinley,' she'll say, and she'd be right.

Mum could be taken away from me if it looks like I've been neglecting her care, and she wouldn't understand that. It would break her heart.

I hesitate, then stab out a few pithy words and hit send.

Can't, sorry. Mother's birthday.

Yes, it's a little white lie, but what the hell? I've been getting quite good at telling little white lies recently. I've developed a talent for it, in fact.

I'm washing my hands when Calum's equally pithy reply arrives with a triumphant chime.

Tough shit, princess. Be there or you're fired again.

I decide to go to the police on my way to the festival. But when I finally say goodbye to Mum and head outside, it's cold enough to snow and the car decides not to start, which makes it feel like the gods are laughing at me.

I prop open the bonnet and peer inside, but have no real idea what I'm looking at. The engine won't even turn over. Is the battery dead? That can happen in cold weather.

223

I find my breakdown recovery card and call for home assistance, but am told it could take anything up to two hours to get to me. Apparently, it's been a busy day for call-outs, and I'm not a priority, being at home.

It's half past four and decidedly gloomy by the time I give up the wait and any idea of reaching the police station today. I dare not stand Calum up.

'Here are my car keys,' I tell Ruby, who's hovering in the hallway. 'I can't wait any longer. Give the mechanic my mobile number when he arrives, and if there's a charge for a new battery, I'll pay over the phone.'

'You're going out?' Ruby looks surprised.

'I've got a publishing thing. Calum Morgan's latest book. He's doing a festival spot.'

Her face is blank. 'Calum who?'

'Doesn't matter.'

'Well, let me give you a lift to the station, at least. It'll be getting dark soon.'

'I don't want to disturb Mum. I'll walk, it's fine.'

'Oh, Celeste's taking a nap,' Ruby says cheerfully. 'I'm sure we can leave her in the house on her own for twenty minutes.'

'I'd rather not risk it. But thanks for the offer.' She follows me to the front door and watches as I head off up the drive on foot. 'I'll try not to be back too late.'

'Enjoy yourself,' she calls after me.

Frustrated and a bit panicked at the idea of being late for Calum's big interview, I speed-walk breathlessly to the bus stop in the gloomy dusk, despite the discomfort of my heels, and catch the first bus that's heading in the direction of the train station.

The upside of not having the car with me is that I'll be able to drink while listening to Calum boring for Britain on stage tonight. But it also means having to walk home from the station later in the dark, which I hate doing. Unless I fork out for a taxi…

It's even colder in central London for some reason. The pavement is icy, and I nearly slip over twice. But eventually, I squeeze into the packed venue, showing my ID at the desk where it seems Calum has told them to expect me.

I'm ushered through to the green room and enveloped in a bear hug by Calum, who's showing off for the others there.

'My editor, Kate Kinley,' he introduces me with every evidence of pride, though I'm surely the least important person in the room.

But two of the older men there, due to appear on a panel in another space at the same time Calum is being interviewed on stage, look me up and down with envious eyes. Their editors, they tell us conspiratorially, are almost as old as them. And male.

I barely have a chance to secure a large glass of gin before Calum is taken away backstage, and I'm shown to my reserved VIP seat on the front row. I sip my drink, wave a greeting to the few other publishing people in the room that I actually know, and prepare to be very bored.

But actually, Calum turns out to be incredibly entertaining to listen to. He makes the audience laugh and wipe away a tear, sometimes with the same anecdote. I find myself frowning along with everyone else when he describes the rough patches he's been through, his years as the CEO of an unsuccessful business and his wreck of a first marriage, and have to remind myself testily that maybe ten per cent of what he says is genuine, the rest bullshit.

I notice, however, that in this breath-taking saga of disaster and redemption, he fails to mention that his second wife has also now left him. No doubt because that would look too much like carelessness.

Afterwards, there's a kind of sprawling, impromptu party between those guests who choose to stay for a drink rather than drifting out with the rest of the audience. I try to slip away as the event comes to a close, but Calum spots me and links his arm with mine, insisting that I hang on until he's had a chance to talk to me in private.

'I have to do some schmoozing. But we still need to talk about the manuscript,' he reminds me. 'Promise me you won't leave yet.'

I force a smile. 'I promise.'

A group of us start out politely sipping our drinks in the bar area while discussing how the interview went and the week-long literary festival in general. But we end up spilling outside onto a raised, spotlit area of decking with tall potted shrubs, behind which Calum is able to smoke unseen by the disapproving venue staff, ignoring the 'No Smoking' signs everywhere. He seems to take delight in breaking the law, deliberately stubbing out his cigarettes in the plant pots and grinning at my discomfort.

His most devoted fans keep turning up, begging him to sign copies of his books or trying to get him alone, something he always strenuously resists, though with tremendous charm.

At intervals, other festival authors come and sit with us for a chat, some of them very interesting.

He greets these writers warmly, but as soon as they've gone, Calum laughs, rolls his eyes and manages to insult them in some indefinable way. Especially the women.

Several times I try to get him to discuss his book with me, since he won't let me go until he's done so. But Calum constantly dismisses me, saying, 'Soon, soon. I'm not ready yet.'

With nothing better to do, I order more tall gins and knock them back, pushing away thoughts of Logan and my mother. I know I shouldn't get drunk. It's one of the cardinal rules for editors at author events. Stay sober! But the alcohol helps me forget what an unholy mess I've made of my life. Always trusting the wrong people, making all the wrong decisions…

By the time they throw us out, shortly after midnight, I can't walk straight anymore, and the alarm bells that jangle at my nerves when Calum slips an arm about my waist don't seem important anymore.

'The festival committee has put me up in a hotel just round the corner,' he tells me, waving goodbye to the others and steering me away down the dark street. 'Come and have a nightcap, Kate. It's too early to call it a night. Then we can talk properly about this book of mine. Just you and me. I think you've worked miracles with it so far, by the way.' His smile is misty, his words slightly slurred. 'Such a talented little editor.'

'Thanks. But I ought to get home.'

'Plenty of time for that. Your mum's birthday, isn't it?' He checks his watch, blinking at the display. 'All over now, I'm afraid. She'll be in bed.'

For a moment, I'm confused, frowning at him. Then I remember my fib about it being Mum's birthday.

'I expect so. And that's where I need to be too.' I hiccup loudly, and clap a hand over my mouth in dismay. 'Pardon.'

He merely laughs, his arm tightening about me. I look down at his hand, which is resting just below my right breast, and wonder how offended he'll be if I push him away.

'You are pardoned,' he says. 'It was a great night, wasn't it?'

'Fab.'

'I'm glad we've managed to get past our differences.' He seems to be manoeuvring me down a narrow alley between high buildings. 'I think you can help me reach a new readership, Kate. A younger readership.'

'Where are we going?'

'Told you. My hotel. This is a shortcut.'

'No,' I say more firmly, coming to a halt beside some yellow, industrial-sized bins. 'It's after midnight. I'm not going back to your hotel.'

'But we need to talk.'

'We can talk on the phone. Or over lunch again. With… with Harry.'

'Fuck Harry.'

I ignore his muttered obscenity and look around, trying to shake off the alcohol haze and regain my bearings.

'Where… Which way's the tube station?'

'Come on now, don't be annoying.' His arm draws me closer. His clothes stink unpleasantly of fag smoke, and my nose wrinkles. 'I've got pink gin in my room. And a bottle of tonic. I bought them especially for you, Kate.'

'Calum, I need you to let me go now.'

'You're such a bloody tease.' The words are spoken lightly, but I sense a real threat under them. 'All you bitches are the same,' he adds, looking me up and down, an unpleasant flicker in his eyes. 'You flirt and flirt. But underneath it, you're uptight and puritanical…'

I have a vague memory of Cheryl warning me not to be alone with him, but even as the thought flashes through my head, it's already too late. Calum pushes me against the brick wall beside the bins. He's much larger and stronger than me, fumbling for my breasts while also trying to kiss me with sour whisky breath. His body weight keeps me pinned there for a terrible few moments, like a caught butterfly.

I struggle, and we lurch together like drunken dancers, Calum staggering backwards with me in tow, both my hands thrust hard against his chest in an effort to escape.

'For God's sake,' he exclaims thickly.

'I *said*,' I pant, fighting to be free, 'get your bloody hands off me.' At last, he releases me, and I make unsteadily for the mouth of the alleyway, my heels slipping on the icy stone. 'Goodnight, Calum. I'll send you an email tomorrow.'

'Don't bother, darling. If you think you'll still be my editor after this—'

'Oh, shut up.'

The author throws a slew of guttural swear words at my back, but to my relief doesn't bother pursuing me, stumbling off into the night instead.

On the train journey home, I want to cry but can't manage it. Instead, I sit staring out of the window at the dark landscape flashing back, lights glittering in the distance, roads and buildings and the occasional cinematic passage of other trains. A few men ogle me but I ignore them.

I pay for a taxi home from the station; sod the expense, it's better than being terrified half to death by walking empty streets, looking over my shoulder at every noise. Besides, I realise belatedly that tonight's little outing comes under work expenses, so I should get the travel money back eventually.

Back home, the car stands icy and silent. I realise that nobody rang me about the charge for a new battery, but can't be bothered to pursue that thought.

Mum's door is closed.

Swaying, I kick off my heels and creep upstairs on tiptoe, thankful that nobody's about to see the wicked state I'm in. Except that Ruby's door creaks open briefly and her indistinct face looks out at me.

'You're in late. You okay, love?'

I mutter something suitably hostile about men, and wave good-night before disappearing into my room. I'm not in the mood to talk. Actually, I'm not sure I'm capable of speech. Not full sentences, at any rate. Which means it's definitely time for bed.

I barely pause to brush my teeth and wipe off my makeup before tumbling into bed and sinking into a thick, mindless sleep.

I'm woken late by an awareness that my phone keeps alternately buzzing and chiming. Someone trying to ring and then leaving a message? This goes on for some time while I lie in a partial stupor, snug under the duvet, ignoring the irritation of daylight pricking at my eyelids.

I feel grim and shaky after last night's excesses. And I have a nagging memory of some fumbled, drunken exchange, and then Calum stumbling away in a dark alley…

My mobile buzzes again, and keeps on buzzing relentlessly. Whoever it is must want to speak to me urgently.

I grope to answer it, wishing I didn't feel so bad. 'Hello?' My voice creaks like a rusty gate.

It's Mark.

'At last. What the hell were you thinking?' My boss sounds so furious that I sit bolt upright in bed, blinking in dismay. 'You are so fucking fired.'

'What?' The light hurts my eyes. 'Why?'

'Very funny,' Mark says in a cutting tone. 'Here's what you need to do. Delete the tweet and make a full public apology, retracting your comments. Say you were drunk or something, that it was meant as a joke. A publicity stunt, perhaps. Maybe then he won't sue us for everything we've got. But I doubt it.' He pauses, and then adds in a bemused tone, 'Jesus, Kate. When you self-destruct, you don't do it by halves, do you?'

Then he hangs up.

I sit there for a moment, staring at nothing, his words echoing in my head. *Delete the tweet…* What the hell is he talking about? What tweet?

I peer through dozens and dozens of notifications on my phone, frowning. The list seems to scroll on endlessly. Messages, tweets, retweets, missed calls…

With an unsteady hand, my heart thumping sickly in my chest, I flick through to my work-linked Twitter feed, where I habitually promote authors and upcoming publications and chat with editors and bloggers about books.

Calum Morgan is a narcissist, a misogynist and a bare-faced liar. Don't buy his self-help books. They are one big fat con from start to finish. #MeToo

My tweet, which was apparently posted at two o'clock this morning, has already been retweeted over a thousand times.

CHAPTER TWENTY-SEVEN

I feel like I'm going mad. Or as though I've woken up to find myself in a new universe, a world I don't recognise and which hates me.

I delete the tweet, though I imagine it's already been screenshotted a few dozen times by now, and indeed some of the amused or scurrilous comments in my notifications indicate that it has.

I hesitate groggily over a fresh tweet, wondering how to explain how that wasn't me and I didn't post it, and then I delete that draft too.

Better perhaps to say nothing for now. Saying more can only make things worse. I mustn't panic, I tell myself carefully. Though obviously, I'm panicking. Of course I am. Given the catastrophic storm hanging over my head, what else is there to do?

At the back of my mind is the horrible suspicion that I may indeed have written that tweet last night. I was drunk, after all, and furious with Calum for assaulting me. Furious with myself too for allowing it to happen in the first place. I'd been warned by Cheryl. I'd walked out on that partnership once already; I ought to have refused to work with the vile man again.

But I let my ambition get the better of my common sense. And this is the result.

I brush my teeth automatically, splash cold water on my face, and then throw some fresh clothes on without bothering to shower. Time is not on my side at the moment. Mark was right about that, at least. I need to act, and act quickly.

I stumble downstairs, my legs unsteady, then stand in the hall, helpless and unsure what to do now for the best.

Should I head straight back into London to the office and explain to Mark in person how it wasn't me that tweeted that libellous remark against our top-selling author? Or sit down and compose a carefully-worded apology to Calum that would discreetly threaten him at the same time as begging him not to sue the company?

After all, I doubt he would wish me to disclose to the world what he did last night. The MeToo hashtag is so weirdly percipient, it's what makes me wonder if I did actually tweet that message and then wipe it from my memory. Because how else would my hacker know what happened?

Though if I did go public about Calum's attack, it would only be his word against mine, and that's not a very comfortable thought.

Ruby comes out of the kitchen, drying up a saucepan, and looks at me in surprise. 'Hello. Should you be up this early? You came in very late last night.' Concern enters her eyes. 'You look a bit rough too. Bad night?'

'Someone's hacked my Twitter account,' I hiss, and catch sight of myself in the hall mirror. God, yes, I look wild. Almost crazy, in fact. My hair is all over the place and my face is deathly-white, except for two burning red spots on each cheek. Like a wooden doll with a painted-on blush. 'I'm in deep trouble.'

'Twitter. That's one of those social media things, isn't it?' She finishes drying the plate, looking rather pleased with herself. 'I don't like social media. It's just another way for the government to watch you.'

I stare at her, then hobble past her into the kitchen. My feet and ankles hurt after walking so far in high heels last night.

'I need… coffee,' I mutter, and slam my phone face-down on the counter. 'And to change my password on Twitter. Christ, I probably should have done that first.'

Ruby puts the kettle on and watches with interest as I struggle to change my password, my fingers clumsy on the tiny onscreen keyboard.

'Someone hacked you? You mean—'

'I mean somebody pretended to be me and posted something publicly in my name last night. While I was bloody sleeping.' I feel angry and impatient, and not in the mood to explain things to people like Ruby who can't be bothered to keep up with modern technology. 'Now it looks like I've got the sack over it. Not to mention that I'm facing a possible court case for libel.'

A memory tugs at me, like a far-off bell ringing. What was it Logan said as he stalked away from me the other night?

I never want to see you again, Kate. But something tells me I will. In court.

I close my eyes in horror, bile rising in my throat.

Logan has been living with us here. He's had access to my phone on numerous occasions. My laptop too, where I also log into my social media accounts. Lazily, I tend to use the same password for most of my accounts these days, because two years ago I tried using a computer-generated one for different sites and then my laptop got stolen, and I had to change all of them by hand because I no longer had access to those passwords.

It's possible he could have guessed my usual password; not only is it David's name and date of birth, but I keep it written down on a slip of paper stuck to the edge of the mirror in my bedroom.

'Logan,' I whisper.

234

'Sorry?'

'Doesn't matter.' I swallow the bile, trying to hold onto my sanity, and update my account with the new password. Then I make the mistake of hurriedly scrolling through some of the more recent notifications, just to see… 'Christ.'

It looks like Calum's vociferous fans have now seen my tweet and have responded to it with violent contempt, bombarding my Twitter feed in their hundreds with messages of hate and aggression. Apparently, for attacking their mild-mannered idol, I deserve to be raped, mutilated, even murdered.

I decide abruptly to delete my Twitter account. That will get rid of one problem, at least. The app asks if I'm sure, and politely points out that I have thirty days to change my mind. I stab the button again to delete the account and throw my phone aside with a groan.

Nobody is going to believe that I was hacked. What the hell am I going to do? My career in publishing is over.

'Oh dear. Sounds like you've been in the wars.' Ruby has made coffee for me in the cafetière. The smell ought to be invigorating. But it merely makes me nauseous. She holds out a steaming mug in my direction. 'You need protein, love. I was just about to do your mum's breakfast. You peckish? I could fry up some bacon and eggs.'

'No, thanks.' Clutching my stomach, I dash to the toilet.

When I stagger out some ten minutes later, I'm tempted just to ignore the world and go back to bed for the rest of the day. My body is advising me to do just that. But one glance at my phone shows me a string of missed calls and text messages, including more missives from Mark, who seems to be demanding to know why my formal apology hasn't been emailed to him yet.

Ruby is making my mother's breakfast. I grab a glass of water, trying not to get in her way.

'I'm sorry I was out so late, by the way,' I say, trying to make amends for my curt manners earlier. It's not her fault my life is falling apart. 'Did anyone turn up to fix the car last night?'

'Yes, and it started first time. Nothing wrong with it at all.'

'How odd.'

'The mechanic said you must have flooded your engine.'

'Hmm.' I'm not sure that can be right, but it's not worth arguing about. My head is thumping. 'Well, I had a rubbish time. But I hope your evening was quiet, at least, and that Mum didn't cause you any trouble.'

Ruby looks unsettled. 'Actually, there was a bit of an incident.'

'Go on.' I gulp down some water.

'You know that special picture…' She pulls a face when I look at her blankly. 'The oil painting. The big one hanging on your mum's wall. Of you and your family.'

'The one my brother finished just before he died, yes.' I nod. 'I love that painting. What about it?'

'I'm afraid your mum went a bit crazy last night. She asked where you were, and I said you'd gone out with… whatever his name is.'

'Calum.'

'That's right. That you'd gone out to a festival with him. And your mum…' Ruby bites her lip. 'I had no idea she'd flip over something like that. I mean, I've never seen her so angry. She was screaming. Saying you had no business going out with anyone but David.'

'Oh my God.'

'She was calling you all sorts. Well, I won't repeat what she said. But it was nasty.'

'I'm so sorry if she upset you.' Back when Giorgios was her carer, Mum did sometimes get a bit hysterical when I went out for the evening. But she hasn't done that in ages. 'Did you remember to give her the meds she usually takes?'

'Oh yes, she took her pills. They made no difference.'

'I'd better go and speak to her.'

It's the last thing I want to do right now. But I can see Ruby is waiting for me to take action of some kind. Though what exactly she expects me to do is less clear. Tell my mother off for behaving poorly? She's a dementia patient and she gets mood swings. Sometimes her mood swings become violent. Ruby's used to caring for people in that situation; she must know how to deal with that kind of outburst.

'Before you do,' Ruby says quickly, 'you should know… Your mother, she damaged that painting.'

'What?'

'I'm really sorry. I was sitting in the bedroom with her, both of us chatting and doing a little embroidery at the same time. You know how I like my embroidery.' When I nod, she gives me a hesitant smile. 'Well, when we got onto the subject of you and men, she started shouting about you and David. I told her to calm down, but the doorbell went. So I left the room.'

'Who was at the door?'

'Logan.'

I stare, not sure what to make of that.

She continues, 'He said he'd left a few things behind and needed to collect them. Just some odds and ends he couldn't find when he left.' Ruby touches my arm when she sees how I flinch. 'I let him have a quick look round the house while I loaded the dishwasher. I hope you don't mind.'

I hug myself miserably. 'Of course not.'

'When he'd gone, I went back in to see your mum.' Ruby hesitated.

237

'I found her standing in the middle of the room, holding my sewing scissors. And that big picture on the wall…'

'Yes?' I prompt her when she stops, baffled by her expression.

'Your mum had completely trashed it.'

'Sorry?'

'She'd stabbed all the faces in the painting. Gouged out everyone's eyes. It was horrible. There was nothing left but great gaping holes where their faces were.' Ruby shudders. 'Except for one person.'

I almost drop the glass of water I've been sipping, my hands suddenly nerveless. 'What? Who… who didn't she stab?' I stare at her, wondering if this is some elaborate joke. 'Are you kidding me?'

Ruby looks offended. 'Good God, love, why would I joke about something like that? I thought she was going to attack me next. I took the scissors away and got her to lie down again. But that painting… I know how much you liked it. Your brother's, wasn't it? I'm afraid it's ruined.'

I put down the glass of water and run down the hall to my mother's room, barely knocking before I barge inside.

'Mum?'

My mother is watching the small television on the low table at the end of her bed. She's sitting up against stacked-up pillows, hands cradled motionless in her lap, a crocheted blue shawl about her shoulders. Her face is intent on the screen as she listens to a news report about a body found in woodlands.

'Mum, it's Kate.'

She doesn't look at me, but lifts her gaze from the television screen to the large family portrait hanging on the wall opposite her bed.

Or what's left of it.

Just as Ruby described, the faces in the family portrait are all stabbed, ripped and gouged out. My father's broad torso in his blue shirt is topped with a mess of canvas fragments, through which I can see the wallpaper behind. My mother's face is equally defaced, and there's next to nothing left of me, even my body violently torn away, just a hint of my jeans below. Ciaran himself still has one ear and a left arm.

Meanwhile, perfect and untouched, staring serenely out of the picture frame with his handsome face unmarred, is my late boyfriend, David.

'Oh my God, Mum, what have you done?'

'Hmm?' She looks round at me at last, her face utterly blank. She doesn't even seem to care.

The news report has moved on, talking about a bad crash in icy fog this morning on the M1, showing scenes of carnage that turn my stomach.

I grab up the remote control and snap it off.

'Mum, the painting… Ciaran's last painting.' I stand staring at the ruined canvas, and tears roll down my cheeks. 'It was so beautiful. All of us together for the last time. I know you lost your temper because I went out. But I still can't believe you'd do something like this. What in God's name possessed you to destroy it?'

Mum says nothing, but looks vaguely from me to the remains of Ciaran's painting. 'I don't know what happened,' she says simply. 'I'm sorry.'

'You're sorry?' I rub away a tear. 'Mum…'

'Perhaps we could stick it back together,' she says helpfully. 'I think there's glue somewhere.' She gives an odd little smile, and begins to sing 'Humpty Dumpty' under her voice, just as she used to do when Ciaran and I were young, ending with 'All the kings' horses and all the kings' men couldn't put Humpty together again.' Then she laughs.

I snap, my temper rising abruptly. 'I can't bear this any longer. I can't bear you. That's it. The last straw.' I put a hand over my mouth to stifle a sob. 'I'm going to put you in a home, Mum. I can't… I can't deal with this. It's beyond me.'

She stares at me, and her lip starts to tremble. 'A home? But you said… You said I could stay here.' Her voice rises too. 'You can't do that. *This* is my home.'

'Not anymore.'

'No, I won't go.' Mum shakes her head, her eyes bulging. 'No, no, no. I'm not going anywhere. This is my home.' I turn unsteadily and walk out, and she yells after me, sounding half-deranged now, '*My* home. Mine. You can't send me away from my own home. I won't go, and you can't make me. Do you hear?'

Out in the hall, Ruby is nowhere to be seen.

I trip over something on my way to the stairs. A half-empty packet of cigarettes. Logan had claimed he was giving up smoking, I recall. He must have gone back to collect the packet he'd thrown into the shrubbery, but then left it here by mistake. So much for that promise!

I grab the cigarettes, rummage for a lighter among the jumble in the telephone table drawer and fling outside into the cold morning, only stopping to slip the heels back on that I kicked off on my way in last night.

I don't smoke and never have done except for a few teenage moments of rebellion against the clean and healthy living my father advocated. But I settle one of Logan's cigarettes between my lips and fumble to light it in the chill wind, my hands cupped about the thin flame.

I suck in the smoke, and cough, my lungs reacting violently. But what the hell… My whole life has gone to the dogs.

Once, I used to go out running, make an aerobics class twice weekly, swim whenever I could. Now, I can't remember the last time I exercised. There simply hasn't been time these past few months, what with juggling Mum's care with the ever-increasing demands of my job. My body is already suffering because of it, so I doubt a cigarette or two will make any difference.

I hear the front door creak open, and turn to see Ruby there.

'Thought I'd give these a try,' I say defiantly, though I feel ridiculous, not even sure how to inhale properly. 'I mean, why not? Ciaran's painting's gone forever. My mother's lost the plot, and my career's in the toilet. I might as well take up smoking. See what I've been missing all these years.'

She watches me without saying anything.

I take another lungful of smoke and nearly throw up again. 'Okay, that's enough. Maybe I'm doing it wrong.' I dash the lit cigarette onto the gravel and crunch it out with the heel of my shoe. 'Is Mum still upset?'

'She's crying, and asking for you.'

'Christ.' I close my eyes. 'I'm sorry I raised my voice to her. I'll go in and apologise. Of course I won't put her in a home. I was just upset. That portrait...' I rub a hand across my face. 'It was my brother's last painting. It's irreplaceable. And I have no idea why she destroyed it.'

'It's not completely ruined,' Ruby comments.

I almost laugh. 'Did you look at it?'

'That nice-looking bloke wasn't damaged. Maybe you could cut him out and frame that part of the picture on its own,' she says helpfully.

'I suppose.' I shiver, and hand her the packet of cigarettes and lighter. 'If Logan ever comes back again, give him these, would you? I think they must be his.'

'Sure.'

I think for a moment, my brain belatedly latching onto something she said earlier. 'Ruby, you don't think it's possible that Logan did that to the painting, do you?'

Her eyes widen. 'Logan?'

'You said he was here. To pick up some things he'd left behind. What if he went in there and… You were in the kitchen, you said.'

'I would have noticed, love. Like I say, it was your mum. I found her with the scissors *in her hand*.'

'But he might have given the scissors to her afterwards. To frame her, maybe.'

I stop, confused. What exactly am I saying? That my ex snuck into my mum's room and deliberately destroyed Ciaran's family portrait of us in some paltry act of revenge? That doesn't sound like Logan to me. But then, if he's been hurting Mum behind my back, trying to force me into putting her in a home and selling the house, perhaps even such miserable spite wouldn't be beyond him…

Ruby peers into the half-empty cigarette packet, and then gives me a sly look. 'So it wasn't you, then?'

I stop on my way back inside. 'Sorry?'

'It wasn't you who gave your mum that cigarette burn?'

'Oh my God, of course not.' I stare at her, speechless and appalled. 'Why on earth would you think that?'

But before I can demand to know how she could ever suggest such a horrific thing, there's the crunch of tyres on gravel, and we turn to see a police car crawling down the drive towards us.

CHAPTER TWENTY-EIGHT

My first thought is that Calum Morgan has already decided to report me for that tweet. Though surely a lawsuit would be more usual than getting the coppers to call round? Unless he's decided it can somehow be categorised as 'hate speech'. I wouldn't put it past him to manage such an insane escalation. The vulnerable victim being oppressed by a cruel world. Or in this case, a cruel editor.

My heart rate accelerates, my stress levels peaking, and I feel ill again. The taste of smoke in my mouth is not helping. After the most appalling start to my day, this is the last thing I need...

'Now, what the hell do you reckon the police want with me?' I mutter, but Ruby has vanished inside, taking Logan's cigarettes with her.

I turn to face the police car, hugging my arms across my chest in the bitter weather.

To my relief though, the officer who climbs out is PC Plimley. At least that suggests she's not here in connection with Calum Morgan.

'Hello,' I say, trying to sound friendly even though I feel far from it. 'This is a surprise. Though a welcome one. Have you made some headway with those threatening letters?'

'Actually,' PC Plimley says, looking awkward, 'that's not why I'm here.' She settles her hat more squarely on her head, and then glances past me through the open door into the house. 'May I come in?'

'Of course.'

Puzzled, I lead the way down the hall into the living room, and spot Ruby standing in the doorway to my mother's room. She's still holding Logan's cigarettes, with that strange expression on her face that was there when she asked if I was the one who'd burnt Mum's shoulder.

Disturbed, I look away quickly. How could she have asked such a thing? Even as a joke it's horrible and distasteful. I've barely smoked before, and would never dream of hurting my mother. Let alone torturing her with a lit cigarette...

But as I turn to close the door behind me, Ruby's still there, watching me closely, cigarette packet in hand.

'So, how can I help you?' I ask PC Plimley with forced cheerfulness, and take up a position in front of the mantelpiece. She too is standing about, studying the room without bothering to conceal her interest. 'Please, sit down.'

She sits on the sofa, perching uncomfortably on the edge, and then takes off her hat and balances it on her knees.

'Can you tell me, Miss Kinley,' she begins in a stilted manner, and I interrupt her at once.

'Kate, please.'

PC Plimley smiles. 'Kate, do you know a person called Giorgios Baros?'

Of all the things I might have imagined she was here to ask me about, Mum's previous carer would not even have made the list.

'I'm sorry?' I blink, confused. She says nothing, not even repeating her inexplicable question, but sits and waits for me to answer it.

'Erm, sure. Giorgios is… was… my mother's carer. A day nurse, you know? He used to come round and sit with her during the day while I took the train into London for work. And a few evenings too, if I ever had to go out. I don't like leaving Mum alone, you see. She's… not well.' I pause, uncomfortable in the silence that's fallen over the room. 'Why do you ask?'

'You used the past tense. So he no longer looks after your mother?'

'He stopped coming, so now I have Ruby. She's with my mum right now, in fact.'

'Ruby,' the constable repeats, gazing up at me.

'That's right.' I fold my arms across my chest, feeling defensive and distinctly confused now. 'I'm sorry, what's all this about?'

'When did Giorgios stop coming? And why? Did you have a falling-out with him?'

'Of course not. He just didn't turn up one day. One evening, in fact. I can probably find you the exact date if necessary.'

'I'd like that, thank you.'

I'm amazed, and a little concerned. 'Why is it important?'

'May I ask, did you make any effort to find Giorgios when he didn't turn up? Did you call him? Send him any texts?' PC Plimley is looking at me enquiringly, and I get the feeling she sees me as a monster for having simply abandoned Giorgios after one no-show. 'Maybe visit his home?'

'All three, actually.'

She gets out her notebook and flips it open. 'Are you able to find me that date, please?'

Dumbfounded, I reach into my jeans pocket and consult my schedule on my phone. It takes a few minutes but finally I find the correct date and give her the details.

'I needed Giorgios to sit with my mum that night while I went

245

to dinner with… with a friend.' I put my phone away, staring at her bent head while she notes down the date. 'Constable, why are you here, asking about Giorgios? Is he all right?'

PC Plimley looks up then, her eyes cautious. 'I'm just doing some paperwork for a colleague. Though I expect he'll want to talk to you himself at some point. As you'll appreciate, Giorgios had quite a few regular patients and contacts in this area, and we need to speak to all of them.'

'But why?' I stumble over the words, catching a look on her face. 'Oh my God. What is it? Please tell me.'

'I'm afraid a body's been found in a stretch of woodlands not far from here,' she says quietly, 'and it's been formally identified as that of Giorgios Baros.' She pauses, her gaze fixed steadily on my face, as though monitoring my reaction. 'I'm terribly sorry to be giving you such bad news.'

I sink into Mum's armchair, staring at her in disbelief. 'I don't understand. Giorgios… He's *dead*?'

She nods apologetically, and makes a quick note in her pad before looking up again. 'So you can see why we're making inquiries in the area. And especially talking to people who were connected to the deceased.' When I flinch, she adds quickly, 'To Giorgios, I mean.'

'I see.'

I struggle with the news, remembering Giorgios's friendly, smiling face and his ever-cheery manner.

'Did he… Was it natural causes?'

'I can't say, I'm sorry.' PC Plimley checks her notebook again. 'Right, you said you went round to his flat. Could you confirm which day that was?'

'I'm not sure. Let me think.'

I stare at the carpet, my head whirling. If Giorgios had died of natural causes, she would simply have said so, surely? Which means it wasn't natural. And the opposite of natural would be… murder.

'It would have been on the Monday,' I stammer, and feel my cheeks go hot as she studies my face. I have no idea why I feel so instinctively guilty when this is nothing to do with me. But just being questioned makes me feel like a suspect. Which is ridiculous. Isn't it? 'Giorgios was supposed to sit with Mum on the Friday night, but didn't show. So I had to find someone else to cover for him. Then he didn't arrive for his usual Monday morning session with Mum, and I desperately needed him to look after her while I went into work.'

'Which is where? Your work?'

I give her the address of the publisher, and watch blankly while she writes it all down. Why on earth does she need to know that?

'Though I may not work there anymore. I think… In fact, I'm pretty sure I've just been fired.'

She stares at me in surprise. 'Oh dear.'

'Somebody hacked my Twitter account during the night and wrote something awful about one of the authors I work with.' The words are just tumbling out and I can't stop them. 'That's actually what I thought you were here for, when I saw the police car. I thought…'

I stop, confused.

'No,' the constable says slowly, a note in her voice that suggests she thinks I'm mentally unstable. 'You thought I was here about your Twitter account?' Her eyebrows rise steeply. 'That must have been one hell of a tweet.'

I shiver, suddenly and inexplicably cold. 'I guess so. I've deleted it now. But too late. It's everywhere.'

'That's too bad. And you were fired over it?'

I nod, looking away.

'Well, I hope you can sort it out and get your job back. There are ways to prove your account was hacked. I suggest you look into that.'

'Yes, I will. Thank you.'

She taps her notebook. 'So, to get back to that Monday morning when Giorgios didn't turn up, what did you do?'

I describe how I took Mum with me in the car to visit Giorgios's flat. 'That was when I discovered he'd gone on holiday.'

Her attention is arrested. 'Holiday? Who told you that?'

'His next-door neighbour. She said he'd put a note under her door or something, telling her he'd be away for a while. I can't remember exactly, I'm sorry. I tried calling him, and texted several times, of course, asking when he'd be back.' I shrug helplessly. 'But I never got a reply.'

'And those messages are still on your phone?'

'Sure.' When she looks at me expectantly, I flick through to the messenger screen and show her my history of text exchanges with Giorgios. 'So that was his last text to me, a few days before his no-show for the Friday evening,' I explain while she scrolls through them, 'and after that, it's just my messages to him. With no replies. I also left voicemail messages for him. So if you found his mobile...'

She nods, and hands back my phone before making more notes.

I re-read my messages to Giorgios, scrolling slowly backwards until I reach his last cheery message to me. It hits me then that he's dead. There can be no doubt about it. Formally identified, she said. But how did he die? And when?

'Did he ever actually go on holiday?' I ask.

'I can't discuss it, sorry.'

I stare down at his last message and feel awful, ashamed of my own increasingly irate texts that follow it.

'You think Giorgios was a no-show on that Friday evening because... because he was already dead, don't you?'

PC Plimley gives me an awkward smile. 'I couldn't possibly say.' Which is as good as her saying yes, as far as I'm concerned. 'Now, if I can take you back to your conversation with his neighbour on the Monday morning, could you possibly describe this lady in detail, to the best of your ability, and also which flat she lived in? Just so we can build up a picture…'

She's a uniformed officer, I think, studying her covertly as we talk. Not a detective. So maybe Giorgios did die of natural causes. Because if they were investigating a murder, I would be talking to a plain clothes detective, surely?

This thought helps me relax a little. Giorgios was a little overweight and not particularly healthy. It's possible he went jogging in the woods and dropped dead of a heart attack or suffered a fatal stroke. If he'd been in a very remote part of the woods at the time, that would explain why his body had only just been discovered. Though it wouldn't explain why his neighbour would claim he'd put a note under her door about some fictitious holiday.

Or maybe he did go on holiday, and died of natural causes or through some dreadful accident while out in the woods on his return.

Though if so, why did he never respond to any of my messages? Giorgios was such a happy soul, and usually very reliable. He wouldn't have ignored my texts and voicemail messages.

PC Plimley shakes my hand at the end of the interview. 'It's possible a detective may wish to speak to you. They'll probably ring first to arrange a time to call round, or you may be asked to go into the station to make a formal statement. Would that be okay?'

I hesitate.

In the silence, I catch a tiny tell-tale creak from outside in the hallway, and turn my head slightly to listen.

'I suppose so, yes. If it will help sort out what happened to Giorgios.'

'Thanks.' Her smile is wan. 'I'm sure we'll get there eventually. And I hope you get that thing sorted out at work. The hacked Twitter account. We did look into the letters you gave us, but there wasn't much to go on and my sergeant decided to take no further action. Not at this stage, anyway. Though if you receive any more—'

'I'll let you know straightaway.'

'Good,' she says firmly, and puts away her notebook. 'You should be careful. Those nasty letters, and now the social media thing… Sounds to me like someone at work has got a real grudge against you.'

I show the constable out, glancing nervously along the hallway as I do so. That barely perceptible creak I heard is still playing on my imagination. Was it just a floorboard relaxing, as they sometimes do? Or was it the sound of someone moving away, having stood outside the door to listen while I was being questioned?

But the hall is empty.

When PC Plimley has gone, I close the front door and lean my forehead against it.

I feel ill.

My legs have a slight tremble and my insides have that grim, hollow, hungover feeling that tells me I should go back to bed and simply sleep it off.

Except I can't.

I have to apologise to my mother first. And then draft an apologetic explanation to Calum. And maybe plead for my job to Mark and the other top executives. Or hire a lawyer.

I close my eyes. Hire a lawyer? Someone like Mr Adeyemi, for instance? I want to laugh but I can't muster the effort. Is there anyone left in my world who can be trusted?

Perhaps returning to bed isn't such a bad idea. I've about reached the end of my ability to deal with the minefield that's my life now.

'What was all that about?'

I turn to find Ruby behind me, her sewing box under her arm.

'Giorgios is dead,' I say dully.

Her brows tweak together. 'The guy who looked after your mum before me?'

When I nod, she makes a little noise of surprise under her breath. At least, I think it's surprise, though her expression doesn't change.

I remember the creaking floorboard just before we left the living room, and suspect that Ruby overheard the entire interview and is simply pretending to be shocked. No doubt she realises – quite rightly – I might be a wee bit pissed off with her if she admitted to listening at the keyhole while I'm being grilled by the police.

'Well, I never.' She inhales sharply. 'Poor bloke. Though what's that got to do with you?'

'I haven't a clue,' I reply shortly. 'Right now, I feel like I'm dying. I just want to apologise to my mum for saying she has to go into a home, and then I'm going straight back to bed.'

I head down the hall towards my mother's room.

'Best place for you,' Ruby calls after me in an approving tone, and disappears into the living room, the sewing box still under her arm.

CHAPTER TWENTY-NINE

There's a faintly unpleasant smell in Mum's bedroom, which I must have failed to notice before. Cigarette smoke? Perhaps Ruby's wrong and Logan really did sneak in here and slash Ciaran's picture to pieces. That would explain the lingering smell. Though it hurts me to imagine him doing such a horrible thing, especially in front of my mother, who must have been terrified.

I push open a window, despite the chill weather, and avoid looking at the painting on the wall opposite.

David's perfect, untouched face is already burnt on my retina though, and I feel his presence so strongly as I sink onto the edge of the bed, it's almost as if he's reaching across the divide from death to life, trying to find me.

Mum is lying on her side, her head turned away. I touch her shoulder, and she flinches, giving a little anguished cry.

My heart contracts with fierce guilt.

She's too scared even to look at me. And it's my fault. I've done this to her.

'Hey,' I say softly, 'it's okay, it's me, Kate.'

She shifts then, and peers round at me, the covers pulled up to her chin. Her face looks drawn, her eyes damp.

'Oh God, Mum, I'm so sorry. I didn't mean it.'

She looks at me blankly.

'What I said before about you going into a residential home,' I explain, and now she really does look frightened. 'No, don't worry. It's not going to happen. I was angry, that's all. I didn't mean it.'

'I… I don't have to leave?'

'Never.' I shake my head, forcing myself to smile, though I feel more like weeping. 'You were right. This is your home. And nobody has the right to make you leave. Least of all me, your own daughter.' I lean over and give her a hug. 'Please don't cry anymore. I'm sorry.'

I help her to sit up, and realise she's still in her nightie. 'Not dressed yet? I thought that's what Ruby was doing in here. But maybe you didn't feel like getting up today. I know how that feels…' Her scrambled eggs on toast, which Ruby must have brought in on a tray earlier, is sitting untouched on the bedside table, the eggs congealed, her mug of tea cold now. 'You haven't eaten your breakfast either. Weren't you hungry?'

She doesn't respond, staring at the ruined painting opposite with wide, horrified eyes as though she's only just noticed it. Which maybe she truly thinks she has, her memory these days almost as destroyed and full of holes as the canvas on the wall.

'Well, never mind. I can fetch you a fresh mug of tea. Are you peckish too? Maybe you could have some early lunch. In fact, I'm not working today, so we could eat together.' I take her hand and squeeze it encouragingly. 'Chicken soup?'

She gives a sharp yelp of pain, and I frown. 'Mum?'

My mother withdraws her hand from mine, pouting in dismay, and then glances up at me accusingly.

'I'm sorry, did I hurt you? I didn't mean to; I obviously don't know my own strength.' Then I realise the skin on the back of her hand looks red, as though she's been scratching it. 'Here, let me see. That doesn't look good.' She shakes her head, trying to conceal her hand under the covers, but I insist. 'Mum, please. I only want to help. Is your hand hurt?'

Slowly, she extends her arm and I take her hand. The back of her hand is a dark red, blotchy in places, with raised weals.

'Oh my God, this is awful. What is it? A rash?' Maybe she's developed some kind of allergy to the washing capsules we've been using. She did last year, and I had to change brand to a sensitive skin type. 'Have you been scratching? You really mustn't.'

She snatches her hand back before I can examine it, her lip trembling as though she's going to cry again.

'It's okay, it's not your fault,' I tell her gently. 'I just wish Ruby had told me, that's all. I could have gone out to the chemist's for something to stop the itching.'

That's when I notice her arm is red too, on the little patch of skin peeking out from below the short sleeve of her nightie.

'What on earth are you allergic to? How bad is this rash? Does it stretch right up your arm?' I push up her sleeve, and gasp. 'Oh, Mum!'

A few inches above the elbow is a ring of fresh bruises, dark red and already beginning to purple in places. It looks like someone has gripped her by the upper arm, perhaps to hold her still and stop her from escaping while they did something to her. But what?

I have to swallow several times before I can speak. 'Mum? Who did this to you?'

She cranes her neck to look down at her arm, and then gives a little moan, shaking her head. 'Can't, can't.'

'Can't what? Can't say or can't remember?' I realise I'm pressur-ising her, and soften my tone. 'Mum, you can tell me. It'll be our secret. Just you and me.'

'A secret.' She nods. 'Yes.'

'So who did this? Can you tell me their name? Man, woman?'

But she only shakes her head, her expression scared now. Her gaze returns to the slashed canvas on the wall.

Following her gaze, I ask carefully, 'Did the same person who hurt you do that to the painting?'

But I've lost her. She's already turning inwards again, her gaze dropping to the hand she's nursing in her lap, and all she mutters is, 'Hungry.' Her voice is so plaintive, it breaks my heart. 'No breakfast.'

'I'll get you some soup. And a cup of tea.'

She says nothing, her head still bent.

I walk round to collect her breakfast tray, and use the opportunity to study her hand at a discreet distance. Is that nasty circular blotch just above her knuckles actually another cigarette burn? That smell of cigarette smoke when I walked into the room…

Christ.

My world explodes in red behind my eyes. What the hell has been going on in this house? And how have I only just started to notice it?

Too busy worrying about my own problems, that's why I missed this. Haunted by David's suicide, flattered by Logan's sexual interest, drowning in work and staggering under the weight of expectation surrounding Calum Morgan's book.

'Mum, did someone burn your hand?'

She sits up with a start, worried again and shaking her head. 'No, no. Can't talk about it.'

'Are you hurt anywhere else?' I ask, trying not to frighten her. 'You can show me. I won't tell anyone.'

Mum hesitates, then pushes back the covers and lifts her nightie. The side of her left thigh is a mass of weals. Someone has beaten her, I realise, speechless with horror.

'Who did this to you?' I put down the breakfast tray and embrace her, tears in my eyes. 'Please tell me, Mum. I won't let them hurt you again.' I try to slow my breathing, to stay calm. 'Was it Ruby?' Her expression doesn't change. 'What about… Logan? My boyfriend. Was it him?' Still, her face reveals nothing. 'Mr Adeyemi?' I run a hand through my hair, at my wits' end. 'When did they do this to you? Today? Yesterday? And how often? Please, Mum, I need to know.'

But she refuses to speak, her lips closed stubbornly.

She's too scared.

I'm not even sure she understands why she mustn't speak, only that she has been threatened with some nameless fate if she talks and so dares not. God only knows what her torturer has said to get inside her head like this. But she's so terrified she can't even reach out to me, her child. And her memory issues have scrambled everything for her. Maybe she genuinely can't remember who did it to her. But she's afraid of what will happen if she discusses it.

This is all my fault.

I don't know what evil monster did this to my mother, or why. But I'm going to put a stop to it forever. Today.

With a supreme effort, I suppress my fury, and even try to sound cheerful when she glances up. 'Chicken soup coming right up.' I'm amazed that my voice doesn't shake; inside, I feel incoherent with wrath, my heart thumping, my body flooded with unfettered adrenalin. 'And two slices of bread and butter, cut into triangles. Just the way you like them.'

I want to kill whoever's been hurting and terrorising my mum. I want to throttle them until the light dies in their eyes. And right now I don't care if that makes me a bad person.

CHAPTER THIRTY

I make us both lunch in a kind of sick stupor, my brain working too fast for my weakened physical state, my body trembling and hungover.

My first instinct was to call the police. But now I realise what that might mean for Mum.

The police would take her away from me, for sure. They'll suspect me as well as Ruby and Logan. We're the people with the easiest access to her, so we're the ones they'll consider most likely to abuse her.

Mum won't understand it if social services take her away. To her, it will be a betrayal. As she said, this is her home.

I've already let her down as badly as it's possible to do.

I can't let her down again by bringing the authorities down on us before I can be sure who's behind this.

I know who I suspect most. But my suspicions are pointless without proof. I need to do this right, or the perpetrator may slip through my fingers before I can properly punish them. But there's a further complication. My weary body has had enough today, and my brain isn't far behind. I can't think straight, my head a mess, my emotions all over the place. And I need to think.

In desperation, I hunt through the medicine cupboard and pop a couple of out-of-date pills, which I had on prescription about eighteen months ago when I was still unable to control my anxiety in the aftermath of David's death. They're antipsychotics, basically.

The little white pills immediately start to take the edge off, and I stop shaking, able to function.

Ruby appears as I'm heading down the hall with the lunch tray. She sees two bowls of soup and smiles. 'Having lunch with your mum? That's a good idea. She's not been herself for days.'

I look at her, and wish I could be sure she's not behind my mother's bruises and cigarette burns.

'Ruby, I'm worried about her. She's got some new bruises. Her arm, her leg and the back of her hand… Well, I think that's another cigarette burn.' I focus on her face; I'm glad those pills have helped me rise above the panic raging through me. I still feel it, the stress and fear. But it's no longer clouding my responses or controlling me. 'What do you know about that?'

'Nothing,' she says.

'Nothing?'

'Like I said.' I hear a crackle in her voice, and decide not to press it. Not yet. 'But maybe you're right.'

'About what?'

'Maybe your mum didn't destroy that portrait of your family. Maybe it was Logan. He was here when it happened, after all. He could have snuck into her room while I was busy elsewhere, slashed the picture and then hit your mother.'

'Why would he do that?'

She shrugs. 'He might have hated that painting. Perhaps because your ex is in it. Some men don't like that kind of thing.'

'But why hit Mum?'

'To frighten her, of course, and stop her from telling anyone it was him. Or maybe she called out for help, and he was shutting her up.' She's frowning, her eyes narrow on my face. 'You look odd. Are you feeling okay? Have you taken something, Kate?'

'No,' I lie.

'Let me carry that tray for you,' Ruby says, and plucks it efficiently from my hands. 'I think you should sit down.'

I don't deny that; my legs are feeling a bit unsteady.

As soon as Ruby walks into the bedroom, my mother's eyes widen, watching closely as she places the soup tray at the end of the bed. When Ruby asks in a friendly tone how she's feeling, Mum says nothing but almost shrinks away from her.

My mother is afraid of her own carer.

It's the first time I've even noticed her response, and I stare, unable to believe I've missed that before today. Have those pills sharpened my senses? Or is this a new kind of delusion brought on by the drugs I've taken?

'Thanks,' I tell Ruby, 'I'll take it from here.'

She smiles and leaves the room without another word.

My mother leans back against her pillows, seeming to breathe easier with just the two of us alone together.

'Here you go, Mum.' I position a tray with legs over her lap, and then put her soup in front of her, with a spoon and plate of bread and butter. 'Chicken soup.'

'Chicken soup is very good for you,' she says sombrely.

'That's right.' I sit with my own bowl on the edge of her bed and take a few spoonfuls, though I'm not hungry. But I want to keep her company while I think what to do.

It would be easier to accept Ruby as the perpetrator than face my fear that Logan is the one who's been hurting her.

I brought him into our house, after all, without asking questions about whether he could be trusted, and it was around then that her condition seemed to deteriorate and bruises started to appear. He has a motive too, while what can Ruby gain from tormenting her own patient?

And there's still Mr Adeyemi. Perhaps I shouldn't neglect him as a possible suspect. There's that bequest he stands to get when she dies, and if she tried to resist him in some way, maybe even saying she wanted to change her will, he might have lost his temper with her.

'Giorgios is dead,' I say suddenly.

My mother looks up from her soup, which she has been stirring slowly round her bowl. 'Giorgios?'

She already doesn't remember him. That's how far she's gone. Once Giorgios was an almost daily fixture in this house, arriving armed with word puzzles and jigsaws, and she would look forward to his visits with a twinkle in her eye, always much brighter and livelier after he'd sat with her for a few hours.

Giorgios was a good carer. He deeply, genuinely *cared*. Now he's dead, and she doesn't even know who he was.

I start to cry. 'Sorry,' I mumble, and push aside my soup.

Mum watches me in mild surprise but says nothing. Then she bends to her soup again, her noisy slurping and the scrape of her spoon against the bowl the only sounds in the room. It's a messy business. She's dropping more soup than she swallows.

'Wait.' Drying my tears, I sit next to her and take the spoon. 'Let me help you.' I scoop up some of the rapidly cooling chicken soup and convey it to her mouth; she opens up meekly, like a baby waiting for apple sauce, and swallows. When the bowl is almost empty, she shakes her head and refuses to open her mouth.

'Can you manage the bread triangles on your own, Mum?'

She takes one and nibbles on it thoughtfully.

261

I take that as a yes.

Her hand still looks red and painful. 'I'll take these bowls out and fetch you something for that.'

But when I reach the kitchen, I stop dead, hearing someone walking about upstairs.

It has to be Ruby. Except that her room isn't above the kitchen. My room is, though, at least partially.

What the hell is she doing in my bedroom?

I stand listening to her footsteps moving back and forth overhead, and feel suddenly afraid. I can't explain it, but irrational or not, I have to fight the urge to grab Mum and run away. This is our house, for goodness' sake. Not hers. Yet somehow I'm beginning to feel unwelcome here, like a stranger.

My gaze lowers from the ceiling to the fridge. On the door, pinned into place by a red London bus fridge magnet, is the flier that came through the door, advertising Ruby's services as a carer.

I've left my phone on the kitchen counter. I snatch it up and hurry outside into the cold afternoon, carefully leaving the front door wide open so I can keep an ear out for Mum.

Scrolling through the numbers on my contacts list, I find Stella from my yoga class.

'Hello, stranger,' Stella says breathlessly, obviously having read my name on the screen before answering. 'Long time no see. You haven't been to yoga in ages. Hang on, I'm just getting a cake out of the oven. Timing is so crucial.' She disappears for a moment, then returns. 'Okay, I've put you on speakerphone. How are you? And your mum? Did Ruby work out for you?'

'Actually, that's why I'm calling.' I hesitate, not wanting to be too open about the reasons for my call. After all, I barely know Stella. But I will have to give her some explanation or she might become suspicious. 'A friend of mine also needs a carer, and I want to recommend Ruby. But this friend of mine says she needs more information. Like, where Ruby did her training, who else she's worked for. I don't suppose you know any of that?'

Stella sounds confused. 'Why not just ask Ruby herself?'

'Well… This friend might change her mind, and then I'd be really embarrassed. I mean, what if Ruby was offended by getting a pass?'

'Yes, I perfectly see that. It could be awkward. Hmmm.' Stella hesitates. 'Not sure if I can help, actually. I've never hired Ruby myself, and I don't know much about her. Except that she's supposed to be amazing.'

'But who told you that?'

'Erm…' Stella is silent for a moment, then says, 'I have no idea. It was just something people were saying.'

'But which people?'

'At yoga? I'm not sure. Why is it so important? Are you having a problem with her?'

'No, not at all,' I lie, closing my eyes.

'Surely she came with references?'

I open my eyes abruptly. 'Yes, she did,' I gasp, clutching the phone. 'Thank you, Stella. You're a life saver. I'll just contact the referees she gave when she first came to me.' I ring off, promising to come to yoga as soon as I possibly can, and then search for another phone number in my list. 'Hello, is that Jules?'

Jules is amazed to hear from me. Three years ago, while David was still alive, we both volunteered for a few days' work at a local charity, where Jules was the administrator. When I saw her name as one of Ruby's referees, I had instinctively felt that she could be trusted.

I walk a few steps down the gravel drive, not wishing my call to be overheard from the house, and briefly explain the situation, again

263

leaving out my real reason for calling, and ask the same questions I asked Stella.

This time, I get a different answer.

Jules sounds troubled. 'Ruby Chambers?' she repeats. 'I barely know the woman. Erm, yes, I worked with her briefly about a year ago when she came to volunteer at the charity offices. She worked the phones, dealt with the public, but then… Well, it didn't work out and we parted company.'

I'm stunned. 'Wait, you mean you didn't write a reference for her? As a carer?'

'Goodness, no.'

'But she gave me a reference from you. With your name and the charity address. You gave her a glowing reference, saying she'd worked for your family as a carer.'

'I definitely didn't write that, sorry. I'm going through a kind of menopausal fog right now,' Jules admits, with a wry laugh, 'but I think I'd remember her working for me as a carer.'

'Oh my God.'

'Are you okay, Kate?'

'I meant to ring you at the time. But I was so busy. I never chased the reference up, never bothered to check…' My mouth is dry. 'I just assumed it was genuine.'

'So this woman faked a reference to get a job with you? That's serious.' Jules draws in a breath. 'Okay, you need to send me what I'm supposed to have written, and then I think you should go to the police. Once you've sacked her, of course.'

'Yes,' I say slowly.

'You are planning to sack her, I hope? Someone who can fake a reference shouldn't be in a position of responsibility.'

'Absolutely.'

'I remember Ruby,' she says, her voice sharpening. 'She was always a bit odd. People complained about her. And she had a way of sneaking up on you and then just standing there, looking at you… It was really quite unnerving.'

I say hurriedly, 'Look, can I call you back tomorrow? Sorry, there's something I have to do.'

I end the call, and turn to see the pale oval of a face framed between partly closed curtains up in my bedroom.

It's Ruby, and she's staring straight at me, unsmiling.

CHAPTER THIRTY-ONE

Bloody woman, I think savagely.

But it could be dangerous to confront her. Knowing what I know now, she strikes me as someone deeply unstable. She's taken over the entire household, lied about her references and God knows what else, possibly tortured my mother in the most cruel and appalling way, and today she's been wandering openly about my bedroom as though she has the right to do whatever the hell she pleases.

It's obvious she isn't bothering to rein in her behaviour anymore, and I have no desire for a violent scene with her. But at least while she's in my bedroom, she's nowhere near Mum.

I stay where I am, turning my back on Ruby deliberately, and ring Mr Adeyemi's office. Jules is right. I need to call the police. But first I need some professional advice.

The deeper I go into this, the more likely it seems that Ruby is the one behind my mother's shocking bruises and burns. Which means Mr Adeyemi is not the enemy I thought he was. But I also need to be very careful what I accuse her of.

Lucy, his receptionist, is apologetic. 'Mr Adeyemi's not in the office today. Can I take a message for him?'

I'm dismayed by this news. 'When will he be back?'

'Not until tomorrow morning at the earliest. But I can make sure he gets your message as soon as he gets into the office.'

'Can't I call his mobile?"

'Oh no, I'm sorry.' Lucy sounds almost shocked. 'Mr Adeyemi hates being disturbed at home. Though if it's really urgent, I can pass you onto his junior partner.'

I hesitate, wondering if I should take the junior partner into my confidence. But my gut instinct tells me the fewer people who know about this, the better. Ruby may have faked her references but that doesn't prove she's been abusing my mother, and I need to be very careful what I say. Accusing her without any real evidence could backfire on me.

'No,' I say at last, 'I only want Mr Adeyemi.' Reluctantly, I leave my name and number with her, and ask for the solicitor to contact me first thing.

'Kate? What are you doing?'

The hairs prickle on the back of my neck at that voice. I turn, pinning a smile to my face.

Ruby is behind me. Her expression is unreadable.

'Me?' I push my phone into my jeans pocket. 'Oh, I just had to make a few calls. Work, you know.'

'Outside?' Ruby glances about the windswept garden, eyebrows raised, as though expecting to find my work colleagues lurking in the bushes, and then looks back at me. 'Isn't it a bit cold?'

'Freezing. Which is why I'm coming in now. My brain was a bit fuzzy, so I decided to get some fresh air. I took a couple of pills earlier, you see.'

'I thought you must have done.' Her smile is superior. 'I can always tell, you know. You needn't have bothered denying it before.

I wouldn't have told anyone. Besides, some people have a problem with pills, don't they?'

'Sorry?'

'Pills and alcohol.' Ruby walks back into the house, and I follow her in silence, staring at the back of her head and wishing I could understand what she's up to, and why. Her behaviour seems utterly incomprehensible to me. 'Some people need that kind of prop in order to live a full life, and others don't. It's sad, but there you go. I'm not judging.'

I'm incredulous.

Is she suggesting I'm some kind of addict? Just because I had a few drinks last night, and then popped a couple of pills to take my mood down a notch or two today?

That hardly makes me a druggie...

All the same, I decide it's better not to contradict her. There's no point causing a confrontation. Though I suddenly wish I'd taken Jules's advice and called the police straightaway. There's something about her that disturbs me. She's not behaving differently, exactly. It's more that I'm seeing her behaviour differently.

I still feel on fairly steady ground, however, and can hold off for a short while at least. I wanted to consult Mr Adeyemi, to be sure I don't need to give her any notice, but I can do that tomorrow, now that I'm more certain he wasn't the one who hurt my mother.

My path ahead seems clear.

I can sack Ruby today, and that should be that. She's unlikely to make a fuss, not when she could go to prison for what she's done. What I want to avoid, above all things, is for my mother to be taken away from me, to be forced to live in a residential home for her own safety. Obviously, if her bruises or burns are discovered before they have a chance to fade, I'll have to take my suspicions to the police and hope their investigation exonerates me. But if I can possibly save my mother the trauma, it'll be worth it.

I ignore the little voice in my head that tells me I'm a coward, and that by not calling the police, I'm secretly saving myself from the horror of falling under suspicion. Which is ridiculous. Of course I don't want to be accused of torturing my mother. Who would? It's nothing to do with cowardice or being self-serving.

But that little voice won't shut up.

The house feels cold and oddly empty. I follow Ruby into the living room and stand in front of the mantelpiece, exactly where I stood when PC Plimley was here. It's hard not to recall the awful news she brought, that lovely, smiling Giorgios is dead, that his body was discovered in local woodlands, as well as what she didn't need to say, which is the unavoidable truth that he must have been murdered…

Ruby faces me across the chilly room, her arms folded across her chest. Her eyes are over-bright, her smile rather fixed. 'Do you have something to say to me, Kate?'

I'm taken aback. 'Sorry?'

'Oh, didn't I tell you? I have a psychic streak. I can tell what people are going to say before they say it. It used to drive my mother bonkers.' Ruby waits, looking at me expectantly. 'Go on, then. Spit it out.'

I lick dry lips, suddenly not sure that sacking her is the right course of action. If she can happily attack my mother, she could attack me too. I'm not a vulnerable dementia patient, it's true. But I am considerably shorter and lighter than her.

Carefully, trying not to make it obvious, I consider what's to hand that I could use as a weapon if she gets violent.

There's a tall brass candlestick that always sits on the tiled hearth behind me. I can't actually see it without turning my head, but I know it must be there. That might hold her off for a couple of minutes.

269

'You're right, of course. There is something I want to tell you, Ruby.' I can't seem to find the right words, more than a little freaked out by the direct way she's looking at me, her gaze never moving from my face. 'It's about my mother. And her care.'

'Decided to let me go, have you?'

Now I'm genuinely unnerved. Maybe she really is a mind reader. 'What… What makes you say that?'

'Just a hunch.'

I search her face for signs of emotion, but there are none. Ruby is neither flushed nor pale. Her gaze is steady, and so is her voice. To a casual observer, she would appear calm and collected. Confident, even.

I'm stunned, and a little shocked too.

Ruby must know that I've found her out. That I've guessed it's her who's been terrorising my mother, not Logan, and definitely not Mr Adeyemi. Yet she doesn't even have the grace to look guilty. And I'm pretty sure now, looking into her eyes, that it's not because she's innocent.

'The thing is,' I stammer, 'I'm worried about my mother.'

'I know you are. That's why you need a carer.'

'Maybe. But what I don't need is someone who *doesn't* care.' There; it's said, it's out. No taking it back now. 'What I don't need is someone who chooses to hurt and humiliate instead. To make up cruel stories and… and drive people away from this house.'

'Cruel stories?' Ruby tuts and shakes her head. 'Oh dear. Remind me, love. How many of those pills did you swallow again?'

'You're fired.'

'I see.' Ruby's chest heaves slightly as she takes a deep breath. Her smile is arctic, but it's still there. 'I suppose that means you want me to leave.'

'Yes.'

'When, exactly?'

'Now would be good.'

'I'll have to pack up all my things. It could take a while.'

'I'll wait.'

Ruby's eyebrows flicker. Her mouth opens and closes in silence. I see her gaze stray around the room, as though looking for something.

'You're making a mistake, Kate,' she says softly.

'I don't think so.'

'Who was on the phone to you outside? Your boss? Your boyfriend?'

'That's none of your business.'

'Whoever it was has filled your head with a load of nonsense.' She takes a step closer, looking down at me. 'You're going to regret this.'

'Is that so?'

'Mothers like yours don't look after themselves. Celeste will have to go into a home now, for sure. Have you considered that?' She stares at me accusingly. 'Did you even bother to ask your mum what she thinks about this? Have you consulted her feelings? Or doesn't the patient get a vote?'

'I've said all I intend to say.'

'And my salary? You haven't given me proper notice. Do I at least get severance pay?'

'You'll get what you're owed to date and nothing more. I'll make sure it's in your bank account by the end of the week. Unless you'd prefer to take me to court?' When she says nothing, I allow myself to smile. 'I didn't think so.'

Ruby continues to stare at me for a few more thoroughly alarming seconds, and then stalks out of the room, leaving the door wide open.

'Better get comfortable,' she throws back over her shoulder. 'It may take me several hours to pack, and to say my goodbyes to Celeste.'

I bite back the urge to tell her in no uncertain terms that she's not going anywhere near my mother again. What would that achieve

271

except to antagonise her further and risk making her resist leaving? Ruby can say goodbye to my mother if she insists, but she'll do it with me in the room. There's no way I would leave the two of them alone together ever again. Not even for a second.

I listen to her heavy tread on the stairs, followed by the sound of her bedroom door closing. She doesn't slam the door, but she might as well have done; the click is so wounded and disdainful.

I sink into the armchair and bend over to catch my breath, gulping at the air as though I've been running.

'Christ,' I mutter, 'that was hard. That was *really* hard.'

And by hard, I mean terrifying, of course. But I'm not ready to admit, even to myself, how much Ruby is scaring me. I've never fired anyone before; that's why my stomach's churning and my head's in a vice, I decide.

I wonder if Mark felt like this when he fired me. Somehow, I doubt it. But it would be some consolation if he'd felt even a tenth of the angst and panic that I'm feeling now.

When I get up, my phone falls out of my pocket. Crouching to retrieve it, I spot a pair of shoes tucked under Mum's armchair, half-hidden from sight by the fringed red blanket that habitually covers the seat, protecting the bottom cushion against stains.

They're black running shoes, slightly mud-splashed, and they belong to Logan. I think he only wore them once while living here, after being inspired to take an early morning run. He must have taken them off in here afterwards, and then the shoes got knocked out of the way, perhaps while Ruby was vacuuming.

'Damn.' I reach under the armchair and drag the shoes out.

Straightening, I look at them guiltily. Ruby hasn't confessed. Why would she? But I'm convinced it was her who hurt Mum. Which means Logan wasn't to blame for any of it. Yet I punished him anyway.

272

And now he's gone.

Carefully, I place the running shoes on the table, and then find Logan's number on my mobile.

He answers after about seven rings, which feels like an eternity. I guess he was trying to decide whether to terminate the call or agree to speak to me. Last time I saw Logan, he was in a towering rage, and small wonder. His girlfriend had just falsely accused him of assaulting her mother. He must have felt so angry and frustrated, yet I simply pushed him away and refused to listen to his protests.

I badly need to apologise. And maybe buy him dinner. Though he'll probably tell me to get lost.

'Hello?' To my surprise, he doesn't sound angry anymore. Instead, he sounds quiet and unsure of himself. 'Kate?'

'Hi.' The word doesn't come out right. I clear my throat and try again. 'Yes, hi. I have your shoes here. Your black trainers?'

There's a short silence. 'Are you holding them ransom?'

I laugh. 'I thought maybe I should drop them round at your place. Or you could come here. Whenever' s convenient.'

Another short silence, during which I can hear the clock ticking on the mantelpiece.

'I thought I was banned from the house.'

'Hardly.' I frown. 'You came round yesterday, didn't you? To pick up some things.'

'No.' He sounds puzzled. 'I haven't been to your house since… since we argued.'

I'm stunned. 'I don't understand. Are you sure? Ruby told me you were here. Yesterday afternoon.'

'Then Ruby lied.'

I close my eyes. 'That's just bizarre. Why on earth would she bother lying about something like that?'

'I've no idea. Perhaps you should ask her yourself?'

He sounds bitter, the uncertainty gone.

'Well, never mind.' I try for a lighter note, pushing aside the vexed question of Ruby's behaviour for the moment. Maybe she lied, maybe she didn't. Right now, I need to mend some bridges. 'For what it's worth, I'm sorry.'

'Sorry about what? Having my trainers?'

'I'm sorry about the argument. Those awful things I said. I was going out of my mind. But I know now that it wasn't you who did all that stuff to my mum.' I lower my voice, very aware of the curious stillness in the house. It feels almost as though the walls themselves are listening to me. 'I think it was Ruby.'

'Are you serious? Her *carer*?'

'I know, talk about ironic.' I run a hand through my messy hair, still feeling shaky and hungover; I need to down a few jugs of water and rest for an hour. But I doubt I'll get the chance. Not now I've just sent Ruby packing. 'Instead of looking after her, it seems Mum's carer has been beating her up. And I had no idea. Which makes me look pretty unobservant. Not to mention irresponsible.' Tears well up in my eyes, and I rub them away impatiently. 'Look, I'm sorry for what I said to you. I truly am. The way I behaved was unforgivable. But if there's any way I can make it up to you…'

'Forget it,' he says gruffly.

I'm not sure how to take that. Does Logan mean I don't need to apologise, he's already okay about it? Or that I can forget apologising because he's planning never to speak to me again?

'Okay. And… the trainers?'

'I'll come over and pick them up. I can't tonight, unfortunately. I'm meeting someone for dinner who might be able to offer me some work.' He pauses. 'How about tomorrow?'

'Evening? That sounds good.'

Then I can cook us all some food, try to make amends.

'I'd prefer morning.'

'Oh, right.'

I stare out at the gloomy afternoon; today's wintry attempt at daylight is already dying. Dusk will fall soon, and with it the temperature. It felt cold enough to snow when I was in town last night. Maybe the sky will finally do what it's been threatening for days, and scatter a shower of icy white flakes across Guildford and the Home Counties.

Mum will be delighted if the weather turns that cold, of course. She's always taken a childlike delight in snow, loving our family ski trips to France and Switzerland, and clapping her hands at the smallest hint of white flakes on the wind here in the UK. All snow means to me is a need for an extra scarf and woollen gloves; I suppose I lack her imagination.

'Kate?'

I realise I've been drifting, staring out at nothing. Dark shadows sliding along the lawn's far edge. Grey skies and the encroaching dusk.

'Sorry, what were you saying? Come over anytime tomorrow, Logan. I don't think I'll be going anywhere all day.'

'What about work?'

I laugh humourlessly. 'Mark fired me.'

'Why, for God's sake?'

'You didn't see my tweet?'

'I'm not online much at the moment. Data costs.'

'Of course.' My mouth twists in a crooked smile. 'Someone hacked my Twitter account and posted something libellous about Calum Morgan. I actually thought it was you.'

'Me?' His voice is blank.

'I know it wasn't, please don't worry. I told you, my head is a mess.'

I turn away from the window, feeling at my lowest ebb. Why am I still on the phone to him? Logan is probably a lost cause after the way I treated him. 'Look, just come round when you like. I'll be in.'

After he hangs up, I wander into the hallway and peer up the stairs. Everything is quiet. Suspiciously so.

As far as I know, Ruby hasn't come downstairs yet. The odd thing is, I can't hear her moving about anymore. There ought to be some noise, surely? She was supposed to be packing. I should be hearing footsteps, creaking floorboards, drawers opening and closing…

Instead, there's just this eerie silence.

I find a tube of antiseptic cream and the first aid kit, and take them through to Mum's bedroom, belatedly remembering her hurt hand.

Every time I think of those shocking bruises on her arm and leg, I want to scream. I want to call the police and have them arrest Ruby for assault. If I don't, she could do all this again to some other unsuspecting patient. In fact, I even stop beside the landline on my way along the hall, and pick up the handset, meaning to dial 999. Then I put it down again, groaning with frustration.

I keep imagining Mum's confusion when the police question her about what happened, plus the very real possibility that she'll be forced to live elsewhere while the authorities investigate, just in case they decide I may be a threat to her well-being.

Ruby strikes me as the sort of person who would lie quite boldly and in a bare-faced way to the police, pretending I'm the one who's hurt Mum. And the only other witness – my mother – would be unable to defend me or point to the real perpetrator.

It would be too horrible.

But perhaps once she's gone, and I've had a chance to gather together as much evidence as I have, I can call the police at that stage. With a solicitor in tow.

That seems like the wisest course of action.

When I open the door, Mum is standing on an old wooden stool in her nightie, struggling to take Ciaran's canvas down off the wall, and she's wobbling dangerously…

'Oh my God!'

I rush to support her before she can topple off the stool. 'Mum, what on earth do you think you're doing?'

She looks down at me, her expression stubborn and impatient. 'I'm taking down the painting. It needs to be fixed.'

'Let me help you down; it's not safe.'

'But the painting—'

'I'll take it off the wall. It's too heavy for you.' I help her down, taking my time, and embrace her thankfully once she's safely on the ground again. 'Mum, you scare me so much sometimes.' She seems to find this amusing, giving a little chuckle. While she watches, I climb onto the stool and take down the ruined canvas for her. It's heavy even for me, thanks to its thick white wood frame. 'Where do you want it?'

She looks about the room vaguely and then points to a space under the window. 'Over there.'

Leaning the canvas against the wall, I crouch to examine its long rips and shreds. David's perfect face looms out at me from amidst the devastation. He was such an attractive man. I brush his cheek with the back of my fingers, part of me still aching to know why he killed himself.

'Careful,' my mother says. 'Your brother painted that.'

'I know.' I straighten and look round at her curiously. She seems more lucid than she has been lately. 'Mum, do you know how the painting got like this?'

'Scissors,' she says helpfully.

'Did you do it?'

277

My mother's outrage is palpable. 'Me?'

'Sorry, I had to ask.' I sit her down on the edge of the bed and smooth cream over the back of her hand. Her skin looks less raw now, thankfully. 'Was it Ruby?'

At that name, her face becomes dark and shuttered. 'Don't know,' she mutters, turning her face away. 'Don't ask, don't know.'

'Okay.' I dress her hand with a clean bandage, winding it round and round while she sits in silence, chewing on her lower lip. 'Mum, there's something I need to tell you.'

She raises her gaze to mine dubiously.

'I've told Ruby to go,' I say softly. 'I've fired her. She's gone up to pack her bags. So you don't need to worry about her anymore.'

To my surprise, she looks horrified. 'Ruby?'

'I've asked her to leave.'

'You can't.' Her eyes widen, and she looks over her shoulder at the door, as though expecting Ruby to burst in at any moment and menace us. 'She'll be angry.'

'I don't care.'

Mum snatches her hand back before I've properly finished securing her bandage, and rocks back and forth, moaning under her breath.

'Oh dear, oh dear. She's going to be so angry.'

'Mum, it's fine.' I shake my head incredulously. 'There's nothing Ruby can do. I'll get another carer. In due time. For now, I'll probably look after you myself.'

She looks aghast. 'You?'

'I'm not completely incompetent. Besides, it looks like I'm back to being unemployed. So we won't be able to afford a full-time carer for a while. I might be able to arrange for a professional to come in once or twice a month so I get a few hours' respite. But the rest of your care will be up to me.' Taking back her hand, I secure the white

278

crepe bandage, making sure it isn't going to come unravelled. My smile is grim. 'How hard can it be?'

The echoing chime of the doorbell makes us both stop and stare at each other in astonishment.

'Who's that?' Mum demands at once, as though I'm psychic.

'I'll go and find out. You get back into bed.' She's looking flushed, and I lay a hand against her forehead, which feels over-warm. 'I don't think you're well.'

'Call the doctor,' she suggests helpfully.

'Maybe I will.'

I head out into the hall to find Ruby standing in the gloom at the bottom of the stairs. To my surprise, she's still wearing her slippers and housecoat, and I see no sign of any luggage.

'Do you need a hand bringing your bags down?' I ask her, trying to be polite and professional about the situation.

She doesn't speak.

There's something oddly menacing about her silence. My hands clench into fists as I come level with the woman, my fingernails digging into my palms. She seemed to accept her sacking earlier without too much heat. I hope to God she hasn't changed her mind and is now planning on being difficult.

The doorbell chimes again.

Ruby says, 'I think you'd better get that.'

I open the front door, and recoil in horror, my heart thumping.

It's Calum Morgan.

He looks dishevelled, his shirt not quite tucked into his jeans, his hair untidy, and there's a hard colour in his cheeks, as though he's been running.

'Well, well,' he says breathlessly, leaning on the door frame. 'If it isn't my editor, Kate Kinley. Or should I say, my *former* editor?'

'Calum?' I swallow. 'What are you doing here? How did you find out where I live?' A rush of hot temper flares in me. 'Did Mark tell you?'

'I'd love to say yes. But your boss refused to give me that information. God knows why. Perhaps he thought I'd want to strangle you and piss on your corpse if I ever saw you again.'

I take an instinctive step back, and then realise my mistake when he tries to barge through the door, putting his shoulder to it.

Panicked, I lean on the door too, putting my own weight against it. Given our relative statures, though, it's not much of a contest and I'm not sure how long I can hold him off.

'Get off my property before I call the police,' I snap, trying and failing to close the door on him. Belatedly, I realise that Calum's mud-speckled ankle boot has become trapped in the door. 'Would you move your foot, please?'

He ignores me, glaring through the narrow gap created by his boot. 'It wasn't hard to find out where you lived, Kate. A few quid on a specialist search brought up your address within minutes. So I thought I'd come round and ask what the hell you thought you were doing, posting that bloody tweet about me?' He bangs on the door and it shudders, but I stubbornly keep my shoulder to it. 'How dare you call me a narcissist? I've worked hard for my success. Don't you know who I am? Do you even understand how many people read my books every year? How many people admire me and find their lives improved by what I've written? I'm a famous, bestselling author. I sold over a million copies of *Get Happy* in the US, did you know that? And they love me in Asia too. They've given me awards. Whereas you…' He looks me up and down in a scathing manner. 'You're nothing, Kate. You're less than nothing. You're just another tiny cog in an increasingly obsolescent machine.'

Suddenly, Ruby elbows me aside and opens the door. 'Listen, love' she tells Calum roughly. 'I don't know who you are and I don't much care. What I do know is that you're trespassing. So unless you want a ride in a police van, I suggest you move your foot and put all this down in a letter instead. How's that?'

Calum glares at me over her shoulder. 'Who the hell is this?'

'I'm her mum's carer,' Ruby tells him in icy tones. 'Now move your foot before I break it.'

He looks taken aback, but grudgingly moves the foot that was stopping the door from closing. 'This isn't over.'

'Yes, it is.' Ruby shuts the door and turns to me. 'Was that the bloke you tweeted about?'

'Yes,' I agree shakily, not sure which is worse, facing down Calum's wrath or being alone again with Ruby.

She makes a contemptuous noise and heads back to the kitchen. 'You don't look too good. Why don't you go and lie down? I'll wait near the door, make sure he doesn't come back. And I imagine your mum could do with a cuppa about now.'

I follow, baffled to see her calmly filling the kettle and putting it back on like nothing's happened.

'Ruby, I don't want to be rude. But I fired you less than an hour ago. Remember?'

'Not very grateful, are you?'

'I beg your pardon?'

Ruby jerks a thumb over her shoulder down the hall. 'I could have left you to deal with that idiot on your own. But I didn't.'

I feel like I'm going mad.

'Thank you for getting rid of Calum. I can't believe he had the nerve to come to my house, especially threatening to strangle me. The man's deranged. But this…' I take a deep breath and nod to the kettle. 'It's not appropriate. I really think it would be better if you just go.'

'Oh, Kate.' She turns and shakes her head, smiling faintly as though I've said something funny. 'I'm not leaving.'

'Sorry?'

'I live here. I'm your mum's carer. This is where I belong. You heard me say so to that lunatic on the doorstep just now, and you didn't contradict me.' Ruby searches my face. 'Did you?'

'Well, no,' I admit slowly.

'So there you go.'

'I wasn't going to contradict you in front of him, obviously. You were doing too good a job of getting rid of him. But you must see how mad this is.'

Her eyelids flicker. 'What did you say?'

'All this, you making tea and telling me to lie down. It's mad. You no longer work here, Ruby.' I decide to be firm with her, just as she was firm with Calum. 'I'd like you to leave.'

'I am *not* mad,' she says with careful emphasis.

I see that I've offended her. 'It was just a figure of speech. I meant… You can't stay here.'

'I can hardly leave you to look after your mother alone.'

'We'll be fine.'

She raises her eyebrows. 'I don't agree.'

'This isn't a debate. You work for me. Or rather, you did.' I am beginning to wonder if I was right first time and she really is mad. That would certainly explain a few things. 'I've terminated your employment. This is no longer your home, and whether you agree or not is neither here nor there. So you need to take your bags, and leave.'

'And did you do what I asked and consult your mother?' she persists, her voice rising. 'Because I feel Celeste ought to be given a say in this.'

'I told her, yes.'

'That's not the same thing. How can I be sure this is what she wants? For all I know you may have lied to her about me.'

'Lied?' I stare at her. 'You've beaten her. You've burnt her with a cigarette. God knows what else you've done to torture her, but she's bloody terrified of you.'

'If that's true, then why aren't the police here? If I'm such a monster, why haven't you reported me yet?'

I glare at her, unable to answer that without admitting my weakness.

I don't have any actual proof that she did any of it. It's all circumstantial. And I'm afraid the police may suspect me instead. Especially if Ruby has anything to do with it.

She was very quick to point me towards Mum's solicitor as a possible culprit for those bruises on her arm. I believed her completely.

What might she say to the police in order to avoid arrest for assault?

Perhaps once I've seen Mr Adeyemi tomorrow, and apologised for having suspected him, he'll advise me on how to proceed.

Ruby has folded her arms and is looking stubborn. 'I'm not going anywhere until I've heard your mother say I need to go.'

'Fine. You want to know if my mother's happy that I fired you?' I leave the kitchen and stride impatiently along the hall. 'Let's ask her, shall we?'

I'm just turning the handle to Mum's bedroom when I feel a sudden weight on the back of my head. It feels like a heavy black curtain tumbling down over me.

My legs crumple and I fall forwards, my last thought one of bewilderment.

CHAPTER THIRTY-TWO

I wake to a cold trickle of water down my face, and groan.

God, my head hurts.

My eyes open on a dimly lit room. It's my mother's bedroom, and I'm slumped on the floor near the window, my back against the metal radiator, which is thankfully cold or I'd have been scalded. My hands are drawn up to one side, supported by something. There's a vague pain in my wrists, which I can't immediately pinpoint.

Mum's face swims into focus a few feet away. She's looking frightened, still in her nightie, wringing her hands unhappily.

'Mum?' I stir, and then freeze instantly into immobility, closing my eyes again as a terrific pain splits my head. It feels like I've fallen downstairs and banged my head on every step on the way down. 'What… what happened?'

There's something huge and oblong lying on the carpet a few feet away. I squint at its white frame first, then the ragged edges of canvas.

Ciaran's family portrait.

'Kate,' someone says softly. 'Wakey-wakey!'

Another trickle of water lands again, this time near my ear. It's coming from above me.

Baffled, I peer upwards.

Ruby is standing above me, dripping cloudy water onto my hair and face from a small glass vase. The flowers lie discarded on the carpet a few feet away.

'Ruby?' My voice is hoarse.

She smiles, and pours a little more over me, several water drops landing in my eye and rolling down my cheek like tears.

'Good,' she says, and puts the vase down, 'you're conscious at last. I was beginning to think I'd have to stab you in the eye or something to get you to wake up. But this is much easier. And less messy.' The smile doesn't quite reach her eyes. 'I hate mess, don't you?'

'What? Are you crazy?' As I jerk upright, I realise my wrists have been bound together and fastened to the radiator. I tug but can't get them free. The white wire wrapped about my wrists simply bites deeper into my flesh. It looks like a charging cable, like the one I use for my mobile phone. 'Did you do this? What the hell is wrong with you?' I tug harder, but it's futile. 'Ruby, let me go at once. How dare you?'

'How dare I?' she repeats, her smile vanishing. 'How dare I? How dare *you* ask such a question of me?' She thumps herself on the chest with a clenched fist. 'Of *me*!'

'Please don't, darling,' Mum whimpers, shaking her head at me in warning. 'Don't make her angry.'

'It's a bit too late for that. Two years too late, in fact. I've been angry a bloody long time.' Ruby takes a deep breath, as though trying to control her temper. Then she pulls the wooden stool forward and sits on it, almost level with me. 'Look at your face. You don't have a clue what I'm talking about, do you?'

I shake my head, watching her warily.

'Poor little rich girl. Daddy's dead and Mummy's lost her marbles. What a sad life you must lead. Apart from the obvious perks, of

285

course. This house, for instance. Your high-powered job in publishing. Oh, except that didn't quite work out, did it? Tsk, such a shame you were fired. And all over a silly little tweet.' Ruby reaches to move a few strands of damp hair out of my eyes, and I flinch backwards instinctively, banging my head on the radiator. 'Now, love, don't hurt yourself. There'll be plenty of time for that later.'

'What do you want?'

Ruby's eyes narrow on my face. 'That's simple. I want what you can't give me,' she whispers, and points towards the ruined canvas. 'I want that.'

'My brother's painting?' I'm confused.

She slaps me, and my head snaps back under the force of the blow.

'No, stupid bitch. I mean him.' Ruby points again, her hand shaking. 'My beautiful David. The man you treated like shit. The man you murdered.'

'I don't understand.'

She slaps me again, and my head cracks against the metal radiator. My mother moans and rocks back and forth, sitting in a huddle on the end of her bed, watching us.

'You can't imagine what it was like,' Ruby says thickly, leaning so close that our faces are almost touching. I can see spittle on her lips and something like fanaticism in her eyes. 'I loved him so deeply. David meant everything to me. Everything.'

'I... I didn't even know you knew him.'

'Why would you?' She makes a dismissive gesture. 'He barely ever spoke to me, not much more than hello and goodbye. Once we talked about the weather, and another time the football results. I was just the woman who looked after his grandad while the poor old sod was dying. No, David never even looked twice. That didn't matter though. Not to me.' She shakes her head, and a single tear trickles

286

down her cheek. 'I worshipped him. I would have jumped in front of a train for that man.'

I don't know what to say. But she's clearly waiting for a response. 'I see. You… knew David, then.'

'I just said so, didn't I?' she snaps.

'Sorry. But why do you say I killed him? I swear, I didn't lay a finger on him.' I swallow, and then whisper, 'David killed himself.'

This time I'm ready for the slap, but it still knocks me back into the metal radiator. Hard too. There's a sickening crunch, and I gasp with pain.

'Please,' I say, 'I'm sorry. I didn't mean—'

'Yes, you did.' She strikes me again, and then again. 'David was in love with you. The same way I was in love with him. And you threw him away, like he meant nothing.'

'He was depressed.'

'Because of the way you treated him.'

'No, no…' My vision is blurred. 'That's not true. That's not what happened.'

'Liar!' She hits me again, her voice rising hysterically. 'You lied to him, and now you're lying to me. I saw his face after his grandad died. David was distraught. He couldn't handle the grief. But you… You just wanted to go out partying and having fun. You didn't care how he was feeling. You refused to listen, because you didn't want to know.'

'I did listen. I did.'

She almost screams at me, 'You abandoned him when he needed you most. You walked away. And he died.'

Something rolls thickly and heavily down from my temple. It drips into my eye, half-blinding me, and I try to blink it away.

Blood?

'You can't know what really happened,' I begin raggedly, though I

287

know she's probably going to punish me again for not agreeing with her. 'You weren't there. You said it yourself, he barely spoke to you.'

'I broke into his flat after he died. I read his diaries. I know what David wrote about you, what he thought…' She breaks off, sobbing.

'It wasn't my fault.'

'Yes, it was. You're a stone-cold bitch. You made David do it. You practically drove him to do it.'

The words strike a chord in me.

YOU'RE SUCH A STONE-COLD BITCH. NO WONDER I KILLED MYSELF.

'You wrote those letters,' I say slowly. 'Those horrible, hateful letters. You sent them to me. At work. And here…' I don't understand. 'Why?'

'They weren't my words. They were David's.'

I shake my head. 'No, he… he didn't write anything like that in the note he left behind. He said he was depressed and couldn't take it anymore.'

Guilt stirs in me though; David did write something in his suicide note about how he wished he could have confided in me. But everyone had reassured me it was just his depression talking.

'You're so full of yourself.' She almost spits in my face. 'He was a wonderful man. Of course he didn't tell you how he really felt. He saved that for his diaries. You want to see what he wrote about you?' She reaches behind herself, and drags her handbag between us. Inside, I can see several small black notebooks. She pulls one out and flips it open to a page marked with a red sticky flag, and then reads aloud, '*My life is over. I tried telling Kate tonight how dead I feel inside since Grandad's death. But she didn't listen. She never listens. My friends call her a stone-cold bitch. But I don't want to believe that.*' There are tears in her eyes. 'You hear that? He was still defending you to the end. But he knew. Deep down inside, he knew how cold you are, Kate. Or

288

he would never have written it in his diary. He killed himself three days after writing that.'

'I didn't know,' I stammer. 'I don't remember him trying to tell me that. But I was dealing with my own grief. My dad, my brother…'

'Bullshit.'

'No, please. Ask Mum, ask anyone. I was on meds for several years.'

'Ask your mum? I might as well ask the wall. Have you looked at her lately?' She jerks her head at my mother, who has buried her face in her hands, still perched on the end of the bed. 'Or were you too busy thinking about your new boyfriend? Lovely Logan. What a pity that didn't work out. Still, he's better off without you. I tried warning him, you know. Sent him a note, saying you were a murderer.' Ruby pulls a face, pushing the creased, leather-bound diary back into her bag. 'But he's blinded by your posh roots and your big house and your money, just like David was.'

'David didn't care about any of that.'

'No, maybe not. He was a good man. And he died because of that.' Her eyes pierce me. 'Because of *you*.'

I DIED BECAUSE OF YOU, KATE. NOW IT'S YOUR TURN.

That's what she wrote in one of her poison pen letters.

She's planning to kill me, I realise. Beyond her, I catch a glimpse of my mother peeking, ashen-faced, through her fingers, and it hits me. Ruby's going to kill me, and then Mum too. She couldn't leave Mum alive. It would be too risky.

And then I realise something else too.

'And what about Giorgios?' I whisper. 'What did he do to you? Or was he somehow to blame for David's death too?'

Ruby pulls back, and I see a change there. A flash of genuine contrition, perhaps.

'I didn't mean to hurt Giorgios. But he didn't know what was good for him.'

'So you murdered him.'

'It wasn't like that. I followed him home to find out where he lived and watched the house. Then I pretended to bump into him at the supermarket. I said I recognised him from way back. After that, it was easy, making friends with him, going out for drinks.'

'Poor Giorgios,' I say bitterly. 'And you call *me* a murderer!'

'It was done for a good cause. For justice. To even the scales.' Ruby glares at me. 'Besides, I tried to persuade him to stop working for you first. Made up a sob story about having been in love with your brother, and how I wanted to look after his mum now she had dementia.' Ruby bares her teeth. 'Only Giorgios didn't believe me. He kept asking questions. *Why had Celeste never mentioned me before? How long had I been seeing Ciaran? Why didn't I just ask to visit occasionally?* He liked your mum; he didn't want to stop working for you.' She hisses between her teeth, her eyes narrowed as though at a painful memory. 'I even offered him money. But that just made him more suspicious.'

I can see how conflicted she is over Giorgios's death, and press on that sore spot, trying to weaken her.

'And I suppose his death was an accident, was it?'

'I didn't plan it, if that's what you mean. We were in his flat. I'd gone round there after the pub to ask one more time if he'd reconsider. And when he said no, and started talking about mentioning the whole thing to you and Celeste…' Ruby shakes her head. 'Well, I couldn't allow that. There was a knife on the bread board. One of those long ones with a serrated edge. He turned away to pick up the phone, and I just…'

She glances round at my mother, who's crying.

'I didn't want to,' Ruby insists angrily. 'Giorgios forced me to do it. I stabbed him in the back, and then kept on stabbing until he stopped moving. There was so much blood. It took me hours to clean the place, make it look like nothing had happened. I even put a note under his neighbour's door, to say he was going on holiday so nobody would get suspicious when he wasn't around. Then I had to drag his body out to my car in the middle of the night. There's an alleyway behind the back gardens there. It took forever. But once it was done, I drove out of town for a few miles and dumped his body in the woods. Tried to cover it with branches as best I could. Drove back, cleaned out the car... I was exhausted.' She closes her eyes briefly. 'But it was worth it, to get this position, to get into this house. You were so keen to have me too, especially after I came round a few times to put the wind up you... watching you from behind the trees, breaking that security light, making you feel unsafe here alone.'

'You're sick,' I whisper, only now realising how cleverly she's been playing us from the start.

'No, actually, I'm highly practical. Not like you.' She looks around at the untidy bedroom, her expression disdainful. 'I'm good at cleaning up messes and sorting things out. Being organised is my superpower.' Her smile is eerie. 'David used to say that sometimes. I kept his gran-dad's place so tidy, you see. Really looked after the old boy.'

'I'm sure David appreciated you,' I say carefully. 'Maybe even felt something for you. Even if he didn't say so to your face.'

'Don't lie to me. I'm not a fool. David wasn't interested in me. And I didn't need him to be. This isn't about him. This is about natural justice. You killed my David. You killed the best person I knew. And for that, you have to die.'

I swallow. 'And my mum? What's she done to deserve this?'

'Nothing,' Ruby says, lifting a shoulder in disinterest. 'Unless you count her role in bringing up a bitch like you, that is. I mean, your kind of personality doesn't come from nowhere. Who's to blame for Kate Kinley if it isn't her own mum and dad? Your dad's already dead and buried. And so's your brother. But I can make your mum pay for creating you.' She leans forward. 'And I can make you pay for killing the love of my life.'

I stare, horrified. 'Is that why you burnt her? And battered her? Because she's my mother?'

'Rich people are easy to hate.'

'We're not rich. Maybe once, but… we're not rich now.'

'You look a lot richer than me, love. I've got nothing. Less than nothing. And I didn't mind that, once upon a time. Back when David was alive. It made me happy, just seeing him around the place. I made little notes for him. Nothing important. Just to let him know how his grandad was getting on. But I know David appreciated the gesture. The next time he came around, he'd say, "Thank you for the note, Ruby," and smile at me… He had such a lovely smile.' Her voice throbs with poignancy. 'I miss it.'

Out in the hallway, the telephone begins to ring.

She turns her head, listening.

'That'll be for you,' Ruby says, and doesn't move.

'I told Logan to come over tonight,' I lie, hoping to frighten her into leaving.

'No, you didn't. I was listening.'

'Then you misheard. Because I definitely told him to—'

'I was listening on the other handset,' she says calmly. 'You didn't say anything of the kind. Logan's coming round tomorrow. By which time, you'll be dead.'

I slump against the radiator, defeated. I've tried to talk my way out of this, but she has an answer for everything. I even tried to bluff but she saw straight through it. Meanwhile, I feel sick and my head is throbbing. My arms ache from being constantly upraised; I try to ease them by rolling my shoulders in their sockets, but it doesn't improve matters. Though I suppose I won't feel them anymore once I'm dead.

'You shouldn't have been so hard on Logan, you know,' she adds, smirking a little when I look up. 'He's really quite nice. A pity he had to fall for someone like you. But I expect he'll get over his disappointment soon enough. Once he sees what you're really like, like the rest of the world already has.'

I stare at her through narrowed eyes. 'Was it you who sent that tweet about Calum Morgan?'

'Didn't see that one coming, did you? You really shouldn't leave your password in your bedroom where anyone can see it. Very careless.'

'Anyone who happens to be in my bedroom,' I point out.

'I don't know why you're so upset. It sounds to me like he deserved it.'

'Maybe,' I say grudgingly. 'Though it cost me my job.'

'I bet your boss went spare.'

'Mark wasn't happy.'

She laughs, seeming to take pleasure in this thought. 'Well, at least you went to that bloody festival thing, even with the car off the road. He should be grateful.'

I catch something in her voice. A note of self-congratulatory triumph. 'You did something to my car too, didn't you? To stop it working.'

'I couldn't risk you going to the police.' She shrugs. 'Easy enough to disconnect the battery. You looked under the bonnet but didn't even notice. Not very good with cars, are you?'

'You seem to have thought of everything. So, are you going to stab me too?' I ask abruptly, hoping to catch her off-guard. 'Like you did Giorgios?'

Ruby licks her lips, and then shakes her head after a moment's hesitation. 'Too messy.'

I watch her, hopeful that she'll change her mind about killing me. She seems less intense than before; maybe she's talked all the hatred out and I can persuade her to let us go.

'To be honest, I thought about torching this place. Get rid of you and your mum at the same time. People would think you did it to yourself, because of that tweet and losing your job, all the public humiliation.' Her smile is chilling. 'I even bought a can of petrol to set the fire. It's in the back of my car.'

My mother is crawling slowly up the bed towards the pillows. She looks beyond exhaustion, poor thing.

'Please, don't do this,' I beg her. 'Let my mum go, at least. Look at her. She's terrified.'

'She made you who you are,' Ruby says stubbornly. 'She deserves to pay too.'

'Please. I'll do anything.'

Ruby scratches her nose, studying me thoughtfully. 'Will you jump?'

'Sorry?'

'Like David jumped. Will you agree to do that? Because if you will, I'll let your mother live.'

My stomach plummets.

Because I understand now what's she planning. David could have taken pills or slit his wrists or thrown himself in front of a train. Instead, he killed himself by jumping from the top floor of one of the multi-storey car parks in town. And he did it in front of me.

I've blocked out the memory of that day because it was so terrible. But her words bring it all back to me...

He rang me just before he jumped that afternoon, asking me cryptically to meet him on the street below the car park, right on the corner.

I turned up on time and stood there for maybe five minutes, looking about for him, confused and wondering where he was. There

294

were people walking past the whole time, carrying shopping bags or going about their business in town. I can still see their faces, the shock when it happened…

At last, my phone rang again.

'Look up,' David said into my ear, his voice strangely breathy.

Thinking it was one of his practical jokes, I glanced up, and saw him outlined against the sky. He was balancing on the narrow rail that guarded the drop from the top floor of the multi-storey car park.

'Oh my God,' I gasped as he lifted one hand in a kind of salute. 'David, what on earth are you doing? Get down from there.'

'I love you, Kate,' he said softly, and jumped.

I wanted to turn away, to close my eyes, but my body refused to obey. Instead, I stood speechless with horror and watched him fall all the way, the phone clasped to my ear, the line still live… until suddenly it wasn't.

'You can't be serious,' I tell Ruby now, feeling about ready to throw up. 'You want me to… to *jump*?'

'That's right. Like David did. From the same rooftop car park.'

I shake my head. 'Not a chance.'

'Okay.' Ruby shrugs as though it doesn't matter to her either way. 'Then I'll lock you and your mum in here, and burn the house down. You can go together. Not a very pleasant way to go for your mum. But if you're lucky, she'll die of asphyxiation before the flames get her.'

Mum has closed her eyes, lying very still on her pillows as though she never intends to get up again. But I want her to get up again. I want her to survive this night. And she will, if I have anything to do with it.

'All right, you win,' I say hoarsely. 'Let my mother live, and I'll bloody well jump for you.'

Ruby smiles. 'Good girl, Kate. I always knew you would.'

Then the doorbell chimes.

CHAPTER THIRTY-THREE

Ruby tries to ignore it at first. But whoever it is keeps leaning on the bell. 'For God's sake,' she says, looking exasperated. 'Who's that at the door now? At this time of day?' She blinks. 'It can't be Irina… I got rid of her, good and proper.'

'What?' I'm horrified, thinking she means Irina is another of her victims.

'You think Irina left of her own accord? That bloody spy was always looking over my shoulder, watching me with your mother instead of cleaning. I didn't like her, and I made sure she never wanted to come back.' Ruby shakes her head, adamant. 'No, it can't possibly be Irina. So who the hell is it?'

'The police,' I lie, relieved to know Irina is still alive, and see her face change.

'What do you mean?'

It's a bluff, and a bold one. But I need to do something. I can't just sit around and wait to be killed, like a sacrificial lamb.

'I called the police earlier. While I was out on the lawn. You saw me on the phone yourself. I had to tell someone about my mum's bruises, didn't I?'

She stares at me, and I can tell she's starting to panic. The confident smile has gone, and she's turning pale.

'You're lying.'

'I'm honestly not. The constable I spoke to said she'd probably call round tonight, or maybe in the morning. It… It just slipped my mind.' I indicate my bound hands. 'Funny, that.'

The doorbell chimes again.

'If you've left the lights on in the hall or living room, and our cars are both outside, it's unlikely the police will give up. Not when it's possible someone in here could be abusing a vulnerable adult.' I pause, and then add speculatively, 'They're more likely to break the door down, actually.'

She jumps up and goes to the door, glancing back suspiciously at my mother. But Mum's still got her eyes closed.

'Not a sound,' Ruby warns me in a hiss, 'or I'll make her pay. Understand?'

'Of course.'

She goes out, closing the door behind her.

Immediately, I start trying to free my hands from the radiator. The wire is so strong though, I can't get enough traction to snap it. And the knot is too tight to undo with my teeth, though I try.

'Mum?' I can't speak too loudly. 'Mum, please wake up!' My mother opens a weary eye and stares at me. 'Help me get these off,' I whisper, showing her my bound hands. 'Quickly.'

Slowly, she clambers off the bed and sways towards me, her feet dragging.

'That's it,' I say encouragingly, and keep tugging on the wire, hoping to snap it. 'Where… Where are your scissors? Did Ruby take them away?' I see the answer in her face and swear under my breath. 'Never mind. Do you have any other scissors? Anything sharp?'

A moment later, I hear raised voices from the hall and almost faint with relief. It sounds like Mr Adeyemi.

Suddenly, the door opens again, and Ruby comes in. She stares suspiciously at my mother, and then closes the door.

'Right,' she tells me, 'it's that bloody solicitor back here again. He's demanding to see you, and I can't get rid of him. So you're going to have to go out there and tell him everything's fine.'

'Okay.'

'If you tell him what's going on, I'll stab your mother in the heart,' she says. 'Simple as that. No warnings.'

'Fair enough.'

I hold up my hands, and she takes a pair of scissors out of her loose trouser pocket and snips straight through the wire.

As soon as I'm free, I surge up and knock her to the ground with as much power as I can manage. Ruby falls awkwardly between the bed and the wardrobe, and I kick her in the head for good measure.

I grab my mother and drag her out of the room. 'Come on,' I say urgently when she resists, 'just another few steps.'

To my surprise, the hall is in semi-darkness, but there's a faint light in the living room. 'Mr Adeyemi,' I shout, heading for the light, 'call the police. It's Mum's carer. She's trying to kill us.'

I stumble over something large in the darkness, and fall heavily to my knees, throwing my hands out to save myself.

Mum stops behind me, and gives a great wail.

The light on the hall snaps on.

I turn my head, momentarily too winded to move.

Behind us, framed in the bedroom doorway, is Ruby, panting and with her face dark red where I kicked her.

'You'll pay for that, bitch,' she spits at me.

I struggle to my feet, and only then see what I tripped over.

298

It's Mr Adeyemi.

'Oh my God,' I whisper, and put a hand on his shoulder, shaking him. 'Mr Adeyemi? Are you hurt?'

The solicitor groans, stirring slightly, but doesn't move.

I look down. There's blood on my hand.

Ruby is heading for us, her face intent, scissors in hand. 'I thought you might try something, love,' she says, sneering. 'So I decided to test you. And now I see that I can't trust you.'

'I take it the deal's off, then?'

'You can joke all you want. But I'm going to kill you both.' Her gaze flicks cruelly between me and Mum. 'The only question is, which one first? Though I suppose it's only right you should watch your mum die. For that kick you gave me.' Briefly, she dabs a hand to her nose, which is bleeding now. 'That hurt.'

'Mum, I want you to go next door. Go on,' I say, almost shoving her towards the front door. 'Find whatever-her-name-is next door and tell her to call the police. Or hide in the bushes. Whatever, just get out of the house.'

Ruby simply laughs.

My mother, distressed but struggling to follow my instructions, tugs on the front door handle, and then looks round at me helplessly.

'I locked it,' Ruby says shortly, not even looking that way. 'You must think I'm stupid.'

She charges me, and I back away, reaching for the nearest thing to hand, which is a small Greek-style statuette on the hall table. It's heavy and made of marble, and Ruby flinches when I take a swing, catching her on the shoulder. But it only slows her down for a moment, and suddenly she's in my face, grappling with me and lunging with the scissors.

I feel a sharp pain in my left side, and gasp, taken aback.

She steps back, and now there's blood on the scissors. We both stare at it. Then she smiles and lunges again.

I swing the statuette wildly, and she falls back, swearing. I think I made contact. But the air is burning in my lungs and I feel curiously lightheaded.

Mum is staring. 'Oh, darling…'

There's a high-pitched ringing in my ears.

Is it real or am I imagining it?

The world tilts sideways, and I stagger. I sink to my knees, and the statuette drops from my grasp. I clasp my stomach and feel something wet. Blood.

Ruby is there, a shadowy figure just ahead.

'Darling,' my mother says again, but I can't hear her properly.

I pitch forward onto my face.

CHAPTER THIRTY-FOUR

I don't know how long I've been lying there in the hall, but when I come to, Mr Adeyemi has moved. He's dragged himself to a sitting position and is on his mobile. That's what wakes me. His deep voice, explaining a little shakily to someone – presumably the emergency services – that he's been stabbed and needs an ambulance. 'Perhaps two ambulances,' he adds, glancing my way, and exclaims, 'Oh, she's conscious.'

'Where… Where's Ruby?' I ask him.

'Gone.' He returns his attention to the call, giving them details of our address. 'Yes, if you could hurry, please. The young woman has a stomach wound.'

He rings off and closes his eyes.

'Where's my mother?'

'Gone too. That maniac took her.'

I take a deep breath and push to my feet, holding onto the wall as I stagger to the landline. 'I have to stop her.'

'You're badly hurt, Miss Kinley.'

'I just need… to be patched up. How about you?'

There's still fresh blood on my hand; I'm smearing a red streak across the pale green and gold wallpaper. My mother would be horrified.

'She stabbed me in the back, and hit me over the head, but I don't think the wound's particularly deep.'

'I'm glad. And I'm sorry... I probably should have said that before. For involving you in this, I mean. I had no idea how dangerous she was.'

'What's wrong with her?'

'It's a long story.' I snatch the handset off the cradle and hit Logan's number. He answers within two rings. 'Logan? Where are you?' My voice shakes. 'I need you.'

'What's happened now?' He sounds weary, and I can't blame him.

'I tried sacking Ruby, and she stabbed me.'

'Jesus Christ.' His voice sharpens, abruptly alert. 'Are you okay? Have you called an ambulance?'

'Yes, and yes. Or rather, Mr Adeyemi called one.'

'Mr Adeyemi?'

'Yes, he's been stabbed too. I thought he was dead at first. But she'd just knocked him out.'

'Sorry?' He sounds disorientated. 'You'd better slow down; I'm not sure I'm following. Where's Ruby now?'

'I don't know. But she's taken Mum with her.'

'What?'

Briefly, I explain about Ruby's obsession with David and her sick ambition to re-enact his suicide. 'She wanted to make me jump too. But I think she's settled for my mother as a second best.' I close my eyes. 'Logan, I need you to take me to... to where David died. You know the place.'

'I know the place,' he agrees sombrely.

'I'm sure that's where she'll be headed. But I can't drive myself. And if she sees the police...'

'Hold on. You're hurt, you said.'

'I don't think it's as bad as it looks. I hope not anyway.' I put a

302

hand to the wound in my side, and grit my teeth. 'But Mum won't survive this if we don't get there quickly. Logan, you didn't see Ruby's face. She's crazy.'

He's silent for a moment. Then he says, 'I'm only a few minutes away, as it happens. I was on my way round to see you; I only pulled over to answer your call. Be there in five.'

I end the call and drop the phone on the floor, too exhausted to bother replacing it on the cradle.

While Mr Adeyemi watches in disbelief, I drag one of Mum's long woollen scarves off the hall stand and wrap it tightly three times about my waist, covering the bloody mess. With a jacket buttoned up over the bulky scarf, I'm good to go. Or as good as I'll be without a paramedic on hand.

'Miss Kinley, I strongly suggest you wait for the ambulance to arrive. Let the police take care of that woman.'

'Thanks for the advice.'

I push my feet into trainers and stagger outside to see headlights sweeping down the drive. A moment later, I'm collapsed in the front seat of Logan's car, and he's helping me put my seatbelt on, because my hands don't seem to be working properly.

'I'm taking you to the hospital,' he says curtly.

'Car park.'

'I've already called the police and told them to deal with it. You don't need to be there too.'

'I absolutely need to be there.' I'm furious with him. 'Ruby's off her rocker. She's got my mum with her and she might do anything if she's cornered. We need to talk her down from whatever she's planning, calmly and quietly, not send in the troops.'

'Be sensible for once in your life. You'll bleed out before we get there.'

'Car park,' I insist thickly.

He swears under his breath, but turns out of the drive towards the town centre. 'You are the most annoying, stubborn, bloody-minded woman I've ever met.'

I close my eyes. 'Thank you.'

I can't say much, but between his guesswork and my monosyllabic answers, Logan manages to piece together the whole story by the time we pull up at the entrance to the car park. It's open twenty-four hours, so he takes a ticket and drives in.

It's all very quiet and empty in the car park. The overhead lights flash across our faces as Logan follows the one-way system at what would feel like insane speed under normal circumstances, tyres squealing, the car climbing ever higher towards the top level.

'You think she's on the roof?'

'Yes, exactly where David jumped from.' I glance at him, feeling sick at those words; his face too is taut, all hard lines and shadows. He was one of David's closest friends. He, more than anyone else, must understand what this feels like. 'Go carefully though. I don't want to spook her.'

To my relief, there's no sign of the police on site. Maybe they went to the wrong car park. Or maybe they're just slower than us in arriving. Though I imagine they probably have more to do than just wrap a scarf around a wound and lurch into a passenger seat. It's early evening now. They could be dealing with drunks or assaults or stab wounds…

'Kate?' Logan's urgent voice recalls me to the moment. 'This is the top level. You were drifting off there for a minute.'

'Sorry, yes.' I sit up, wincing. Then I point. 'Look, over there.'

It's all coming back to me now.

I came up here a few months after his death. Parked up on this level, and walked to the spot where he jumped, near the corner of the building, where a few snapped and flapping 'Police Do Not Cross' tapes still marked out the spot for the investigators. I may have said a little prayer for him, I don't remember now. But I certainly left a plastic-wrapped bouquet of flowers behind on the ground, with a note attached.

For David, RIP. I'm so sorry. All my love, Kate xxx

Next time I came up here, a few weeks later, the flowers had gone. The place looked ordinary, cars coming and going, business as usual. I never returned after that.

Tonight, there are only two cars on the roof.

Ours and Ruby's.

I see Ruby immediately. She's wrapped in her long black coat and standing perfectly still, looking down over the guard rail to where David fell to his death on the street below.

Reliving the awful moment, perhaps, though she was never there.

I wonder if she's praying too.

At the sound of an engine in the quiet car park, Ruby turns and glares, no doubt recognising Logan's car. Then she hurries back to her white Fiat, parked a few feet away, and throws open the front passenger door, where presumably my mother is waiting.

'Okay, she's seen us.' On my orders, Logan has pulled up about five car lengths away. He looks round at me in the dark interior. 'What should I do?'

'Stay here and make sure the police are on their way.'

'Kate, stop and look at yourself. You can barely stand, let alone walk over there and start negotiating with a mad woman.' He takes my hand, his face intense. 'Let me go instead.'

'What good would that do?' I ask bluntly. 'She doesn't care about you.'

'I could try to persuade her—'

Ruby leans forward and is speaking to my mother inside the car. Her voice is raised, almost shouting, but I can't hear the exact words.

I don't have any more time to waste.

'She won't listen. Not to you, Logan.' I open the car door. 'But she'll listen to me. Because it's me she really wants, not Mum.'

'Kate, please—'

'Hush.' I climb out of the car with difficulty, grimacing with pain as I do so. 'Look, I need you to explain the situation to the police as best you can. There's no point them coming in here mobhanded. Oh yeah, and remind them she's probably still got those scissors.'

I shut off his protests by slamming the door shut behind me.

It's just me and Ruby now.

CHAPTER THIRTY-FIVE

Ruby is struggling to drag my bewildered mother from the front seat of her car. My mother, bless her, is strenuously resisting this effort, one frail hand gripping the door frame and the other batting Ruby away.

It's a pathetic sight. The evening is cold, and my breath is steaming on the wintry air. Mum, barefoot and still in her nightie, must be freezing. Her silvery hair lifts on a gust of wind, and for a moment she looks more like a ghost than a flesh-and-blood woman. And if I don't intervene, she soon will be.

Mum's hand slips on the icy metal, and she falls back with a cry. Ruby seizes hold of her and begins hauling her toward the guard rail.

'Ruby!' I shout, staggering across the car park, holding the tightly wound scarf in place over my wound. 'Stop it, and let her go!'

In the distance is the scream of police sirens, growing steadily closer. The sound terrifies me, as I'm sure seeing a host of police cars converging on her will only panic Ruby into doing something more dreadful and unexpected.

'I'm here now, see?' I say more persuasively. 'You don't need my mum.'

'You can both go together.' Ruby has not relinquished her grip on my mother, but she stopped at my shout and is looking back at me, her face suspicious. 'Her first, then you.'

'That's not going to happen.'

'I stuck you in the guts, love. You're bleeding out.' Ruby laughs at my confusion as I glance over my shoulder, belatedly realising she's right; as I walk, I'm leaving a trail of bright red blood spots behind me on the concrete, like gruesome breadcrumbs. 'You can't stop me. You're not strong enough.'

I come to a halt. 'Okay then, fine. Throw my mother over. But you won't get me if you do. And it's me you want, isn't it?' I pause, meeting her arrested gaze. 'For David,' I add softly. 'For this to be justice.'

Ruby hesitates.

Behind me, I hear Logan get out of his car.

Her gaze flashes bitterly that way. 'Don't interfere,' she yells at him, 'you hear me? Or both of them die.'

'I'm not going to interfere,' he says, but takes a few steps away from the car.

'You were his friend,' Ruby says accusingly. 'You came with David once to visit his grandad. I was his live-in carer, you know. His grandad was a very sick man. He had dementia too, like Celeste here, but it was cancer that got him in the end.' She gives a short laugh. 'You don't remember me from those days, do you?'

'I'm sorry.' Logan shakes his head, and takes another step forward. I try to warn him with my eyes to stay where he is, but he's not looking at me anymore, only at Ruby. 'I did go with David once to visit his grandad. But I don't remember you, no.'

Her eyes spark at that, and her hands tighten on my mother's shoulders, keeping her close. I'm suddenly afraid she will try throwing her over the guard rail; they're so close to it, only a few feet away. But

Ruby seems to want to talk first. 'Did… Did David ever mention me?' She pauses, looking at him almost eagerly. 'Did he ever talk about me to you?'

Logan makes a helpless gesture. 'Not that I recall. Should he have done?'

'He saw me several times a week for nearly three years. Whenever he looked in on his grandad, in fact.'

'Jack.'

'That's right.' Ruby sucks in her breath. 'I was always there for Jack. Nothing was too much. I wanted David to know that, to see how much I was doing for his grandad.'

'I'm sure he appreciated it.'

'Yes.' Ruby nods slowly, staring at him. 'He did. He might not have said so, but I knew. Just like I knew how much Kate was hurting him.' Her eyelids flicker. 'After Jack passed, I moved house to be nearer David. I didn't like to bother him; he had his own life. But sometimes, when he went out for a coffee at the weekend, I'd sit opposite him in the café, and just smile. He'd smile back too, and I knew it was a comfort for him to see me.' Her face hardens as the sound of police sirens fill the air, followed by the sound of rhythmic thumps as the cars begin to ascend the ramps at speed, heading for the roof. 'Then he started bringing Kate into the café, and going shopping with her, and sometimes he'd take her back to his flat.'

'You were spying on him,' I say incredulously. 'On us.'

'I was keeping an eye on him. I promised Jack before he died. I said, "Don't worry, love, I'll keep an eye on your boy." And he died peaceful, because of that.' She looks at me with open hatred. 'But David didn't die peaceful, did he? You split up with him. You drove him to take his own life.'

'I didn't split up with him. I just said… let's spend some time apart. Let's take five. He'd been acting so strangely. Constantly not turning up for dates, or picking fights and accusing me of seeing other men. I loved David, he was… God, he was kind and beautiful. But he was broken too. And we both needed some space.'

'What David needed was to be loved. To be held and comforted. Not pushed away like he meant nothing.' Ruby's eyes spit rage at me. 'I would have loved him properly. I would have been there for him, whatever he did to me.'

'David wasn't himself,' Logan says quickly, taking another step towards us. 'It was nothing to do with Kate. He'd been depressed for a long time, even before he started seeing her. And he admitted to me himself that he was treating her badly.'

'Liar,' Ruby snarls, and turns, dragging my mother nearer the edge.

'No,' I scream, and rush forward.

'Stay where you are, both of you. Unless you want her to die.' Ruby pushes my mother half over the guard rail. She looks back at me, her face aglow with a kind of madness. 'Come to the edge, Kate. And when you get here, climb up on the rail. If you do that, maybe I'll let your mother go.'

With an eerie siren wail, the first police car rises over the peak of the top ramp, blue lights flashing on the night air, and accelerates towards Logan.

'Do it now,' Ruby shrieks, thrusting my mother further over. 'Or else.'

'Okay, okay, I'm doing it.' I hurry to the edge, and peer over. The rail is narrow and the drop is staggeringly high. I feel sick and unsteady, but swing my leg up and try to hoist myself onto the rail. 'Oh, Christ.'

'Kate, don't,' Logan shouts, sounding anguished.

'Shut up,' I mutter.

If I had any choice in the matter, I absolutely would not be doing this, I think furiously. But it's me or my mother. And I can't let it be my mother. I couldn't live with myself afterwards, any more than David could live with his depression a moment longer. Though why he chose to punish me by killing himself right in front of me, I will never know. Perhaps he too, like Ruby, thought I was a cold bitch who had driven him to suicide.

Somehow, I clamber onto the rail, and lie astride it, clinging on for dear life and too scared to open my eyes.

'Now, let her go,' I moan. 'You've got what you want.'

'Stand up. Jump.'

'Let her go first.'

'I want to see you jump. Then I'll let her go.'

I can hear more police cars arriving, doors opening and slamming, voices on the air. Logan is explaining the situation, giving them names. I'm desperate for them not to interfere, listening to my mother whimpering with fear a few feet away as she dangles head-first over the street in a chill wind.

'No, you'll push her off once I've jumped.'

'I promise I won't.'

'I don't trust you,' I shriek.

There's a short silence. I can hear Ruby's breath panting.

'Fine,' she says, and I hear my mother's moan as she's pulled back from the rail. 'I'm sending her back to the car.'

I open my eyes, and crank my neck round, desperate to make sure my mother is safe. My side is pressed against the guard rail, so painful it's like an ice pick slowly skewering my internal organs. I see my own blood on the concrete, and experience a nauseating wave of faintness, and then raise my eyes in time to catch the white ghost of my mother in her nightie, shuffling on bare feet towards the Fiat…

My view is suddenly blocked by Ruby's grim figure.

'Right, now jump,' she says, and prods me with something sharp. The scissors, I realise.

'Not yet. I need to see her safe first.'

'She's safe enough.'

'Logan, help my mother. Come and get her.' I hear running footsteps, and Ruby steps aside to show me Logan supporting my mother with a police officer on her other side, the two men carrying her away as quickly as possible, her bare feet lifted off the ground to protect them. 'Thank God.'

The scissors are thrust into my leg, and I yelp.

'Now stand up and jump,' Ruby yells. 'Like David did. Or I'll push you over, do you hear me?'

Sod that, I think.

Grabbing the scissors as they're shoved towards me again, I wrestle her for them one-handed, still balanced precariously on the narrow rail hundreds of feet above street level. She howls with fury, and would probably have pushed me off, but I quickly roll towards her and let myself fall the other way, onto the car park concrete.

The jolt is sheer agony, and I give a high-pitched yelp.

She follows me into a crouch, screaming with frustration, trying to heave my body up again, to get me back on the rail.

My hand jerks sideways, still clutching the scissors between us, and they spin away from us both. There's blood in my eyes again.

Vaguely, I see her gaze follow the scissors.

Then she bends and hisses at me, 'You know why David asked you to come here that day? Why he wanted you to see him jump?' Her face leers into mine, inches away, her breath hot. 'Because I told him you'd been cheating on him. I sent him anonymous notes, listing all the times you'd been unfaithful.' Her face cracks at last into a kind

312

of rictus, her mouth agape with pain, her eyes tortured. 'I never meant for him to die,' she sobs. 'I wanted him to be free, so he'd see how perfect we were for each other. I would have been everything to him. David was mine, not yours. He was always mine, mine, mine!'

The police are running towards us, shouting a warning to get down on the floor. As though I'm not already on it. One of them grabs her by the arm.

'No,' Ruby gasps, and tears herself away from him. With a mad lunge, she throws herself over the guard rail, and disappears, still screaming, 'Mine!'

A sickening, familiar crunch follows.

I close my eyes.

EPILOGUE

The doorbell rings just as I'm sitting behind the desk in my father's old study, finishing an outline for my proposed thriller. I've been working on it for several weeks now while researching the background, and I'm beginning to feel satisfied with the structure at last.

When I go out into the hall, Logan is already there. 'I'll get it,' he insists.

'You look very fetching in that pinny,' I tell him.

He shoots me a mock-threatening look, and throws open the front door. 'Mr Adeyemi,' he says, and shakes the man's hand in welcome. 'Come in, Celeste is expecting you.'

Mr Adeyemi nods at me as he takes off his coat. 'How are you, Miss Kinley? I've just finished that course of rehabilitation therapy for my back. I know you had some trouble. Are you feeling any better?'

The stab wound Ruby gave me caused some serious issues at first. I was in hospital for almost ten days after that night in the car park. But the infection that set in was eventually resolved with antibiotics, and the scar is healing nicely now.

'Much better, thank you.' I grin. 'I just have to be careful with sudden movements for a while. Not to reopen the wound, you know?'

'She has to lift her left leg when she sneezes,' Logan murmurs. 'It's quite entertaining to watch.'

I return the mock-threatening look he gave me before.

Mr Adeyemi pauses before the new addition to the hall: a small, oak-framed portrait of David, with soft lighting above it to provide a focal point and a gold scroll beneath bearing his name and dates.

'This is marvellous,' he says, studying the painting in surprise. 'But I don't understand how it was possible.'

'Logan had it cut out from the original canvas for me. It proved impossible to fix the damage Ruby did to the rest of us, but… David was still intact. So here he is, in pride of place. And with a beautiful new frame.'

'It's lovely indeed. A fitting tribute to his memory.' He gives me and Logan a curious look, then smiles. 'Well, where is the lady of the house? I have promised to come once a week to talk with her. Dr Forster apparently believes this will be helpful.'

'I imagine Celeste will be pretty pleased too,' Logan says. 'She likes you.' He pauses. 'A lot.'

Mr Adeyemi allows himself a small smile. 'And I like Celeste. A lot.'

'I'm glad to hear it.' I show the solicitor through to the living room. 'I'll let you two talk for a while. Then I'll bring some tea through in about half an hour. How's that?'

'Perfect.'

'Mr Adeyemi is here,' I announce breezily, and Mum, who has been playing with her tangled knitting on the sofa, looks up in delight.

'Abayomi!' she exclaims, astonishing me by actually remembering the man's first name. She pats the sofa cushions next to her, her smile a blessing. For a while after Ruby's death, I thought she would never smile again. But as the weeks have passed, she's gradually come out of her shell and is almost her old self again. 'Come and sit with me. I'm knitting, do you see?'

'Hello, Celeste,' he says deeply. 'You are looking well.'

I smile and leave the two of them together.

Logan has removed his pinny but is still in the hall, admiring David's portrait. 'Your brother had such a gift,' he says. 'What a waste for him to die so young.' He takes a deep breath. 'For both of them to die so young.'

I curl my arm into his. 'Finished baking your cake?'

'Finished writing that synopsis?'

'More or less.'

'The cake's in the oven. Don't let me forget to take it out. Then I'll have to get back to work.' Logan has been offered a position at a rival firm; it's only part-time for now, but he hopes to make it full-time eventually. He shoots me a look. 'So you know whodunnit now?'

'I'm alternating between two theories,' I admit, cuddling into him with a wonderful sense of happiness. I'm much happier staying home with Mum as her carer while writing thrillers to keep my brain active, and the book deal I've just been offered should help keep us going for a while. Having Logan come back to live with us felt like the end of a terrible nightmare, with a glorious new dawn ahead. So we both have a few money worries; so what? We'll work it out together. 'But I should know by the end of the book.'

Logan shakes his head in smiling disapproval. 'I applaud you for deciding to give up editing and take up novel-writing instead. But surely you learnt as an editor that an author needs to plan her books thoroughly before writing them?'

'But that would spoil the surprise,' I say innocently, and laugh at his expression.

316

Acknowledgements

This one is for my regular readers and supporters, who are such an inspiring and loyal group of people. You are the ones who keep my fingers on the keyboard and who never fail to remind me that there are readers waiting – often impatiently! – for each new book. That's so important for a writer, especially during dark days when the going gets tough, and it's easy to forget what's at stake each time you sit down to a manuscript in progress. So, thank you for reading and rating my novels, for being there for me on social media, and for keeping me in touch with the important stuff.

Inge Street, for instance, and Pierre L'Allier. You are the readers I'm thinking about as I write this. Thank you, Inge. Thank you, Pierre. This one's for you.

My grateful thanks also to my marvellous agent, Alison Bonomi from LBA, who has been there for me through difficult times too, my number one supporter and friend. Thank you, Alison, and thank you also to the whole wonderful team at LBA!

Thank you also to my editor for this book, Alice Rees. Your enthusiasm got this idea off the ground in the beginning, and your editorial suggestions made this book tighter and better, so thank you. And thank you also to the hard-working and inspirational publishing team at Lume Books: James, Rebecca, Rufus, Imogen. You are all brilliant!

Finally, a huge thank you to Steve for being such a considerate husband, and to my kids Kate, Becki, Dylan, Morris and Indigo, for putting up with an absent-minded writer for a mum, and for making me endless cups of tea!

Lightning Source UK Ltd.
Milton Keynes UK
UKHW040638011021
391497UK00002B/415

GREAT WESTERN S
IN
SHAKESPEARE COUNTRY

Bob Pixton

GREAT WESTERN RAILWAY

PASSENGER BY
LONDON
(PADDINGTON)
TO
**STRATFORD
ON AVON**

SHAKESPEARE EXPRESS

Kestrel Railway Books
PO Box 269
SOUTHAMPTON
SO30 4XR

www.kestrelrailwaybooks.co.uk

Printed by The Amadeus Press

ISBN 978-1-905505-13-5

Front cover: A member of the station staff, along with a handful of passengers, waits for the train to stop at Grimes Hill & Wythall Platform in 1957. Consisting of three coaches, the 4.30pm from Moor Street will terminate at Henley-in-Arden after stopping at all stations along the line; No 5104 is in charge. *(TJ Edgington)*

Back cover: Stratford-upon-Avon has always been a great draw for visitors, and the Great Western Railway was not the only railway that publicised its attractions. *(Alan Bennett Collection)*

Great Western Steam
in
Shakespeare Country

Introduction

The Great Western Railway's lines serving this, essentially rural, part of Warwickshire took a very long time to arrive. Opening in 1852, was a line from Birmingham, south-east towards Oxford and the capital. Hard on its heels, was another line south to serve the small market town of Stratford-upon-Avon, to cater for the needs of the large number of tourists who visit the Shakespeare attractions. Apart from some brief activity to serve Henley-in-Arden with a small branch in 1894, matters rested until the turn of the 20th century. Opening to passengers in 1908, was the third line to create the triangle – the Birmingham & North Warwickshire Railway. This linked Stratford-upon-Avon with Birmingham directly through the Forest of Arden, and was built in a time that many people regard as the "Golden Age of Railways", from 1880 to 1915. During this time, trade and industry was booming, with railways all over the country expanding to fill their needs. Workers were becoming more affluent, and travelled in increasing numbers, not only on excursions to beauty-spots, but also to their work as commuters.

Railways through this part of rural Warwickshire have been given different names according to the audience. Many people would identify with James Inglis who, as General Manager of the GWR in 1904, referred to the route from Cheltenham to Birmingham passing "through the Garden of England". He was, of course, referring to the Vale of Evesham and the surrounding market gardening areas when writing in the GWR Magazine. He was advocating this new line as it would "open up such areas of production to the large markets of numerous cities and towns". He added that the line would add "to the comfort and well being of all classes". A handbill promoting a service from Birkenhead to Bournemouth in 1910 extolled the virtues of this through service being of "comfort, and with all the attractions that a journey through country of great scenic and historic attractions can afford".

In the 1920s, the GWR was unashamedly brazen in its marketing to foreign visitors, especially Americans, calling itself "The National Holiday Line" and "The Line of the American Pilgrim". In 1935, the company argued that the total income from tourism to the country's economy was roughly comparable with the country's exports of woollens or coal. The company issued numerous booklets and handbills to encourage tourists to visit the area, and the concept of "Shakespeare Land" was promulgated in North America through a series of radio broadcasts as well. The North Warwickshire line was also useful in taking race-goers to the courses at Stratford-upon-Avon and Cheltenham, both of which had their own special platforms. The GWR publicity machine left no stone unturned, and produced booklets, pamphlets and sheets about almost every pastime that people enjoyed, applauding the virtues of angling, camping, walking and golf – all by GWR of course! Nowadays, the North Warwickshire line is marketed as "The Shakespeare Line".

LE PAYS DE SHAKESPEARE LE PAYS DE SHAKESPEARE

CHEMINS DE FER BRITANNIQUES   Imprimé en Angleterre

Competition between rival railway companies was alive and well in this "Golden Age", and prompted new ventures. With the GWR having lost its chance to capture the line up the Lickey incline decades previously, its empire was separating into two parts: Birmingham and the north, Bristol and the west. The development of the North Warwickshire to link up the two segments was a sensible step – the line would be independent of the MR, and enabled the company to offer long distance trains from the south west to the Midlands and beyond.

Life wasn't all plain sailing for the GWR, however. Soon after the through route opened, the MR challenged the company over the use of the spur at Yate from its main line onto GWR metals for the run into Bristol. The MR wanted the GWR to pay a toll and use its line through Mangotsfield into Bristol, but the courts sided with the GWR.

The North Warwickshire Railway was not a line that the GWR really wanted, nor fully exploited. Yes, the line provided an unconstrained alternative to the MR line to Bristol from Birmingham for a major part of the route, and yes, the line did tap into the opportunities provided by opening up new lands and markets. However, perhaps the real reason why the company built the line was to spoil the area for other railway companies. A shorter line from Birmingham to London could have been achieved by using part of it and then bypassing just north of Oxford to somewhere near Brentford, as advocated by other companies. With their own financial difficulties much more prominent, the supporters faded away, leaving the GWR with an opportunity to build the line. Only in the heyday of summer excursions did the line become an important part of the system, with its finest hour being in the post World War II era of holiday travel – a bubble all too soon punctured by motorways and package holidays. Ironically, a derailment of one of the many freight trains diverted onto the line to preserve pathways on the ex-MR line, caused the demise of the sections north and south of Honeybourne.

This book serves to offer the reader journeys along the lines. First, is a trip along the original main line from Birmingham Snow Hill to Leamington and then along the branches to Stratford-upon-Avon. Completing the triangle is a return up the North Warwickshire line to Birmingham Moor Street. Inevitably, covering such a long period of time and new technologies, not all the pictures live up to the title. It has been with great reluctance, and with no possible alternatives available, that other types of motive power have occasionally been used. Pure GWR!

Acknowledgements

A great many people, organisations and societies have helped me put this volume together. The staff at The Shakespeare Birthplace Trust, Warwickshire County Record Office, Henley-in-Arden Heritage Centre and libraries along the lines at Stratford-upon-Avon, Leamington Spa, Solihull, Shirley and Acocks Green, have all gone out of their way to help me, for which I am most appreciative. Without the help, advice and organisation at the Kidderminster Railway Museum, this book would have been devoid of many of its best pictures, so many thanks to the staff there, especially Audie Baker and Robin Smith. Numerous people gave freely given of their time and energy to find answers to my questions – I thank you all. This list includes: Dorridge Residents Association, Knowle Residents Association, Henley & Beaudesert Castle Society, the staff at the GWR Steam Museum in Swindon, Mrs E Handley, Ian Baxter of Chiltern Railways, Ed Chaplin, Laurence Kingston, John Tolson, Alan Bennett, Jonathan Dovey and (for his encyclopaedic knowledge and understanding of the train reporting system) Derek Frost. I apologise if I have omitted any other names. Last of all, thanks to the cafés and tea rooms in the Heart of England for sustenance.

Bibliography

Readers can find more details of certain aspects by looking in the following books and magazines:

The Alcester Branch SC Jenkins & R Carpenter
Birmingham Snow Hill, a First Class Return Derek Harrison
The Elegance of Edwardian Railways Geoffrey Williams
The English Landscape in the 20th Century Trevor Rowley
The Greatness of the GWR K Beck
Great Railway Stations of Britain Gordon Biddle
Great Western Lines & Landscapes Alan Bennett
The Great Western Railway in the Twentieth Century OS Nock
GW Coaches from 1890 Michael Harris
GWR Engineering Works, 1928-38 R Tourret
GWR Reflections K Beck & N Harris
GWR Steam in the Midlands Michael Mensing
Locomotive Engineers of the GWR Denis Griffiths
The North Warwickshire Railway CT Goode
Operating BR History, No 7: Through the Links at Tyseley LC Jacks
The Oxford, Worcester & Wolverhampton Railway Bob Pixton
Paddington to the Mersey Hendry & Hendry

Railway Blunders Adrian Vaughan
Railway Nostalgia around Warwickshire Hibbs
A Regional History of Great Britain, Volume 7: The West Midlands Rex Christiansen
The Rise of the Commuter Village of Dorridge G Bradley
Salute to Snow Hill Derek Harrison
Shakespeare's Country, part of Odhams *Britain Illustrated* series
Shakespeare's Railway John Boynton
Signal Box Register, Volume 1: GWR The Signalling Record Society
An Illustrated History of the Stratford-on-Avon to Cheltenham Railway Audie Baker
The Stratford-upon-Avon & Midland Junction Railway JM Dunn
Track Layout Diagrams of the GWR and BR WR, Sections 28 & 30 RA Cooke
Train Formation & Carriage Workings of the GWR WS Becket
Wartime on the Railways David Wragg
Warwickshire Railways M Hitches

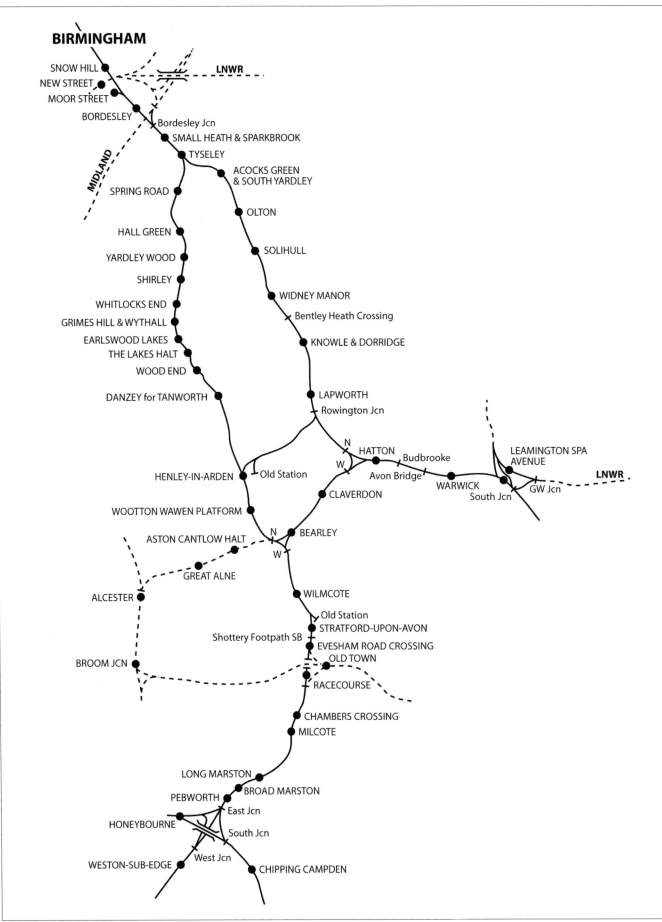

BIRMINGHAM

SNOW HILL
NEW STREET
MOOR STREET
BORDESLEY
LNWR
Bordesley Jcn
SMALL HEATH & SPARKBROOK
TYSELEY
ACOCKS GREEN & SOUTH YARDLEY
MIDLAND
SPRING ROAD
OLTON
HALL GREEN
SOLIHULL
YARDLEY WOOD
SHIRLEY
WIDNEY MANOR
WHITLOCKS END
Bentley Heath Crossing
GRIMES HILL & WYTHALL
KNOWLE & DORRIDGE
EARLSWOOD LAKES
THE LAKES HALT
WOOD END
LAPWORTH
DANZEY for TANWORTH
Rowington Jcn
N
HATTON
Budbrooke
LEAMINGTON SPA
AVENUE
W
Avon Bridge
LNWR
HENLEY-IN-ARDEN
Old Station
WARWICK
GW Jcn
CLAVERDON
South Jcn
WOOTTON WAWEN PLATFORM
N
BEARLEY
ASTON CANTLOW HALT
W
GREAT ALNE
ALCESTER
WILMCOTE
Old Station
STRATFORD-UPON-AVON
Shottery Footpath SB
EVESHAM ROAD CROSSING
OLD TOWN
BROOM JCN
RACECOURSE
CHAMBERS CROSSING
MILCOTE
LONG MARSTON
BROAD MARSTON
PEBWORTH
East Jcn
HONEYBOURNE
South Jcn
WESTON-SUB-EDGE
West Jcn
CHIPPING CAMPDEN

The Main Line South to Leamington Spa

The GWR Station in Birmingham

Snow Hill. A station here was not in the original Birmingham & Oxford Junction Railway proposals, instead, the lines were to enter the then LNWR station at Curzon Street. It took an extension to the Act to enable a line from the start of the Duddeston Viaduct at Adderley Street (north of Bordesley station) to Great Charles Street (on the fringe of the town centre – Birmingham didn't become a city until 1889). At the latter point it was to lie side by side with a line from the north, the Birmingham, Wolverhampton & Dudley Railway, and by this manoeuvre, both companies would have an equal share in Snow Hill station. To the east, the site was bounded

by Snow Hill (below) and to the west by Livery Street (above). Such is the lie of the land that the southern approach would be in a 596yd tunnel, while the northern exit was on a viaduct over the roads there. Trains from Paddington started to enter the station from 1852, but the lines north were not ready until 14th November 1854. All these views are after the Edwardian rebuild. *(Birmingham Reference Library & BPC)*

Snow Hill.
The previous northern boundary of the station was Great Charles Street and the southern boundary was Monmouth Street. In 1863, the Great Western Hotel was opened, and being built above the tunnel entrance to the south of the station, enabled passengers to walk through the building to reach the platforms. The hotel wasn't a success, the company taking over the upper floors as offices, and the ground floor being altered to a restaurant.
(Lens of Sutton)

The company planned to rebuild the hotel before World War II, and American visitors to Stratford-upon-Avon might well have been prime targets to stay here. A facing of Portland stone would have made it match that of the re-built Leamington Spa station exterior, during the 1930s, the buzzword was "modern".
(BPC)

BIRMINGHAM (SNOW HILL) STATION RESTAURANT

HE premises of the Great Western Hotel, Birmingham, were acquired by the Company in connection with the extensive alterations at Snow Hill Station. The upper floors having been converted into General Offices, the whole of the ground floor has been adapted as an extensive first-class popular Restaurant.

This establishment is open daily for Breakfasts and Luncheons, and a speciality is made of Afternoon Teas. The facilities afforded for obtaining well cooked and quickly served food at moderate prices are equal to any in the city of Birmingham. The entrance is from Colmore Row, or by means of a covered way from the Station platform. The Grill Room, in Livery Street, is open from 8.0 a.m. to 10.0 p.m.

The Restaurant and suite of rooms are available for public and private Dinner Parties, Concerts, At Homes, etc.

DINING ROOM, BIRMINGHAM (SNOW HILL) RESTAURANT.

36

The dining rooms were mentioned in the company's booklet, *GWR Hotels & Catering*, in 1927.
(BPC)

6

Snow Hill Concourse, 1947.
With improved services locally and nationally, and in spite of a rebuild of the original station which took place in 1871, the station couldn't cope. Around the turn of the 20th Century, between 350 and 400 trains were being handled daily, so between 1906-1913, without closing the station, it was rebuilt again. A passenger walking under the hotel entrance to the station would end up in the main booking office. This was constructed in white Carrara Ware under a tall arched roof, and opened in 1912 with access for foot and horses from Livery Street. Even at this late date, some of

the seven booking windows still have "Third" above them, and any grand features have been spoilt by excessive, intrusive advertising. Wide steps led down to the two island platforms. A small army of people worked at the station – 351 in 1933.
(Millbrook House Ltd)

Snow Hill. The two lines from the south across Bordesley viaduct faced about 500 yards of 1 in 45, mostly in a tunnel. Inexperienced drivers often thought they could shut off steam and coast into the platforms; when they didn't, one of the station pilots would rescue them. Emerging from the tunnel, the up and down lines widened into four, passing around the two island platforms. Two more lines sprang from the innermost platform lines, so that goods trains could bypass the platform lines. The girders are for the crossing of Great Charles Street. Looking south in circa 1924 (left) and extending north from here was a 500ft-long shed at right angles to the lines, with a wide gap down its centre to allow smoke to leave. Looking north in 1958 (bottom) we see the crossovers between the central lines and the platform lines creating two platforms on one face. The signals controlling such movements can be seen by the canopies. North of here were four bay platforms, to the left and the right. In the distance is the elevated slim-based North signalbox with its 224 levers. Being all electric there was no point rodding. This box and the smaller South box (96 levers) were replaced in September 1960. Note the dress code of the interested parties – school uniform being worn without a hint of embarrassment. The open, airy, northern end contrasts with the smoky cavernous southern end.
(Both Stations UK)

Trains at Snow Hill. The name wasn't adopted until 1858, and until quite late in its life the station nameboards just said, "Birmingham". Plans to rebuild Snow Hill at street level with a roof-top car park were shelved due to the electrification at New Street. In 1963, the LMR took over the former GWR lines in the area, and Euston to Birmingham trains were electrically hauled from 1967. Some suburban services staggered on until 1972, before complete closure took place; the hotel and offices were demolished at the end of 1964. In October 1987, a modified version of the earlier rebuilding plans resulted in the reopening of Snow Hill station.

Top: Local passenger workings and stock removals to carriage sidings at Bordesley and Small Heath were often undertaken by a 2-6-2T. Here, No 6116 arrives at platforms 6/7 with a south-bound stopping train in 1961. This train is the 5.38pm all-stations to Knowle & Dorridge, and it was followed by the 5.45pm from Moor Street all-stations to Stratford-upon-Avon along the North Warwickshire line. On Saturdays, passengers travelled by the 5.52pm for stations along the main line. *(HD Bowtell)*

Middle: Heading a northbound train of iron ore wagons is 2-6-0 No 5312, probably destined for the steel works near Wolverhampton. It has just left the tunnel and is crossing Great Charles Street. *(R Carpenter)*

Bottom: Preparing to leave platform 12 is Hall class 4-6-0 No 6980 *Llanrumney Hall*. This is probably the 5.45pm to Worcester, stopping only at Whitlock's End, Grimes Hill, Wood End, Henley-in-Arden and Wootton Wawen before arriving at Stratford-upon-Avon at 6.35pm. Continuing south, it will join the OWW line at Honeybourne, reaching Worcester at 7.45pm. Passengers would not take this service if that was their destination, as the 5.40pm from Snow Hill to Cardiff would get them there in half the time, even though it departed from the city facing in the other direction! *(Milepost 92½ Picture Library, AWV Mace Collection)*

8

The Broad Gauge

When the line opened from Oxford to Birmingham on 1st October 1852, broad gauge trains passed along the lines here, indeed, on the opening day, *Lord of the Isles* ran into the back of a goods train! Mixed lines ran to Birmingham, but there were only narrow gauge lines beyond. This was because authorisation for that line happened while the Gauge Commission was deliberating on the matter. One of its conclusions was, "that a break of gauge is a very serious evil", which sounds like typical Victorian melodrama! Whatever the merits of the broad gauge, it had a tremendous effect on the GWR, which, instead of putting its energies into improving services, caused them to be diverted into converting its existing lines to standard gauge. Thus, until the early 1890s, the company was very introspective – always looking in on itself and not competing more vigorously.

All London expresses were broad gauge to start with, and from the opening, up and a down trains took 2hr 45min including stops at Oxford and Leamington. These timings were for Gooch's famous 8ft single engines, and are even more remarkable considering that the Didcot avoiding line wasn't opened until 1856. Trains along the rival LNWR line from Euston to Birmingham took more than 3 hours. Timings for GWR trains varied over the years, usually taking longer, and in 1869, the service became standard gauge throughout. In 1880, the 4.45pm from Paddington took the same time as at the opening of the line, but it was not until 1896 that the time was bettered by ten minutes. Train times were reduced to 2hr 20min in 1902, and the magic 2-hour expresses started in 1910 with the Aynho cut off reducing the distance, but keeping to this schedule proved hard for all expresses to and from the capital.

Some "convertible" engines were built. Designed after the decision was taken change the gauge, these 2-4-0 engines were built with their driving wheels outside the frame so that they could run on the 7ft 0¼in track, but after the changeover, the wheels were simply removed and replaced inside the frame.

Top: A typical broad gauge express passenger train headed by a 4-2-2 locomotive at an unknown location. (*BPC*)

Middle: Unidentified broad gauge 4-2-2 together with its crew – location unknown. (*Kidderminster Railway Museum, VR Webster Collection*)

Bottom: A "convertible" 2-4-0 locomotive, built to aid the changeover from broad to standard gauge. (*BPC*)

9

Moor Street, 1964. The quadruple lines to New Street are crossed next to the road access to Moor Street; they are below the brick retaining wall, on the left, with the GWR lines to Snow Hill crossing them on the concrete bridge. Having crossed Bordesley viaduct on the level, Modified Hall 4-6-0 No 6995 *Benthall Hall* is slowing down, but not too quickly, as it is entering a short section of a stiff 1 in 45 gradient. On the left, at the start of

the viaduct, is a bracket signal with upper quadrant arms; the left-hand post is for the up main and the right hand post is for transfers across to the up relief lines – the most commonly used line has the tallest post. Above the coaches is the paraphernalia for Moor Street station with the goods shed dominating the view to the right. It was probably the prohibitive cost of widening the two lines north of here to create south facing bays at Snow Hill that led to Moor Street being built at all. *(BWL Brooksbank, Initial Photographics)*

Bordesley Viaduct, 1958. This was the view from Moor Street signalbox looking towards Bordesley across the widened viaduct. The two main lines are on the left, and on the down main is an express, 6014 *King Henry VII* is bringing the speed of its 12-coach train down ready for the approach to Snow Hill. Some of the coaches are bound for Birkenhead. Joining the main lines is the pair of relief lines and from them, to the right, is the trackwork to serve Moor Street station, behind us. The patch of fresh ballast on the down relief line marks the place where trains from the new station could gain access to the up and down main lines using a crossover. This had been removed two years previously and transfers now took place just before Tyseley

station. The up goods and shunting line are on the right of the viaduct, and the "cash register" style of signal, with its back to us, indicated the line a train was to go to in the goods depot. While other railways fully embraced streamlining, the GWR only dabbled; this engine sported some aspects of the idea for six months from March 1935. *(Kidderminster Railway Museum, C Thompson Collection)*

Bordesley Viaduct, 1949. Looking north from the end of Bordesley station, we see the original line to Curzon Street on the right curving away on Duddeston viaduct; the Bordesley end was used as sidings serving a cattle station for many years. Curving gently away ahead is the main line to the city centre. The controlling signalbox is Bordesley North, and the photographer is standing in between the main lines, up to the right. Dictating movements along the down main is this fine example of a GWR bracket signal. The main route (the taller post) is for Snow Hill, while trains could turn off left to Moor Street. For the latter route, the distant arm is fixed and cannot be altered, to ensure that train speeds were brought down prior to a stop ahead. At this time, trains could come along the down main line and, almost at the last minute, swing into Moor Street station by a crossover on the viaduct – removed in 1954. On the left is the pair of relief lines, which allowed trains to directly access Moor Street station or to join the main lines. *(Millbrook House Ltd)*

Inset: Viewed in 1966, this box had just one year left. Interestingly, the locking room windows are all concentrated together and appear to be openable; it has tiles rather than lead flashing. Originating in 1918, this wooden box had 47 levers and replaced Station signalbox at the end of the platforms on the down side. Unfortunately, when this section to Bordesley South was quadrupled, it was in the path of the relief lines. *(D Allen, Kidderminster Railway Museum)*

Duddeston Viaduct, 1949.
When the Oxford to Birmingham line was being planned, it was to terminate at Curzon Street by passing across the roof tops of the area on a viaduct. That station served several other railways, notably the lines to London, to Liverpool and Manchester, to Derby and to Gloucester. Not only was it already extremely congested, but this line would have to cross some of them on the level to access the station. Directly in front of us, across the lines, was to be part of the viaduct (parts of it visible curving away to the right). The connection to Curzon Street, behind us, was never made, but parts of the 1853 viaduct are still with us today. *(M Whitehouse Collection)*

Bordesley Station, 1958. This was the second station at this site. The original was slightly to the north with a pair of platforms facing each other, but with the quadrupling of the lines, this new station with staggered platforms was opened in March 1918. Either side of this platform would pass main line trains with a down suburban train at one face of the island to the right. Although closed now, it sometimes opens its doors for Birmingham Football Club matches, which since 1906 have been played at St. Andrews. *(Stations UK)*

Inset: Bordesley Station, 1964. You could blink and miss this rather uninviting entrance to the station at street level. Stairs took passengers to the elevated platforms above the Coventry Road; its awnings can be seen in the top left. *(RM Casserley)*

Bordesley Junction. Mention the GWR and shunting, and most people picture a shunting truck like this. The GWR was not alone in having such vehicles, but they were used extensively by the company. Apart from containing special equipment, useful in day-to-day shunting activities, the biggest reason for them was safety. By riding on the trucks, staff could be ferried around the yard quickly and safely, compared to walking around a poorly-lit yard with all manner of trip hazards and quietly-moving wagons. While these trucks didn't eliminate accidents, they were an attempt to speed up the operations in the safest possible way. *(Unknown)*

Small Heath, 1943. A small two-platform station opened with the line in 1852, the booking office being on the overbridge, and when the line was quadrupled through the station in 1913, the two existing platforms became islands. As part of the extension of the station, large awnings were built on both islands for passenger protection. We are looking from between the fast lines with the relief pair being to the left and a pair of goods lines being on the extreme left; a train will soon arrive from behind us along the down main. Ahead were opportunities to move onto the relief lines, and then onto the up goods line. *(BPC)*

Small Heath Sidings, early 1960s. This area was rapidly developed as the chief sorting place for GWR goods trains in the area. Engine servicing also took place here, and at one time there were two four-road engine sheds, which closed in 1908, being replaced by Tyseley. Not only was there a goods yard on the down side, but reception, sorting and departure lines were on the up side. Typical shunting engines were pannier tanks, and a pair is illustrated here. While to most people the GWR is typified by King and Castle class engines, they were not ubiquitous, and in fact the 1938 returns for the company show that

around 20% of its (almost) 100 million miles of travel was performed by such humble engines as shown here. This is not surprising really since for the last fifty years of its existence, it had over a thousand of such engines. The up signals are interesting – underneath the arm on each is a "cash register" display, into which could be put a notice telling the driver which route to take, when the appropriate lever was pulled by the signalman; it appears that there is a choice of four routes on each post here. *(Milepost 92½ Picture Library, AWV Mace Collection)*

Tyseley, circa 1955. Looking north from the end of the down relief platform, we see an up express putting out plenty of smoke. Castle class 4-6-0 No 5010 *Restormel Castle* races past the large goods shed, still with writing from pre-war days on it; note the loading gauge on a line by the shed. The bracket signal in front of us is for the down main, indicating which route a train is to take at the crossover ahead. A train is signalled for the line to Snow Hill – the left-hand pair of signals would mean Moor Street. This double junction was wrecked by a down train on 22nd May 1967 and taken out of use. On the left are the carriage sidings and the engine shed. *(J Davenport, Initial Photographics)*

Tyseley, 1955. Although slightly over three miles from its next stopping place, Snow Hill station, the driver of this Castle class engine will be keeping a watch on his train's speed. The train is passing along on the down fast line through the station; the nameboard on the platforms is rather a simple affair. Passengers for the Birmingham Railway Museum are encouraged to alight here now. *(P Kingston)*

Tyseley Junction, early 1960s. Passing along the down relief line is a parcels train headed by Grange class 4-6-0 No 6840 *Hazeley Grange*. Its destination isn't here (otherwise the single arm on the bracket signal would have been pulled off) – its most likely destination is the massive goods shed at Hockley, and to get there the train would have to pass through Snow Hill station. Looking very much like an enlarged version of the Moguls they replaced (some parts of the latter engines were reused when some of this class were built) they were actually heavier, and so more restricted in their range of routes. One of the chief differences between them was that the 4-6-0 engines had the No 1 boiler making them more powerful. *(J Moss)*

Tyseley Junction, around 1910. At the start of 1907, four running lines were opened from north of Tyseley station as far as Olton. The two tracks to the east were for up trains with the southern pair for Birmingham-bound trains. Tyseley South signalbox opened in the same year, a month before the North Warwickshire branch, on 13th November – at 70ft long and containing 136 levers it was a very large structure. Although slightly blurred, this picture is of historic value as it shows a down train passing to the immediate left of the signalbox; its partner is the other side of the box. Over two weeks in 1913 the extra pointwork was added and the lines were paired by speed, so the signalbox had the down relief to the right and the up relief to its left. *(PJ Garland)*

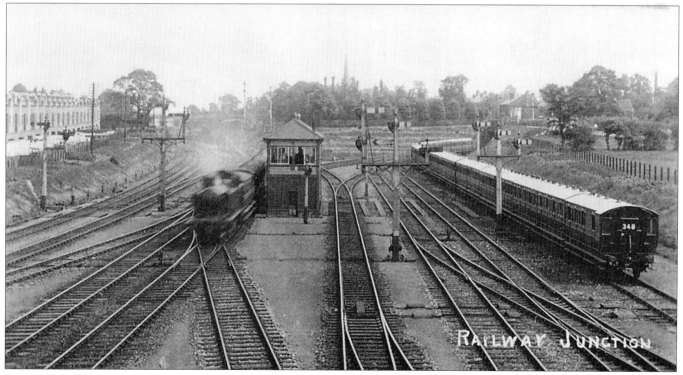

Acocks Green, around 1905. In its account of the opening of the line on 30ᵗʰ September 1852, *The Illustrated London News* called this place, "Haycocks Green". This copy of an old postcard shows a collection of passengers waiting for a Birmingham-bound train, possibly a society special. The influence of the broad gauge is well evident in the gap between these two tracks; the crossover dates from May 1879, and the signalbox at the end of the up platform

probably came into being then too. Under the bridge can be seen the up refuge siding which, together with its down counterpart, was added in June 1892. At that date, the platforms were both extended southwards. *(R Carpenter)*

Acocks Green, 1957. Fifty years before this picture was taken the main line here was quadrupled and the station rebuilt with the wooden buildings (seen previously) replaced by substantial brick affairs. Looking towards Birmingham from the island platform that serves the relief lines, this view shows the extensive canopies for passenger protection; on the adjacent overbridge is the booking office. Judging from the nameboard, the station has acquired another district of Solihull in an attempt to win more passengers. Hauling a stopping train from Moor Street to Leamington is 2-6-2T No 5163. *(TJ Edgington)*

16

Acocks Green, 1959. Illustrating that motive power other than Prairie tanks was used on suburban trains is this view of Mogul 2-6-0 No 6349 in May. It is standing at platform 1, usually the line for up fast trains. However, at this time of the day there was a steady avalanche of passenger trains leaving Birmingham. Less than ten minutes previously, the 5.52pm from Snow Hill would have stopped at platform 3, as the 6pm express conveying passengers from Birkenhead to the capital tore along the up fast line. No sooner would the dust have settled from that episode than the 6.05pm all stations to Leamington would arrive with the 6.25 selective stopping train from Moor Street hard on its heels. Note the roll of canvas above the cab to protect the footplate crew against the weather. During World War II, it also stopped the glow from the fire being seen by enemy aircraft. *(M Mensing)*

Acocks Green Exterior, early 1960s. The place chosen to build the booking office for the quadruple lines from 1907 was where Sherbourne Road crossed the railway line. Around this time, the staff would have comprised a stationmaster, junior and senior porters, similar graded clerks, a parcels clerk and a lamp man. *(J Moss)*

Left: Olton, around 1900. Heading south, the line skirts Olton Mere, a 31-acre feeder reservoir for the Warwick & Birmingham Canal dating from 1790. Olton is a local expression of the words "old town", that is, the oldest part of Solihull, and was mentioned in Domesday Book. Standing on the down platform, waiting for a train north, the photographer is looking towards Birmingham. The signalbox and crossover date from 1879, ten years after the station opened. There were adequate facilities here of brick construction with cute chimneys. Note how the platform is made of bricks and the numerous advertisements. A newspaper article from *The Birmingham Post* of 3rd February 1930 illustrates a reason for multiple lines on heavily used routes. It reported that one of the driving wheels of the Dover to Birkenhead express "came off and rolled down the bank". It continued, "The mishap blocked the down main line traffic for some time. The train was eventually hauled back to Solihull and thence to Birmingham. Single line working was adopted while a breakdown gang attended to the disabled engine, a work that lasted some time." Unfortunately, there is no mention of the engine apart from the fact that it had six driving wheels. *(BPC)*

Middle: Olton, 1959. Due to the frightening figure of over a million men being out of work in 1929, the Government of the day passed the Development (Loan Guarantees and Grants) Act, which authorised the payment of interest for some years for capital schemes that public utility undertakings performed. To relieve congestion on its southern approaches to Birmingham, the GWR came up with a scheme to quadruple the lines from Olton just under eight miles to Lapworth. It involved building new stations as well as extra lines, and here, two island platforms were created with the fast pair of lines passing around the structure to the right. In the 1950s, Mr AG Noble was stationmaster, with about 90 trains stopping at the passenger-only station each day. Annually, 300,000 passengers were booked and 11,700 season tickets sold. On the extreme left can be seen the roof over the new station entrance at road level; platforms were accessed by a subway and steps. *(Stations UK)*

Olton Exterior, 1948. A subway led to steps to access the platforms. *(RS Carpenter)*

18

Olton, 1948. One of the legacies of World War II was that immediately afterwards, our plentiful natural energy resource, coal, was proving very difficult to develop to its potential. Ironically, while we exported good quality locomotive coal from South Wales, we imported inferior American coal (unsuccessfully) to fuel our engines. Consequentially, thoughts turned to adapting locomotives to burning oil instead. To start with ten 2-8-0s and eight 2-8-0Ts were modified, all for working main line freights in the company's main coal producing area, South Wales! Then, in Autumn 1946, some Halls and Castles were also altered. One idea was to have Cornwall as an oil-fired area to the exclusion of all-coal burning engines, due to the cost of transporting the coal. Here, Hall class 4-6-0 No 3953 (ex-6953) *Leighton Hall* passes through the station on the up fast line. There was enthusiastic Government approval to convert over 1,217 engines, and construct oil depots at a number of running sheds, but after much money had been spent (probably by the GWR, not the Government) perhaps it was the realisation that payment would have to be made in foreign exchange, which the country was short of, that ended the experiment. To most informed railway commentators this was a massive blunder as the economic benefits of oil-fired steam engines would have been such that cheap and reliable motive power could have lasted well until electric engines could have replaced them. All the oil burners were converted back to coal within a couple of years; this engine only burned oil from April 1947 to September of the next year.
(RS Carpenter)

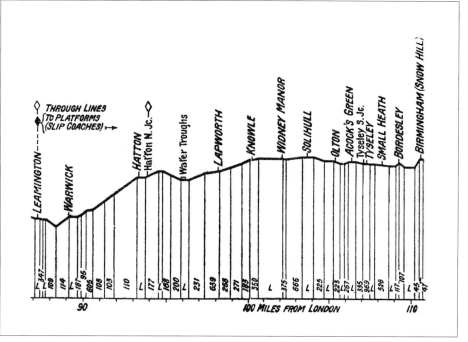

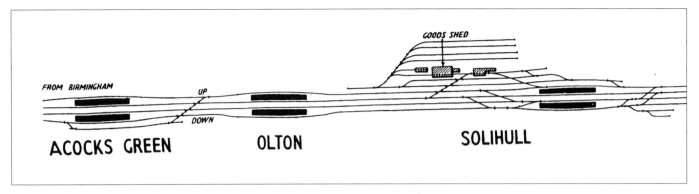

FROM BIRMINGHAM   UP   DOWN   GOODS SHED

ACOCKS GREEN   **OLTON**   **SOLIHULL**

Quadrupling of Lines, 1930s. As mentioned in *Warwick County News* for 1st February 1930, "The widening of the line between Olton & Bentley Heath is to be undertaken by Cleveland Bridge & Engineering Co. Ltd., from Darlington. The works include the demolition of the old stations at Olton & Solihull and the widening and reconstruction of no less than 17 bridges. It is high time Olton & Solihull had stations in keeping with their modern developments as residential & trading centres." At the 11th March 1930 meeting of Solihull Rural District Council there was much discussion about the cost of widening the roads when new bridges were being built. The County Roads & Bridge Committee agreed:

• Some to be widened, Blossomfield Road bridge from 25ft 6in to 42ft, at a cost of £1,118.
• Some to remain as they are, Rising Lane bridge, Lapworth; Darley Green bridge, Knowle.

The discussion seemed to centre round the cost of such works (£17,343) the loan part adding three farthings (¾ of an old penny) on the rates.

Testing the Bridges. The new underbridges were tested by running four King class engines, coupled in pairs and running side by side, at speeds up to 60mph one Sunday morning. Here Hillfield Road has no less than four King class engines passing across it; on the left are 6017 and 6005, on the right are 6001 and 6014. *(Solihull Public Library)*

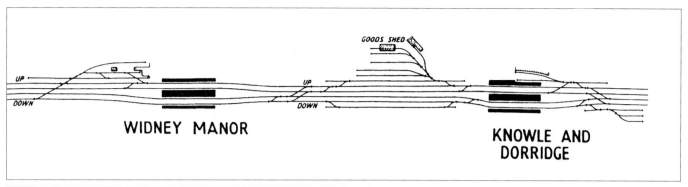

WIDNEY MANOR

KNOWLE AND DORRIDGE

Height Testing the Bridges. Measured lengths of wood were put under the bridge in readiness for the engines to pass over them. Here the heaviest engines the company had (King class locos at 89 tons with an axle loading of 22½ tons) pass along the down slow line over Blossomfield Road just south of Solihull station. *(Solihull Public Library)*

Olton, Warwick Road Bridge. Coincident with the quadrupling of the line was the widening of the road here from 36ft to 60ft. To keep the weight down, the five 152ft span girders were of a lattice construction, but even then each one weighed about 160 tons. *(BPC)*

Solihull, 1864. Although of very poor quality, this picture is of great historic interest. Not only does it show the considerable buildings on both platforms dating from its opening with the line, but it also shows mixed gauge track and the primitive method of operation by the point lever in the left foreground. Built as a broad gauge line when opened in 1852, the extra rail was added, and standard gauge trains ran to Birmingham from the early 1860s. *(Millbrook House)*

Solihull, no date. After their introduction in 1898, engines like this performed well on express trains along this line. Here, Bulldog class 4-4-0 No 3393 *Australia* is at the up platform, which has been extended towards Birmingham. By 1908, a footbridge had been built and between it and the coaches, is evidence of the signalbox that was built for 1890. By this time the whole district was becoming more prosperous, and there were extra sidings and refuge sidings. A legacy of the broad gauge is the wide gap between the tracks. *(BPC)*

Solihull, circa 1958. One of the reasons for the Government's 1929 Act was that the public utilities would be able to cope with demand when trade picked up after the depression. To this end, goods facilities here were concentrated in a new yard, efficiently organised with a large shed, a 6-ton power crane and facilities for end loading. Beyond the shed, livestock could be accommodated. Looking from the Streetsbrook Road overbridge we see the layout well and 0-6-0PT No 9753 on (probably) the 10.15am Leamington to Tyseley train. It appears that some of the freight train has been left in the adjacent loop while the yard is shunted. The yard was also served by the 8.25am Bordesley to Oxford train. Access to the yard was from the down main line by crossing the up main, along which is train is signalled. The station is in the background, with a train expected along the fast lines to the left. *(BPC)*

Solihull Exterior, 1993. As part of the 1929 Act, the old station was demolished and a new one built slightly to the south. Seen here 60 years after opening, is the small brick booking hall and offices, with a blue-tile-lined subway under the four running lines and steps to the platforms. Nowadays, buses crowd the forecourt, ferrying passengers locally and to the National Exhibition Centre, as well as to the borough's international airport. *(BPC)*

Solihull, 1955. A busy scene with three of the four platforms occupied. Facing us is 2-6-2T No 5194 ready to set off north with a stopping train to Birmingham along the down fast line. On the left are the coaches of a train using the up main line, possibly an express. Meanwhile, there is much activity on platform 3 with probably a suburban service having arrived from Birmingham. In the evening peak periods, some trains were strengthened (for example, the 5.28pm from Snow Hill) often to 10 coaches. The 5.10pm was also heavily used, and the stock increased accordingly. *(R Carpenter)*

Solihull, 1949. Due to a shortage of motive power, compounded by indifferent coal, the new Western Region of BR was loaned engines like this Fowler 2-6-2T from the London Midland Region. The bracket signal to the rear of the train controlled a set of crossings that allowed up or down transfers, while the single arm that the train is passing controlled relief line transfers. At the down end of the station there were other points that enabled trains to terminate around the relief platform. Indeed, in the 1910 timetable, this was a common place for services for Birmingham to start. On the right are two lines, one used as a carriage siding, and (as the picture was taken in July) this could be stock for an excursion. Such stock was often prepared at Tyseley carriage sidings during the week, then put out to store in sidings like this ready for the weekend. In between the coaches is the down refuge siding.
(Millbrook House Ltd)

Widney Manor, 1899. A train has arrived on the first day of opening on 1st July. The station was in the middle of nowhere, so quite how the company justified the expense would be interesting to know. Some two years previously, a covenant had been struck with the local landowner, the Greswolde family, that a station would be maintained here for 15 years, to be served by no less than six stopping trains a day and one stopping goods train on each weekday. Large canopies stood out over both platforms, with a covered footbridge connecting this, the Leamington platform, with the other for Birmingham. Notice how, in time-honoured GWR fashion, the steps for the footbridge commence right at the end of the canopies giving passengers continuous protection from the weather. *(Solihull Public Library)*

Widney Manor, 1961. The quadrupling of the line in 1933 retained the layout of the original lines, and added a pair of relief lines to the south. Thus, the site of the original down platform became the place for an enlarged island platform for down main and up relief trains. These can be seen in this view north with a new down relief platform being built to the left. With the time just after 6pm, the 5.50 express for London (Friday's only) is about to explode through the station along the up main. Its relief

train from Birmingham would follow about 10 minutes later. Starting with the 17th June 1957 Summer timetable there were new diesel trains. A half-hourly service to Birmingham was provided, and an extra million passengers were attracted. From 4th March 1968, with the availability of the new New Street station (with its ex-LMR lines electrified) local services were switched from Snow Hill. This necessitated an extra 10 minutes on journey times, with a resultant increase in car congestion. Happily, 10 years later, and with new stations at Moor Street and Snow Hill, this decline has not only been reversed, but aided by a progressive fares policy, even more passengers are using the trains. *(Milepost 92½ Picture Library, AWV Mace Collection)*

Widney Manor, 1956. With the time after ten past seven, the evening calm would be broken as this express passed through on the down main line – King class 4-6-0 No 6005 *King George II* hauls the 5.10pm London to Wolverhampton on 7th August. The train will be trying to pick up speed after its unusual stop at Knowle & Dorridge, two miles before at 7.09pm; Snow Hill is about 15 minutes away. Not only does this picture illustrate well the expansive curves of the enlarged station, but also its signals; the controlling box is just off to the left. Sighting problems have been solved in two different ways – for up fast trains the curve means that the signal has been cantilevered out over the line, while for down fast trains, the signal is obscured by the footbridge, hence its elevation and lower repeater arm. *(M Mensing)*

Widney Manor Signalbox, circa 1905. This was a typical "standard" box in the era from 1896 until the Grouping; note the finials at the joint of the ridge tiles. Opened with the station and extensive goods yard around 1898-9, its 27 levers were increased to 44, probably during quadrupling of the line. The plates with the letters "S" (left-hand end) and "T" (right-hand end, just visible) were used to indicate to crews of passing trains when the Signal Lineman or Telegraph Lineman were needed – before telephones were provided, this was the only way to call for maintenance staff. It is likely that they have been placed here purely for this posed photograph. *(Lens of Sutton Collection)*

Widney Manor, 1959. Having left Moor Street station at 5.20pm, this 4-coach train will stop at all the stations to Leamington, except here! Well able to cope with its load is 2-6-2T No 5163 on 10th June – many commuter trains along the line approached 10 coaches. On the left is the signalbox while the goods shed, complete with 1½-ton crane, is obscured by the engine, which incidentally, still has GWR written on its side tank almost 30 years after it was built at Swindon. There is an interesting use of an old vehicle in the goods yard on the right. *(M Mensing)*

Widney Manor, 2008. With just two lines in use, the opportunity to rebuild the station was taken. The place of the former relief lines is now a road and car park, and any desire to increase the capacity of the line is now very restricted. *(BPC)*

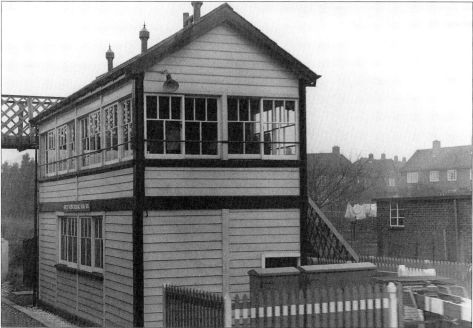

Bentley Heath Crossing, 1911. Just south of Widney Manor station, the main line is crossed on the level by Mill Lane. South of the crossing, a small 15-lever signalbox was provided from 1875, and when in 1901, loops between there and the Knowle station were brought into use, an enlarged frame for the box was supplied. Looking north towards the box, this view shows a mixed freight train passing along the up main line. Heading the train is GWR Bulldog class 4-4-0 No 3354 *Bonaventura*, with the name and number on a combined plate on the side of the cab. Probably the first five vehicles are fitted, including a Mica and an LSWR van, so helping with the train's brake performance and speed. *(G Williams)*

Bentley Heath Crossing, Exterior, 1975, With the quadrupling of the line in 1932, a new completely wooden 49-lever box was built (unique along this stretch of line) north of the crossing. So busy was the line that up and down goods loops were also provided. Not only did the box control the main, relief and loop lines, but also a series of crossovers north of the road crossing that allowed down-main-to-relief and up-relief-to-main transfers; access to a Ministry of Food cold store came off of the down relief. A footbridge allows pedestrians to cross the line without the need to open the gates. *(BPC)*

Bentley Heath Crossing, Interior, late 1940s. Behind the signalman is the wheel that operated the level crossing gates. On the shelf to the right are the block instruments that not only tell him the state of occupancy of each line, but also enable him to communicate with the boxes either side of him. To move the levers the signalman has to pull the catch handle, on the back of the lever, which releases a catch at the lower end of the lever to permit the points and signals to be moved. *(Joe Moss Collection)*

Bentley Heath Cavalcade.
I have taken this opportunity to illustrate some of the many classes of GWR engines that plied this route.

4-2-2 No 3056 *Wilkinson* is heading south with a rather motley collection of vehicles for the 3pm from Snow Hill to Leamington, arriving at 4.02pm in 1910. The second to last carriage was the sort used as slip coaches when modified. On the roof, either side of the raised central portion, would have been two longitudinal cylinders to create the vacuum necessary for the brakes of the slipped portion when released from the train. *(BPC)*

Saint class 4-6-0 No 2902 *Lady of the Lake* travels south in 1910. This 2-cylinder engine was built at Swindon in 1906, and lasted until August 1949. *(HW Burman)*

Star class 4-6-0 No 4034 *Queen Adelaide* approaches Bentley Heath in 1913. This engine earned revenue for almost 42 years, and was only withdrawn two years after the last of the class it was replacing was built. The first vehicle, a siphon, has GW written across its end. *(HW Burman)*

0-6-0 No 673 passes one of the signal posts in the area just before the outbreak of World War I. With its 5ft 2in wheels, this type of engine was the forerunner of the 2301 class, itself the progenitor of the 2251 class. The lightweight nature of these engines made them very versatile and useful for branch line work. *(HW Burman)*

County class 4-4-2 No 3814 *County of Chester* passes with an Oxford to Birmingham express in the late 1920s. A very interesting signal is controlling its progress along the down main line. Not only are the signals hoisted skyward in a most un-GWR-like manner, but there are lower repeater arms too. *(WL Good)*

No book about GWR steam would be complete without a comment about its most famous and travelled engine, King class 4-6-0 No 6000 *King George V*. Following its construction at Swindon in double-quick time in 1927, and after its arrival in America, it acquired a bell, mounted on the front buffer beam, and two commemorative medals that were placed on the cab sides. Originally planned to carry the names of cathedrals, but altered when invited to America, our representative took the name of the reigning monarch. *(WL Good)*

Knowle, 1891. When the line was being surveyed, the local landowner, George F Muntz, "allowed the Oxford to Birmingham Railway to pass through his land at Dorridge providing that the London trains should stop at a station in Dorridge. Muntz laid out his estates near the station for the building of villa type residences for Birmingham industrialists who, like himself, wished to dwell away from the built up city *(less than 14 miles and half a hour away)*." Originally, the station was called Knowle

hence Station Road from that village, two miles to the north. I wonder how many of the 1901 population of 2,093 made the trip behind a horse drawn carriage at a cost 6d, and taking 20 minutes? The Forest Hotel in Dorridge was said to have been built by Mr Muntz so that he could stay there the night before travelling by train to London. The gap left between the lines after the removal of the broad gauge meant there was sufficient room for a water column, seen in this view north. Note that the up signal is not only visible under the covered footbridge, but faintly seen above it. *(BPC)*

Knowle & Dorridge Exterior, 1952. From July 1899, the latter village's name was added, and in May 1974, the original village was dropped from the name. This is currently the limit for supported travel, being at the edge of the borough boundary. Quadruple lines were opened here in May 1933 – the extra pair of lines was to the south west of the station, with the old down platform becoming an island for down main and up relief trains. This booking office, complete with carved names, leads onto the up main platform with the footbridge (part of which can be seen to the right) starting under the canopy. *(RS Carpenter)*

Knowle & Dorridge, 1951. The nameboard stands out proudly as a freight train passes on the up relief line; note the well-tended flower beds. Dating from 1911, this Churchward-designed 2-8-0 engine No 2833 will have been revenue earning for 40 years. Ten of the class were converted to burn oil after World War II. An interesting insight into the way the company worked can be gleaned from some unusual sources. At the 14th February 1907 meeting of the GWR (London) Lecture & Debating Society, the topic was "Goods Train Working", and the presenter stated that between 1901 and 1906, the tonnage carried by the company had increased by 25%. Remarkable as this was, it was achieved with a decrease of mileage of 12½%, and even better for the company's shareholders, by an increase of 27% in their earnings per mile. Timekeeping was improving too – the years leading to World War II, were a golden age for railways in this country. *(BPC)*

Knowle & Dorridge, 1963/4. A goods yard was built just north of the station on the north-east side, and a shed was provided, measuring 120ft by 40ft, and complete with a 1-ton travelling crane inside. This was the site for car-train operations, whereby holiday makers could put their car onto a train to be reunited with their vehicle at their destination. Seen here on the right, were two sidings for unloading up to 14 horse boxes for the Knowle racehorse traffic. A parcels train, hauled by Hall class 4-6-0 No 6925 *Hackness Hall*, has been signalled to pass along the up main line. The four platforms and their canopies show up well. Quadrupling the line demanded more signalling control than the 1875 box could provide, and a 1932 replacement with 74 levers was one of three in the county, the others being at Solihull and Lapworth.
(Milepost 92½ Picture Library, AWV Mace Collection)

North of Lapworth, circa 1960. On the up relief, seen just before entering Lapworth station from the north, is 2-6-2T No 4140 hauling a weed-killing train. It consists of two modified long wheelbase vans and several tanks sandwiched between brake vans. Looking out from one of the vans is an operative making sure the spray (seen near rail level) is working correctly; covers were held over the running lines to prevent spray getting on to them. Other weed-killer trains used old tenders for their source of water. In between the lines on the left, opposite the rear brake van, can be seen the ATC ramps in the down lines. *(BPC)*

Lapworth, Exterior, 1900s. A superb view of the facilities for this settlement, which at that time was a lot smaller – is this the original Park & Ride? The district is more well-known in canal circles than in railway ones because two systems come close together near here, and were connected in 1802. They are the Warwick & Birmingham Canal and the Northern and Southern sections of the Stratford-upon-Avon Canal. The latter canal linked the River Avon with the Worcester & Birmingham Canal at Lifford. Canals in the area had an effect on the price of heavy goods, and (for example) the price of coal fell. They were also well-used carrying bulky materials such as bricks, flour, stone and lime, and cheap machine-made bricks soon destroyed the local trade. The buildings for the station were modified when the lines were quadrupled, the former down-side buildings, becoming an island platform, and the up-side buildings becoming the main entrance.
(Warwickshire County Records Office PH352/108/25)

Lapworth, around 1910. The current station very much resembles the situation at the opening in 1852. There were two platforms for a simple station for the small village of Kingswood, and a crossover between the two running lines and a controlling signalbox were in place by 1875 – but not in the places in this picture. The peripatetic signalbox started off at the end of this, the down platform, but in 1888 it occupied a similar place on the up platform, only to arrive back on the down side (a short distance north from its former site) six years later. Although the Birmingham & North Warwickshire line had been opened by the time this photo was taken, the signs still encourage passengers to "Change for Henley-in-Arden". Discernible on the embankment is an up signal well away from the line – without knowledge of the route, it could easily be missed by the driver of a train. *(Kidderminster Railway Museum, H Bromwich Collection)*

Lapworth, 1920s. An auto train waits at the up platform. While it is tempting to think of this branch being ideal for steam rail motors, a powerful reason for their abandonment was a surplus of small tank engines constructed at the same time. Because of the inherent inflexibility of steam rail motors, these tank engines were increasingly used on auto trains, often hauling trailers made from converted rail motor carriages. *(Warwickshire County Records Office PH352/108/23)*

Lapworth, 1929. Looking towards Leamington, this view shows the enlarged station rather than the one built for the opening of the line in 1852. Both platforms have been extended with a bay added to each, this happening in 1894. As can be seen, the up line had a refuge siding leading to a fair-sized goods yard. A similar refuge siding existed on the down side. *(Clarence Gilbert Series)*

Lapworth, 1964. The GWR decided to quadruple the lines from Olton to here in 1933, and to make Lapworth its terminus for many suburban services. To aid this, it made the down platform into an island, and had the new face connected to the up and down lines. When trains drew up to this new platform face, the main lines would be left free until the train's return departure. The platforms were extensively rebuilt with the footbridge extended to a footpath on the down side of the lines. Racing through the station with a northbound express train is Hall class 4-6-0 No 6903 *Belmont Hall*, a year before its withdrawal. Interestingly, the side of the canopy has a graceful curve on it – probably original. This was an era of well-tended flower beds, and some companies ran a "Best Kept Station" award scheme. *(Joe Moss)*

Lapworth, 1964. About to shatter the peace on the up platform is a train of empty stock with Castle class 4-6-0 No 5056 *Earl of Powis* in charge. When this engine first entered service in June 1936 it carried the name *Ogmore Castle*, but in September of the next year it was decided to transfer the "Earl" names from the 3200 class 4-4-0s to Castle class engines; the original name being given to another member of the class, No 7007, in July 1946. However, at Nationalisation in January 1948, this engine was renamed *Great Western*, and the poor name finally found a resting place with another Castle class engine, No 7035, in August 1950,

where it remained until withdrawal in June 1964. To the right of the train is a loop that is drawn out northwards into an up refuse siding, and extended to the extreme right as a goods yard. About half-way along the train, the vehicles are passing over a facing point that allows up trains to pass onto the line visible to the left of the engine for the terminal side of the island platform. This line also connected with the down main line as well as the relief lines seen over to the left. The steel posted bracket signal on the left has the taller post for the down main line, with the smaller post for the arm to indicate to down trains that they are to move over to the down relief line a couple of hundred of yards ahead. The signalbox, dating from 1894 when it had 35 levers, and enlarged to 78 levers in 1932, is just off the picture to the left. *(Joe Moss)*

Lapworth Frame, 1986. When the adjacent signalbox closed on 1st September 1969, a ground frame was built to operate the trailing crossover at the northern end of the up platform, reminiscent of the situation at opening. Currently, the station is poorly served by trains every two hours, and a couple extra during peak periods; it is unstaffed. The anticipated development of the area hasn't been to the scale expected when the station was enlarged, and there is little opportunity to encourage "Park & Ride" as there is only a small station forecourt. *(JGS Smith)*

Rowington Junction. This was the starting place for the short branch to Henley-in-Arden. Although linking the town by rail to the outside world was a relatively easy aim, the 1861 plan took 35 years to come to fruition. This view is along the main line south of Lapworth towards Hatton, and by this time (probably circa 1950) there was no facing access to the branch. With most of it having been removed in 1917, the stub end acted as a siding trailing into the down main line. A crossover, and hence the need for the signal, between the up and down lines enabled trains to proceed south. As a block post, especially in the summer when there were more trains, the signalbox was retained until 1957, but by that time, few of the 25 levers it contained were in use. *(Railway & Canal Historical Society, Cook Collection)*

Henley-in-Arden Station, early 1900s.
Reflecting the mood of the local population, *The Birmingham Argus*, on the day after opening, said that Henley had slipped from, "considerable prosperity" to "no importance", and added the thought that the line could revive the town's fortunes. To support that view, the reporter added that, "Henley has been long out of this world, and it does not seem reluctant to come into it". The carrying of passengers and children provoked the comment that some of them had never seen a train before.

Above Left: A single platform of 295ft opened north of the town on 6th June 1894, across the River Alne at the end of a short lane. There was an engine shed opposite the station buildings, littered with advertising hoardings. Gas lights had the station's name etched in the glass, and the well-tended flower beds must have taken considerable time and attention. A single track shed was provided which was home for a 0-4-2T of the 517 class until its closure in 1908. Over the fence from the platform were the offices of Truelove the coal merchants, who also had depots at Knowle, Lapworth, Earlswood and Solihull. At the end of the platform, adjacent to the offices are milk churns indicating the nature of the main freight activities. *(GM Perkins)*

Above Right: It has been possible to travel to central Birmingham in 45 minutes since its opening. One such service is shown around 1905 with "double-ender" tank 2-4-2T No 3606 at the head of the train; today's journeys take five minutes less along the North Warwickshire line. After the latter line was opened, Henley-in-Arden had good connections to Birmingham, Stratford-upon-Avon and, with changes, London. However, patronage declined, and the economies needed during World War I meant that closure of the branch would not cause much hardship. This happened from 1st January 1915, with goods services following a year later, and a year later, in 1917, the central part of the branch was closed permanently. Half a mile at the Rowington Junction end was retained as a siding, and about 10 chains (220 yards) was kept at the goods yard end to allow shunting. *(R Carpenter Collection)*

HENLEY-IN-ARDEN BRANCH.

		Week Days.																	Sundays.		
		a.m.		a.m.	Mxd.	a.m.		p.m.	Mxd.	p.m.		p.m.		p.m.		p.m.	Mxd.	a.m.		p.m.	
Kingswood	dep	7 4	...	9 28		11 12		2 40		4 58	...	5 45	...	6 53	...	7 55		10 0	...	4 6	... ...
Henley-in-Arden	arr	7 16	.	9 41		11 24		2 53		5 10		5 57		7 5	.	8 8		10 12		4 17	... ...
		a.m.		a.m.		a.m.	Mxd.		p.m.		p.m.		p.m.	Mxd.	p.m.	Mxd.	a.m.		p.m.		
Henley-in-Arden	dep	7 53	...	8 55	...	10 15		...	1 30	...	4 30	...	5 16		7 22		9 10	...	5 5	... ...
Kingswood	arr	8 5	.	9 7	.	10 28			1 42	..	4 42	..	5 29		7 35		9 22		5 17		

Accident at Henley-in-Arden, 1899. At around 7.40 am, the early morning through train from Birmingham was coming into the station. The line was subject to a 20mph speed restriction, lowered to 10mph for the last part by the platform. The line here was on a falling gradient at 1 in 55, and this, coupled with wet rails, resulted in engine No 3356 going too fast, and running through the stop block. It and its first two coaches ended up in a field four feet below the rail level. No-one was hurt – there were few passengers and the footplate crew had leapt out as the engine passed the platform. The driver was held to be at fault and was fined.

Above: 1902 timetable.

Right: 1884 timetable.

Below: Rowington Troughs. To reduce the time trains spent in stations, and to allow non-stop trains, water troughs were built some distance from main stations. The LNWR introduced them very early on, but it was a while before the GWR adopted them in the late 1890s, and here, closer to Leamington than Birmingham, was a convenient stretch of flat ground. Special attention had to be paid to the drainage of the trackbed as it was subject to constant deluges. Adding to this difficulty would be the possibility of water freezing in cold weather. The troughs were topped up from a 40,000 gallon water tank alongside the track, with its roof just visible above the first coach. By this process it would not take long to top up the 3,500 gallon tender. Heading south, hauled by a County class 4-4-0, is an interesting mixture of coaches. *(BPC)*

GREAT WESTERN RAILWAY.
OPENING OF NEW LINE
BETWEEN
KINGSWOOD
AND
HENLEY-IN-ARDEN

On WEDNESDAY, JUNE 6th, 1894,

The NEW LINE between KINGSWOOD and HENLEY-IN-ARDEN will be Opened for PASSENGER and PARCELS TRAFFIC, and on and from that date,

A SERVICE OF PASSENGER TRAINS
Will run as under :—

		WEEK DAYS.											SUNDAYS.	
		T A.M.	A.M.	A.M.	P.M.	P.M.	P.M.	P.M.	P.M.	T A.M.	T A.M.	P.M.	A.M.	P.M.
Wolverhampton (Low Level)	dep.	—	7 45	9 52	12 10	1 5	3 32	3 40	4 23	5 25	6 10	8 35	4 25
Birmingham (Snow Hill)	,,	7 0	8 32	10 35	1 5	2 7	4 15	5 8	5 20	6 25	7 10	9 20	6 40
Kingswood	arr.	7 31	9 9	11 10	1 45	2 35	4 51	5 32	5 52	6 59	7 45	9 55	7 17
London (Paddington)	dep.	—	6 30	10 2	—	1 30	—	—	—	—	4 45	—	2 30
Oxford	,,	—	8 45	11 54	—	2 53	3 15	—	—	—	6 9	7 25	5 27
Leamington	,,	—	8 55	10 1	22	—	4 15	5 10	—	5 40	7 15	9 5	7 7
Kingswood	arr.	—	9 21	10 39	1 51	—	4 42	5 33	—	6 7	7 42	9 30	7 32
KINGSWOOD	dep.	7 34	9 25	11 15	1 58	2 40	4 55	5 37	5 53	7 0	7 50	10 0	7 37
HENLEY-IN-ARDEN	arr.	7 45	9 36	11 26	2 9	2 51	5 6	5 48	6 4	7 11	8 1	10 11	7 48

		T a.m.	a.m.	a.m.	p.m.	p.m.	p.m.	p.m.	T p.m.	T p.m.	a.m.	p.m.
HENLEY-IN-ARDEN	dep.	7 54	9 4	10 19	12 34	2 17	4 25	5 14	6 13	7 20	9 12	7 2
KINGSWOOD	arr.	8 5	9 15	10 30	12 45	2 28	4 36	5 25	6 24	7 31	9 23	7 13
Kingswood	dep.	9 9	—	11 10	1 45	2 35	4 51	5 32	6 32	7 45	9 55	7 17
Leamington	arr.	9 32	—	11 35	2 9	3 0	5 15	5 50	7 10	8 5	10 20	7 43
Oxford	,,	10 50	—	1 53	4 0	4 17	—	7 12	8 55	9 16	1 0	—
London (Paddington)	,,	12 15	—	3 20	—	5 45	—	8 40	—	10 45	3 38	—
Kingswood	dep.	8 9	9 21	10 39	12 51	2 59	4 42	5 34	6 25	7 32	9 30	7 32
Birmingham (Snow Hill)	arr.	8 50	9 48	11 20	1 25	3 37	5 18	6 12	7 3	8 8	10 10	8 13
Wolverhampton (Low Level)	arr.	10 3	10 45	12 7	2 1	4 28	6 14	6 59	7 52	8 57	10 55	9 3

T These are Through Trains between Birmingham and Henley-in-Arden.

Rowington Troughs, 1933.
The 560ft long troughs were authorised in July 1898, opening on 1st October 1899. To stop the water running out, the track at the ends of the toughs were on a gradient of 1 in 360 for a short distance; white boards, seen to the right, indicated the precise start of the trough. The driver of Mogul 2-6-0 No 6385, at the head of ex-SECR stock from the Kent coast, will be keeping an eye on his speed, as the water scoop worked best between 20mph and 50mph. Until the troughs were opened, it was customary for trains to stop at Oxford or Leamington to take on water. Afterwards, non-stop

trains for Birmingham could take water here, and Leamington could be served by a slip coach. In 1901, the 2.10pm from Paddington would take on water at Goring (west of Reading) and here. Cold weather was a problem, and in the very bad winters of 1917 and 1947 the troughs were shut for many days, engines had to get water at stations or other places where there were water columns. *(BPC)*

Hatton North Junction, 1950. A Castle class 4-6-0 in full flight! No 4092 *Dunraven Castle* heads an up express past the signals at Hatton North Junction. On the bracket signal are three posts – the middle one carrying the up main's arms. The top one is the home signal for here, and the lower arm is the distant for Hatton South some 1,100 yards to the south. The smallest post is for entry into the up loop while, on the left is the pair of arms for the branch. The engine is about to pass over the ATC ramp, which told drivers the state of the signals ahead. *(G Coltas Trust)*

Hatton North Junction, circa 1960. Hall class 4-6-0 No 5955 *Garth Hall* has passed through Hatton station, and is about to pass over North Junction with a down express. The engine obscures the start of an up loop. Built as an up refuge siding in 1892, it was converted into a loop in 1901. This picture, and the next one, was taken from a metal footbridge that still takes a footpath over the line adjacent to the 25-lever frame signalbox which was opened to control the junction. Just beyond this point, would be the place where up trains slipped a portion for Stratford-upon-Avon, it coming to a halt in Hatton station after the main portion of the train had long gone. *(BPC)*

Hatton North Junction, 1962. Heading onto the down main from the branch is Modified Hall class 4-6-0 No 7912 *Little Linford Hall* on 20th July. Brought into use in 1897, the curve from Branch Junction box had a loop added in 1901. This curve was often used as an alternative to the North Warwickshire line to reach Stratford-upon-Avon. The 1960 timetable shows that the 8.32am from Stratford-upon-Avon, having stopped at Bearley and Claverdon, would use this curve to access the main line. Next it would call at Solihull before arriving at Birmingham Snow Hill at 9.18am. *(BPC)*

Hatton South Junction, 1943. Pictures taken in wartime are rare. Even if you had the camera and materials there was always the risk that the authorities would think the worst of you taking a picture of anything that could help the enemy. Coming out of the up goods loop onto the up main line is a lengthy coal train made up of a collection of private owner wagons, all looking different. The loop here could hold 57 wagons as well as an engine and a brake van. Heading the train is USA class S160 2-8-0 No 2138, a long way from its home shed at Leeds. Note the air brake pumps to the right of the smoke box door. About 2,100 of these engines were built and sent worldwide. 796 were sent to Britain, but 18 were lost at sea due to U-boat action. 416 were taken into service for the railways here, the GWR and LNER sharing 360, and the LMS having about 50. Some 362 were stored in various places, many around here and along the OWW at Kingham, ready for D-Day. *(Kidderminster Railway Museum, VR Webster Collection)*

Hatton South Signalbox Interior, 1960. While there were signalboxes at opposite ends of Hatton station and a single branch platform line between them, there was a potential problem – single line working without a token. This was solved by the construction of a new South box on the down platform, and the abolition of the two old boxes. Opening on 8th January 1937, this 84-lever box had the track diagram facing the branch platform with the front windows facing the main running lines. On the shelf are the instruments used to communicate with adjacent boxes, and to indicate if a section of track is occupied or not. Grade One relief signalman Jack Vine is on the right. *(J Moss)*

Hatton, 1963. A station opened here with the Oxford to Birmingham line in 1852. The up and down platforms were altered in 1860 to accommodate the branch to Stratford-upon-Avon, with the down platform becoming an island; the entrance was probably moved to the up buildings. Connecting the island platform with the up platform is a footbridge, which once boasted a roof (it has the GWR initials on the corner triangular piece) and on the island platform is the South signalbox. The rods and wires that control the points and signals leave the building by the gap in the platform support wall. Until 1913, a turntable existed in the space to the left, accessed from the branch platform line. *(Joe Moss)*

Hatton, 1957. Hatton station is between several small villages, and is where the railway line and the canal are next to each other; a handful of houses are sandwiched between the two. Looking from the island platform, we see the ageing wooden and corrugated iron buildings on the up platform. While down trains slipped coaches for Stratford-upon-Avon at Leamington, up trains slipped them here. In 1875, coaches were slipped from three expresses a day, and attached to Leamington to Stratford-upon-Avon local trains. Until 1909, when the track layout was altered, such local trains caused problems because there were no facing points on the down line. A local train from Leamington would have to pull into the station, and then be reversed into what became the down goods loop, before starting off again along the branch line. *(Joe Moss)*

Hatton, 1949. The lengthening evening shadows of the road overbridge nicely stop short of Bulldog class 4-4-0 No 3377 – a single coach of 3rd class accommodation is probably adequate for the early evening service from Leamington to Stratford-upon-Avon. The station nameboard reads, "HATTON JUNCTION FOR BEARLEY & STRATFORD ON AVON". With the closure of the branch from Bearley to Alcester in 1944, that town has been omitted from the new nameboard. Hatton station was the nearest for Budbrook Barracks, home of the Royal Warwickshire Regiment until its closure in 1960, the village of Hampton Magna now incorporating many of its houses. The siding on the extreme left was used for loading horse boxes, which together with a similar siding at the other end of the up platform, accounted for the goods facilities here. *(M Whitehouse)*

Hatton, 1957. About to round the curve through Hatton station is the 2.20pm from Paddington, its first stop being at Snow Hill at 4.18pm; coaches were carried for Birkenhead. Even though train ID numbers had been introduced in 1934, they were replaced by a 4-character system displayed on the smoke box. The first number was the class of the train as denoted by the headlamps, but in this case, the rest of the characters had not been put on, hence the empty holders. King class 4-6-0 No 6005 *King George II* did this type of work for most of its 35-year existence. There is a fine display of GWR signals here – on the left is an up signal, while the bracket signal is for movement from the branch platform to the up main (left-hand arm) or to the down goods loop (right-hand arm). By the small hut on the right, almost at the site of South signalbox, is a post with three signals on it. Top for entry to the siding to the left, middle for the branch platform, and bottom for passage onto the down main by the crossover in front of us. The cluster of signal posts in the background control exit from the down refuge and down siding – sometimes goods trains were backed into here to await their passage north or south. *(P Kingston)*

Hatton, 1960. Having buffered up to the rear of a freight train north of Warwick, 2-6-2T No 4176 is easing off with most of the bank scaled. The station marks the end of the banking section for some down trains, but not the top of the gradient which is some distance north of here. After coming to a halt at the down platform, the engine will cross over to the up main and run down the gradient to Warwick. On crossing over again it will lurk in the down bay for its next duty. *(Colour-Rail, J Moss Collection)*

Hatton Bank. All modes of transport linking Birmingham with Leamington had to travel down into the River Avon valley. For barges on the adjacent Warwick & Birmingham canal, there were 21 locks enabling boats to descend 146½ feet in just over two miles. The speed of up trains would need to be watched carefully while some down trains would have to be assisted from Leamington. The gradient from Leamington gave them a boost until the line passed under the canal, but between the level section through Warwick station (around milepost 90 to just after post 93) and the level section through Hatton station, the bank was steep enough for some freight trains to need assistance. Most of the incline was at 1 in 110 – not the steepest of main line gradients, but sufficient to reduce the speed of an express train to about 30mph. To relieve congestion on the ascent, what started as a down refuse siding became a goods loop in 1911, and was eventually extended all the way to Hatton station in 1914. The actual summit of the climb is not until milepost 94½, north of the junctions at Hatton. The loop could accommodate more than one train, with the second train being allowed to draw up to the signalbox at Budbrook crossing, a third of the way along the loop.

Top: Taking special care with its speed is the driver of Castle class 4-6-0 No 7019 *Fowey Castle* before it acquired its double chimney in September 1958. In the search for improved performance after World War I, this class of engines was very economical, and at the World Power Conference in 1924 its designer, Collett, produced data backing up his claims. This competitive era produced a design for a "Super" 4-6-0 engine to be called the "Cathedral" class, but which became the King class. *(BPC)*

Bottom: Even though they were built especially for this type of role (heavy mineral trains) help at the rear was sometimes needed for these powerful engines. Here, 7200 class 2-8-2T No 7246 is assisted by a 2-6-2T along the down goods line. Having buffered up behind the train at Warwick, the banker will ease off at Hatton, and when a suitable path becomes available, will coast back down to its waiting place in the down bay at Warwick station. Meanwhile, the train, if it is iron ore for South Wales, will descend an even steeper slope to Stratford-upon-Avon. The train engine started life as a Churchward 2-8-0T No 4234, but due to changing economic circumstances, it was altered by Collett in 1938 by increasing the length of the frames, and adding a rear pony truck so that the coal capacity could be increased from 4 to 6 tons. *(G Coltas Trust)*

41

Above: The photographers on the bridge will have been well rewarded by a fine display of smoke as the two engines hurried up the bank. However, Joe Moss, hoping to have a picture of the engines framed by the bridge's arch, was disappointed as the same smoke rather spoiled the effect. Here, the more powerful engine, Hall class 4-6-0 No 6911 *Holker Hall*, leads a smaller, yet only slightly less effective Mogul. The detachment of the lead engine and the insertion of the banker together with the re-assembly of the train engine all took time, but the GWR thinking was that this was the safest and most efficient way to use bankers for passenger trains. At Snow Hill the banker would be removed. *(Joe Moss)*

Right: Warwick, 1950. Looking south from St. Mary's church, this view shows rural Warwickshire with its tourist attraction, the castle, started in 1375, hiding behind the trees. The town's population in 1801 was 5,592 – around twenty times that of neighbour, Leamington. However, while the number of residents here doubled over the next fifty years, its neighbour mushroomed, having three residents for every two in the county town. In *Holiday Haunts* for 1936, the GWR describes Warwickshire (apart from a comparatively restricted industrial area on the northern border) as "like one vast park of green fields and noble trees, with occasional villages of an intimate charm, mellow old manor houses and historic towns. The chief impression left today (despite the troops that have marched and fought in it, especially in the Civil War) is one of an utter and all-enfolding peace". *(BPC)*

Warwick, 1938. Passing Cape Yard is ROD 2-8-0 No 3026 with a freight train that trails back to Warwick station. On the left is an up refuge siding, which in 1944 was converted into a loop. Two workmen seize the opportunity to break from their task to watch the passing train, and perhaps wonder about the person taking such a humble photograph. In most areas of the country, coal was delivered to yards such as this in 10-ton wagons that the men are standing in. It was their job to make the coal stacks seen to the right of the wagons, and they did this by simply shovelling the coal out of the wagon onto the ground by hand. Occasionally, they would get out of the wagon to rearrange some of the larger pieces to form wall, and move some of the coal about to even up the stack – their job didn't cease if it rained, either. The sidings here were used initially when the Royal Agricultural Show was held at nearby Warwick Racetrack, illustrating the essentially rural nature of the area. *(G Coltas Trust)*

Warwick, 1955. The railway infrastructure stands out well in the snow. A train has just departed along the down main line underneath the imposing bracket signal. On the left is the bay for banking engines and on the up side, a train is expected along the main line as the signal is on – the lower arm being off indicating that the train will stop in the station. Waiting while the passenger train occupies its route is ROD 2-8-0 No 3028 with a fitted freight. A few moments later, a stopping passenger train, hauled by a familiar 2-6-2T, passed by on the up line disturbing all the snow. *(N Simmons)*

Warwick, 1960. The small bay that had existed at the Hatton end of the down platform was enlarged when the platform was increased in 1892. A platform to the left was also added, but quite when the water column was installed is uncertain. A common use of this bay was to house engines that would assist trains up the gradient ahead, and it was a convenient time for them to replenish their tanks, as 2-6-2T No 8109 is doing. *(P Kingston)*

Warwick Exterior, 1963.
A short road connects the Coventry Road with the station. The main station buildings are on the down side with a subway to the up platform on a steep embankment. Not easy to spot is the use of two different colours of brick, especially around the doors and windows to give a pleasing effect.
(P Kingston)

Warwick, circa 1924.
A small group of passengers awaits a train on the down platform. The 1892 extensions to the platforms (especially the up) are noticeable, and on that platform is the signalbox which, since 1909, had been doing the work of both the North and South boxes. Notice the number of adverts.
(Stations UK)

Warwick, 1935. Arriving at the down platform is 2-6-2T No 5544 some seven years after its construction at Swindon – notice the sloping tank and sliding cab shutter. With 4ft 7½in driving wheels, these engines were sprightly performers on stopping passenger trains. The stock is interesting – a 70ft "Toplight" non-corridor set dating from 1911, which with their 57ft relatives, dominated the Birmingham suburban scene. The freight facilities at the end of the platform allow for side- and end-loading, with a gauge to ensure wagons were within permitted limits. A double slip is hidden by the dock edge and operated by the two levers beyond the ground signal. Until 1895, a wagon turntable performed the function of the pointwork here. Seen very faintly in the distance is a pair of signals on one post, the lower of which is the distant for the next box along the line – Warwick Avon Bridge.
(RK Blencowe)

Warwick, 1959. The goods yard for the county town was east of the station on Coventry Road. It consisted of three loops, two of which passed through this large shed on the up side. On the down side were a siding (later enlarged to two) and a loading dock at the Leamington end of the down platform; entry and egress was controlled by South signalbox until 1909. A 6-ton crane was available. Rushing past the site is Hall class 4-6-0 No 5912 *Queen's Hall* with an express in June. *(P Kingston)*

Warwick, 1959. When the signalling arrangements were altered in 1909, the Warwick end of the goods yard was controlled by the new signalbox, and the Leamington end by this ground frame with just a handful of levers in no more than a 6ft by 4ft "garden shed". When the rails were removed in April 1961, it ceased to have a use. *(P Kingston)*

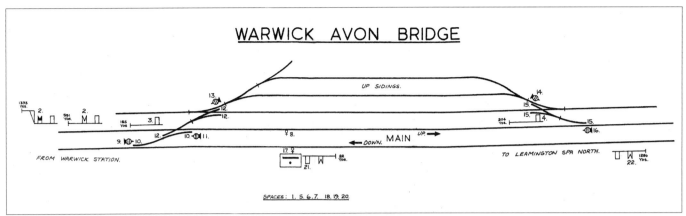

WARWICK AVON BRIDGE

SPACES: 1, 5, 6, 7, 18, 19, 20.

Avon Bridge. On leaving Warwick heading south east, and after passing over the River Avon, the line descends at 1 in 114 to go under the Warwick & Napton canal, and then has to climb at 1 in 109 on its way to Leamington. About ¾ mile from Warwick, and 1¼ miles from Leamington, was the site for three loops on the up side whose access was controlled by the 22 levers of the aptly-named Avon Bridge signalbox; the loops had access to Avon power station. Before World War II, much of the coal in the country was delivered in private owner wagons, and municipal generation of electricity was in its infancy. The journey from colliery to merchant and back to colliery varied between 14 and 23 days. Between 1936 and 1938 Fredrick Fox, a coal factor, bought sufficient wagons and devised a system that took only four days. Fox sold his idea to the Warwickshire & Leicestershire Power Company, which ran a plant here from 1920. The plant ceased operations in 1972, and was demolished in 1974; the site is now occupied by a Tesco supermarket. *(The Signalling Record Society and Derbyshire Records Office, courtesy Keith Turton)*

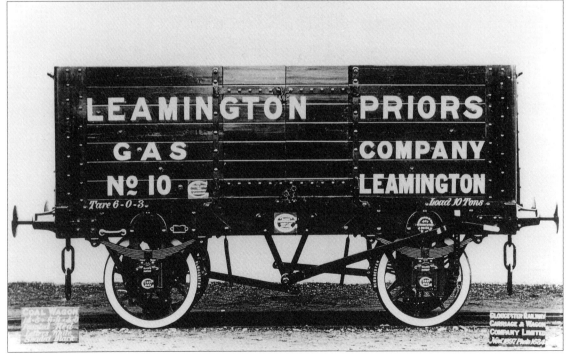

46

Leamington

It is difficult for us to appreciate life in rural areas 200 years ago. At that time the population of Leamington was a mere 315 people, mostly living south of the River Leam in what later became "Old Town". The surrounding land was dominated by farming, a way of life that was only broken by the opening of a canal through the town in 1800. The town is in the floor of the Avon valley with barges ascending and descending. East of Leamington, the Warwick & Napton Canal (opened, 19th March 1800) descends 146ft from the Oxford Canal in 20 locks. West of Leamington, the Warwick & Birmingham Canal climbs a similar height by the 21 steps at Hatton in just over two miles. Goods could pass between London and Birmingham using these canals, which linked up with the Oxford and Grand Union Canals, together with the Birmingham & Fazeley Canal, to provide a through route. However, their effect on Leamington will have been limited. Coal from the Midlands was probably the chief commodity unloaded here, with lime (from quarries south-east of Leamington), bricks and grain also featuring.

Hidden away in the municipal archives is a quotation from the Pump Room Committee, "Leamington owes its existence as a Town to the discovery and exploitation of its healing springs, and to the Spa which made these available to the public which … came in their increasing numbers to gain health and enjoy quiet refreshment of mind and body here". Mineral springs were developed into bathing places from the 1780s, and the Royal Pump Rooms opened in 1814 at a cost of £30,000. Most of this new building took place north of the River Leam across the bridge in "New Town". In 1819, a gas works was established by the canal side.

In 1837, the opening of the London & Birmingham Railway some 10 miles to the north-east changed things forever. With most people never moving far from their birthplace, this was a great distance, but travel was a luxury of the wealthy, as the majority of the local population had neither the time nor the money to spend on such non-essential items. However, the railways encouraged movement both of people and goods, and with the country becoming more prosperous people bought more goods.

It wasn't too long after the opening of the first railways that rival companies sought to develop their lines, and it was the GWR that opened a line through the town on 1st October 1852, the population having exploded to 15,724 the previous year. Originally, the Oxford & Rugby Railway was to pass through Banbury and Fenny Compton before linking up with the London & Birmingham line at Rugby – there was no mention of Leamington at all. Another railway, the Birmingham & Oxford Junction, was to drive south from the Midlands and link up at Fenny Compton, but there was still no mention of Leamington. In fact, the most direct route between Banbury and the Midlands would have by-passed the town to the south as well, but persuasion from the town's businessmen saw the line pass through Warwick and Leamington.

A branch from the LNWR line at Coventry meant that costs could be shared by building a joint station. However, indecision meant that the LNWR went ahead and built their station, leaving the GWR to build its own. It would have been more logical for a branch from the main line to Stratford-upon-Avon to follow the river valleys, but instead, trains have to toil up Hatton bank and then descend into the town of Stratford-upon-Avon.

Top of this page: The Lower Parade, Leamington. *(BPC)*

Opposite page, bottom: Leamington Gas Wagon. In 1838, an Act established Leamington Priors New Gas & Coke Company with an entrance on Ranelagh Terrace and houses in Priory and Gas Streets. When the railways arrived, their coal was cheaper than that delivered by the canal. It was delivered to the railway sidings nearby, and carted to the gas works. *(HMRS, Keith Turton Collection)*

THE LEAMINGTON STATION.

INLAND & MARINE SPAS

ON THE GREAT WESTERN RAILWAY

Leamington Exterior at the Opening. In the *Illustrated London News* for 16th October 1852, was a report of the opening of the line between Oxford and Birmingham on 30th September. The magazine carried a line drawing, which is probably the only picture of the roof over the tracks. The *Leamington Year Book* for the following year describes the station as, "Four lines of rails (broad gauge) with their respective platforms are included under one roof. The length is 270 feet, the breadth 76 feet. The roof is carried on 96 pillars ... rising 30 feet from the level of the rails. Nearly half the space of the roof at the ridge is covered with glass, the remainder is boarded and covered with blue slates." North of the up platform, an excursion platform was created outside the train shed. Access to the platforms was afforded by a subway at the eastern end of the station, and eventually this linked the forecourts of both railway companies.

Inland & Marine Spas. The GWR produced many booklets to encourage people to travel, and *Inland & Marine Spas* described the town thus: "'Leafy' Leamington, one of the most perfectly equipped Spas in England, has much which rivals any of the ... Continental Spas. The title of 'Royal' was given to Leamington Spa following the visit of Queen Victoria to take of the healing and strengthening waters almost directly after her accession to the throne. In the famous Jephson Gardens ... there is a spaciousness that charms at once, sweet-smelling flowers and groups of aromatic shrubs bloom everywhere, and spreading trees offer grateful shade. The Grand Pump rooms itself is exactly opposite." Although patronage had swelled the population to over 25,856 by the census of 1901, twenty years later, it had only grown to 26,888. Attractive and informative as the GWR publicity material was, the railway company was fighting a rearguard action. While little industry came to the town before 1918, it was the development of the Lockheed Works in 1931, and the growth of such industries during World War II that drove the population to 36,500 in 1945. Employment in car-related industries around Coventry has brought further expansion since then.

Leamington Exterior, around 1902. The main station building was this single-storey affair at the western end of the down side. The land falls away to the east so much that at the eastern end of the platforms, a road (Lower Avenue) is crossed by a bridge. In this structure were the booking office, waiting rooms and lavatories. This building was described as being "strongly built of brick and plaster, in the Anglo-Italian style". On the right, accessed from the platform, was a refreshment room, while on the left are the parcels facilities. This was big business for the company, and it had an office in the Parade. The number of items increased from 74,542 in 1903 to 99,615 ten years later. While the 1923 figure was almost static compared with the previous decade, by 1933 it had climbed to 123,473 items. *(BPC)*

Leamington Up Platform, early 1920s. It was a very brave Churchward who, as General Manager of the GWR at the turn of the last century, persuaded the board of directors to buy a French engine. Not only did they do that, but on his advice they bought two more. Here is one of the pair bought in 1905 with an up express. Although the De Glehn engines were noted for their smooth running, there seemed little difference between the French engines and the GWR's own Atlantics. Having slender rods and motions compared to typical GWR mechanisms, led Churchward to liken them to "watchmaker's work". However, their influence (especially the bogie) spread far and wide – even to Stanier on the LMS and Thompson on the LNER. Here is No 103

President in charge of a Wolverhampton to Oxford express at the up platform. To the rear of the short train made up of an interesting set of coaches, complete with destination boards, is an engine; it was the practice to add previously slipped coaches in this manner, and by this manoeuvre, through coaches from Stratford-upon-Avon to London were offered. After being allocated to Oxford, and covering just over ¾ million miles, much of it along this line, the engine was withdrawn in March 1927. *(R Carpenter)*

Leamington Down Side, circa 1936. The two central lines under the train shed were originally used to store coaches, but by 1910, they had been straightened and made into running lines. By the late 1880s the central portion of the train shed had been removed, leaving portions that were of limited use. After a small extension to the platforms by 1886, they were lengthened again in 1901. By the time of this picture, the original goods shed at the end of the down platform had been rebuilt half a mile or so west to make way for a bay platform at the Birmingham end, a parcels bay adjacent to that, and some carriage sidings as well. While the workmen in between the lines have the benefit of a lookout, accidents were all too common. *(Kidderminster Railway Museum, AT Locke Collection)*

Leamington Spa just after World War I. A Saint class 4-6-0 engine rests with a northbound express at the down platform. In the adjacent bay there looks to be a branch train, probably for Stratford-upon-Avon, with passengers transferring to it. Prominent, is the long footbridge which took a footpath across both company's lines. Passing from Old Warwick Road, the

bridge had a set of steps to the GWR up platform before coming down to the road outside the Avenue station of the LNWR. It had been extended over the new lines following the extensions of 1901, but quite when the steps connecting it to the up platform were removed is unclear; it probably coincided with the introduction of platform tickets at the station in 1914. At this time, the GWR was a considerable employer in the town, with something like 100 people having jobs centred on the station.
(Millbrook House Ltd)

THE "SAFETY" MOVEMENT

CHAPTER I.

—

INTRODUCTION.

HUMAN lives are cheap. Dirt cheap. Men risk them for nothing. They sell them like old crocks. They do, really. Men will take their lives in their hands to save a few yards' walk, or to save waiting a minute or two. They'll even do it for fun.

THERE are risks inseparable from every calling. It's a pity, but there it is. Of course, sensible men try to avoid them. Self-preservation is a natural instinct. There might be excuses for lack of foresight or want of thought, but what shall we say of men who, in cold blood, actually adopt dangerous and forbidden practices, and risk their lives for so small a purpose as saving a little time or trouble?

A BIT of straight talk to the men of the railway service on the subject of personal accidents is needed. Many a man in usual and simple duties places his life and limb— and those of his mates—in peril through sheer want of ordinary care. No one has any right to display such indifference in the routine of his work as to cause injury to his fellows or, for that matter, to himself, but it is done almost daily. Worse than this. After regulations have been carefully framed by the railway company for the purpose of guarding against personal injuries, and brought under the notice of every man concerned, they are often flung to the four winds of heaven, and risks and dangers deliberately created.

IS it any wonder that accidents happen? Of course the men judge that it'll be all right. In many cases it is. But sometimes it isn't. It's the all-right cases that make men venturesome. Even narrow squeaks don't make them careful.

THE TRAGEDY OF THE FOUR-FOOT.

"BEFORE Crossing the Line look in both directions " is advice that has been emphasised over and over again. Yet it is disregarded with appalling frequency. Hundreds of men have paid the penalty with their lives. Read these typical cases: An unfortunate yard foreman at Leamington stepped on to the line without looking to see whether or not a train was approaching; an express was upon him almost at once, and the poor fellow was killed. A widow, five children, and an aged mother were left to mourn his loss.

Before Crossing the Line,

LOOK

in BOTH Directions.

The Safety Movement. In 1914, the GWR issued a small booklet to each of its 80,000 employees, so concerned were they about safety. The Board of Trade report on accidents for 1912 stated that "1,500 railway men were injured owing to their own misconduct of caution". In one month (October 1913) six were killed on the GWR, the causes including:

- Crushed between vehicles
- Falling between train and platform
- Being knocked down by rolling stock.

Above: Page 8 of the booklet included the sad story of a Leamington man.

Rebuilding Leamington Spa Station. By the early 1930s, the facilities at the station were becoming very run down and in need of extensive repair, so in 1936, the company decided to replace much of the infrastructure that was part of the original 1852 station with wider, longer platforms, a lower approach road and a new set of buildings. A new subway, at the eastern end of the station under both company's lines, meant that the footbridge could be removed.

Station Approaches, 1937. The sloping nature of the land is well illustrated in this view during reconstruction. The land immediately in front of the booking office has been levelled, and the subway entrance leading to the up and excursion platforms is in front of us. Linking the booking office and the subway was a set of wooden steps to the right of the temporary booking office on the forecourt. The down side part of the wooden canopy at the subway entrance has had to be removed – it used to proudly proclaim the name of the owner. The demolition and construction cost just over £55,000. *(Warwickshire County Records Office S5696: 3/5188)*

Station Interior, 1937. A street-level booking office led to the platforms via a 15ft wide subway and steps; both platforms had refreshment facilities, and electric lifts were provided for the conveyance of luggage. On the longer, wider platforms are new canopies with the ironwork for the roof visible to the rear. Pausing at the down main platform with an express is Saint class 4-6-0 No 2914 *Saint Augustine* of 1907 vintage. Note the absence of the footbridge except for a short section on the left. *(G Coltas Collection)*

Exterior, 1938. The company was very keen on publicising itself, so even before the building is complete, the name stands proudly above the canopied entrance. The heap of rubble is obscuring the entrance to what will be the public subway. The Friends of Leamington Spa station maintain an extensive garden on this site today. The new three-storey entrance building was of brick with Portland stone facings, and with its neat, clean lines must have been a wonderful contrast to what it replaced. Above all the buildings were modern, and so they captured the public's attention – a similar plan for Snow Hill station would have left a lasting impression on American visitors. The bulk of the work was completed by the time war spoilt the euphoria of having new facilities. *(BPC)*

Booking Office Clock, 2008. This picture was taken 100 years on from the day the North Warwickshire Line opened on 1st July 1908. *(BPC)*

The LNWR Side – Leamington, around 1950. Due to railway politics of the day, Leamington had a GWR station, but not a joint one with the LNWR. Standing on the end of the platform for Rugby-bound trains the photographer is looking towards the up end of the GWR station, on the right. The LNWR double track, controlled by these magnificent signals, rises to pass over Lower Avenue and will run parallel to the GWR line for ¼ mile on their routes east. To its right is a low brick wall, and beyond that are the two goods lines that pass to the north of the GWR station to allow their goods trains to bypass the station. Controlling passage along the up goods line is the signal with a white hoop on it. Of course, such trains would have to wait for a pathway before proceeding, and the water column could be used during such a wait. To the left of the brick building can just be made out South signalbox, which not only controls the progress of trains at the up end of the station, but also along the end of the line rising as it passes between the two brick buildings. This is the link between the two systems which was in operation before 1886 – there was a connection through exchange sidings at the down end of the station as well. *(Joe Moss)*

52

GWR Local Services

Leamington Spa, 1957. Built at Swindon in 1933, and designed by Collett as light passenger tank engines, this member of the 5800 class was not fitted for auto-train workings. It has arrived with a shuttle from Stratford-upon-Avon, and will soon retrace its steps. Not being auto fitted meant that the engine always had to lead the train – with auto trains, the train could be driven from either the engine or the modified leading coach. Small shunting engines would have been used to retrieve coaches slipped from northbound express trains, some trains slipping more than one coach – at Bicester for local stations beyond, and at Leamington for Stratford-upon-Avon. The only disadvantage of travelling in a slip coach was that the passenger couldn't make use of the dining car. After collecting the coach it would form a local train to Stratford-upon-Avon. For the return trip, the slipped coach would be brought to Leamington, where the engine would run round it and wait in the excursion platform. When the up express arrived, the engine would add the coach to the rear of the train. Sorting everything out at Old Oak Common for the next day must have been quite a challenge. *(TJ Edgington)*

Leamington Spa, 1959. Built in 1936 at a cost of £5,093, this railcar was one of a batch of three numbered 14 to 16. In 1950, the mileage of all such units was recorded, and this one was found to have covered just over half a million miles. Typical duties included the shuttle between Leamington and Stratford-upon-Avon, clocking up either 117 or 173 miles a day, depending upon which duty it had been allocated. All the seats were second class, and as they could be driven from either end, this type of vehicle superseded the non-auto fitted 0-4-2T. *(P Kingston)*

Leamington Spa 1957. With the time creeping towards 4.20pm, Hall class 4-6-0 No 6947 *Helmingham Hall* is almost ready to depart for its home shed town of Worcester on 16th February. The all-stations journey to Stratford-upon-Avon will take about 30 minutes. Honeybourne will be reached by 5.20pm with all the stations along part of the former Oxford Worcester & Wolverhampton line to Worcester being called at before arriving at its destination at 6.06pm. *(P Kingston)*

GWR Main Line Services

Leamington Spa, 1958. Two lines arrive from the south east into the station area on a series of viaducts and bridges. Adjacent to the South signalbox, two lines branch off and pass to the north of the station as goods lines. The two that continue into the station also divide into one pair for the platforms and another that pass straight through the middle. About to pass onto the latter down line is the "Inter

City", one of the few non-stop trains from the capital to Birmingham. A member of the celebrated King class speeds through the station, reminiscent of trains that carried slip coaches years ago. That operation would have taken place by the signals in the distance. Coaches for Stratford-upon-Avon would have been slipped from the 11.25am, 2.15pm and 5.35pm expresses as "through coaches for Stratford-upon-Avon". As the train passed over the canal bridge there was a slip signal, and at a predetermined point (a landmark, such as one of the road bridges) the Guard would activate the slip mechanism to release the coach from the train. Through trains, especially aimed at the American tourist market, were tried from 1927 leaving Paddington at 9.25am, and returning from Stratford-upon-Avon at 5.30pm. However, they failed to appear in the 1932 timetable, probably due to lack of passengers. *(P Kingston)*

Leamington Spa, 1956. The weight of the Kings restricted them to the main lines from Plymouth and Birmingham to London. According to GWR thinking at the time of their introduction (1927) their power made them admirable for the "Two-hour" expresses along this route, but after nearly 30 years in service, fractures were found in the bogies frames, leading to their

temporary withdrawal in early 1956. The region simply didn't have enough powerful engines to maintain its timetable, so seven Pacific engines were loaned from the London Midland Region. Here, on 18th February, with the time around 3.24pm, 46210 *Lady Patricia* drifts into the station. After a stop at Banbury the capital will be reached two hours and fifteen minutes after the train, carrying through carriages from Birkenhead, had left Snow Hill. *(P Kingston)*

Leamington Shed, 1963. For over 50 years, an engine shed had been located on the up side of the line beyond Leamington station towards Warwick with a capacity for three engines. This must have been hopelessly inadequate, as from September 1906, a new shed was built some ¾ mile to the east of the station, beyond the link between the LMS and GWR lines, which opened two years later. The four-road straight shed was situated on the up side of the line, complete with a 65ft turntable and coaling facilities. Adjacent, were five loops for storing carriages, and from July 1959 they were modified for use as a diesel refuelling facility for DMUs on Birmingham suburban services. *(R Carpenter)*

Bottom left: Leamington Shed 1932. Prior to the 2-6-2T becoming the standard GWR engine for suburban passenger services (ten being allocated here in February 1954) engines such as these were used, nine being allocated here in 1911. First introduced in 1900 with a 2-4-2T wheel arrangement, they were called "Double-enders". The design incorporated several new ideas such as an enclosed cab and a water scoop capable of being used in either direction. The vent, sticking out from the middle of the side tank, had to be enlarged as collecting water at high speed caused the tanks to split. In 1921, 17 engines were allocated here, ranging from 2-4-0T Metro tanks to ROD 2-8-0s, with passenger engines such as 36XX 2-4-2Ts and Bulldog class 4-4-0s being the commonest. By 1932, 19 engines were allocated here. *(G Coltas Collection)*

Bottom right: Leamington Shed, 1953. This rather unusual view of GWR facilities is taken from the LNWR line to Rugby. Ahead is that company's GW Junction signalbox, with the controlling bracket signals for trains to proceed along their lines towards Avenue station. Adjacent to that structure, the line passes across the Warwick & Napton canal, on the other side of which another signalbox can be made out in the distance – this is the GWR's South Junction box (called East Junction until 1914) at the start of the viaduct approaching that company's station. On the left are the GWR's facilities for its steam engines. The coal wagons will have been pushed through the brick structure with a large water tank on top to replenish the tenders and coal spaces of tank engines. This involved men shovelling coal from the wagons into a half ton container on wheels, which was then pushed to the overhang and emptied into the engine's coal space. The shed closed on 14th June 1965.
(Milepost 92½ Picture Library, AWV Mace Collection)

The Branch Line to Stratford and Beyond

With the altitudes of Leamington, Stratford-upon-Avon and Honeybourne being similar, it would be reasonable to assume that the railway surveyors followed easy contours to link the towns up. While this is true for the southern approach, one would have thought that the valley of the River Avon from Leamington would have been followed for the northern one. However, this was not to happen, so trains have to struggle up the Hatton bank, leave the main line and then descend, at a steeper gradient than before, to their destination. Trains were often banked up each gradient.

Down Train for Stratford-upon-Avon, 1942. Approaching Hatton is railcar No 29 with an extra coach to give increased accommodation. It is no ordinary coach, but an auto trailer, probably a converted steam railmotor. One advantage that steam auto trains had was that they could operate in either direction without the need for a reversal. However, when paired with a diesel railcar, the trailer would need to be detached before a return trip. At Leamington, this was done in an interesting manner; arriving at Leamington shed with the trailer in tow, the train would pull into the line leading to the carriage sidings. The railcar would be detached and enter one of the loops. Next, the brakes of the trailer would be released, and it would run into another of the loops, as they were on a falling gradient. All the railcar needed to do now was come up the slope, reverse onto the trailer, and away they could go. It was interesting and fascinating to observe, but time-consuming and potentially hazardous. In the previous year, this railcar, one of five, cost £6,240, it would be difficult to buy a small family car for that price today. *(VR Webster)*

Hatton, 1956. A passenger alighting from an up train from Birmingham would have this view of the station's island platform. At the end of the brick building is the Gents' lavatory with its entrance protected by a wooden screen, and hanging from it are three fire buckets. The station nameboard around the 1930s had said *Hatton Junction for Bearley Alcester & Stratford on Avon*. However, to reflect various line closures, the word Alcester has been blanked out. Passengers changing trains here used the footbridge and had the benefit of a refreshment room in the main building, beyond which is South signalbox. On the right, is a grounded coach body serving as a cycle store. While down trains were able to slip coaches for the branch at Leamington, up trains slipped them here, and afterwards they were attached to the rear of branch trains. Slip portions from up trains ended as a World War I economy measure, never to be reinstated. *(RM Casserley)*

Hatton, around 1960. Passengers will have climbed the stairs and crossed the lines by the GWR-built metal footbridge. Looking down and to the south we see the platform they had alighted onto. Access to the station would have been through the wooden building that contained the booking office and ladies waiting room and lavatory. The brick wall to the left, bearing several buckets of sand in case of fire, screened the gentlemen's facilities. Seating was provided by two benches on the platform with the company's initials on the supports. Beyond the access road, the rural nature of the area is apparent with just a couple of houses and the canal behind them. The surroundings have altered little over the years. *(J Moss)*

Hatton, around 1950. Looking north from the footbridge, this view shows the signalling arrangements for the junction. On the left is the down island platform with the road bridge dictating the height of signals for visibility. Of the four distant arms in view, only the down main line's arm is not fixed. On both bracket signals, the left-hand arms are for the branch and the right-hand arms are for the main line. The roof of the footbridge was removed later in this decade for maintenance purposes, and to aid the sighting of these signals. *(J Moss)*

Hatton Junction, 1929. The 9¼-mile line from north of Hatton station was promoted by the Stratford-upon-Avon Railway Company in 1859, and opened in October 1860. A single line of mixed gauge was sufficient to cope with the numerous coaches serving Shakespeare's home town. Looking from the road bridge we see the scene before the 1936 signalling alterations. In 1897, to accommodate new arrangements for the junction, the North signalbox was moved some thirty yards to the position shown here. At the same time, North Junction signalbox was opened, so this box was renamed Middle box. Curving away to the right is the main line to North

Junction, Lapworth and Birmingham. On the left is the branch to Branch Junction and Stratford-upon-Avon. Notice how branch trains could access all three running lines through the station and the bidirectional running permitted by the signals. *(Clarence Gilbert Collection)*

Hatton, 1956. From almost the same vantage point, over 27 years later change has arrived. Gone is Middle signalbox like North box before it, and the layout of sidings has altered. A new South box opened on the island platform replacing Middle and South boxes. Interestingly, the up signal post now only needs to carry a single arm. Drifting along the up main line is an unidentified 2-6-2T. It has probably helped push a freight train "over the knob", by North Junction. Having eased off, this engine would then have used the trailing crossover by that signalbox to gain this line. Warwick and the down siding would be its destination. Allowances were made for around a dozen trains a day to be banked. Notice the ATC (Automatic Train Control) ramp in the down line adjacent to the engine. The area in the triangle created by the lines here was once used for the disposal of a trainload of more-than-ripe bananas when the mechanism for carrying them broke. The ripening led to fermentation, and the heat generated caused some fires to start. Water applied by the fire brigade only made matters worse, as did subsequent downpours of rain, and the smells and steam from the area apparently went on for many years. *(RM Casserley)*

West Junction, 1950. Having cleared Hatton station, this freight train is passing the former Branch Junction box at Hatton West Junction. Bending away to the left is the curve to meet the main line at North Junction. This section came into use from 23rd July 1897, and here was the start of the single line to Stratford until the branch was doubled in 1939. Signalled in the up direction is a train towards Hatton station, the other arms being for the curve north and a loop from it, with a capacity for 55 wagons. The gradient from Stratford-upon-Avon to here was more severe than that on the main line. Banked trains would come to a stop on the branch, the banking engine would be uncoupled, and at a suitable time, it would return down the gradient. 28XX class 2-8-0 No 3815 hauls a fitted freight down the gradient towards Stratford-upon-Avon. It will need the extra braking power of the wagons as the weight of itself and the tender would be insufficient to stop the train. *(Millbrook House)*

Hatton West Junction, 1969. A train from Hatton station is heading south, and is about to pass the signalbox sometime between singling of the line (12th January) and closure of the box (1st September) 1969. A scene reminiscent of how the line operated for most of its existence has been captured. To ensure that two trains don't collide on the single line, the signalman is handing the token (a metal loop) to the driver with the train slowing to a walking pace for the collection. At the other end of the section, the driver will give the token to the signalman there. This is one of many sections of line that have been singled and now, due to increased traffic, they are a bottleneck to traffic. In the background, on the right, are the signals for the now two lines here; the right-hand post is for the single line to North Junction, while the left-hand post is to Hatton station. *(Kidderminster Railway Museum, D Wittamore Collection)*

Claverdon, 1931. About a mile and a half along the branch was the station to serve the village of Claverdon. At the opening, the single line had a short siding for local coal merchants, and this later became a loop. *(Clarence Gilbert Collection)*

Claverdon, 1939. By July 1939, the line was doubled under a Government scheme, and opened on the 2nd of the month. As can be seen in this view towards Hatton, the old platform looks very much intact serving just the up line. In the background, is the new signalbox with the loop for delivering coal not yet ballasted. About to pass under the road bridge is a local stopping train for Hatton with 2-6-2T No 5163 pulling an interesting couple of coaches. *(G Coltas Collection)*

Claverdon, date not known. This track-level view puts the two stations into perspective. Under the road bridge can be seen the single platform that served from 1860 until 1939. On this side of the bridge are the two 150-yard long platforms with identical buildings on each, connected by a new concrete footbridge. The buildings housed waiting rooms and toilets. This view is looking north towards Hatton, the gradient being upwards. *(Railway & Canal Historical Society, Cook Collection)*

Claverdon, date not known. At road level a new set of facilities was built to the west of the line including a booking office and a room for parcels. Construction began in March 1938. *(Railway & Canal Historical Society, Cook Collection)*

Claverdon, 1939. Looking south we see that passengers have alighted from a typical two-coach formation local train. On the rear coach are the words, "Leamington Stratford and Worcester"; this was No 1 set. *(WA Camwell)*

Claverdon, 1957. Having left Stratford-upon-Avon fifteen minutes previously, this train is half-way through its journey to Leamington stopping at all stations. Making light work of its slim, but adequate load, is 20-year old Grange class 4-6-0 No 6851 *Hurst Grange* on 22nd April. This class of engine was designed in the Churchward era to replace the worn-out 2-6-0 Moguls. However, this class of engines was slightly heavier, so was restricted from certain routes; it was the Manor class of engines that really filled the gap. The signal controlling down trains from the end of the up platform has been removed. *(TJ Edgington)*

Claverdon, 1964. Waiting at the down platform is Castle class 4-6-0 No 5042 *Winchester Castle* heading a train from Leamington. The engine was built in Swindon in 1935, and would be in service for almost thirty years, a figure regarded by some companies as the expected lifespan of an engine – not by the GWR though!
(Warwickshire County Records Office: PH167/92)

South of Claverdon, 1938. It wasn't until July 1939 that the line was doubled from Hatton West Junction to Bearley. Having been given the road from the signal protecting Mother Cooper's crossing at Edstone, diesel railcar No 4 continues on its journey to Hatton. On the right is Bearley East Junction's distant signal. Two railcars were diagrammed to shuttle between Leamington Spa and Stratford-upon-Avon, with forays to Honeybourne. Diagram 'A' required the unit to be in revenue earning service for only just over a third of its thirteen-hour day. There was a 2½ hour period in the morning and 3½ hours in the afternoon when it was simply doing nothing – a far cry from today's cancelled services due to stock shortages. *(Kidderminster Railway Museum)*

Approaching Bearley, 1956. Descending the incline into the Avon valley from Hatton will take all of the driver's skill. Having controlled his train's movements down the slope from Hatton to here, he will have the steep 1½ mile gradient at 1 in 70 into Stratford-upon-Avon to contend with. Fortunately, as the headlamps show, the brakes of the wagons containing iron ore, are connected to those of the engine making his life much easier. 28XX class 2859 of 1919 vintage has passed Bearley's easily-visible distant signal on its way to South Wales. As many as six trains a day would make this trip through Honeybourne and Gloucester with empties travelling via Hereford and Worcester. Prior to the GWR constructing the first 2-8-0 in the country in 1903, refuge sidings were built for trains not exceeding fifty wagons. When these engines were introduced with their massively increased haulage capacity (70 loaded or 100 empty wagons on many routes) their timetabling needed to be very carefully done until sidings could be enlarged to cope. *(RC Riley, Transport Treasury)*

Bearley, around 1910. The photographer is standing on the bridge that carries the line across the main road to Birmingham; Bearley village is about a half a mile to the left, 4½ miles south of Claverdon. Access to the station is along the lane on the right, the house being the dwelling of the station master. The layout enabled trains to pass with platforms being provided for both lines on the loop. The main station buildings were on the Hatton-bound platform, with a shelter for down passengers. The larger canopy is on the platform on the right, for Hatton and Leamington. The station buildings housed a booking office, waiting room and lavatories. In the distance is the controlling signalbox, Bearley East Junction, with some of its rods and wires in front of us. Access to the platform for Stratford-upon-Avon, as well as the branch to Alcester, would be by walking across the two lines on the wooden crossing at the ends of the platforms. The lane leads to the goods shed and goods yard. *(Warwickshire County Records Office: PH352/25/2)*

63

Bearley, early 1920s. By this time, the loop had been lengthened about 800 yards towards Hatton. As the original set of points was retained, there were effectively two loops. It appears that there is little apart from the Great War between this picture and the previous one until the nameboard is inspected. It used to read BEARLEY JUNCTION FOR ALCESTER HENLEY IN ARDEN AND NORTH WARWICKSHIRE LINE STATIONS, but a word is now missing from the second row. Although the branch to Alcester was made in 1883, services for both goods and passengers were withdrawn from 1st January 1917, and the track removed, hence the removal. Relaying meant that the reopening could take place from 1st August 1923. *(Stations UK)*

Bearley, 1937. Just arriving from the Alcester branch is an auto train, composed of 0-4-2T No 4801 and trailer coach No 76. Sometimes mixed trains ran along the branch line, with the engine sandwiched between a coach, or coaches, at one end and goods wagons at the other. This view is south with the signals for the departing branch on the extreme left. After leaving the station, the single branch line heads west to meet the MR at Alcester, 6½ miles distant through rural Warwickshire following the River Alne. The second opening of the line lasted until World War II. However, due to the relocation of a factory from Coventry at Great Alne because of enemy action, it reopened in 1941. Passenger services were withdrawn in 1944 and freight services in the 1950s. The short curve from Bearley East Junction to North Junction survived a little longer, as it formed part of a diversionary route when the main line was being repaired. *(RJ Buckley, Initial Photographics)*

Bearley, 1959. Iron ore from Northamptonshire was moved along the branch via Stratford-upon-Avon, Honeybourne and Cheltenham to the steelworks in South Wales. However, the single line branch was becoming a barrier to such traffic, so the decision to double the line from Bearley to Hatton was enacted in 1939, causing some alterations at the station here. In this view north towards Hatton, the extensions to both platforms can be seen, as well as the construction of a footbridge – necessary now that the line was busier. The awning for down line passengers looks bigger than the shelter it is attached to. Two sidings were added behind the signalbox as well as one to the goods yard. On the left is the empty goods shed. *(Stations UK)*

Bearley East Junction, 1956.
Prior to the opening of the branch to Alcester, Bearley was a crossing place on the Hatton to Stratford-upon-Avon single line. Standing in the goods yard looking south, this view shows the signalbox that became operational by 1872. With the opening of the North Warwickshire line in 1907, its frame was enlarged to 31 levers, and further to 37 levers in 1938, in readiness for the doubling of the line. An early-morning freight to Honeybourne has been given permission to proceed towards Stratford-upon-Avon; the lower signal of the left-hand pair is operated by the box in front on that line, Bearley West Junction. The right-hand pair of arms is for the branch to Alcester, which meets the North Warwickshire line a short distance away at Bearley North Junction. That box operates the lower of the two arms. *(Kidderminster Railway Museum)*

Road Transport. While today's rail network seems passenger orientated, this hasn't always been the case – indeed, until the late 1950s, freight earned the major share of the revenue for a line. Although outside the scope of this book, figures for the Alcester branch illustrate this decline well, hence the empty goods shed at Bearley.

Date	Revenue from freight	% of revenue from freight	% of revenue from passengers
1925	£7101	82%	18% (£1554)
1938	£1418 (down 80% from above)	69%	31% (£630)

As can be seen the drop in amount of freight carried on this rural branch line was 80%. One of the reasons for this was the large number of surplus reliable vehicles (and men who could drive them) after World War I. These men used pay-offs to set themselves up as road hauliers, carrying what they liked (or not) at the rate they could set themselves. There was no way that the railways (by law, common carriers of all freight wherever the customer wanted) could compete. Railways also had to pay rates to local authorities that hauliers did not, and damage to the roads was paid for from the rates while damage to the railways was paid for by the railway companies themselves. One way round this competition was for small freight traffic to be sent to railheads for onward delivery by motor vehicle. Here is one such motor vehicle with would-be drivers receiving instructions in safety. Large numbers of these Scammell "mechanical horses" and their trailers, including the covered type, were used for around thirty years. *(BPC)*

Wilmcote, circa 1900. About a mile and a half south, the village of Wilmcote is skirted by the line with a station situated adjacent to a road bridge. As at Claverdon, a single platform sufficed with its names on the glass of the gas lights and well looked-after flower beds. In this view towards Stratford-upon-Avon, the pointwork for the small goods yard at the end of the platform can just be made out. Lime and cement were the chief products, as well as the typical agricultural needs and products (witness the milk churn). *(HMRS)*

Wilmcote, 1924. With the construction of the North Warwickshire line from Tyseley, a junction was created at Bearley West in 1907, about a mile north of the station. The line from Bearley station (and East Junction) was doubled to West Junction at that time too. Faintly visible through the road bridge is the original station, as a new one was built on the other side of the bridge. Opening on 9th December 1907, it had two platforms joined by a fine covered footbridge. The signalbox was moved from the down side to the up side, as shown through the road bridge. *(Stations UK)*

Wilmcote, 1959. Little changed over the years, apart from the complete removal of the original platform. Electricity has replaced gas for platform lights, and much more modern pictures show the covered footbridge still in good repair. On leaving the station, the line soon descends at 1 in 75 for the best part of a mile. This caused difficulties for northbound trains, which often had to be banked, and this was one of the reasons why a shed was needed at Stratford-upon-Avon. *(Stations UK)*

Wilmcote, 1964. Although many lines have refuge sidings, it is rare to see pictures of them in use, let alone with a train entering or leaving. This train, heading north, has passed this point before; it will have pulled into the station and then reversed into the siding, either to let a faster moving train proceed ahead, or to wait for a passage through the network ahead. Getting its train going up the gradient towards Bearley West Junction is Modified Hall 4-6-0 No 7926 *Willey Hall* on the morning of 15th May. *(M Mensing)*

Stratford-upon-Avon

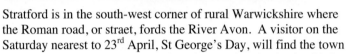

Stratford is in the south-west corner of rural Warwickshire where the Roman road, or straet, fords the River Avon. A visitor on the Saturday nearest to 23rd April, St George's Day, will find the town impassable due to the number of tourists, as that day is also Shakespeare's birthday, and it seems that the whole town comes out to enjoy the pageantry. The town is rich in old buildings, some seen in this 1950 photograph of the High Street (above right). In adjacent Henley Street, and still standing, is the house where Shakespeare was born in 1564 (back cover, top). Half-timbered houses of the Tudor period abound, a good example being the Falcon Hotel in Chapel Street, but there are many more.

The town has always been a favourite with visitors, especially from America, and since the 1970s, Japan – all trying to discover "real England", and with the railways eager to transport them here. Among the many postcards issued by the GWR was this one of Stratford shown above left. The Royal Shakespeare Theatre (below) dates from 1932, replacing an earlier theatre that was destroyed by fire in 1926 (back cover, middle). With seating for about 1500 people, much of the money to build this Grade II* listed building was raised in America. A redeveloped theatre here opens in 2010. *(BPC and Alan Bennett Collection)*

Stratford-upon-Avon, 1943. An up goods train is leaving the goods yard on its way to Tyseley. Having probably originated at Honeybourne, it will have stopped here and reversed into the Birmingham Road yard. After removing and adding wagons, the train is heading north again under control of Earl class 4-4-0 No 3210. Wartime pictures like this are extremely rare, as anyone taking pictures of infrastructure was though of as being "up to no good". The railways felt that they were badly treated by the Government during World War II, and statistics to support their view comes from the Ministry of Supply – the GWR estimated that in 1946 it would need 25,000 chairs (the iron pieces that rails rest in on the wooden sleepers) every year for the next three years, based on the fact that in 1938 they had used 19,000 chairs. They were granted 12,500. Due to the backlog of repairs, the company could only count on 4,441 coaches for use on any day in 1946; in 1938 they had used 5,819 daily. A survey done in 1956 showed six iron ore trains heading for South Wales with most stopping for water here – note the parachute water tank. The weekend survey logged just one empty returning. *(VR Webster, Kidderminster Railway Museum)*

Stratford-upon-Avon, 1934. The terminus of the line from Hatton was north of the canal adjacent to the main road to Birmingham. At the opening on 10th October 1860, the Stratford-upon-Avon Railway was mixed gauge so that broad and narrow gauge trains could use the branch. It was worked by the GWR, as the parent company had neither engines nor rolling stock. While the train shed seen here survived, the station offices didn't, as five years after opening, they were dismantled and rebuilt at the town's new station. The Birmingham Road site was used for some years as a departure point for excursion trains. The goods depot came under Worcester, and here 21 staff would have been employed. Receipts went up from around £29,000 in 1903 to around £35,000 at the time of the picture. *(LGRP)*

Birmingham Road Goods Station, 1963. After the departure of the passenger services south across the canal to the new station, this site developed into an extensive goods depot. Typical of the motive power for shunting in the yard, local trips and banking duties was this Collett "22" 0-6-0 No 2210, usually positioned at the neck to the goods yard when idle. As an outstation of Tyseley shed, engines such as this would probably stay here for a week. Another engine, clean and fresh from the parent shed would come light engine, crews would swap over, and the old engine would be taken for a washout and repairs. Some members of this class received tenders from pre-war scrapped ROD 2-8-0 engines – recycling isn't a new phenomenon. *(Joe Moss)*

Birmingham Road Goods Station, 1968. Flowers brewery had extensive sidings to their premises as did the local gas works, hence the gas holder in the background of many pictures. Across the main Birmingham Road was a brick and tile company that had a siding from the goods yard. This was worked by a horse pulling wagons across the road, and later it became a scrap metal yard. In the 1950s, it was the custom for an afternoon trip to be taken to the "Old Town" station, the former LMS yard, to exchange wagons with the yard here. Coal for domestic purposes would have been big business in the yard, with town deliveries by horse and cart until just after World War II – the depot had six vehicles and three horses. Difficulties in obtaining supplies due to the rail strike caused one merchant, WH Jackson, to cease operation in 1955. Some of the buildings were used for the storage of animal feed and fertilisers reflecting the main industry locally. As a consequence of the post-war reorganisation, "smalls" traffic (under one ton) was concentrated at sub-railheads such as here (the former LMS doing something similar). Goods were then delivered by "mechanical horses" to addresses in the town and by larger lorries for the more rural areas (for example Shipston-on-Stour, Long Marston and Milcote). *(J Tolson)*

Stratford-upon-Avon, 1963. This fine specimen of a bracket signal is on the original route of the line south across the canal to the new station from the junction with the original terminus – now the goods yard. In 1911, new lines were built from the goods junction to a new layout at the station. The original crossing became a down loop with connections to the down platform, the road being granted by the right-hand arm. The other two arms have white hoops on them indicating that they are for shunting purposes, leading to an unloading bay (middle arm) or to the engine shed (left-hand arm). On the right is the coaling stage with wooden cladding. Compared to many such buildings,

this offered quite a degree of protection from the elements for the workers. Their job was to shovel coal from the mineral wagons on the right into the coal spaces in the engines waiting below the protuberance on the left of the shed. On the top of the shed was a water tower supplying several water columns in the vicinity. The allocation in 1921 consisted of five engines, the most numerous being 3251 class 4-4-0s. By 1934, just two more engines had been drafted in here. *(Joe Moss)*

Stratford-upon-Avon. Languishing in the loading dock is another example of a Collett designed engine, No 2292. This double sided dock was very useful for unloading horses destined for the racecourse in the town. It was not uncommon for a van of fish to arrive in the early morning, and to be unloaded at this dock; the loading gauge ensures that vans will not foul the bridges. The two schoolboys on the right are probably looking in their *ABC Combined Volume* to find out if they have seen this particular engine before. The owner's crest is displayed on the side of the fine covered footbridge in the background. *(RK Blencowe)*

Stratford-upon-Avon, 1958. On the left, is the original alignment of the line to the station with the hump over the canal clearly visible as a down loop and an occupied carriage siding. In 1911, major improvements were made at the station, involving the building of a two-road engine shed to supersede the cramped single-road site south of the station; it measured 155ft by 38ft. At the end of the shed was the canal with the building in the background being accessed from the goods lines north of the canal. Originally built as a two-road shed, it was the closure of the former LMS shed that precipitated the laying of the siding on the left in 1957. As a sub-shed of Worcester, it employed 24 people in 1929. On the shed is a Prairie 2-6-2T, with a 2251 class 0-6-0, 2-8-0 "Austerity" and a Fowler 4F 0-6-0 behind a water column. There wasn't a turntable here, but there was one at the "other" railway, and there was always the triangle at Bearley that could be used to turn engines around.
(Transport Treasury)

Stratford-upon-Avon, Arrivals from the North.
An express from Birmingham runs into platform 1 on 15th June 1957. In charge is Castle class 4-6-0 No 5045, complete with Hawksworth straight-sided tender. From its construction in March 1936, this engine carried the name *Bridgwater Castle*, being renamed *Earl of Dudley* in September 1937. The signalman in Stratford-upon-Avon East signalbox will have pulled a lever to allow the top arm of the post in the background to fall, indicating that the train is to proceed. The bottom arm hasn't been pulled, showing that the train is to stop in the station. For sighting purposes the tall up starter signal is on the wrong side of the line. *(RK Blencowe)*

On a wet miserable day in the early 1960s, Churchward-designed 2-8-0 No 2824 brings empty coaches into the down platform ready for an excursion (C10). The smoke vents for the engine shed can be seen on the left, while a typical GWR water column stands at the end of the down platform.
(Mile Post 92½ Picture Library, AMV Mace Collection)

Stratford-upon-Avon, Northern Departures
With the curve from the station, the bridge across the canal, and then the 1 in 75 up to Wilmcote, the exit from the station is anything but easy for train crew for the first two and a half miles. Two bankers were employed at the station, one for goods trains and one for passenger trains. Those for the latter usually buffered up and pushed from the rear as far as East box, and for the former as far as Wilmcote. However, trains needing assistance along the North Warwickshire to Earlswood, had to have the extra engine coupled at the front, meaning that it would not be available for quite a time to do other duties, and the footplate staff would have to return tender first with little protection from the elements.

Above: 1963. Leaving the station is a special train for the Midland & Great Northern Society on 5th October hauled by LNER class B12 No 61572. Giving the train crew a breather is the banker, 2251 class 0-6-0 No 2210, seen previously on shed. *(TJ Edgington)*

Right: Around 1955. Train crews from both engines are anxiously looking back to the station for the signal to proceed. Meanwhile, many passengers, wondering why they had spent so long (around 5 or 10 minutes) at the station stop are equally anxiously peering out of their windows. Some might be just curious about the noise and jolting they had experienced as the assisting engine was inserted between the coaches and the train engine. Here, 2252 class 0-6-0 No 2257 is assisted by an unidentified Grange class engine. *(Milepost 92½ Picture Library, AWV Mace Collection)*

Stratford-upon-Avon, around 1910. In the early 1860s, the town had two single lines both ending at opposite ends of the town – this one south from Hatton, and another north from Honeybourne; passengers would have to make their own way between them for a through service. Extending the two single-line railways, and connecting them in the town was not too much of a problem, the real dilemma was where to site the new, single passenger station. It was to be built next to a road crossing, but would it be the Alcester or Evesham road? On 17th September 1861, the town council decided on the Alcester Road site, so a temporary wooden platform and buildings were duly erected there and used from 1st January 1863. This temporary arrangement sufficed for a couple of years, with a new set of offices being completed at the end of 1865, a wooden roof providing protection for passengers. It wasn't until 1891 that the up platform was erected, complete with a footbridge for access. It also had a bay platform facing north, hidden from our view. A local train hauled by 0-6-0 No 1753 has arrived at the down platform.
(Shakespeare's Birthplace Trust)

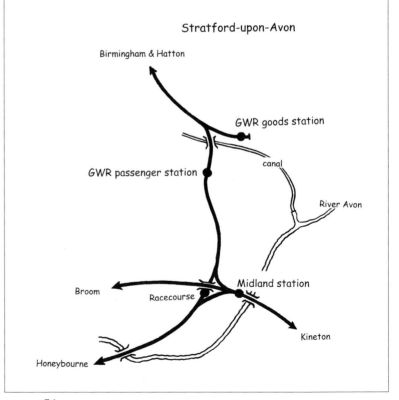

Stratford-upon-Avon

Birmingham & Hatton

GWR goods station

GWR passenger station

canal

River Avon

Broom

Racecourse

Midland station

Kineton

Honeybourne

Stratford-upon-Avon, around 1910. Standing on the Alcester Road bridge and looking north, this view shows how the station was enlarged from 1911. The up platform has now become an island by the bay to the south west being extended to create a loop joining the main line beneath us; a loop siding was later built to its left. A catch point prevents rolling stock sliding out onto the up main line. The brick building on the old up line has been removed to widen the platform, and an entirely new building has been built with a 222ft roof above a general waiting room, refreshment and tea rooms. Arriving from the north is an auto train, probably from Hatton or Bearley. Given the publicity that the company lavished on the area, it took a surprisingly long time for it to create a station worthy of its trade. However, the timing (soon after the opening of the North Warwickshire line) shows where the real pressure for change came from. The standard GWR brick buildings were augmented by the addition of an extensive awning to the south to give more passenger protection, and for the storage of bicycles. The remodelling was

largely due to the growth of American tourist traffic, and I wonder how many would agree with the comment in the *GWR Magazine* about the new buildings: "The general appearance of the station combines, with a sense of fitness for its utilitarian purpose, an appreciable element of architectural effect." *(Warwickshire County Records Office: PH352/172/118)*

Stratford-upon-Avon Exterior, 1st July 2008. On the centenary of the opening of the North Warwickshire Railway, this was the view. Notice that there are two sets of brick buildings, with contrasting brickwork around the windows, and a large space under the canopy in the middle for passengers to exit. The entrance is the doorway on the right. *(BPC)*

Stratford-upon-Avon, 1934. Passengers have been able to stand on this site looking towards the Alcester Road since 1863. Visible under the bridges is the West signalbox, and at right angles to the GWR is another railway line crossing half a mile south of the GWR station – the East & West Junction Railway. Until that line's station was opened, its trains would have arrived at this platform at the GWR station, but this arrangement only lasted from July 1873 until June 1875, when its temporary station opened, to be replaced by a permanent one from 1876. The siding on the left was part of the alterations opening in 1911. In it are some horse boxes, unheard of today, but a profitable business years ago. The population here was only 8,500 in 1900. The nameboard calls the place "Stratford-on-Avon", but in post World War II times, "upon" was used, and the suffix "General" was added to differentiate it from the LMS station. *(Mowat Collection)*

Stratford-upon-Avon, 1929. When the American Ambassador to England came to the town, it wasn't at this station that he arrived (much to the annoyance to the GWR, I suspect) and it gave a lot of publicity to its rivals for the "Shakespeare Line" when he came to open the aptly named, Harvard House in 1909. The station was designated Grade 3 in the GWR system, was of intermediate size, and had a staff of 37. The alterations and enlargements were a success for the railway company, with receipts doubling from 1903 to around £24,000 at the time of this picture. The company made half as much again from carrying freight.
(Clarence Gilbert Collection)

Stratford-upon-Avon, 1953. Having just arrived with a train from Birmingham, 2-6-2T No 4571 pauses at the 550ft-long platform. Despite the canopy being sufficient to accommodate all the carriages, this attention to detail didn't satisfy all, as witness a letter to the local paper in 1910: "There should be a convalescent home for Stratford's (GWR) trains...because many of these vehicles must be very tired judging by the long rest they require at every station and the hours of enforced leisure at each junction." The station's main entrance is on the right with the footbridge at the end of the canopy. On the left is a bracket signal for trains to move south from the terminal face of the island platform and the adjacent loop. Behind that are some Ministry of Food buildings in Lodge sidings, added during World War II.
(G Coltas Collection)

Stratford-upon-Avon, 1956. When the train moved away, the view to the 580ft-long island platform would show the wonderful set of steps from the covered footbridge, complete with company motif. Unusually, there are two sets of steps from the bridge onto the island platform, one set facing each way. Again, the canopy is sufficient for the length of normal local trains. The company prided itself on the fact that passengers would be under continuous protection from the elements from the moment they arrived outside the station until they exited from the station at the end of their journey. Approximately twice as many passengers booked tickets here in 1959 compared to 1938. *(HC Casserley)*

Stratford-upon-Avon, Departures to the South. Standing next to the pointwork for the up loop we see Castle class 4-6-0 No 5074 *Hampden* pausing at the end of the down platform with an express. It had only carried that name since January 1941, having been named *Denbigh Castle* from July 1938. On the right are the facilities for engines to take on water – the column, the handle for turning on the supply, and the heater for cold weather. To the extreme right is the flexible end of the column over a funnel leading, as does the grill on the slope, to a drain. This train will not be using the facility, as it has not drawn forward enough for the column to be swung round to the inlet at the far end of the tender's 4,000-gallon tank. At the Grouping there were just a handful of services between Birmingham and Bristol along this route. Stopping places were here and Cheltenham Malvern Road,

taking around 2¼ hours. On Saturdays in the summer, it was a different matter – another six trains used the route, and to relieve pressure on the main line stations, the platforms at Birmingham Moor Street were pressed into service, and many services used the St Philip's Marsh lines (thus avoiding Bristol Temple Meads station) on their way to the West Country. *(TJ Edgington)*

View from Alcester Road Bridge, 1961. This was the roadside view taken next to the water tank. Having just left the down platform is an express heading south, probably for Cheltenham and beyond. Hauling it is an unidentified Castle class 4-6-0 engine, complete with Hawksworth straight-sided tender. Waiting in a curious place is a northbound freight train hauled by a Stanier 8F 2-8-0. One way to cope with the gradient beyond the passenger station was to wait until both the signalboxes along the line (West and East) could offer a clear line, and allow the train an uninterrupted attempt at the bank; this explains the position of this train. The signalman in West box will pull a lever to lower the top arm of the left-hand pair of signals, and shortly afterwards, the signalman in East box will do likewise for the lower arm. With the right of way confirmed the driver will proceed through the station northwards.
(Shakespeare's Birthplace Trust)

Stratford-upon-Avon, Departures to the South, 1957. This view was taken slightly further south, where Shottery footpath crosses the line. This was protected by a short-lived signalbox from 1899 until 1902. Passing south with an express is Castle class 4-6-0 No 5061 *Earl of Birkenhead* on 25th February, probably bound for Cheltenham. In the background is the up siding, with West signalbox and a large water tank adjacent. *(BPC)*

Stratford-upon-Avon, 1935. Gleaming in chocolate and cream in the up siding is diesel railcar No 4 awaiting its next turn. This was one of the first generation railcars with no buffers, 40 seats, a small buffet area and two lavatories. They were designed for express services at speeds between 75 and 80 mph, hence its two engines. The diesel service only sold the number of tickets that they had seats for, and soon it was augmented by steam stock, as it became so popular. An additional service ran through to Swansea which, by the outbreak of World War II, also called at Henley-in-Arden and Hall Green. In 1934, railcars such as these were introduced on a Cardiff service running non-stop through here. Being unable to be expanded from just one coach, even with a supplementary fare payable, and being "air-brushed" out of public timetables to discourage short journey passengers, they were still too successful as more passengers wanted them than there were seats. Of course, passengers for Welsh cities could travel north from Snow Hill via Worcester and Hereford. A large water tower, built in 1886, is behind the West signalbox. The bracket signal tells drivers of up trains that they are to pass into platform No 3 (left-hand pair) or platform No 2. The adjacent box only controlled the top (red-painted) arms, with the box in front (East box) controlling the lower, yellow-painted, distant arms. *(R Carpenter)*

Stratford-upon-Avon, 1950. Having just passed over the footpath across the line, a stopping train will be slowing down in preparation for the station stop about half a mile north. Hauling the train from Worcester is 4-4-0 No 3377, while fellow engine No 3455 waits in the siding ready for its next duty, probably banking a train up the gradient at Wilmcote. Although this section was part of the line that joined the two original stations in the town, it wasn't doubled until late on – Stratford station to Shottery footpath in 1902, and Shottery footpath to Evesham Road crossing in 1899. *(Millbrook House Ltd)*

Evesham Road Crossing, 1958. Two of the three main road level crossings in the town became bridges – Alcester Road in 1861 and Sanctus Road in 1864; Evesham Road remained a crossing on the level. When the two termini were linked in the 1860s, a short section was doubled, starting here, for about 350 yards to the south for the junction with the "other" railway. Opening on 17th October 1904, was a short (100ft-long) railmotor halt south of the crossing. As many stations did, it closed during World War I on 14th July 1916, never to reopen. Dating from 1891, the 13-lever box was replaced by a modern flat-roofed 50-lever structure on 24th April 1960. Its extra levers allowed the closure of a box to the south, and the addition of Racecourse Junction between 1960 and 1965. An Act of 1842 stated that level crossing gates must be kept closed across roadways, except when required to be opened to allow lines to be crossed. Clearly with the increasing numbers of motor vehicles this was impractical, and in 1933 the law was altered so that gates on level crossings should be closed across the railway. *(Transport Treasury)*

Evesham Road Crossing, 1938. One can almost hear the sequence of different sounds leading up to this picture. If the windows of the signalbox were open it was perfectly possible for the public to hear the pinging of the bells that the signalmen used to communicate with each other. Workmen are repairing the decking of the crossing, so a warning would have been shouted to them by the lookout. This would be followed by the noise of the gates swinging across the lines to shut off the road. From inside the cabin would flow the sounds of the catch handles being released, and the clank as the levers were thrown. Signal wires would twang, and the top signal would make a clang as it moved from stop to proceed. The lower signal arm, operated by another signalbox, would then follow suit after a

short delay. Depending on the urgency of the situation, there would then follow a short delay before the sound of a steam engine approaching from the north. It would whistle some distance before the crossing, and this magnificent, fairly new, Castle class engine would come into view. The train would be visibly picking up speed as its coaches were dragged over the crossing, and the Doppler effect made it seem to fade away more quickly than it arrived. Levers were thrown in the box, the gates opened, and the men continued with their work after their welcome break. *(Kidderminster Railway Museum)*

The Line South to Honeybourne

At just under 8½ miles, the branch from the main line at Honeybourne was the slightly shorter of the two branches to Stratford-upon-Avon. It was the Oxford Worcester & Wolverhampton Railway that took until July 1859 to build and open it, having obtained an Act to build a branch from the south in 1846. I suspect even that date was only due to the competition from the line from the north – left to its own devices the OWW might have taken even longer. This line was "narrow gauge" (compared with the GWR) and was worked by that company. Fortunately, the two lines in the town were joined to create a through route that became part of a longer distance line from the Midlands to the West Country. What a pity towns like Bradford and Manchester didn't have this vision.

Looking North from Sanctus Street Bridge, 1958. About to pass under the bridge is the southbound "Cornishman". Controlling train movements is Evesham Road Crossing box, seen above the fourth coach. To allow the named train to proceed, its signalman will have pulled levers to move the top arm of the right-hand pair in the left distance, and the upper arm on the bracket signal. Drivers of cars waiting at the crossing will see the end of this train disappear, and will prepare to cross. However, they will be frustrated, as another train is expected on the up line; the two signals on the left-hand post in the distance have been pulled to the off position for a train to pass. On the bracket signal, the arm on the right would be for the chord east onto the SMJ at East & West Junction. *(RC Riley, Transport Treasury)*

Looking South from Sanctus Street Bridge, East & West Junction, 1957. Just south of Evesham Road crossing would have been the site of the terminus of the line that arrived from Honeybourne in July 1859. It was abandoned in 1863, as the line had been connected north to the line from Hatton at Alcester Road. In 1873, the East & West Junction Railway arrived in the town from Kineton, a little over nine miles to the west. As its station wasn't ready, the company sought to use the GWR station, and to access it, a double junction was built which can be seen curving away to the left. Although the Honeybourne to Hatton line

was single at that time, it was doubled from a point just in front of the junction (probably where the trailing crossover is) to the Evesham Road crossing. Thus the E&WJR used the Alcester Road station for just under two years until its station was ready in June 1875, the curve being retained after that time. Controlling events is the 18-lever brick signalbox on the left called, at this time, Stratford-upon-Avon West Junction. In the distance, the main line is curving to the right before passing under a bridge. In 1873, Royal assent was given for a line to pass from the East & West Junction line west to Broom Junction on the MR. The GWR only gave its permission when the new railway offered to build its bridge over the GWR line wide enough so that the line underneath could be doubled at a later date (this was done in 1908). *(RC Riley, Transport Treasury)*

East & West Junction, 1957.
Bringing a train from the south is
seven-year old Modified Hall class
4-6-0 No 7918 *Rhose Wood Hall*. It
would be withdrawn in another eight
years – what an expensive waste!
Passing over the junction for the
curve to the LMS line, it is bound
for Stratford-upon-Avon, and has
just passed a magnificent GWR
signal post with the top arm allowing
it to proceed. The lower arm is a
distant signal for the next box in
front, Evesham Road Crossing. It is
highly likely that the train left
Worcester Shrub Hill at 1.25pm, and
all stations would be stopped at
before arriving at Leamington – a
level of service we can only dream
about today. Until 1948, there were
two trip trains a day between the two
company's goods yards, but (as far
as I can make out) there is no record
of any passenger movements over
the connecting curve.
(RC Riley, Transport Treasury)

East & West Junction, 1957.
Standing in the "V" formed by the
lines enabled these two views of
southbound summer express trains to
be taken. Castle class 4-6-0 No
7017 *G. J. Churchward* heads the
down "Cornishman". Having left
Stratford-upon-Avon General at
10.19am, it is on its way to
Cheltenham where it is due to arrive
just after 11.00am. To assist
signalmen and station staff, the train
carries the reporting number 825 on
boards in a metal frame on the
smokebox door.
(RC Riley, Transport Treasury)

East & West Junction, 1957. As
the train was so popular, a second
portion would arrive ten minutes
later. Carrying the reporting number
826 is Hall class 4-6-0 No 6990
Witherslack Hall. On very busy
days there could be up to three
others following the main train in
quick succession. This titled train
ran along the route for only ten years
from 30th June 1952 until 10th
September 1962. It was then routed
along the MR Lickey incline.
(RC Riley, Transport Treasury)

Leaving Stratford-upon-Avon, 1933.
South of the town, the north-south GWR line is crossed by the east-west MR joint line. This picture was taken from the parapet of the overbridge for the latter line, looking north. The curve from our line to the SMJ line is in front of the large building on the right in the background. The line south from East & West Junction was doubled to Milcote in 1908. Heading south in September is an auto train for Honeybourne hauled by GWR 517 class 0-4-2T No 1424. There were 9 or 10 such trains, taking around twenty minutes stopping at the two stations and a varying number of halts.
(Kidderminster Railway Museum)

Racecourse Station, 1956. Slightly south of the SMJ, the GWR line became single again until it was doubled in 1908. This picture was taken from the parapet of the overbridge looking south, before any connections were put in. There were no facilities, simply the 550ft-long up and down platforms with nameboards. They were constructed from wood with tarmac on the top, and opened on 6th May 1933. After depositing their passengers, trains would proceed either to the main station or to Long Marston, where the engines would detach, run around their coaches, and wait to come back in a procession to collect their passengers later.
(Historical Model Railway Society)

New Curve (Racecourse) Junction, 1964.
In 1960 a curve was built from the ex-East & West Junction line south to meet the ex-GWR line just south of Racecourse station. As iron ore trains from Northampton to South Wales were causing congestion along the line to Hatton, this alternative route (27 miles shorter) was tried, with the advantage that the need for extra engines to bank trains up Hatton and Wilmcote banks was eliminated. This curve would also allow closure of the joint line east from here to Broom. The photographer is standing by the side of the GWR line looking east. Leaving the joint line is a fitted freight hauled by Hall class 4-6-0 No 6944 *Fledborough Hall* on 23rd May. Above the train is an upper-quadrant LMS-type signal, while the home signal is a typical tubular-steel post of a lower-quadrant type. Alas, the iron ore traffic did not last, and the chord was closed on 1st March 1965.
(M Mensing)

Stratford-upon-Avon's Other Railway

Born out of the desire to transport Northamptonshire iron ore to the steel works of South Wales, the amalgamation of the lines that made up the Stratford-upon-Avon & Midland Joint Railway was not a success. Known as the Midland Counties & South Wales Railway between 1866 and 1870, its nickname was the "Slow, Moulding & Jolting". Passing from Broom Junction in the west to Olney in the east was a single line linking two parts of the Midland Railway's empire. It had connections with the LNWR at Blisworth, the GCR at Woodford and the GWR at Fenny Compton and here. The MR line crosses over the GWR line at right angles here. All through its existence, curves were added so allowing better movement of trains.

Station at the End of New Street, 1966. The *Stratford-upon-Avon Herald* for 1st July 1873 described the station as, "a small but substantially erected brick building standing on land formerly known as Church Farm". The passenger station at Stratford-upon-Avon had a wide space between its platforms – perhaps the original station was to be an island platform rather than the two platforms that were built? In its heyday, the station boasted an extensive engine shed and a large turntable. Passenger train services here were withdrawn in 1952, and later in that decade, all the loops on the SMJ were lengthened to accommodate trains of 60 wagons. Looking west from the ends of the platforms, this view shows the trimming of the edges to allow wider ex-GWR engines to use the route. Ahead are the curves to meet the GWR line, north at East & West Junction and south at Racecourse Junction. Straight ahead would have been the main single line, a short climb over the GWR line, and then to Broom Junction.
(Railway & Canal Historical Society)

West from Stratford-upon-Avon along the Joint Line 1957. This is not the only place where there are connections between the GWR and the SMJ lines – east, at Fenny Compton on the main Oxford to Birmingham line, the two company's metals came side-by-side. This connection has been improved over time and is now the entrance to the MOD depot at Burton Dassett, some 3½ miles from the main GWR line. To add extra capacity to the LMS line in World War II, the line from Clifford Sidings was doubled to here. A freight train has just passed over the River Avon, and entered the station. Fowler 4F 0-6-0 No 43971 has buffered up behind, and the train is heading west. *(RC Riley, Transport Treasury)*

1958. Having done its job, the banking engine runs back into the station that last saw regular passenger trains six years previously. Curving away to the right in amongst the sidings is the chord to meet the GWR line, and clearly visible is the single line to Broom Junction, rising up at 1 in 60 to pass over the GWR line. In 1942, a west to south connection was put in at Broom to allow trains from the East Midlands to pass to the South West and Wales, avoiding Birmingham and the Lickey incline.
(RC Riley, Transport Treasury)

Experiments on the LMS Line, 1932. A motor coach was trialled by the LMS in an attempt to combine the flexibility and cost of road travel with the speed, lower fares and fuel consumption of rail travel. On arrival at a specially prepared siding in the goods yard, the driver exchanged the pneumatic rubber tyres for metal-flanged rail tyres. The "Ro-Railer" then ran into Stratford-upon-Avon station to pick up passengers before setting off for Blisworth along the railway. This wasn't the only such vehicle built by Karrier Motors of Huddersfield but the experiment here lasted only a few months until June 1932. *(BPC)*

Milcote, 1924. Looking north towards Stratford-upon-Avon we see the arrangements that existed when the line was single. The nearest line was all that existed, being served by the platform we are standing on. The station's facilities were concentrated in the building in front of us, and the level crossing was controlled by a signalbox, just protruding from the left-hand side of the dwelling. *(Stations UK)*

Milcote, 1924. In 1908, the doubling of the line to the north was extended through Milcote. A new set of platforms was opened with small brick buildings housing such facilities as a waiting room and gentlemen's toilets in them. Looking south from the down platform, this view shows the well-tended flower beds and gas lamps, with the level crossing of Milcote Lane at the ends of the platforms. Beyond, is the signalbox with the station building above it. *(Stations UK)*

Milcote, early 1960s. The station had the rather long title of "Milcote, Weston & Welford", indicating that it was probably near none of these villages, but in the middle of rural Warwickshire. Heading south over the level crossing is a freight hauled by Mogul 2-6-0 No 6362. In 1907, the train would have been leaving the single-line and entering the double-track section; the next year it was double track throughout. *(R Carpenter)*

Long Marston, 1910. By arrangement and appearance, this station could be mistaken for Milcote some 2½ miles to the north. The similarities focus on the building and the signalbox before the level crossing, but here the up platform has only a wooden shelter and is opposite the down platform, on which is a group of railway employees and passengers posing for the photograph. The down train, destined for Honeybourne, is passing the down refuge siding adjacent to the level crossing. Milk churns on the up platform illustrate the main activity in the area. There was a small goods yard to the south of the station, as well as an up refuge siding. From the GWR's perspective, doubling the line was an economic success – the station doubled its goods between 1903 and 1920 and receipts rocketed from £2,000 to £7,000 per annum. *(Stations UK)*

Long Marston, 1967. While staff numbers might be a fraction of their former levels, and the platform is overgrown, there is evidence of continuing railway activity here. A lengthy metal bicycle shed has been built on the down platform, and a steel footbridge has been found necessary for safety reasons due to the level of activity. Perched at the end of this platform, as if suspended in the air, is an interesting signal to protect the level crossing from up trains. Beyond it, several wagons rest in the down refuge siding. *(Stations UK)*

Long Marston, 1957. Viewed south from the end of the down platform is the start of the lines serving an ordnance depot established during World War II. Notice the oil drums next to the corrugated iron shed and the small yard crane and loading dock serving the local community. Since 1931, the station master here was also responsible for the stations at Milcote and Pebworth, rather like a vicar having more than one parish. The bracket signal is interesting in that the two arms are different lengths. Normally, local goods facilities are accessed by trailing connections and crossovers. However, as this was the entrance to a busy depot, a facing slip allowed trains to enter the sidings directly. Heading towards Stratford-upon-Avon is a stopping train headed by Mogul 2-6-0 No 6357 on 15th June. *(RK Blencowe)*

Long Marston, around 1960. The down "Cornishman" is about to shatter the peace and quiet of this country station with an unidentified Castle class engine in charge. Having left Cheltenham over 40 minutes previously, it will soon arrive in Stratford-upon-Avon. Ten years before, almost half of all holidaymakers went away by train, but ten years later, almost three-quarters went by car. On the left is the local loading dock complete with large corrugated shed and 1½ ton crane. *(J Moss)*

Long Marston, around 1960. The railway company ferried visitors to Stratford-upon-Avon from, for example, Birmingham, and returned them later in the day by special train – similarly, to and from the racecourse for its meetings. With limited capacity in the town, other areas were pressed into service to store empty carriages ready for the later exodus.

Above: Having occupied one of the loops for the adjacent depot, carriages are brought across the down main line in preparation for their journey north by Grange class 4-6-0 No 6851 *Hurst Grange*.

Below: After waiting for the previous train to clear the section, it is then the turn of another train to proceed north. Prairie 2-6-2T No 4165 is emerging from the up refuge siding. *(Both J Moss)*

War Department Sidings, Pebworth, around 1960. Standing on the road bridge half a mile south of Long Marston enables the concentration of freight operations here to be well shown. On the left is the start of the up loop – until 1941 it was a refuge siding, and on the extreme left (just visible by the fence) is a vehicle on the, now, up refuge siding. One can almost hear the exhaust of the down fitted-freight hauled by Standard class 9F 2-10-0 No 92000 on its way towards Cheltenham, possibly for a destination in South Wales. Just about to be obscured totally by the front of the engine is a small hut that housed the West ground frame. It controlled access onto the down main line via the bracket signal on the right. Seen above the train are two sets of loops that fed the depot here. This line was regularly used by freight trains on direct and indirect routes. An example of the latter would be the 3.50pm from Acton (West London) to Bordesley via Oxford and Stratford-upon-Avon. Tyseley-based 28xx class 2-8-0 engines were permitted to haul 70 loaded wagons on this turn. *(J Moss)*

Long Marston, 1960. In preparation for the Allied invasion of Europe during World War II, several depots were constructed to store materials that would be needed, both for the assault, and to supply the Army when abroad. To serve the vast number of sheds, over 25 miles of internal railway was developed here, and more than 400,000 tons of goods were despatched by rail in both 1943 and 1944. For moving wagons over the system, several War Department engines were used, such as 0-6-0ST No 160, with two ex-LT&SR coaches to move workers. *(R Miller)*

Pebworth Halt, 1967. Just over a mile south of Long Marston, a lane crossed the line. In common with many places along the route, a halt (Broad Marston) had a brief life there from 1904 until 1916. A few hundred yards further south was another – Pebworth Halt, opened on 6th September 1937. This view towards Long Marston shows the platform's open construction, the platform being 8ft wide and 150ft long. *(Stations UK)*

Honeybourne's Junctions. At the opening there was a 3¼-mile single line from Long Marston to Honeybourne where the Oxford to Worcester main line was joined. At the start of the 20th century, the GWR attempted to improve its service between the Midlands and the West Country by proposing a new, double-track line. This was to leave the Stratford-upon-Avon branch just before this line curves west to Honeybourne station. The new line would pass south to arrive at Cheltenham, and by this route, two parts of the company's empire would be connected. So, ¾ mile before Honeybourne station, East Loop Junction was established. Trains either went south along the new line, or west along the original line towards the station (East Loop). A quarter of a mile along the latter, North Loop Junction was built. There, trains to Honeybourne were met by trains from the south, also on their way to the station (West Loop). Trains from the south, before passing under the OWW main line passed West Loop Junction, and went either north to East Loop Junction, or along the West Loop to the station. There was also a chord between East Loop Junction and the main line at South Loop Junction to enable trains to pass from Stratford-upon-Avon to the Oxford direction.

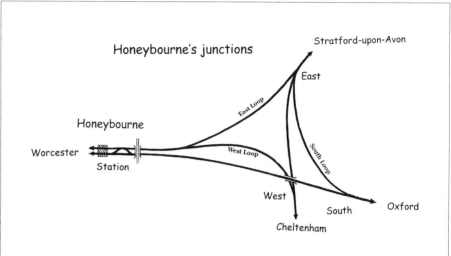

West Loop, 1955. Emerging from the bridge carrying the Oxford to Worcester line over the Stratford-upon-Avon to Cheltenham line is an auto train from the latter town. Ex-GWR 1400 class No 1402 hauls its coaches at the start of the curve that makes up West Loop towards Honeybourne station, a mile or so to the west (right of picture). Up above are the signals for the main line on its approach to the station from the Oxford direction.
(Kidderminster Railway Museum)

West Loop Sidings, 1963. Trains for Cheltenham would pass under the OWW line and head south. A short distance along the line was deemed a suitable place for BR to build some extra facilities for the flow of iron ore traffic from Northampton to South Wales, and in both directions they built three loops. To facilitate the flow of trains, they shut West Loop signalbox on 24th April 1960, having built a modern flat-roofed box by the northern end of the loops. Looking south we see the connection from the down main line passing to the left of the new signalbox to enable trains to access the loops. Meanwhile, on the up side there is plenty of activity. Heading north is a freight train hauled by Standard class 2-10-0 No 92222, as sister engine No 92137 waits in the headshunt for the loops. It was in these loops that engines took on water, and train crews were exchanged. After operating for only six years the loops were closed.
(Kidderminster Railway Museum)

Winchcombe, 1976. With the decision to concentrate passenger workings on the ex-MR line via the Lickey incline, the parallel idea was that freight workings should be diverted elsewhere, and consequently, the line to Cheltenham became better used. However, in August 1976 there was a derailment of a train of hoppers, and the expense of repairing the trackbed encouraged BR to close the route. The pathway is still *in situ* with preservationists keen to extend their operations north from their Toddington base.
(Kidderminster Railway Museum)

Ex-Honeybourne North Loop Junction, 1957.
Being in the middle of nowhere, pictures of these junctions are virtually non-existent. The only GWR connection in this picture is that the units were built at Swindon! This six car "inter-city" DMU is heading for Cardiff, having left Birmingham at 12.25pm. Its normal route, would have been under the OWW and on to Cheltenham, but that line was blocked at Winchcombe for permanent way works. So, to pass west along the OWW the train is about pass along the East Loop into the station here. On the right is the north to west curve (West Loop) from under the OWW to the station. The signals being passed by the front of the train are for North Loop Junction – the controlling signalbox and its 31 levers had a short life from 1904 until 1933, when its function was transferred to Station South box, on the main line. The train's route will now be to Evesham, then along the ex-MR line to Ashchurch and Cheltenham. Across the background are some wagons on the line that the train should be taking.
(M Mensing)

Stratford-upon-Avon Branch. Although the main and branch lines at Honeybourne were originally part of the same railway company, and were granted permission within a year of each other, their construction and openings were separated by many years. The main line was formally opened on 7th May 1853, but the branch

needed a Parliamentary extension before it opened on 12th July 1859. Typical of the engines seen at the station was this 2-2-2 No 51 *Will Shakspere* (sic), although branch trains usually had to make do with humble tank engines. With so little footplate protection, it must have been pretty grim travelling into driving rain at 40mph. *(Real Photographs)*

Honeybourne, 1930s. This picture was taken from an overbridge adjacent to the station looking east towards Oxford. The branch line from Stratford-upon-Avon curves in from the left to lie alongside the main line to Worcester. On the right is Station South signalbox with a fine exhibition of some of the signals it controlled. The nearest pair, with their backs to us, are on tall posts to allow for sighting over the bridge we are standing on. The nearest bottom arm is fixed, meaning that it is always "on", so the driver of a train on that line must be prepared to slow down and stop at the next signal. *(Lens of Sutton)*

Honeybourne Junction, 1959. These two views east give a good impression of the facilities here, far in excess of the demands of the local population. At the opening, just two platforms sufficed. The station nameboard is a novel in itself, reading. "Honeybourne Junction for Stratford-on-Avon Branch Warwick Leamington Birmingham Broadway Winchombe and Cheltenham", all in capitals – no opportunity for business was lost! The valance for the canopies has nice curves on it, illustrating the care given to even the smallest features that gave stations such a pleasing look. Milk churns were a common site at the station illustrating the main economy of the area.

This page, top: For the 1906/7 extension, a new pair of lines was added to the north of the main line. The old up platform had another face added to make it an island, and a new platform (No 4) was constructed, on which we are standing. They were all connected by the large covered footbridge. The 2.30pm auto coach from Cheltenham has just arrived. *(E Wilmshurst)*

Opposite page, top: The photographer is standing on the original down platform, now platform 1. At the original up platform, now the up main platform, stands a Pannier tank engine No 9476, complete with auto coach. Meanwhile, on the up branch platform, rests 5101 class 2-6-2T No 6137, probably on a Leamington to Worcester service that has just arrived from Stratford-upon-Avon. *(HD Bowtell)*

Signals at Honeybourne, 1964. This view is along the down branch line from platform 4, from just in front of the overbridge. The restricted site has caused the arms to be shortened. Branching off to the left can be seen a 1942 down loop whose access would be indicated by the lower arm. The white diamond means that the line is on a track circuit, and a train's presence will be shown on the track diagram in the signalbox by means of a light. Hence, the driver, if stopped by the signal, has no need to inform the box, according to Rule 55. *(Joe Moss)*

Below: Honeybourne Station, 1958. The massive covered footbridge allowing access to all platforms shows up clearly. The two lines on the right were added as part of the station's enlargement, being used mostly for branch trains. Here, the Cheltenham branch auto coach is on the left in platform 3, with Pannier tank No 5418 in charge. Using platform No 4 as a refuge is a fitted freight with at least one-third of the wagons having brakes connected to the engine's. Although Modified Hall class 4-6-0 No 7915 *Mere Hall* is waiting on the down branch, it could head north towards Stratford-upon-Avon or south towards Cheltenham. Alternatively, by using the double junctions ahead, it could pass onto the main line towards Oxford as an up train. To avoid congestion on the main lines around Banbury, quite a few through goods trains between Birmingham and London used the North Warwickshire line, and joined the ex-OWW here. While this eased matters on the main line, it shifted the problems to here. Bankers were expected to assist a minimum of 17 trains (one per hour) up the bank. With few refuge sidings and a lack of loops on the North Warwickshire line, any delay caused severe congestion and further delays. *(Mile Post 92½ Picture Library, AWV Mace Collection)*

Honeybourne, 1939. Railways serving the Avon valley, both here and at Leamington, encountered problems with gradients, and many up trains needed assistance if they were to maintain good progress, so banking engines were provided here at the bottom of the incline. Ageing GWR 0-6-0 No 2580 awaits its next turn in the sidings adjacent to the station. A mile west of the station, a dispersal depot was built as part of the preparations for the D-Day landings. Shunting engines for the Sheen Hill depot were also seen shunting the extensive sidings around the station.
(RJ Buckley, Initial Photographics)

Honeybourne South Loop Junction, around 1955. Setting off up the bank is 2800 class 2-8-0 No 3863 with an up freight train. In the distance, at the rear of the train can be seen the plumes of smoke from the banking engine. The box is for the convergence of the south loop with the main line. Dating from 1907, it had 23 levers, one of which has been pulled to lower the top left-hand arm. The two arms on the shorter, less-used, route are for the south loop to enable down trains from the main line to turn north and proceed to Stratford-upon-Avon directly.
(Restoration & Archiving Trust)

Main Lne at Honeybourne, 1964. No account of Honeybourne would be complete without a view of an express train, and here is Castle class 4-6-0 No 7020 *Gloucester Castle* bound for Worcester. Descending trains could go too fast, and 100mph was not uncommon through the station area. In the enlargements of 1906/7 a down loop was provided round the back of Station South signalbox, in which descending freight trains had to stop and release the brakes that they had pinned at the summit. Following the improvements in 1909, afternoon departing passengers from London for Stratford-upon-Avon had a choice of which direction they approached the town. Throughout the day, there were connections and slip coaches from the north, usually via Leamington, but a passenger could catch the 4.45pm for Worcester. Coaches were removed at Moreton-in-Marsh, and following the express down the bank they would arrive here. The train was then split into a Stratford-upon-Avon portion (arriving 7.05pm) and a Cheltenham portion (arriving 7.35pm). Both timings were better than the route via Leamington or Swindon. *(BPC)*

North Warwickshire Line to Birmingham

Although set in rural surroundings, residents of the towns in the Forest of Arden thought that they deserved better communications – after all, Birmingham was less than 25 miles away. Stratford-upon-Avon was well connected with the GWR main lines, to the north at Hatton with the London to Birmingham line and to the south, at Honeybourne, on the London to Worcester line. However, both were single-line branches, so the town felt snubbed, and cherished the idea of its own direct line or superior service to Birmingham. Similarly, although a line was authorised in 1861, nothing more had been done to connect Henley-in-Arden to Kingswood on the main line.

Consequently, at a meeting of interested parties at the Swan Hotel in Henley-in-Arden in 1892, a plan was drawn up for an independent railway from Stratford-upon-Avon through Henley-in-Arden to terminate in Birmingham. The termini at both ends were to be near existing GWR stations, and two other lines proposed at the same time would have connected the new line to the GWR's Alcester branch and the SMJ line at Stratford-upon-Avon. Being connected to the "opposition" (the Midland Railway) in the area at two places should have stunned the GWR, after all, the proposals would mean a distance to London thirteen miles shorter than its own. However, perhaps the GWR viewed a 553yd tunnel at Camp Hill, a viaduct at Bordesley, extensive earthworks along the line, and a Birmingham terminus as not being an attractive proposition to investors. Arrogantly, the GWR asserted that if the proposed scheme fell at the Parliamentary hurdles then it would (magnanimously) build a similar line. However, Parliament liked competition and the Birmingham, North Warwickshire & Stratford-upon-Avon Railway (BNW&SR) scheme was accepted in 1894.

Perhaps woken from its lethargy by the other company's proposals, the GWR decided to improve communications with the towns in the Forest of Arden, and two piecemeal additions were made. Firstly, in 1894, they connected the main line to Henley-in-Arden, but the town had to make do with a single track branch. Secondly, in 1897, they built a north curve at Hatton, so creating a triangle of lines there in an attempt to spike the opposition's guns. This allowed trains to travel directly between Birmingham and Stratford-upon-Avon without the need for reversal in Hatton. The fastest town-to-town trains would now take 40 minutes.

The GWR started to look upon such proposals as part of a bigger picture. Fortunately for them, supporters of the BNW&SR did not come forward with the expected monies, so watching from the sidelines paid off, and an order to construct the line passed to them in July 1900. Alterations to the original plans meant that the line was to connect with the Hatton to Stratford-upon-Avon line south of Bearley and with the GWR main line at Tyseley. With this line, and another from Honeybourne to Cheltenham, the GWR would have its own Midlands to West Country link independent of the MR. The construction of Moor Street station in Birmingham can be viewed as the original independent proposals being justified. The line hardly stimulated commuters to flock to Stratford-upon-Avon, its population rising by only 2,000 to 11,616 between the line's opening and 1931.

This steam navvy, one of eleven used, was typical of the machines used to build railways, superseding the armies of men typical of schemes 50 years earlier. By adding baulks of timber at one end that had been removed from the other, the machine proceeded across the terrain making and fine-grading the cutting. The spoil is being loaded into a horse-drawn wagon, which will be pulled along the contractor's rough track. *(GM Perkins Collection)*

Construction of the line

It took less than two years to build the line to a standard fit for the conveyance of goods, and another seven months to have the passenger facilities ready. With only a double line approach from the south available to the GWR, the extra suburban business generated by the new line meant that the development of Moor Street station, just before the main lines plunge into Snow Hill tunnel, was inevitable. However, its opening didn't take place until trains had been running on the line for a year. Passing through gentle Warwickshire countryside resulted in few constructional problems for the contractor, CJ Willis & Sons, who started in the largest town on the route, Henley-in-Arden.

Looking along the Stratford Road in the summer of 1906 (above) we see a bridge being built for the line that would connect the original station to the new line, and allow the branch from Rowington Junction to be closed. The old station survived as a goods depot until 1962. Below is the finished article viewed from the other direction. *(Both GM Perkins Collection)*

It was part of the contractor's skill to organise the construction so that the spoil from cuttings became consolidated into the line's embankment, wherever possible. To move the spoil, steam engines were used, and here is a pair of Manning Wardle 0-6-0 tanks called *Sidley* and *Newport*. Another engine languishes in the timber shed, its temporary nature emphasised by the wooden props to keep the sides up! The rough nature of the track seems to have claimed a victim – it looks as though the front engine is there to pull the rear engine back onto the track.
(GM Perkins Collection)

This was the field that in 1906 was destined to become Henley-in-Arden station. The land has been levelled for the real track, and the cutting graded. Some work has been started on the construction of the platforms using bricks brought in along the contractor's tracks. Note the Scots Pine tree in the middle of the picture – it reappears in a view of the completed station on page 103.
(GM Perkins Collection)

The line between Tyseley and Bearley opened to goods traffic on 30th December 1907, but the passenger facilities weren't ready until 1st July of the following year. Looking south from what will become Henley-in-Arden passenger station, the double track, complete with signal, is ready. Although substantially constructed, the interior touches to the buildings are being completed, as well as the roof on part of the footbridge and the platform surfaces.
(LGRP)

Leaving Stratford-upon-Avon, **May 1959 – Train Engine.** At around 6.10pm, the main part of the northbound "Cornishman" leaves the station. In charge is Castle class 4-6-0 No 5070 *Sir Daniel Gooch* taking it non-stop to Birmingham Snow Hill station. The origins of the name date back to the days of the broad gauge, running to Plymouth, and later, to Penzance. The name was revived and given to the Wolverhampton to Penzance service from 1952, but in the 1960s it was extended to Bradford. The post-war train stopped at Snow Hill and Stratford-upon-Avon. *(M Mensing)*

Banking Engine. With the sound of the train engine disappearing into the smoke a disinterested watcher would be surprised to observe the end of the train, twelve or more coaches long, with another engine puffing away like mad coming past the end of

the platform. 2251 class 0-6-0 No 2257 performs that duty with "the shape of things to come" waiting on the left to make its return trip to Birmingham. Communication between the train engine and the banker would be by a series of whistles. Having started its job close to the signalbox just under the Alcester Road bridge, this engine will do all it can to assist the train, and will ease off as it passes East signalbox. Then it will pass through the station, returning to the siding by the West signalbox to await its next duty. *(M Mensing)*

August 1952. With the time approaching 5.00pm on the 30th, holidaymakers would be just over 40 minutes from Birmingham Snow Hill. The train, the 2.05pm from Weston-Super-Mare, is leaving Stratford-upon-Avon hauled by Grange class 4-6-0 No 6828 *Trellech Grange* aided by banker, 2-6-2T No 5138. It was standard GWR practice for the more powerful engine to lead at the front. This meant uncoupling it in the station, moving it away, backing the banker onto the coaches, and connecting the couplings and brakes. Next, the train engine would back onto the banker, and again, couplings and brakes would be connected before the whole procession could proceed; four minutes were allowed in the 1960 timetable for these manoeuvres. This pair will travel all the way to Birmingham Snow Hill, where the banker will be released to find a pathway back here. However, it will have been unavailable for banking duties for some time, so on summer Saturdays, Tyseley shed would have supplied additional engines for the large number of trains that might require assistance. *(R Carpenter)*

Wilmcote, 1957. With the time just after 7.30, the 6.40pm all-stations train along the North Warwickshire line deposits its passengers from Moor Street. The flower beds are well tended, and the lamps have the station's name at the top of one piece of glass. A new station opened here after the line was doubled in 1907, and the original station and the signalbox are visible through the arch. *(TJ Edgington)*

Wilmcote, 1992. The station is north of the summit of Bishton Bank, just over a mile of 1 in 75, and one of the reasons for having banking engines. Note the fine 1883 footbridge still in use, and the "competition" having renewed the arch on the bridge with a concrete beam. Featherbed Lane leads from here, across the adjacent canal to Mary Arden's house. The platforms are no longer pristine, and the flower beds are growing bushes, but the train's timings are approximately the same. *(RK Blencowe)*

Left: Bearley West Junction, 1987. A mile north of Wilmcote station is the divergence of two lines. Heading north to Bearley and Hatton is the original 1860 line, while arriving from the north-west is our line, the North Warwickshire. Viewed from a passing train, we see the signals that control the junction. The taller one on the right is for ours, the most used line, and the arm for the line to Hatton, restricted by a 35mph speed limit, is on the left. The controlling signalbox opened when the junction came into being in 1907, and is still in operation, its area extending to cover the Stratford-upon-Avon district from 1998 as well. Deliveries of coal and water were usually dropped off from a passing train making an unscheduled stop. *(BPC)*

Below: Bearley West Junction, 1969. Looking north, this view shows the stairs end of the signalbox that controls the joining of the North Warwickshire line (on the left) to the original branch from Hatton to Stratford-upon-Avon (on the right). Dating from 1907, this brick-built box had 25 levers which were enlarged to 30 in 1974. From 1998, it controlled movements around the Stratford-upon-Avon area. *(Kidderminster Railway Museum)*

Bearley North Junction, 1953.
Fractionally more than half a mile round the curve, a train from Stratford-upon-Avon would arrive here on the right. A train is expected on the North Warwickshire line as its signal is off. Trains heading for Stratford-upon-Avon would pass along the double track on the right with a signal post with two arms for West junction in the distance. In the centre distance is another two-armed post for the 1876 single line to Bearley East junction and station. This spur saw action in the early 1950s when the main line was under repair. Trains left the main line at Tyseley, passed to here, and then went via Bearley station to rejoin the main line at Hatton. Protecting this junction are two signals with their backs to us; notice the steel guy ropes to keep the signal post from falling over.
(PJ Garland)

Bearley North Junction, 1947.
Looking out from the 35-lever signalbox this picture shows the track layout and the down signals well. On the left is the fine bracket post with home and distant signals for both routes. The left-hand pair is for the curve to Bearley station, and the one to the right is for Stratford-upon-Avon, with West junction just round the curve. The top arms would have been controlled by the box we are in, and the lower arm from the next box ahead, West junction. Heading towards Birmingham is an express hauled by Star class 4-6-0 No 4058 *Princess Augusta*. This class was the forerunner of the highly-successful Castle class of engines, which had a slightly bigger heating surface, cylinders and power. However, many people regard the progenitors as the better engines, and indeed, many of them were rebuilt as Castles.
(PJ Garland)

Bearley North Junction, 1946. Hauling a stopping train to Birmingham is 2-6-2T No 3152, one of the 3150 class designed for this purpose – heavy suburban passenger traffic. The two lines are separating in preparation for the tracks to pass under the canal that the photographer was probably standing next to. The tall down signal post also has a co-acting arm at a lower level, partially obscured by the engine's exhaust.
(PJ Garland)

Bearley North Junction, 1947. This view is looking north from the signalbox, showing the 1813 aqueduct carrying the Stratford-upon-Avon canal over the lines – the longest canal aqueduct in England. A short section of the trackbed of the original branch from Bearley to Alcester was used by the North Warwickshire line, so there were two junctions here. The younger line from Stratford joins the Alcester branch behind us, and in front of us, it leaves the branch. Aston Cantlow and Great Alne are stations along the single line on the left to Alcester, where the MR line from Evesham to Redditch is joined. The Stratford Canal, completed in 1816, was financed by William James, a product and benefactor of the Forest of Arden. He was born in Henley-in-Arden, and married a yeoman's daughter from Tanworth-in-Arden. *(PJ Garland)*

Rural Warwickshire, 1970. With animals weighing almost a ton each, it would be important to get the timing of such activities right, if they were to survive and the train wasn't to be damaged. However, the current two trains an hour would be hard to collide with! In the background is the Bearley aqueduct, and this view has changed very little over the century that the line has been open, although the carts would have been horse-drawn with wooden wheels with steel tyres. Were the green, brown and cream of GWR trains selected to fit in with such a landscape? *(Coventry Evening Telegraph)*

Wootton Wawen Platform, 1930. The summit of the line is some ten miles away near Earlswood Lakes. The company seems to have set a standard that the gradient shouldn't be steeper than 1 in 150, and for most of the two miles from Bearley North Junction to the platform here, that is the gradient. The station's illumination was on fine lamp posts, complete with the station's name on the glass of the gaslights. On the down platform was a typical GWR "pagoda" waiting shelter, and at the far end of the platforms is a bridge over Gorse Lane, illustrating the rolling nature of rural Warwickshire. Unmanned structures such as these were very profitable to the GWR, and its experiences of them in the Stroud valley had shown that within a matter of months their capital outlay had been recouped; clearly they hoped for a similar result from here. Tickets would have been issued by the guard. Possibly, this should have been called a "Halt" due to the almost total absence of buildings and staff. *(Clarence Gilbert)*

Wootton Wawen Platform, 1969. This platform would be where trains from Stratford-upon-Avon, seven miles away, would stop; access is down long slopes from the Alcester Road bridge. Very little seems to have changed in the intervening years, except the roof on the shelter on the opposite platform. *(Stations UK)*

Wootton Wawen Platform, 1957. Two trains left the city at the same time, 5.45pm, to pass along this line. From Moor Street would be the all stations to Stratford-upon-Avon, arriving 67 minutes later. From Snow Hill would be the train for Worcester, which on 28th May was hauled by Hall class 4-6-0 No 6904 *Charfield Hall*. Somewhere around Small Heath, this train would roar through the station while the previous one would be picking up passengers at the relief platform. In procession they would then pass along the North Warwickshire line with this train stopping only at Shirley, Henley-in-Arden, Wilmcote and (surprisingly) Grimes Hill, Wood End and Wootton Wawen, arriving in Stratford-upon-Avon 17 minutes before its partner. *(TJ Edgington)*

Henley-in-Arden, 1908. Almost two miles north of Wootton Wawen, through open rural countryside, the market town of Henley-in-Arden is reached. Standing on the island platform, this view shows the station's facilities well. As befits the largest town along the line, there were brick built buildings on both platforms, each with extensive awnings. The footbridge incorporated a footpath, hence its extra steps at each end. Adjacent to the steps to the down platform and footpath was a large water tank, just visible above the platform canopy. The Scots Pine tree above the footbridge can also be seen in the picture showing the construction of the line on page 97. Quite why the platform awnings do not extend to the footbridge, leaving a gap for passengers to get wet, is a mystery. Notice the bracket signal next to the signalbox – the right-hand arm would give the road to the goods depot and the line to Lapworth. (The GWR didn't use hyphens, apparently.) *(BPC)*

Henley-in-Arden, circa 1949. Looking towards Stratford, we see a short loading bay or horse dock siding and a water column at the end of this platform. The crossover beyond the platform was to allow trains that had terminated here to cross to the other line in preparation for the return journey to Birmingham. Still standing today are the signalbox, some semaphore signals, the footbridge and the buildings by the station's entrance. However, the latter are completely boarded up, and the buildings on the island platform have been removed and replaced with a bus-stop type shelter. In 1983, there was talk of closing the five miles from here to Bearley. Not only would this save money, but it would enable a quicker service to Stratford-upon-Avon – by 17 minutes said the experts. Fortunately it hasn't happened, and the station is still open to hourly trains in each direction. *(J Moss)*

Henley-in-Arden, 1957. Arriving with a train from Birmingham is 2-6-2T No 3101. This was one of a just five built with 5ft 3in driving wheels, whereas the other 41 members of the 3150 class had wheels 5in larger. Although only 17 miles from Birmingham, the town is in the middle of rural Warwickshire; this journey would have taken about 45 minutes, which commuters probably found too long. Note the ironwork for the benches which incorporates the company's initials. *(R Carpenter)*

Henley-in-Arden, 1952. The up platform was built as an island with a run-round loop to the extra face. This enabled services from Birmingham to terminate here, for the engine to detach, and then run round to the other end of the coaches ready for departure north later. This is exactly what has happened with Standard class 3 2-6-T No 82001 in June, not long after it was built at Swindon. In 1911, a late evening excursion to Bristol was scheduled to pass through here, but unfortunately, the signalman thought it was a steam railcar, and sent the train into the loop. The first two carriages were, fortunately, locked out of use, and unoccupied. Apart from some infrastructure damage, little prevented the resumption of normal services the next day (a Sunday), but the driver and fireman were scalded when they returned to the engine to shut off the steam to prevent a boiler explosion. *(PJ Garland)*

Henley-in-Arden around 1950. As well as providing a place for storing coaches from terminating passenger trains, the loop was also used to hold freight trains sometimes. Here, ROD class 2-8-0 No 3044 waits for a northbound passenger train to clear before proceeding. Very long trains would be split, and both lines occupied, causing operational problems if a terminating passenger train needed to run round its coaches. Note the roofless section of the footbridge serving the footpath. The lower parts of the lamp posts are painted white – a throwback to the blackout in World War II. *(PJ Garland)*

Henley-in-Arden, circa 1950. The view from the footbridge towards Birmingham shows the track layout well. Beneath us are the two lines for the loop on the up side with a water column. To the right are the main lines with the up starter signal on the wrong side of the line to aid sighting. The brick signalbox has a facing point next to it to allow trains to pass into the loop on the up side. In 1964, this was removed and replaced by a trailing pair of points just by the start of the platforms. As the main line curves away to the left, to the right is the connection to the original station in the town, over 1,000yd long, and accessed from Kingswood on the line from Leamington to Birmingham. On this branch was a refuge siding to reverse goods trains into when they were late running, and a passenger train was expected. It could hold 42 wagons and a guards van as well as the engine. *(J Moss)*

Henley-in-Arden, circa 1960s. The GWR publication, *Rambles in Shakespeare Land & the Cotswolds*, describes the town thus: "Henley-in-Arden is a name that breathes romance and the town itself does not belie its name, for it is a picturesque, unspoilt place". Along with its namesake on the Thames, they epitomise everything that is "English". Heading north up the gradient to Earlswood is Standard class 4-6-0 No 73036 leading an unidentified pilot engine. Express trains would reach the city in about 30 minutes. The GWR rules for banking engines stated that if, after the gradient there was level or a falling gradient then the assisting engine should be inside the train engine, and also, if only one of the engines had a pony truck then it had to lead. To enable these rules to be obeyed, the normal four-minute stop at Stratford-upon-Avon would lengthen to as much as ten. Note the new position of the up starter signal.
(Kidderminster Railway Museum, J Tarrant Collection)

Top: Henley-in-Arden, circa 1950. The station was purely a passenger and parcels concern, all freight being handled at the original station, which closed to passengers on 1st July 1908. For a short time after the construction of the North Warwickshire line, it was possible to arrive at the town by both routes, but in 1916, the original line was closed beyond the link to the goods station, so that all trains had to come from the new line. Goods trains would be drawn onto the branch (as here) and, after reaching the link, pushed into the goods station. 0-6-0PT No 9733 is working the branch with a short freight, having set off at 9.25am from Bordesley with a pick-up freight. The train called at Shirley at 10.20, then at Earlswood and Henley-in-Arden. Having finished the job, the guard is looking ahead to see that they have been given the route across the main lines to the loop on the up side ready for the return trip – the circle on the signal arms indicates they are for goods traffic. In the 1950s, the train would proceed back to Tyseley some time after 2.30pm, again following the stopping train to Moor Street. Danzey would be the first port of call where loaded wagons would be delivered and empty ones picked up. Earlswood, Shirley and Hall Green's empty wagons would be collected on the way to Bordesley Junction. *(PJ Garland)*

Middle: Henley-in-Arden Goods, late 1940s. After arriving in Henley-in-Arden station the goods train would stop in the down platform where the guard would collect the staff to allow it to go onto the single line to the goods yard. Reversing, the complete train would arrive by this shed and Goods Junction ground frame, coming to a halt with the engine by the point in front of us. It is in the wrong position for shunting the yard, but using the staff, the point could be altered to the position we see and the train would set off down the slight gradient towards the old station. By pinning down the wagons' brakes, and uncoupling the engine from the wagons, it could be moved into the shed siding. With careful release of the wagons' brakes, they could roll down the gradient, the engine could emerge, couple up to the guard's van and shunting could commence; the capacity of the yard was around 40 wagons. For the return journey, wagons would be assembled onto the guard's van, pulled onto the head-shunt, the point changed, and the train pushed to the passenger station before proceeding. *(BPC)*

Above: Looking up the approach road we see the external side of the former passenger station buildings, now a residence for the station master at the "new" station, and in the middle are the cattle pens. Henley-in-Arden had a market on Mondays, and cattle would pass along the main road (High Street) to and from here. On top of the former engine shed was a water tank that supplied troughs to water the animals. On the left are the back sidings used by coal merchants and for general merchandise. *(J Moss)*

Right: Adjacent to the cattle pens was a brick stable, with facilities for one horse. During World War I, as the fourth part of mobilisation, around 1 in 8 of the nation's horses were "called up" for service in the regular army. In those days, much of the movement of goods around rural areas was done by horses, so such a reduction must have had a major effect. *(BPC)*

Bottom-right: Henley-in-Arden, circa 1950. At 38ft long and 13ft wide, this box was the largest along the line, and the inside has probably changed little over the 100 years it has been there. The 57 levers were locked and released by a catch handle at the back, and underneath was the locking room where mechanical interlocking ensured that only certain combinations of lever movements could be performed, and only then in a particular order. This action would, through rods and wires, alter the points and signals. The wires still twang, and the signals still make a noise as they move (albeit upwards now) to herald the impending arrival of a train. *(J Moss)*

Opposite page, bottom: There was an impressive brick goods shed, with offices in the extension on the left, and a 5-ton crane. Local merchants have sheds to store goods such as fertiliser and animal feed, built on stilts to protect their contents from vermin. After World War II, two lorries carried out local deliveries, one of which is seen next to the shed. *(J Moss)*

Danzey, 1908. Approximately half way along the almost five miles of 1 in 150 gradient up from Henley-in-Arden is a station mid-way between the villages of Danzey and Tanworth-in-Arden. The official passenger opening was just a few weeks ago when this view south was taken. The platforms were well supplied with gas lights and, even though there was an adjacent overbridge, a footbridge complete with lights was supplied to connect the platforms. This has now been replaced by a concrete version. In the 19th century, the Post Office added "in-Arden" to avoid confusion with Tamworth, also in Warwickshire. However, Wilmcote, near Stratford-upon-Avon, is a very similar name to Wilnecote, south of Tamworth, but its name was not changed. *(Stations UK)*

Danzey, 1910. On the down side was the controlling signalbox (22 levers) and on the up side was a small goods yard, accessed by a trailing slip. Between the lamps, with the station's name written on the glass, can be seen the milepost indicating 10½ miles from Stratford-upon-Avon. A train for Birmingham is expected judging by the fact that the signal is off. *(R Carpenter)*

KNOWLE (WARWICKSHIRE).—Copt Heath G.C. Membership 350. 18 holes. Professional, T. Green. Close G.W.R. Stations, Knowle and Solihull. Visitors, 3s. 6d. per day; 5s. Saturdays and Sundays; 15s. per week; 40s. per month.

LEAMINGTON SPA (WARWICKSHIRE).—Leamington G.C. Membership 330. Professional, B. E. Hobley. 18 holes. 1 mile from Station. Visitors, 2s. 6d. per round; 3s. 6d. per day; 12s. 6d. per week; 30s. per month. Buses run within quarter mile of links.
Leamington & County G.C., Whitnash. Membership 400. Professional, T. Walton. 18 holes. 1½ miles Leamington Spa Station. Visitors—Gents., 3s. 6d. per day; Ladies, 2s. 6d.; Saturdays, Sundays and Bank Holidays, 3s. 6d.; 12s. 6d. per week; 30s. per month.

STRATFORD-UPON-AVON (WARWICKSHIRE).—Stratford-upon-Avon G.C. Membership 400. Professional, H. Leach. 18 holes. 1 mile Stratford-upon-Avon (G.W.R.) Station. Visitors, 2s. 6d. per day (Saturdays and Sundays, 3s. 6d.); Bank Holiday weekends, 5s. per day; Gents., 15s. per week; 42s. per month; Ladies, 10s. 6d. per week; 31s. 6d. per month.

WOOD END (WARWICKSHIRE).—Ladbrook Park G.C., Tanworth-in-Arden, nr. Birmingham. Membership 350. Professional, A. E. Holton. 18 holes. 3 mins. Wood End Station. Visitors, 2s. 6d. per day; Saturdays and Sundays, 5s.

As if the Shakespearean attractions of Stratford-upon-Avon were not enough, the Great Western made much of the various leisure pursuits that were available in the area – in this case, golf.

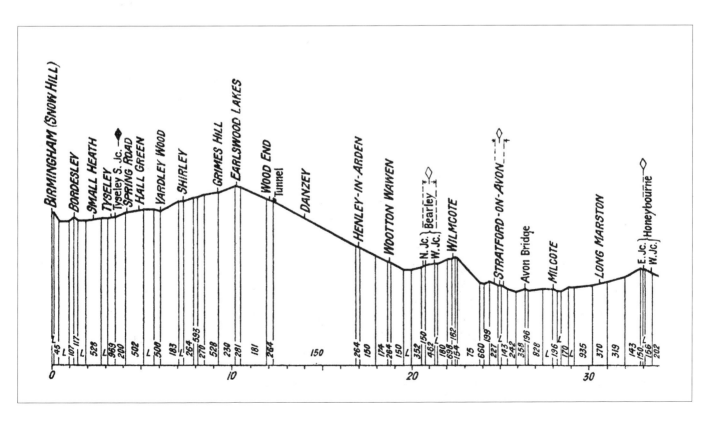

Danzey, around 1908. While this elevated view adds little to our knowledge of the infrastructure, it does serve to illustrate the passenger service soon after the line opened, steam rail motors being used. *(HW Burman Collection)*

Consisting of a single coach underframe, rail motors housed a small engine at one end and a driving space at the other end, with seats for 52 passengers in between. This meant that they could be driven from either end, eliminating the necessity for reversals. They were first introduced a few years earlier along the Stroud valley line, prompting the construction of simple platforms at convenient places between the conventional stations. When this line was opened, around 100 units had been built, but by this time, some limitations of the original design were becoming obvious. *(Kidderminster Railway Museum)*

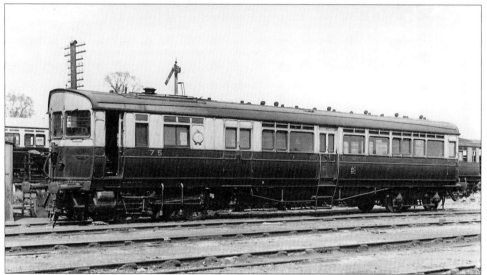

The limited hauling capacity of rail motors meant that they were unable to haul another coach without a serious loss of performance, especially if there were any gradients to contend with (although such pairings were made, as in this picture). An additional coach also removed any benefit gained from speedy turnarounds, and firemen found conditions rather warm, as well. Because of these limitations, no more steam rail motors were built, and instead, small tank engines were modified to be sandwiched between two or four modified coaches. Known as auto-trains, they had all the benefits, and fewer of the disadvantages, of their predecessors. After World War II, 2-6-2T locomotives took over many of the turns along the line, with diesels superseding many of them from 1957. Altogether about 85 of the over 100 rail motors were rebuilt as non-powered trailers. *(BPC)*

Danzey station buildings, 1964.
When building this line through rural Warwickshire, the GWR decided that for the major centres of population it would provide substantial brick buildings, employ permanent staff, and all but express trains would stop. This level of provision can be seen at Earlswood Lakes and Yardley Wood. At the other end of the scale, it would provide simple unstaffed stopping places called "Halts", as we have at Wootton Wawen (opened as a "Platform") with others at The Lakes and Whitlock's End, although these are of a later date. There were also "in-betweens", needing more facilities than a halt, but whose income did not justify brick buildings. Danzey and Wood End are perfect examples of such Platforms, although for some reason this suffix was never allocated to Danzey. All the buildings were of corrugated steel with similar style pitched roofs.

Exterior. The main building, on the Birmingham side shows a Ford Anglia 105E and (probably) an Austin A40 in the car park. There is a notice trying, even in those days, to encourage passengers to park and ride... bicycles!

Interior. Having walked onto the platform, passengers could buy a ticket, and use the waiting room or the toilets. The platforms were built to normal standards, and to access the other platform, passengers were expected to use the concrete footbridge.

Down side. As fewer passengers were expected to make the trip to Stratford-upon-Avon, a simple shelter was provided. Fire buckets were hung on the end wall, and passengers could read adverts while they waited, one location being the Cambrian Coast (served by the GWR of course!)

(All Roger Carpenter)

Danzey, 1957. While country branch lines are favoured by railway modellers, some try to telescope track layouts to unrealistic levels – six coaches and an engine could comfortably be accommodated here. The 5.15pm from Moor Street has made its penultimate stop, terminating at the next station. Stopping at all the stations along the line, the journey time to here of 42 minutes wasn't very inviting to passengers who had other travel options. After running round, the train would become the 6.20pm from Henley-in-Arden to Snow Hill. Note the height of the pine trees seen almost fifty years previously. *(TJ Edgington)*

Near Wood End, around 1924. Heading away from the tunnel is outside-framed 0-6-0 No 1203 – note the coal rails on the

tender to increase its capacity. The train is composed of a motley collection of wagons, several of which would have been privately owned. The engine is one of Dean's, which were very successful on branch lines all over the GWR system, and which some regard as forerunners of the highly successful 57XX series of pannier tanks produced by Collett from 1929. The side retaining walls by the tunnel mouth have a nice curve to them. *(BPC)*

Wood End Tunnel, circa 1950. I am not sure why the company decided to build a tunnel rather than extend the cutting – its short length can be gleaned from this elevated view. It took ten months to construct, being completed in November 1906. The tunnel was started from the south, but a lack of ventilation meant that the contractors had to sink a 40ft shaft from the surface. Part of the tunnel collapsed, and the only exit was up through the shaft. *(J Moss)*

Wood End Platform, circa 1950. Looking north we see the curving nature of the line and platforms, which are of brick construction. The original wooden footbridge was replaced with a concrete one that had a connection to a footpath as well. There were waiting shelters on both platforms and on this, the one for Birmingham, there was a gentlemen's toilet, as well as a booking office similar to Danzey. Signs of under use are beginning to show, with weeds starting their invasion. *(J Moss)*

Approaching The Lakes Halt, 1964.
Hauling an interesting load of empty mineral wagons, as well as a breakdown crane, is 0-6-0PT No 3635 on 28th September. The sinusoidal nature of the line around here is well shown by this and other pictures. In its heyday, being a trainspotter at this station must have been quite exciting – on summer Saturdays in the late 1950s, there were over a dozen long-distance trains booked from Birmingham to Cheltenham along the North Warwickshire Line, not counting excursions. Destinations were Paignton (5 trains) and Penzance (3 trains), and other resorts included St Austell, Weston-super-Mare, Kingswear, Ilfracombe and Newquay. The capacity of this route to the south west would be used to the full, and without it, the ex-MR line wouldn't have been able to cope. Sometimes it didn't, causing massive delays.
(RJ Buckley, Initial Photographics)

The Lakes Halt, 1969. This station was not part of the original plans, being opened on 3rd June 1935 to serve the village of Terry's Green. Access to the platforms was down two inclines from the adjacent road, and passenger protection was offered by these two wooden shelters. These 100ft-long structures were built where there was easy access, and the company thought it could make a profit. In the early days, rather like today, passengers were encouraged to help punctuality by being alert in getting in and out of stopping motor trains, and the company even warned that the advertised times "at the haltes are only approximate – the Cars may start a minute or two earlier". *(Stations UK)*

Approaching the Lakes Halt, 1964. Coming from the Birmingham direction is a freight hauled by Modified Hall class 4-6-0 No 7908 *Hensall Hall*. Having few wagon brakes under his control, the driver will need all his skills if the train isn't to push his engine down the gradient. The highly successful 1928 Hall class of 4-6-0s designed by Collett were meant to be a replacement for under-powered 2-6-0s and 4-4-0 classes as they became worn out. Starting in 1944, his successor, Hawksworth, altered the design by (amongst other things) increasing the superheating area by over 10%, and with increasingly inferior fuels they performed well. Superior as they were, this didn't stop the engines having a very short life span – just 15 years for this one, and a waste of money that was destined to show that BR was a drain on the taxpayer.
(RJ Buckley, Initial Photographics)

Approaching Earlswood Lakes, 1965. Two hundred years ago the lakes didn't exist, but after an Act of 1815, they were constructed to collect water to feed the Stratford-upon-Avon canal some distance to the south, water being pumped to it by a steam engine. Coming almost to the end of around 8 miles of uphill gradient, mostly at 1 in 150, is a northbound freight train. In charge is Hall class 4-6-0 No 6956 *Mottram Hall* on 10th February. Note the Hawksworth straight-sided tender with its capacity of 4,000 gallons of water and six tons of coal. On the right is an up refuge siding. *(RJ Buckley, Initial Photographics)*

Leaving Earlswood Lakes, 1965. Having laboured for around 7 miles from Tyseley with variable (but on average about 1 in 300) gradients, the train crew might think they are in for a rest. However, they now face a slightly longer trip down at a stiffer 1 in 150, and will need to ensure that their train doesn't push them too much. With all the wagons' brakes connected to that of Standard class 2-10-0 No 92221, it shouldn't be too much of a problem. On the right is the site of the recently-cleared small goods yard, although the loading gauge has been left behind. At the rear of the train can be seen the signalbox with the GWR-style water tower beyond. The signals in the distance are lower quadrant ones, while those nearest us are of the upper quadrant type. *(RJ Buckley, Initial Photographics)*

Earlswood Lakes, 1965. Some up trains needed extra power if they were to make good time up the gradient to Birmingham. Here, Standard class 2-6-4T No 80072 has helped such a train, and as it departs northwards, the banking engine will shut off steam and stop in the station. By means of a trailing crossover it will pass onto the down line and return to (probably) Stratford-upon-Avon. *(BPC)*

Earlswood Lakes, 1957. On its way to Birmingham is a stopping train with 2-6-2T No 4170 in charge. At the end of the platform is a water column, and there was also one at the end of the down platform, both being fed from the water tank on the extreme right. The apparatus next to it was used when the weather was icy to prevent the water from freezing. A covered footbridge enables passengers to transfer from one platform to the other. *(TJ Edgington)*

Earlswood Lakes, 1908. This was the scene very soon after opening, looking towards Stratford-upon-Avon. Both platforms have generous facilities, with the booking office being on the down side. Placed so as to be opposite the Guard's compartment on the approaching train is a large parcel. It is ironic that the Lakes were promoted by the GWR as a pleasure ground to attract passengers, since they put up fences to stop people using them during construction of the line. A running battle ensued with the local inhabitants who thought that their footpaths and access to the Lakes were being obstructed. *(BPC)*

Earlswood Lakes Station.

Earlswood Lakes, 1949. Standing at the end of the down platform gives a good view of the signalling arrangements. Ahead of us is a crossover and single slip, to access the goods yard off to the left. Allowing movements into the yard would be the ground signal between the running lines, while the tall starter signal in front of us would prevent any progress along this line while those movements were happening. A short loop with a cattle dock sufficed at the opening, with a longer siding being added not long afterwards – probably for deliveries of coal and agricultural goods. In the up direction can be seen two signals with their backs to us. The taller post is for passage along the main line, while the smaller post (with a hoop on its arm) was for the up refuge siding, which joined the main line at that point. Controlling

movements along the line here was the signalbox on the right, its 31 levers ceasing to be pulled after 1981. It was identical to the still-open box at Shirley. Trains from Birmingham also have the opportunity to refill their water tanks, and beyond the platform is a corrugated iron hut, probably for storing oil and paraphernalia for lamps, with a crossing made of sleepers to access the signalbox. *(J Moss)*

Earlswood Lakes, 1965. On the other side of the bridge to the station, there was a down refuge siding, seen here on the right. Note the catch point that would derail any train trying to move out onto the main line without the permission of the signalman. Heading south at the head of a seemingly endless freight train is Hall class 4-6-0 No 6922 *Burton Hall* passing the raised upper quadrant signal. *(RJ Buckley, Initial Photographics)*

Grimes Hill & Wythall Platform, 1959.
A mile north from Earlswood Lakes, the line passes under Norton Lane where the station offices are. These pictures of the station were taken from that bridge. As fewer passengers were expected to travel south, a simple waiting shelter on the down platform suffices. Originally this was a typical GWR pagoda-style building. The germ of the threat of closure of the line started with the outbreak of World War II, but prior to that the line enjoyed around 30 journeys in each direction. Over successive years this was reduced to only 16 by October 1943, and only one long-distance express survived. By 1946, the service had risen to 22 trains and there was some reintroduction of express trains. However, the shortage of men and materials, coupled with the poor state of the railways, meant that restoration to pre-war service levels was slow, and by this time, increasing car ownership and road building was having an effect on passenger's thinking. *(Stations UK)*

Wythall Booking Office, 2008. Adjacent to the bridge is a small wooden booking office on Lea Green Lane, a slope leads down to the down platform. Passengers for Stratford-upon-Avon walk across Norton Lane bridge before passing down the ramp to access trains. *(BPC)*

Grimes Hill & Wythall Platform, 1964. Heading a mixed freight train south is Hall class 4-6-0 No 6995 *Benthall Hall*. In ten years time the name boards will be shortened by the removal of the first name. At the end of the Birmingham platform, a post with a small "6" on it informs the driver where a six-car DMU was to stop. When lines were first built out from London by the Metropolitan Railway, it made great play of the fact that the city could be reached easily by its trains, and sold plots of land to build houses on. In 1912, the GWR began advertising short-distance traffic to its lines from Paddington to Reading, High Wycombe and to the branches and loops that connected them. It published a booklet called *Homes for all – London's Western Borderlands*, containing details of estate agents, builders, schools and season ticket rates, and the following year it tried to market this line with a similar booklet, *Homes for all – Birmingham's Beautiful Borderlands*, which cost a penny. Publication of these booklets ceased on the outbreak of the war, but after it finished, a large number of houses were built by Birmingham City Council to the south of the city. However, as they were well served by trams, rail penetration was not a significant factor in their growth. Other railway companies tried this method of attracting more passengers. *Where to Live* was produced by the GNR in 1914, and *Homes in the South West Suburbs* was published by the LSWR in the same year. *(RJ Buckley, Initial Photographics)*

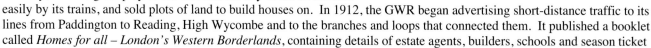

118

Whitlock's End Halt, 1939. Many trains stopped at all stations along the line, some stopped at none, and others stopped at some stations by request only. This is one of the latter heading towards Stratford-upon-Avon. 4-4-0 engine No 3202 with express headlamps hurries past with a short train of non-corridor coaches. Even though the railways didn't stimulate the growth of all the towns along the way, the GWR was good at seeing a market for its services. To assist in this process, it opened the halt here on 6th July 1936, only ¾ mile from Shirley, and a mile from Grimes Hill. That centre it described thus: "Within 15 minutes of leaving Snow Hill, the busy toiler...can alight among the green fields. Snow Hill is only 2-3 minutes walk from the centre of Birmingham". *(RJ Buckley, Initial Photographics)*

Whitlock's End Halt, 1959. Within walking distance of this stopping point are several small settlements, for example, Dickens Heath, Whitlock's End, Major's Green and Trueman's Heath. However, the facilities were anything but inviting. On both platforms there was a simple wooden shelter and slopes in both directions. Looking south from the adjacent road, Tilehouse Lane, this shot illustrates the rural appeal of the area. To the north, the line crosses the Stratford-upon-Avon canal as it passes west to Lifford to meet the Worcester & Birmingham canal. *(Stations UK)*

Shirley, early 1960s. After passing under Haslucks Green Road, the line curves west through Shirley station as this view north shows. Although the station was in the village of Haslucks Green, and the larger settlement of Shirley is along the A34 almost a mile east, the GWR probably thought that the latter name sounded more attractive, and would pull in more trade. Certainly this is true today, as the station buildings are open and in use for their primary purpose of serving passengers. Note the regularly spaced electric lamps on the platforms and the overgrown and unused loading dock to the left. Behind the schoolboy is a signalbox, and at the end of this, the Stratford-upon-Avon platform, is a home signal to protect a trailing crossover just beyond the ends of the platforms. This is used by today's trains to regain the line back to the city after terminating here. *(J Moss)*

Shirley, around 1930. The track layout here was quite straightforward. Apart from up and down refuge sidings, on the down side was a loop and three sidings. One led to the cattle pens, and two were much longer to serve the goods yard, probably for coal and general goods. At this time every house had coal fires and domestic deliveries in 1cwt sacks were weekly, or fortnightly if there was sufficient storage in the household. There was also a substantial brick goods shed and a 10cwt crane to assist in loading bulky items. Passing along the line, shunting as required, is 2-6-0 Aberdare class No 2646. Although not very glamorous, more of the GWR's profit was being produced at this time from freight than passengers. *(R Carpenter)*

Shirley, Soon after Opening. One of the reasons for the construction of the line was for the GWR to have an independent line towards Gloucester, instead of being at the mercy of the MR and its Lickey incline. A southbound train, most likely for Cardiff or the west of England, is about to pass through the station hauled by Bulldog class 4-4-0 No 3453 *Dominion of Canada*. On the right are some cattle pens (surprising so close to a built-up area) and on the left, at the end of the Birmingham-bound platform, is a small corrugated hut for track staff. For their safety, a set of boards has been made into a walkway across the point rodding and signal wires. *(R Carpenter)*

Shirley, 1964. Looking from the covered footbridge at about 6pm on 24th June, we see a healthy number of passengers sheltering from the sun under the extensive canopies as they wait to join a train. I suspect that a considerable number of passengers will alight, as this is the 5.45pm from Snow Hill – one of the fastest commuter runs from the city. Castle class 4-6-0 5091 *Cleeve Abbey* will take the train forward via Stratford-upon-Avon and Honeybourne to Evesham. Originally this engine was Star class No 4071 before rebuilding to this form sometime between 1937 and 1940. On both platforms were buildings housing a waiting room, ladies' waiting room and gentlemen's toilets, with a booking office and a parcels office on the down side. *(RJ Buckley, Initial Photographics)*

Shirley, 1970. Controlling the passage of trains along the line was this platform-mounted signalbox with rods and wires passing through a gap in the platform wall in front. Measuring 29ft by 12ft is this excellent example of standard GWR signalling practice from the 1896-1921 period – still working today. The floor of the box would be eight feet above rail level, but being on the platform it appears lower. Inside, some levers remaining from the original 31 can be seen. The resignalling of much of the West Midlands area will concentrate all control at Saltley in its "West Coast Traffic Control Centre", after which the three boxes along the line (here, Bearley West and Henley-in-Arden) will close, together with Leamington along the old main line. *(MA King)*

Shirley, 1964. Heading south is an express freight train hauled by Grange class 4-6-0 No 6845 *Paviland Grange* on 24th June. The arrangement of the canopies and the buildings that support them is similar to Henley-in-Arden; the canopy continues about 20ft beyond the buildings at this end. This not only allows the steps of the footbridge to begin in the dry, but allows a gated exit onto the station forecourt on the right. Along with Olton, Solihull and Dorridge stations, Shirley has become a focal point for local bus services in an attempt to encourage interchange with passenger trains, and the cross city service from Worcester, Kidderminster and Stourbridge terminates here. This, together with the hourly service to Stratford-upon-Avon, provides a 20-minute service through the city. *(RJ Buckley, Initial Photographics)*

121

Yardley Wood, 1959. Just over a mile north of Shirley, after skirting Trittiford Mill Park to the west along the River Cole, is the station for Yardley Woods, as the district was originally called. This view is towards Birmingham under Highfield bridge (No 12) where the line ascends for a short distance at 1 in 500. Even at a modest station such as this, the amount of maintenance necessary to just paint the railings was substantial. When multiplied by the number of stations you get an idea of how big organisations like the GWR were. *(Stations UK)*

Yardley Wood, 1964. Having been helped by the descending gradient, a down express freight train roars along through the station hauled by County class 4-6-0 No 1011 *County of Chester* on 21st September. Notice the lack of number plate on the smokebox door and the characteristic straight-sided tender. The entire class of 30 post-war, Hawksworth-designed, engines had double chimneys, and were rated 6MT by BR – more powerful than most ex-GWR engines, but less so than the Castles and Kings. The small waiting shelter, complete with a reasonably-sized awning is smaller than that for Birmingham-bound passengers. Interestingly, despite having brick buildings, it was opened as a Platform, but soon lost this suffix. *(RJ Buckley, Initial Photographics)*

Yardley Wood. Between the set of shops on the main road and the up platform buildings is a brick booking office. Passengers for the Stratford-upon-Avon direction would have to buy their tickets from here, and then walk across the line on the main road to get to their platform. The down pipes from the guttering are built into the recess in the walls. *(BPC)*

Hall Green, around 1919.
This fascinating view is looking north with York Road bridge in the background. At the end of this platform is the controlling signalbox, and beyond it, a very tall signal post. A bracket signal on the opposite side of the line is obscured by a blemish on the photograph. A trailing slip giving access to the small goods yard on the up side, complete with 3-ton crane, is at the end of the Birmingham platform. As a precaution during World War I, station names were painted over on lamps, and the paint is still present on the lamps here. The adjacent River Cole

powers Birmingham's only working water mill at Sarehole, dating from 1771. Originally the area was called Haw Green due to a family name. In its *Homes for All* booklet, the GWR described Hall Green as having "bracing air, well wooded in parts and open in others, it offers many an ideal excursion to the pedestrian". *(BPC)*

Hall Green, around 1919. Facing Stratford-upon-Avon from the 6-foot way we see why the up signal (seen previously) and the down one (its head just visible) were so high. The station's footbridge, followed by bridges over Stratford Road and, in the distance, Bank Road, all transpire to make sighting difficult for train drivers; notice the much smaller down starter signal at the end of the platform. The line is ascending, and will continue until Earlswood Lakes, some 6 miles to the south. On the right is a complete set of waiting rooms, lavatories and the booking office, with a large awning. For Stratford-upon-Avon bound passengers, accessed by the covered footbridge, a waiting room and the obligatory male facilities were considered sufficient under a smaller awning. Illustrating the nature of the traffic are the milk churns awaiting collection – refrigeration for all was some 40 years away. *(BPC)*

Hall Green, 1958. A greyhound stadium in York Road opened in 1927. Famous residents have included Tony Hancock, Nigel Mansell and JRR Tolkein, and it has been suggested that the Shire Country Park, along the banks of the River Cole on its way to Small Heath, inspired some of the scenes for his books. The flowers and the well-tended planted area, illustrate a level of care and attention that would soon cease. On this platform are two trolleys, with attendant staff, showing that some traffic in parcels was enjoyed. On the down side can just be made out the buildings of High Grade Steel, which were accessed just after the 29-lever signalbox. *(Stations UK)*

Hall Green, late 1940s. Looking south from York Road bridge you can see Hall Green station in the background. On the extreme left can just be seen the signalbox, bracket signal cantilevered out for sighting purposes and the connections to a steel stock holder's premises. On the right is the goods yard with the lines on the extreme right populated by coal wagons. Shunting would be done by Aberdare class engines and later by pannier tanks. North Sea gas was to alter this picture for ever, as few homes stayed with solid fuel. Modellers wishing to copy this small suburban station would need a considerable space for an extremely modest layout. *(R Carpenter)*

GWR Staff

Attitudes in Edwardian days to the employment of women were very different from today's equality. At the outbreak of World War I only around 2% of GWR employees were women, but with large numbers of men released for war work, their numbers rose to nearly 10%. However, due to the insistence of the men's unions, their roles were considered temporary, and by 1920, their numbers had shrunk to 3%. A similar pattern could be seen as a result of World War II, with numbers rising to 15%, but by Nationalisation the figure had dropped back to 10%. Nevertheless, the idea that the railways were a male preserve had been broken forever.

Above left: Hall Green, late 1920s. Of around 25,000 GWR employees who saw action in World War I, approximately 10% did not return. Probably most of the employed station staff have come to pose for this picture, so typical of times that were soon to end. All are male, and in addition to the fact that many men did not return from the war, women who had performed their tasks equally during the conflict, sought to be employed in their own right. After World War II, employers were bound under the Re-instatement in Civil Employment Act to employ returning servicemen in their old jobs, or a suitable alternative. *(Lens of Sutton)*

Above right: Lapworth Station Staff, 1913. Although unstaffed now, this was the complement of the railway employees just before World War I, and all were male. Seated on the right is the Station Master, Mr E Newton with the Porter, Mr G Edgington behind him. Next in seniority would be the seated Clerk, Mr A Finney and then the "whipping boy" as the Junior Porter (with an assertive stance) Mr WA Edgington. *(Kidderminster Railway Museum, H Bromwich Collection)*

Tyseley, 1948. Sandwiched between the quadruple running lines to the north and a pair of goods lines (and the engine shed beyond) to the south, was an extensive set of loops for carriages. In the May sunshine, some of the Carriage & Wagon Dept staff pose – notice the different dress according to their position – driver, cleaner, fireman, clerk or foreman; this is one of the few such pictures with women in. Taking a break from performing its duties is 0-6-0PT No 9635 and, interestingly, the shunting truck – so typical of the GWR. This one is over 30 years old, has 18in round buffers and vacuum connections, useful for moving coaches as their brakes could be used, and higher speeds could be reached secure in the knowledge that the train could stop! *(PJ Garland)*

Spring Road Platform, 1939. Getting into its stride is GWR Duke class 4-4-0 No 3284 *Isle of Jersey* on 9th May. The lightweight load of three coaches was typical of the day. Of 1895 vintage, this class was soon to be superseded by newer GWR 4-6-0 engines. Until 1927 this type of engine would have been responsible for the express trains to destinations beyond Stratford-upon-Avon. This was because at Stonehouse, south of Gloucester on the MR line to Bristol, there was a weight restriction on the viaduct. Strengthening of this structure enabled larger and more powerful engines to be used. In "GWR-speak", a Platform meant a longer, more substantial stopping place than a Halt, but without the brick structures of a "real" station. They were manned by senior grade porters called "platform attendants", who booked tickets, parcels and milk for the auto-trains that stopped here. West Road bridge is in the background, with a corrugated iron booking office at the top of the ramp.
(RJ Buckley, Initial Photographics)

Spring Road Platform, 1958. Under the road bridge, the line can be seen turning west towards Tyseley. The parapet of the bridge provides a good contrast for the yellow painted fixed distant arm for the junction ahead. Buildings of a similar material and construction are on both platforms, but there are superior facilities, including a gentlemen's toilet, for Birmingham bound passengers. The large building in the background is Acocks Green Garage – a bus depot. *(Stations UK)*

Spring Road Booking Office, 2008. Having suffered from fire at the hands vandals, this was a most un-GWR-like booking office (left). Lurking to the rear is the Portakabin replacement (right). *(BPC)*

Spring Road Platform, 1964. A Birmingham-bound freight train, hauled by Standard class 2-10-0 No 92164, ambles along the up line. Although the gradient isn't severe (down at 1 in 500, steepening to 1 in 200) the curve ahead would mean that the footplate crew would have to pay special attention to their speed. Passengers for Stratford-upon-Avon would stand on the left-hand platform – notice the numbers on the lamps indicating where drivers of 4- and 6-coach trains should stop. As few passengers would be waiting for such trains the facilities were minimal. *(RJ Buckley, Initial Photographics)*

North of Spring Road Platform, 1964. With the junction to the main line a short distance round the bend to the left, the driver of Castle class 4-6-0 No 7013 *Bristol Castle* will want to pick up speed if he is to live up to the express passenger train headlamp code. A combination of the speed restriction imposed by the curve and the noticeable start of the gradient means that the train speed will be low until the driver comes round the bend sufficiently to see the signal. His train, the 17.45 from Snow Hill, will need to clear the line for the 17.45 from Moor Street all stations train that will follow it down the line. Ahead is just over six miles at an average gradient of around 1 in 300 to the summit of the line at Earlswood Lakes. The newly-painted signal on the right is the distant post for the signalbox at Hall Green, some ¾ mile south. *(RJ Buckley, Initial Photographics)*

High Drama on the North Warwickshire Line

Facilities such as those seen along the line could not survive after World War II, with roads having the capacity to absorb seemingly endless growth, along with their taxpayer's subsidy. Rural lines like this were a drain on the taxpayer, and were destined to become cycle-paths. Built as a spoiling operation by the GWR, Stratford-upon-Avon could be served well by trains from Hatton, as it had been before the line opened. Thus the scene was set for the most remarkable chapter in the line's history. To illustrate events I've put captions around views that opponents would have picked – ones with no passengers. What is interesting is the desire to close the line in 1969 came enough years after the Buchanan report of 1963 for its predictions to have been digested and acted upon. Talking about city centres it said, "the pleasantness and safety of surroundings will deteriorate catastrophically". He could equally have been commenting on rural life, but his words went unheeded by those with power and influence.

Wood End Platform, 1969. It is possible to discern that the line here is still on a gradient. With vandalism to electric lights and windows, together with encroaching vegetation, stations took on a very forlorn air. Add to this the continual maintenance of a tunnel and a downwards spiral would develop. Car ownership had increased from just below 1 million in 1930 to over 12 million by the time of this picture, so with "economy" being the buzz-word, this line was eventually put under the microscope. Consequently, the die was cast for closure of this line, and a replacement bus service introduced to serve communities from Wootton Wawen to Spring Road. With the last trains due to run in May 1969, views like these were about to be consigned to history. *(Stations UK)*

The Lakes Halt, 1969. Set in rural Warwickshire, close to the reservoirs for the Stratford-upon-Avon canal, is this halt with platforms some 130ft long of wooden construction with a tarmac surface and old sleepers for the edges. When this line was put up for closure a users' group looked into the matter in late 1966. Not surprisingly, they concluded that, "a trail of havoc and hardship would result if the line was closed". However, this was brushed aside with assurances that suitable replacement bus services could be provided, but these had been shown to be costly and slow, and would encourage car usage. It took the dramatic move of an Appeal Court ruling, just three days before the expected closure, to prevent such happenings. *(Stations UK)*

Shirley Station, 1959. Waiting for a train to the city we see the tranquil scene between departures. Note the extensive canopies and covered footbridge, all to keep non-existent passengers dry, but at what expense? Later, in 1969, the West Midlands Passenger Transport Executive was set up, subsidising the line from the city to Grimes Hill, with the rest of the line receiving financial support from the Government. The current train operator, London Midland, has a policy for all the stations along the North Warwickshire line beyond Earlswood Lakes (excluding Henley-in-Arden): "Trains will only stop on request. Customers wishing to alight must inform the on-train staff and those wishing to join must give a hand signal to the driver". It is still possible to stand at the exact spots where these photographs were taken. *(Stations UK)*

Tyseley Junction, circa 1960. A freight train from Stratford-upon-Avon passes along the down goods line with 2-6-0 No 6332 in charge. The arrangement for the branch is well displayed. Access to it could be from the up main line, to the extreme left, or the up relief line, to the left of the signalbox. Passenger trains from the branch could proceed onto the down main (almost obscured by the tall signal post) or to the down relief (and the goods lines from it) by pointwork hidden by the box. The main lines are down to Birmingham and the North Warwickshire lines are up to Birmingham, so the train will be received as an up train and passed on as a down train by the signalbox staff.
(R Carpenter)

Tyseley Station, circa 1908. At the end of the 19th century, the main line from London approached Birmingham from the south-east through Solihull. A pair of running lines was sufficient, and small stations were opened at Acocks Green, Olton and Small Heath. Tyseley station was built approximately mid-way between the last two stations, opening on 1st October 1906.

Built as a four-platform station, it accommodated a section of quadruple track that started at Olton, a mile to the east, almost to Small Heath a mile to the north-west. There were generous facilities on both island platforms with a booking office on an adjacent overbridge and steps leading down to both platforms. Some of the station staff have come to pose on the southern island which, at that time, had down lines on each side. Thus, the up and down main lines would be the pair in view, with the relief pair passing by the outside faces of the islands.
(Millbrook House)

Tyseley Station, circa 1908. Although published before, this view has so much information it is worth showing again. Illustrating the GWR's idea of passenger comforts, the steps down from the street level booking office lead directly under the canopy. Waiting at the down relief platform is an unidentified rail motor, typical of those seen in the early days along the North Warwickshire line. Prior to the opening of Moor Street, such trains terminated here, and passengers had to change for the last leg of their journey to the city. Signals for goods trains (those with white hoops on) abound, and in fact the two lines to the left of the carriage are goods lines. In the distance is the provision for carriages in the form of loops and a four-road shed. Rail motor No 98 was allocated here in 1909, and was used on the service until 1914. At its construction, in 1907, it cost £2,173 and ran 446,801 miles before being converted to trailer No 215 in April 1935. *(Lens of Sutton)*

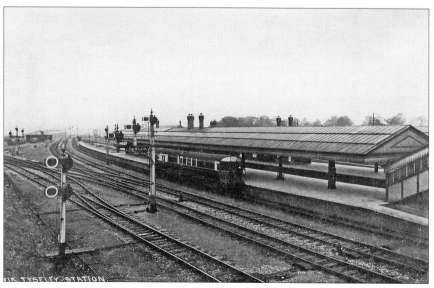

Tyseley Shed, 1964. Opening in June 1908 was a shed destined to be amongst the largest on the GWR system. It consisted of two turntables, side by side, in a rectangular building. On the right is an engine parked with its chimney under a smoke hood that would enable the corrosive sulphurous exhaust fumes to pass up and out of the building. Unlike many other sheds, I am not aware of this shed ever needing to be re-roofed as a consequence of smoke erosion. Coaled and being turned onto a vacant track is an unidentified (due to the number plate having been removed!) Grange class 4-6-0 engine. *(J Moss)*

Tyseley Shed, 1933. A double-sided coaling station was provided with two elevated sidings running through the middle. Coal wagons in the sidings could be unloaded in the shed into tubs that would be pushed to the opening protected by lean-tos. Here, their contents would be emptied into the coal space of waiting engines. To service the engines a massive water tank was needed: it is above the coaling stage, its capacity being 98,000 gallons. Directors of companies are always concerned about running costs, and comparative figures for the "Big Four" in 1938 showed the GWR to have lower repair and renewal costs than the LNER. Costs per engine mile were also much lower, as the engines burned less coal and consumed less water. Although closed to steam on 7th November 1966, an adjacent facility still runs steam-hauled excursions to Stratford-upon-Avon at weekends in the summer. *(PJ Garland)*

Bottom-left: Tyseley Shed, 1932. Not only did the shed provide the engines for passenger, freight and shunting duties in the area, it also supplied engines for longer distance trips. Some engines were bought from the Railway Operating Division of the Royal Engineers in World War I. 2-8-0 No 3001 is an example, and it would be used for long-distance freight – to London, for example. In contrast, engines that hauled London-bound passenger expresses were usually shedded at Wolverhampton's Stafford Road rather than here. As these trains were often of twelve coaches or more, they needed the most powerful engines on the GWR – the King class. LNWR trains to Birmingham were usually hauled by less-powerful engines such as Patriots and Jubilees. *(R Carpenter)*

Bottom-right: Tyseley Shed, no date. The entrance to the engine shed was adjacent to the carriage sidings, but at a lower level. Engines such as this were powerful and had good acceleration, enabling them to be used on both freight and passenger trains – mostly in the Welsh valleys. This example, No 6681, is one of a group of fifty engines that Collett had the company buy from an outside manufacturer, Armstrong Whitworth, in 1928, as Swindon's rate of production wouldn't have been fast enough for his purposes. *(BPC)*

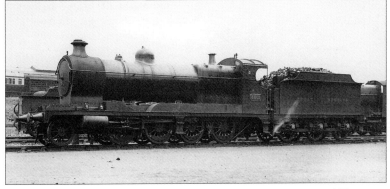

Small Heath, 1960. Looking towards Tyseley from the relief island, this view shows an up goods to the left. The Birmingham Small Arms (BSA) factory was developed adjacent to the canal and the railway from 1861, with rail access to the up goods line; an enemy bomb in 1940 unfortunately killed 53 workers there. Having probably been dragged out of Tyseley carriage sidings, the coaches are about to be delivered to Snow Hill station. Grange class 4-6-0 No 6856 *Stowe Grange* is heading along the down main through the station. *(M Mensing)*

Bordesley Junction, 1963. At Bordesley there was the north-south main line and also, passing east-west, the MR line from Saltley to Camp Hill. In 1861, a single line curve was built from here on the main line east to meet the MR line at Bordesley Junction Midland. In 1941, as part of the war-time extensions to the system, the curve was doubled and today it is the main route for cross country trains. Having battled up the gradient from Saltley, probably with the aid of a banker, Grange class 4-6-0 No 6852 *Headbourne Grange* has left the Camp Hill line. This can be seen passing across the left background, and the train stands ready to enter the extensive GWR yards at Bordesley. *(Restoration & Archiving Trust)*

Bordesley, 1965. North of Small Heath station, the Birmingham & Warwick Junction Canal is crossed, necessitating a small rising gradient on both approaches. A short distance south of Bordesley station, the MR line from Camp Hill crosses the GWR line by the bridge in the background. Heading north along the down main is an oil train with 2-8-0 No 3864 in charge. Note the lack of any use of high-visibility clothing by the worker on the up relief line. An up express is probably expected along the main line on the left, judging by the setting of the signals on the fine bracket post. *(RJ Buckley, Initial Photographics)*

Bordesley Viaduct, 1949. Originally there were two lines across the rooftops of the Digbeth area of Birmingham, the River Lea and Grand Union canal necessitating a viaduct of 60 arches and 2 girder bridges. In 1913, these were extended by the addition of a pair of relief lines and a goods line. A long siding from the latter was useful for shunting the goods shed at Moor Street. Approaching Bordesley North signalbox, and heading south across the viaduct, having just left Snow Hill station, is the 9.12am from Wolverhampton to Paignton with an unidentified Hall class engine in charge. Across all the running lines is a ladder-like connection ending in the line on the far left, which has a piece missing. This is because beyond this point to Moor Street it is an up goods line, but up to this point from Bordesley Junction it is a down goods line, and the missing track prevented conflicting movements. *(Millbrook House Ltd)*

Bordesley Viaduct, 1912. For the opening of Moor Street station in 1909 there were only two lines across the viaduct and a double junction to the platforms sufficed. Controlling the access to the station is this bracket on the tall down signal post. When the viaduct was widened to accommodate extra lines, the supporting arches had to be carefully built as there were to be two sheds at road level as well as the shed at rail level. It would take four years for the complex work to be completed while still allowing public roads to operate beneath the viaduct. *(BR)*

Moor Street Station, Exterior, 1960. At the opening on 1st July 1909, the buildings were built of wood and were of a temporary nature. Later, they were replaced by the brick structure that stands there today. This view is looking up Moor Street with the pair of lines passing through to Snow Hill station being below the store on the extreme left. The large poster alludes to special regulations that existed for travel on Saturday trains, especially in the summer, as they were so popular. A new canopy has been added over the entrance with the ironwork from the passenger entrance from Snow Hill above it (below), and the words and GWR crest picked out in gold. *(J Tarrant Collection, Kidderminster Railway Museum)*

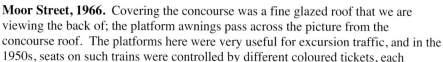

Moor Street, 1966. Covering the concourse was a fine glazed roof that we are viewing the back of; the platform awnings pass across the picture from the concourse roof. The platforms here were very useful for excursion traffic, and in the 1950s, seats on such trains were controlled by different coloured tickets, each corresponding to a particular train, which was great as long as the ticket collector wasn't colour blind. To haul such trains, engines would arrive tender first from Tyseley. The corner of the goods shed is on the extreme right. *(H D Bowtell)*

Signalling Arrangements, Moor Street, 1964. This impressive signal gantry stood at the end of the island platform. The taller of the arms indicated the route out from the platforms onto the up main line, while the smaller post was for the relief line. This bracket signal replaced one with two arms and displays to indicate which route was to be taken. Underneath each arm was a white area, into which could be pushed a notice telling the driver which route to take, when the appropriate lever was pulled by the signalman. This device rendered larger, more expensive, bracket posts unnecessary, and some workers nicknamed the display "cash register" as it mimicked the action of manual cash machines. Here, the choice of routes was restricted as the relief to main crossover, ahead, had been removed in 1954. The controlling signalbox behind was originally almost where the photographer is standing. However, when the goods depot was built and the viaduct enlarged, this box was commissioned – probably some time in the autumn of 1913. The original wooden box went to Foxhall Junction and this tall (13ft 6in) narrow-based (12ft by 54ft) box survived until 1969. It contained 118 levers – almost double the original's 61 levers. Note how the wooden cabin protruded over the brick base. It controlled the lines to both Moor Street passenger and goods facilities, as well the lines across this end of the viaduct as they quadruple. *(BPC)*

Moor Street, 1956. This was a very cramped site and there were special regulations to ensure that the restricted accommodation didn't become inoperable; on the passenger side, it was ideal for short suburban trains hauled by tank engines.

To allow the engines by the buffers to be released from the terminal platforms a novel feature was installed – there was a piece of moving track that enabled an engine to move across to the parallel track, and so be released. So that there was always a piece of track at the end of the line a third piece of track was hidden under the platform which moved across to fill the gap. Here we see 2-6-2T No 8109 of Leamington shed being moved from one terminal road to another. This feature was designed (in 1909) in such a way that the large tender engines could just be accommodated. On the left is the later addition of a second platform with a single face, with the wagon hoist to shed "B" in the background. *(BPC)*

Moor Street Goods Station, 1966. Not too long after the passenger station opened there was an opportunity for the railway company to buy an adjacent plot of land, which they turned into a goods depot, opening on 7th January 1914. There are a large number of vans and the goods shed is over to the left. On the extreme left and in the centre of the picture are two metal sheds on stilts. These are two of the three wagon hoists to the lower level goods depot, all of which fed onto traversers from which the sidings were accessed. *(HD Bowtell)*

Moor Street, Lower Shed "B", circa 1916. Access to shed "A" was from Park Street and to "B" from Alison Street. Delivering goods to and from the depot was originally performed by horse and cart. At the opening of the depot in 1914, 24 horses were transferred from the Hockley stables, and others soon followed; previously all goods for the area had to be carted the two miles from there. The large number of lorries available at the end of World War I started the decline in equine transport, although in 1947, there were still 245 working horses in the Birmingham area. Records show that in 1929, 193 people worked at the goods depot here. Illustrating why goods traffic was lost from the railways is the handling method. Men walked into the wagons and carried out or trolleyed the boxes, stacking them on the platforms and then onto the waiting dray. *(BPC)*

Moor Street, 1987. After the closure of Moor Street to passengers and goods the infrastructure was not demolished, fortunately. With New Street unable to cope with the demands being made upon it, the re-opening of the line across Bordesley viaduct to Snow Hill was decided upon. At the northern end, services to Stourbridge were able to switch to their former home again, but at Moor Street, two new platforms to serve the main lines were built. This is the scene on 4th February with a 5th October reopening date. Trains can still access the former terminal roads, and rumours abound as to their future use. It is highly likely on the centenary of Moor Street in 2009, that a journey to the capital will take the same time, but with many more stops and a greater frequency. *(BPC)*